Swan

Under the Tuscan Sun

In Tuscany

Bella Tuscany

The Discovery of Poetry

Ex Voto

Swan

{ A NOVEL }

FRANCES MAYES

BROADWAY BOOKS

NEW YORK

Broadway Books titles may be purchased for business or promotional use or for special sales. For information, please write to: Special Markets Department, Random House, Inc., 1540 Broadway, New York, NY 10036.

Visit our website at www.broadwaybooks.com

First edition published 2002

Book design by Pei Loi Koay

Library of Congress Cataloging-in-Publication Data
Mayes, Frances.
    Swan: a novel / Frances Mayes.—1st ed.
      p. cm.
    1. Mothers—Death—Fiction.   2. Exhumation—Fiction.
   3. Georgia—Fiction. I. Title.

PS3563.A956 S93 2002
813'.54—dc21

                          2002019705

ISBN 0-7679-0285-8
International edition ISBN 0-7679-1436-8

Excerpt from *Breathturn* by Paul Celan, translated by Pierre Joris. Copyright © 1995 by Pierre Joris. Reprinted by permission of Sun & Moon Press.

10 9 8 7 6 5 4 3 2 1

For Ashley

But in you, from
birth
foamed the other spring,
up the black
ray memory
you climbed to the day.

PAUL CELAN

BREATHTURN

[TRANS. BY PIERRE JORIS]

Peaches and fireworks and red ants.
Now do you know where you are.

C. D. WRIGHT

DEEPSTEP COME SHINING

Of those so close beside me, which are you?

"THE WAKING"

THEODORE ROETHKE

Swan, pop. 7,000, county seat of J. E. B. Stuart County. An attractive town with broad avenues and well-preserved late-nineteenth-century architecture, Swan is situated on a forested rise between the Altamaha and Ocmulgee rivers. Origins are unrecorded, but the area formerly was held by Creek and Seminole Indians and later was populated by Scotch-Irish and English settlers, who farmed and engaged in timber clearing for northern companies. During the early unincorporated years, it was known as Garbert, but in 1875 it was chartered as Swan by the Town Council and Mayor John Repton Mason. The name change recognized the migratory whistling swans once common in the swampy environs. The first industry was a cotton mill established by Mason, who engaged the Washington architect Ransom Gray to design an elliptical town plan inspired by Bath, England, Mr. Mason's original home. The chief crop today continues to be cotton, but local farmers have diversified and now raise pimentos, tobacco, corn, and sugarcane. Other industries include poultry ranches, a trouser factory, turpentine and fertilizer plants. Population has declined from a high of 11,000 to 7,000 due to the closing of J. R. Mason Mills. An active Chamber of Commerce is engaged in attracting new light industry to the area. The Cottonmouth Countdown is a colorful annual festival every July. The Jeff Davis Museum exhibits memorabilia from local combatants in the War Between the States. The Ogelthorpe Hotel is an outstanding example of late plantation architecture in the Georgia vernacular. Other attractions include Sassahoochie Springs, with ancient oaks surrounding a large spring believed to be bottomless.

FROM *A GUIDE TO GEORGIA PLACES*
BY ADAM LUMPKIN ADAIR

July 7, 1975

J. J. STOOD ON THE END OF THE DOCK, feeling as if the four pilings might rip loose in the current and send him rafting. But the dock held. He loved the smell of rivers. In July heat, in wavy air, in the throbbing of cicadas, in the first light on the river, he was what he would call happy. A full moon angled down between pines, casting a spiraling silver rope across the curve of the water. He watched the light, flicking through his mind for words to describe it. *Luminous, flashing.* Ordinary. The light seemed liquid, alive, annealed to the water, too changeable for any word. The river rode high after two storms. A cloud of gnats swarmed his foot, then moved as a single body over a swirl in the current. He stepped out of his faded red bathing suit—automatically he pulled on this suit every morning when he got out of bed—and climbed down the ladder into the water. His morning libations, he called this routine. In all the good months, and sometimes in the cold ones just for sheer cussedness, he dipped himself in the river early in the morning. Near the dock he could stand on the bottom, feeling the swiftness or languidness of the current, sometimes jumping as a fish nipped at the hairs on his legs and chest. He floated for a minute, listening to water whirl around his head, letting himself be carried, then turned his body sharply and swam over to the crescent of washed-sand beach his parents had cleared years ago. From there he could walk out of the river and follow a trace covered in pine needles back to the dock. He noticed a fallen sourwood sapling, tangled with muscadine vines, and leaned to pull it out of the water. As he jerked loose the roots, a wedge of earth cleaved from the bank, spilling dirt onto his wet legs. At his feet he saw something white—a bone, a stick bleached by the sun? He waded back into the river and rinsed off.

Maybe what he glimpsed was an arrowhead. J. J. had found hundreds. He turned over the earth with his foot. There—he picked it up, blew off the dirt, and washed it. Never had he found one of these. He held a perfect bone fish spear, three inches long, with exquisitely carved barbs like a cat's claws on each side. He admired the skill—the delicate hooked end of each barb would bite into flesh while the fisherman dragged in the fish. At one end he saw slight ridges where the line was tied over and over by the Creek Indian who once fished these waters. Ginger, he thought, Ginger should see this. But his sister's green eyes were light-years away. He pawed through the dirt and pulled out other roots from the bank, but found only a smashed can. What a beauty, this small spear in the palm of his hand. He took in a breath of pine air as far as he could, the air driving out of his head the familiar surge of what felt similar to hunger and thirst. Ginger was not there, so to whom could he show his treasure? He regarded it intently for himself. He had no talent for needing someone else. He shook his hair and banged the side of his head to knock the water out of his ear. Rainy night in Georgia, he mocked himself. Last train to Clarksville.

He dressed in khaki shorts, not bothering with underwear. Six-thirty and already hot, heavily hot, steamy hot, the best weather. Nothing to eat in the refrigerator but some rice and a piece of left-over venison from a week ago, when he'd brought Julianne, the new schoolteacher from Osceola, out here. She'd said it was so interesting that he lived way in the woods all alone. As down-to-earth as she looked, she turned out to be afraid for her feet to touch the bottom of the river. She'd hung on to his back, her laugh verging toward a squeal, and he felt her soft thighs on his. She was hot to the touch, even under water. But then she couldn't eat venison because she thought of Bambi. She cooked the rice, which, as he remembered, had hard kernels at the center of the grain. Then she looked at his wild salad as though it were a cow pie. J. J. often went for days eating only greens he picked and fish he caught. He chewed slowly, watching her. If she was beautiful, as Liman MacCrea had promised, why did he think her skin looked so stretched tight across her face that it might split like a blown-up pork bladder? And eyes that close together made a person look downright miserly.

Then he'd rubbed his temples and looked again. A pleasant face, kind and expectant. Warm. What is she wanting? he wondered as she smiled. Then he noticed her teeth, which were ground down, like an old deer's.

"Pokeweed and lamb's-quarters? I've heard of dandelion greens before. Can you eat these? That's so interesting." She pushed the fresh, pungent greens around with her fork. With the one bite she took, grit crunched between her teeth. Something she saw in his eyes appealed to her, some waiting quality. Not just a flirt or the good ol' boy he sometimes appeared to be, he was someone to solve, she told herself as she changed into her bathing suit in his room. She looked carefully at his things, comparing her own box bedroom to his, her pink chenille spread and the prints of Degas dancers on the wall, the lace curtains and view out onto an empty street, to his crammed bookcases, twenty or more ink pens, mounted fish and deer heads, his rough Indian blanket on the bed. I have no way to reach him, she thought, and would I want to? She felt suddenly tired but practiced a big smile in the mirror, lifting her thick chestnut hair off her neck. Her teeth gleamed white and even. The new red maillot certainly showed off her Scarlett O'Hara waist. "Cherry Bomb," she whispered. Cherry Bomb had been her nickname at Sparta High, when she was Homecoming queen. But that was twelve years ago. She wished she had washed the lovely greens because she was not about to eat grit.

J. J. thought if she said "so interesting" again, he'd drive the fork through her eyes. He poured glasses of bourbon. "Let's toast your seventh-grade class who gets to spend all that time with you." She lowered her eyes with pleasure, which shamed him. Was he becoming a God damned hermit? He wondered how he would feel with her legs wrapped around him. Lost in outer space? He knew he'd find fault with Christ Almighty. She played the flute, had a degree in music education. So what if she turned freaky in the woods? Still, he had felt a tidal wave of boredom flood through him, a craving to be alone so intense that he shuddered. Although he'd expected to be driving her home at one or two in the morning, top down, a little night music, he was burning up the road at nine-thirty.

He made a pot of coffee and heated Julianne's leftover clump of bad rice with some butter. The kitchen table was littered with chert, flint, a flat stone, and two antlers. Lately, he'd tried to teach himself flintnapping, using only tools the Indians had used. He'd ordered *A Guide to Flintworking* and driven over to a rock shop in Dannon to buy pieces big enough to work. He wanted to make a stone knife for gutting fish, but so far he'd split a lot of stones and created a pile of waste flakes and chips. One try, by accident, actually resembled a scraper.

He held up the fish spear to the sunlight at the window, admiring the fine symmetry. Balancing coffee, bowl, and notebook, the spear held lightly between his teeth, he pushed open the kitchen door with his elbow. Yellow jackets worked the scuppernongs, and bees burrowed into the rose that sprawled among the vines, his mother's yellow rose, still blooming and her gone an eon, a suicide. He did not want to think about that. She had loved the cabin as much as he did. Her rose had long since climbed from the arbor and bolted into the trees. He placed the fish spear on a piece of white paper and opened his notebook to record his find. July 7, he wrote. The early sun through the grape arbor cast mottled light onto the table. He might love the light at the cabin even more than the water, but no, they were inseparable. The emerald longleaf pines tinted the light at all hours, casting a blue aura early and late, and in full sun softened the hard edges of objects. He moved the paper into a splotch of sun. The bone looked like ivory. First he measured the length, then in light pencil carefully he started to draw. What kind of bone, he wondered, maybe boar, maybe beaver. How long would it have taken the Indian to carve it?

He quickly went over his lines in black with his Rapidograph. Drawing, he thought, never captures the thing itself. At least mine doesn't. Maybe Leonardo da Vinci could get this right. But Leonardo never heard of the Creeks, or of the belly of the beast, south Georgia. Easy to get the *likeness*. The unlikeness is what's hard. Where the object ends and everything around it begins, that's the impossible part to negotiate. He held up the spear and turned it around. He decided to look at it under his father's microscope. He might find a speck of blood from the fish that swam away with the spear in its side. Too bad Ginger's not here, he thought. She ought to see this.

GINGER CROUCHED IN THE HIP BATH, running the nozzle over her dusty body. Her damp field trousers and shirt heaped on the floor seemed to exude more dust. She bathed fast. This far into the Tuscan summer, the well might go dry, leaving her to cook and sponge off with bottled water until a rain came, raising the water table again. She slipped into the hot cerise dress with straps she'd bought at the Saturday market in Monte Sant'Egidio, thinking, I'm thin again. Marco will like this dress. She allowed herself to think of the pleasure of his hand on her back, guiding her across the piazza. His *Italian* hand. She loved his foreignness. She sucked in her breath. Lithe, she thought. Amazing what miracles a few months of digging and hauling can accomplish. She changed the sheets, boxed the pillows, stacked her books neatly on the bedside table. Stuffing her nightgown and robe in a drawer, she stopped in midgesture. A memory hit her of Mitchell, whom she'd married at twenty-four. Mitchell in bed, reading *Time,* all scrubbed and expectant in pressed boxers. For most of their three years together, he spent his nights waiting while Ginger outwaited him downstairs, reading or listening to music until he dozed off and she crept to bed, carefully lifting the magazine off his chest and turning out his light. What was it? she asked herself. Not him. When they dated, she'd thought she would fall into *his* love, his certainty; she would begin to feel something. She would sit, crawl, walk. She would be like everyone else with a silver pattern, a honeymoon in Nassau, a foil card of birth control pills, curtains to choose, recipes. Mitchell was so fine, she thought, patient. Anytime he walked in a door, she'd been happy to see him. What a disaster.

Her hometown, Swan, would talk for years, and still, about Ginger not coming downstairs on her wedding day. At first she'd been just late, then Jeannie Boardman sat down at the organ they'd trucked in for the day and began to play "Clair de Lune" and "Moonlight Sonata." Finally, Aunt Lily, after throwing a hissy fit outside Ginger's locked bedroom door, had served the champagne, puffs filled with crab salad, cheese straws, platters of macaroons and ladyfingers. The guests had eaten with appetites piqued by the shock of Lily announcing that Ginger was not feeling well and we should all enjoy ourselves.

Secretly, Ginger had looked down on the garden through the veil of curtains at all of them, whispering and laughing. The ice swan centerpiece with rose petals frozen inside, a local tradition, melted and lurched against the side of the punch bowl. She wished she could touch her tongue to its cold beak. She'd wanted to be radiant, a laughing bride stepping out of her grandfather's house into a bright future. She'd wanted to climb onto the roof and fly down on them. Wanted this not to be happening. She wanted her mother undead, her father restored to himself. She wanted Mitchell not to feel misery and humiliation. She could not go. She could not *have*. It had not been a decision but a state of being.

Later, J. J. had reported that their cook, Tessie, washing glasses in the kitchen, hummed "I Come to the Garden Alone" to herself as a way to keep calm but every few minutes muttered, "Those chillin, those chillin." Tessie had worked for Catherine and Wills Mason ever since Ginger was a baby, then for Lily ever since the children moved to the House. When J. J. had made a foray into the kitchen for a shot of bourbon, he'd heard her low singing—*and he walks with me and he talks with me and he tells me I am his own*—as she held up each glass to the window, checking for lip prints. The lowering afternoon sun reflected bright rainbow circles onto her black uniform and her dark face.

"Hail, Tessie," J. J. had toasted her. "Another memorable afternoon at the Mason patch." He'd left his dinner jacket somewhere and had pulled open his collar. She watched him pour the shot of bourbon straight down his throat, just like his daddy used to after their mama died. The corners of her lips pulled down and she turned on the hot water full force.

Mitchell and his parents had secluded themselves in the living room, where his mother quietly cursed the day he'd ever brought Ginger into their home, and didn't he know Pattie Martin, who'd always been crazy about him, would not have pulled a stunt like this in a million years?

Caroline Culpepper, Ginger's maid of honor, had talked softly at the door, but Ginger had only said, "I'm sorry, Caroline, but you might as well go on home." Not even J. J. could get Ginger to unlock her door until the last guests drove away. When she did, her dress lay in a jumble on the floor, and the satin shoes, akimbo in different corners of the room, evidently had been tossed at the wall. She looked splotched and ugly sitting on the floor with her knees drawn up. She'd gotten only as far as putting on her underwear and the garter that was supposed to have been tossed to the groomsmen. She stretched out her leg and ripped off the puckered blue elastic. J. J. just stood in the doorway, shaking his head. "Well, now you've done it," he said.

He barely could hear her. "I woke up this morning from a dream that Mother had come to the door. I was getting ready to go out, spraying perfume in my hair. And she looked at me with a smile and said *you are pathetic.* My will just keeps withering, J. J." Then she'd cried, wouldn't speak until the next day. He'd brought her a robe and sat with her, not even having to ask anything else.

Three days later she and Mitchell were married in the garden, where the wicker baskets of flowers had drooped. His parents had refused to come, then refused to speak to her for seven months, his mother having said to Mitchell that he would rue the day he married her. Oh, wasn't she right? Ginger had worn a pale suit and J. J., standing with his arms crossed, had stared at the run in her stocking, alert to the possibility that she would bolt. But she was as pallid as the ivory linen she wore, and she swayed as if she were just up after a spell of malaria. J. J. told her later that she looked like a dog staring in a mirror without seeing the reflected dog.

Lily and Tessie had warmed up the limp leftover cheese straws to crisp them, and the dozen guests they'd called back wouldn't have missed it for the world. J. J., who gave her away, had felt that she was not really going anywhere.

"Sugar, you just got a case of jitters. Everyone gets them, you just got them *bad*," the guests repeated as the cake was cut. Mitchell would have been raving mad if he were anyone else. Instead, he stayed close, his arm always protectively around her.

GINGER HEARD MARCO'S CAR DOOR SLAM. She had not thought of Mitchell in weeks. She wished now that she'd been able, even once, to make up their bed with the pleasure of anticipation. Now, four years since she'd seen him, and still the idea of his body, his perfect body, made her shoulders tense and rise.

From the upstairs window she saw Marco kick the car door closed because his hands were full. He never arrived empty-handed. Striding up the path to the house—there was something of the faun or satyr about him—he was smiling. Ginger smiled to think of him with hairy haunch and goat feet. She loved his black, black curls and tanned skin. ("Is he olive-complected?" Aunt Lily had asked her, trying to be tactful.) Ginger had never known anyone whose natural facial expression was a smile. He must have been born laughing.

The candle she placed on the bedside table, meant to be lighted before a saint, would burn quickly. She smoothed the bed and scattered across the pillows wild mint and yellow sunflower petals from the basket she'd filled earlier. A tremor of joy ran through her. Like a prisoner, she explained to herself, who digs a tunnel with a spoon and finally breaks out in the woods—I'm free, I will be happy. While most women would look on the fulfillment of sex as a deep pleasure, her first emotion was pride, as though she'd broken the record for the hundred-yard dash, or accomplished a high pole vault. Her bare soles on the cool tiles made her want to dance.

Climbing down the ladder stairs to the kitchen, she saw the terrace doors opened to the early evening air and the slope downhill to the river Nesse. What they call a river in Italy hardly qualified as a stream back home in Georgia, but she loved the chuckle of water in the night. She'd rented the farmhouse because it faced the Nesse. All winter she'd slept with the window cracked just to hear the sibilant slide of cascades pouring over rocks, the sweet gurgle where water surged over a dam built by children in summer. Now the flow had slowed to a faint trickle.

Marco, handing her yellow and apricot roses from his mother's garden, embraced her at the same time. "You've transformed! Your neck doesn't have any more rings of dirt." Her eyebrows flew up, two circumflexes, two bent wings. He touched her face with his palm: she felt as smooth as a holy-water font. He thought she sometimes hid behind her cameo-perfect face, but tonight, no, she looked vibrantly *here*. His sister-in-law criticized Ginger's nose— bony, she said—but Marco thought it must be like an English queen's nose. His lips brushed her ear, her raucous hair—a blaze he'd warm himself by anytime.

She felt his compact, muscular body as a jolt (the prisoner, now up and running for the woods), breathed in his soapy shaving scents. He smelled good always; even after hours of work in the sun he smelled horsey, like wet earth and oats. After making love, his underarms let out an acidic, lair odor. What a good animal, she thought, submitting to his arms. Good, she thought. I didn't shy away.

He held a box up, almost out of reach. "Don't open! This is for later."

She grabbed and shook the box.

"No! Give it back. You're terrible!" He took the box inside.

Ginger clipped sprigs of rosemary. "We're having roast chicken with potatoes—surprise, surprise!" Ginger had a limited interest in cooking, though she loved to eat. Roast chicken with herbs was her idea of triumph in the kitchen.

"I could smell it from the car." On the table, a millstone set on top of a thick stone column, she crisscrossed two grapevine cuttings and placed the plates and glasses. His feet up on the low terrace wall, Marco sipped the Campari she brought him and watched the swallows dip and glide, devouring, he knew, thousands of bugs. "*Rondini*," he told her, "those birds—swallows. We watch for them because they are graceful. They fly high when it is dry, low after rain." He only seemed to teach her nouns.

He watched Ginger against the darkening cobalt sky, where a mellow moon like a worn gold watch hung suspended over the mountains. As she moved back and forth from the kitchen to the table, he observed that she had an odd quality of just having landed, something like an annunciation angel, with coral robes barely settling as she pointed her lily toward the Virgin Mary. Other American women he'd met were solid and demanding; they knew what they wanted. Ginger was slippery. She seemed usually vivid at times, like now, whistling "There's No Business Like Show Business." He loved her legs, which he considered wholly American. (The one thing that irritated Ginger about Marco was his habit of stamping certain things generically American.) When he'd studied in Virginia for two years, he'd found the southerners exotic. Ginger had joined his Etruscan research group as an intern after her first year and a half of graduate work at Georgia, while she decided whether or not to continue. Some fear he didn't understand seized her when she contemplated writing a dissertation. To him she seemed a born archaeologist, took in at a glance what other associates hardly saw after it was pointed out to them.

As they excavated the site side by side all day, he had his eyes on her—squatting in the dust as she brushed off an artifact, stepping over the rivulets that sprang from underground springs and ruined their work. American, he thought. It's because she's foreign that she's familiar and unfamiliar—sometimes far from him, with her lower lip bitten and her chin angled up as if she were viewing him from the long end of a telescope. He loved her, but thinking of building a life together confused him. Maybe she was too different from his old girlfriends, from Lucia and Cinzia, his brothers' wives, who moved into Bella Bella, his parents' house, without a murmur and fell into the family as though they'd always been there. He could not see Ginger moving into the other side of the top floor—not that he would want that himself—blending into the rhythm that everyone in the house seemed to find. If Lucia shopped, Cinzia shelled the peas and did the laundry, while his mother presided over the kitchen. They all told the two children what to do, usually contradicting each other, so the children learned to choose among the instructions, essentially doing as they pleased.

As the only unmarried son, he was exempt from all operations of the house, though he helped his father in the vegetable garden more than his brothers did. The house, alive with smells of ironing and stewing, the boys' sweaty hair, an array of boots in the cantina, various colognes and cleansers—the collective odor of family—would it admit the stoic posture, the diffident, aloof Miss America? He summoned a picture of Ginger standing in a doorway having to ask how she could help. No, that would not ever be the scene. They would have their own house, like this one, in the country, and make trips once a year to the States, where her family operated like the labyrinthine, plotless Faulkner novels, and trees grew out of dank swamps. When Cinzia watched TV on the divan, her head sometimes lobbed onto his mother's shoulder. He'd seen Ginger step back from contact, but when the two *baci* on the cheek were un-avoidable, she smiled afterward, touching her fingertips to her face.

After the chicken, Ginger brought out the salad. He stretched his arms and pounded his chest with his fists. *"Luna, luna,"* he shouted. "Moon, moon." No hurry, he remembered, let it play. Let it loop and rewind and play again.

Tonight they were celebrating their team's find—an intact Etruscan six-step stone staircase with a mythological head carved into the base. Gaetano, a classmate of Marco's and a palynologist, had driven up in the afternoon from his work site at Pompeii to consult with him on the faint imprints of plants they'd also discovered. He brought Marco vials containing scents he had re-created from remains he'd discovered in a recently unearthed apothecary shop.

Ginger and Marco lingered at the table. She brought out a bowl of the season's last cherries and a paisley bedspread so they could lie down and look as long at the stars as they wanted. "See that constellation." She pointed. "That's one of Hannibal's elephants coming over the Alps."

"That, *amore,* is Orion." He dangled a cherry above her lips and she snapped at it.

"And that—you see up there to the left the Model T Ford? And there—the tilt-a-whirl."

"What is tilt-a-whirl?"

"A tilt-a-whirl you ride at a carnival. It slings you round and round." He doesn't even know what a tilt-a-whirl is, she thought, and I'm so glad for all he doesn't know. The vacant eyes of her father flashed through her. She could see the horizon in those eyes.

"Are you as good at anything else as you are at astronomy?" Marco rolled on his side and kissed her arm. She threw her other arm around him and moved closer. "Oh, wait a minute." He ran into the house and returned with the box. "Gaetano brought these when he drove up from Pompeii this afternoon. You'd just left—too bad."

He unwrapped tissue paper from around a vial, which she recognized as the cloudy aqua blue of ancient glass. She'd heard that

Gaetano had found a cache of dried unguents, oils, and perfumes last year. He'd spent months analyzing and reproducing them. Marco unwrapped two more. "Let's go upstairs."

Behind her on the ladder stairs, he ran his hand up her leg, his fingers brushing the edge of her panties. She lighted the candle and pulled off her dress in one motion. He had no way of knowing what that action meant to her, but caught a flash of her pleasure. As Marco slowly unbuttoned his shirt, she thrust her arms under his arms, her head against his chest. "Let me hear your heart."

"Let me *show* you my heart." They lay crossways on the bed, which dipped in the middle where light from the moon pooled. Marco reached over for one of the vials and twisted the wax-sealed stopper. He held the opening to her nose. She inhaled the fresh scent of lemon with a smoky, burned edge behind the fragrance. He poured the gold oil into his palm. "Wait for me," he said. He slid down and rubbed his hands together. She closed her eyes, her arms folded behind her head, and felt his hands around her foot, rubbing in the warmed oil. He pushed against each toe, pressed the ball and heel, and gently worked his palm against her instep. The other foot. Her feet stung with pleasure. She looked at Marco at the side of the bed, intent, as she sometimes saw him concentrating at work, but his body had a sheen of silver outline from the candle, and his mouth was parted like that of a small boy sleeping. *Mitchell, we never,* flitted across her mind.

He opened the second wax seal and waved the vial under her nose. She touched her finger to the mouth of the vial and he tipped it. "Grass and cloves." They were kissing deeply, but he moved away, straddled her legs, and began lightly to brush the ancient scent onto her breasts, circling his hand over her nipples, then in larger concentric motions. The oil sent an electrical charge into her blood. Slowly, even the part of her she always held in reserve ignited. *So this is what they mean.* In the last instant of unyielding, she thought fleetingly, *there must be life after death.* She moistened her hands on her breasts and reached down to caress him. "I can't take much more," he said.

Ginger pushed him over on his back, opened the smaller third vial, and emptied the contents on his chest, quickly spreading the oil. The fecund, grapy heart of the wild iris steeped into her hands, running along his sides and down his body. *Water falling over rocks.* He heard the small cries that came from his throat. Startled by the new sound, he laughed, said "Bless Gaetano," wrapped his arms around her back and up through her hair, and they had their love.

July 8

CASS DEAL TURNED HIS PICKUP into the gates of Magnolia Cemetery. He stopped at his caretaker's shack for a cup of instant coffee. A scorcher coming up, he thought. The magnolias over in the Confederate Corner were heavily in bloom, sending out their sweet stench. He hated the smell. So many of the coffins that rolled out of the Ireland Funeral Home hearses held a single magnolia on the polished mahogany. Elegant, he'd been told, but he figured it was just cheap. Sure made cleanup easier. He poured hot water over the acrid granules. Not many of the grand funerals anymore. Just get them in the ground and go. People live too long these days, outstay their welcome. Cass, at seventy, did not put himself into this category.

He threw his rake and bucket into the pickup bed and drove toward the new part of the cemetery. Funeral Friday at two. He had a grave to dig and prepare before the funeral home people came out to set up their tent and rows of chairs, which tended to sink into the soft earth under especially heavy mourners. He rolled slowly along the grassy lanes, hardly glancing at the granite angel in the Williams plot, the jar of yellow glads on old man Conrad's grave, and the diamondback stretched on the grave of the Adams child, who died of infantile paralysis. Collapsed lung, wasn't it? The new part of the cemetery sloped toward a swamp. Snakes often came up to warm themselves on a convenient stone. He passed the Mason plot, the only one with a fence. The iron gate long since had rusted open, and the tangled roses that Wills Mason planted for his shameful wife always drooped in the heat. A mess and Cass was not paid extra for cleaning up, even though extra work was required here. They did sometimes send their own help out to prune. Just beyond the Mason's, he spotted trash on the ground and stopped to pick it up. A smashed Dr Pepper can and a white handkerchief. Dirty, too. He threw them in his bucket and gunned the truck. He caught the flicker of ribbons from four standing wreaths. Raw red hump of dirt and Merrilee Gooding lying under it. Who'd ever think someone that pretty could up and die? They say Dr. Strickman took out a tumor the size of a football. Her blanket of red roses looked like dried blood. Just goes to show how quick it is from can to can't.

Morning sun exploded through the slash pines at the edge of his domain. Rain two days ago. The ground would give easily. He'd long ago lost count of the number of graves he'd dug, but he knew to the minute how long it used to take before he got the Bobcat a few years back—five hours and ten minutes steady unless he encountered a limestone shelf. That was trouble. The Bobcat saved his back. Quicker now. Rake, level, drive the backhoe to the site, make sure the dirt lands in a neat clump. Then he'd get Aldo out to pour the cement liner. He knew everything about his job after forty years at it. That's what he liked about the dead, he often said; you always know what to expect from them. Once he found two skeletons and some beads and broken pots about four feet under. A professor from the college over in Douglas had taken them away and no one ever heard any more about them. Creek Indians, he'd told Cass. He'd hit water sometimes. The Ireland people just hoped the bereaved didn't see the coffin float for a second before the dearly beloved settled into the ground.

———

LILY MASON AIMED rather than drove her Lincoln out Lemon Street toward Magnolia Cemetery around nine o'clock. After Tessie had called and said she'd be late to work on account of a sick neighbor, Lily had bathed, dressed, and then put together her own breakfast of black tea and two chocolate cookies, a vice she permitted herself, along with a cordial in the afternoon before her nap and a strong gin martini before supper. Gin, she thought, tasted pure and clean, the way water ought to taste and didn't. By quarter of nine, she had fed CoCo, her green parrot, and wandered in her garden among the larkspur, lemon lilies, invasive verbena, and rusty camellia bushes. She needed to tend to the irises on the slope down to the pond. The spent flowers had dried to ash blue on their muscular stems. CoCo squawked at her from his wicker cage. He had spent his early bird-hood in a machinist's shop, so instead of words he made car sounds, a metallic clattering and shrieking that amused Lily but no one else. The jessamine, she saw without any intention to do anything about it, tangled into the spirea's drooping arcs of white blooms. This summer everything wants to escape its boundaries, she thought. Bridal bouquet, they called spirea, but no bride ever carried it down the aisle—too common. If she'd ever been a bride, she would have carried blue delphiniums, white roses, and trailing ivy. Ginger's bouquet—but she didn't remember. It must have been half-dead by the time she stood right here clutching it in the garden.

Lily snapped off two flowers to take out to her parents' graves, imagining that she could show them to her mother as she used to. "Look at the white star inside this morning glory. Isn't that something?" she might say, or "That daylily—it looks freshly dipped in yellow paint." But she was not fool enough to speak to them aloud. She slipped her clippers into the glove compartment and laid a newspaper on the back seat. Her closest friend, Eleanor, was meeting her at Magnolia Cemetery to pick roses, then they were going to the Three Sisters Café for coffee and a chat.

———

ELEANOR LAID A BUNCH of purple foxgloves across her husband's name carved in north Georgia granite, Holt Ames Whitefield. Four years ago, after his death, she'd fallen into the habit of visiting at his graveside every morning except Thursday, her beauty parlor day. She'd had a marble bench erected and she sat there a few minutes, sometimes reading to herself a daily meditation from *The Upper Room*, sometimes just remembering the trips they took to Haiti, Jamaica, California, and Alaska. Those frozen aqua waters and the ship cracking through ice, the sudden looming icebergs against a pure blue sky—she couldn't help but think death must feel like that. It was still impossible to think Holt—Holt!—would not return. Sometimes when she took in the mail, she thumbed through the junk, half expecting a letter from him. The sudden red arterial hemorrhage from his throat after the surgery and he was gone. "His time was up," Father Tyson had said, a remark that caused Eleanor to cut the contents of her donation envelope in half. She and Lily agreed on the subject of Father Tyson. Eleanor smiled to remember her friend's dismissal of him as "neither useful nor ornamental." But poor Holt. Who's to say his time was up? When she was a fresh widow, she used to curl into the fetal position every morning when she woke to realize that he was not there. Finally, after four years, the sharp edge of pain subsided. Now she was at ease in the mornings and liked to look downhill toward the cypress trees standing in black water and the white floating hyacinths.

She was irritated to hear Cass Deal's motor and to see his red machine charging at a grave site in the distance, lifting and dumping forkfuls of earth. Where is Lily? she wondered. She said aloud a few lines from a poem Holt liked—he had been the high school English teacher and she had been the math teacher—remembering as she said them that she used to be annoyed when he shifted to his oration voice and quoted verse.

> Some say the world will end in fire,
> Some say in ice.

From what I've tasted of desire
I hold with those . . .

She could not remember the rest. Would desire lead one to favor fire or ice? She wasn't sure; Holt would have to finish it for himself. Not that for an instant she thought she was communing with him. Dead is dead. Father Tyson can hold forth all day and dead is still dead. She just liked seeing his name and dates so solidly present. 1906–1971. *Q.E.D.*: Existence proven for as long as granite lasts.

She shaded her eyes and spotted Lily's car speeding around the curve before the cemetery gate. Good. Plenty of time. Eleanor's bridge group was coming to her house for lunch. Hattie at this moment must be stewing the hen for the chicken salad, she thought, and taking out the starched pink linen place mats she brought back from the Jamaica trip. The bridge club met every Tuesday for lunch and a few rubbers. Over the years two tables had dwindled to one, and, frankly, Eleanor was not sure how much longer she would be willing to listen to her friends discuss their phobias and aches. Lily had become exasperated and quit three years ago. Now the others enjoyed being able to win. Lily had remembered every bid, every card, and was prone to trump brilliantly. When partnered with Eleanor, no one else had had a chance.

Eleanor intended to fill her house with bunches of the lovely Lady Godiva roses that just went to waste clambering all over the fence of the Mason plot, a double waste, really, those scented perfume clouds—blackberry, melon, lime water—floating over the dead. They flourished almost all May and June, and even now into July, a profusion of rambling pink double-bloomers, their canes twisting between the iron fence spikes. Of course by August, everything gave up and wilted. She and Lily had gathered them before, although Lily never wanted to take any home. Eleanor already envisioned them on her sideboard in the silver pitcher. She should have left Hattie a note to polish it.

She slung open the car door, making sure it caught and would not slam back on her ankle. She felt as strong as she had at sixty-five, though less agile since the left hip replacement she'd had over in Tipton two years ago. They'd installed a new metal hip to replace the bone that crumpled as she jumped over a ditch to pick black-eyed Susans. She'd had to sit in the ditch until a passing tobacco farmer saw her, hauled her out, and took her all the way to the hospital. A nice man, he was. After she'd recovered, she sent Holt, Junior out to his house with several jars of her peach pickles and plum chutney.

Eleanor drove over to the Mason graves just as Lily swung the cream puff, as her nephew J. J. called it, inside the gate. Eleanor watched her run over the edge of Annie Ruth Steepleheart's grave. Lily swerved and lurched back onto the path toward the Mason plot. Eleanor closed her eyes. Lily was such a wild card in the deck.

With both feet on the ground, Eleanor hoisted herself out of the car and felt inside her bag for the scissors.

"Am I late?" Lily slammed her door. She pecked the air near Eleanor's cheek. She'd known her all her life. Eleanor, a few years older, had taken Lily in when she was a new teacher at the mill school, but all her good advice came to nothing: Lily hated teaching. After Lily's daddy, Big Jim, died, she resigned and devoted herself to gardening. She and Eleanor were the founding members of the Robert E. Lee Garden Club and had talked on the phone and swapped a cutting, recipe, or magazine article almost every day since. As Lily saw Eleanor flicking open her clippers and rolling up her sleeves, she flashed on her, radiant and capable, presiding over a long table at Christmas dinner when Holt, Junior was a baby, at the beginning of their close friendship.

"No more than usual. How are you, sugar?" She saw that Lily had hennaed her own hair again. The orangy cast of the dye shone like cheap mahogany furniture. Otherwise, Lily's coiled chignon pinned high looked the way it had at fifteen when they'd run into each other at club dances at Carrie's Island and boys swarmed around Eleanor. Eleanor had glimpsed Big Jim holding forth at a table where Lily bit her lip and sipped lemonade and her mother, Florence, looked supremely bored. Lily would have been a fine wife for someone, Eleanor thought loyally, if she hadn't been overshadowed by her parents when she was young. She had remained a daughter rather than making that necessary transition into her own woman. Later, she was raising Ginger and J. J., for which, surely, she would have stars in her crown.

They scanned the voluptuous roses hanging in bunches like ready-made bouquets. "I like that blouse. Is it new?" Lily was prone to wear old clothes, so anytime she appeared in something decent Eleanor praised it. "Yellow is a good color for you."

"Ginger sent it for my birthday last year." Lily muzzled her nose into a full bloom. "If Paris could get that scent into a bottle, women would pay any price." She would not, of course. A dusting of talcum was fine for her. She snipped stems and handed an armful of roses to Eleanor, who took them to the car. As Lily clipped, something caught her eye, a quick glimmer—a blue jay wing? She leaned down and squinted. Through the cascades of bloom, she glimpsed a pile of clay on the other side of the fence near the graves. What on earth? She pushed through the gate and stopped.

Immediately, she reeled away, suddenly unable to see. She looked up at the sky and tried to focus. The early morning buffed blue was turning to the bleached midday paleness, which would stay that way until twilight, when farm dust turned the lower horizon a streaked rose and orange. Harmon Dunn, the druggist, said he saw blue and gold confetti when his retina detached; maybe hers had come undone. She blinked several times, then opened her eyes slowly and turned back to the sight she always would see incised on her eyeballs. A surge of rejection pushed through her. "Eleanor," she managed to say, but Eleanor was spreading roses on the back seat of her car. Blue dress, black hair. "No," she whispered. A gash in the ground, stone smashed, bronze coffin turned upside down. Catherine. Preserved, darker but preserved, lying on the side of her own grave.

Then Eleanor was beside her. "My stars above!" Eleanor heard her own burble as though her throat were filled with water, then she tried to regain herself so she'd know she had not simply flipped, as her older sister, Rebecca, had when she walked out of the dentist's office and had no idea where she was. Rebecca ended up in a crib in a rest home in Crossaway, curled up like a baby. Eleanor had to faint or scream, but she only stood steadily, taking in the inconceivable sight of Catherine Mason, dead and buried for years, tumped out of her grave.

Lily grabbed the gate. No sound came from her except for a stopped moan, as though she'd had her breath knocked out. A memory rushed through her. *How do you like to go up in the swing, up in the sky so blue? I'm soaring through the pecan tree, my hands grasping the ropes, feet out straight, but my mother pushes my swing too high, I'm falling through the air. Falling and falling.* She grabbed Eleanor's arm. From the swamp, a breeze blew up, just enough to scatter rose petals across the graves of the other Masons. A bank of them had gathered under Catherine's feet.

Eleanor's brain began to tick. She must help Lily. Oh Lord, Catherine's feet, her feet, her bare feet splayed out with red polish still on the toes. Eleanor remembered Alan Ireland handing back Holt's polished wing tips when she took in his burial suit. "We won't be needing shoes," he'd said dryly. Catherine lay perfectly composed, as she had in the coffin, her hands crossed over her stomach. Rigid as stone, Eleanor expected. The light caught Catherine's hair and it still shone. But her skin had turned leathery, almost gold, like the worn-out suede jacket in the back of her closet. Holt. He, too, would still be recognizable, thanks to all the chemicals the Ireland boy pumped into him. Eleanor would not want to be seen like that.

"Oh no, Eleanor, look, Daddy's . . ." Lily gestured to the other side of the plot. Eleanor took in at a glance Big Jim Mason's grave sloshed with black paint. She put her arm around Lily and firmly steered her to the car.

CASS ADMIRED THE PRECISION of the hole he'd dug. He sat down for a smoke before he rode back to the shack. He saw the two ladies clipping roses over in the Mason grounds, then a few seconds later watched them both get in Eleanor's car, leaving Lily's Lincoln blocking a crossroad. Eleanor was about the only regular morning visitor. Most of the locals came on Sundays, if at all. That old maid Lily Mason shouldn't just leave her car wherever she pleased. But that's the Masons for you, he thought. He watched Eleanor tear up the path as she pressed the accelerator too quickly and spun gravel behind her. The pair of them, Cass thought. One of them a speed demon; the other old biddy will uproot a telephone pole one of these days—her son ought to stop her from driving. Matter of time. But that Holt, Junior wore his pants hiked up around his waist. Pansy, some said. It would be a cold day in hell before he could stop his mama from doing anything she pleased.

LILY FEARED FOR HER HEART, which gonged against her chest. She slumped over, her face in her hands. Eleanor scratched off, tossing the roses she still held to the floor.

"Stop, Eleanor, I'm going to throw up." Lily opened the door and leaned out as her stomach wrenched. When she pulled the door shut, she closed it on the tip of her little finger. Eleanor leaned over, shoved down the handle, and jerked Lily's arm inside. The flattened fingertip and pushed-in nail turned purple. Lily began to whimper. Eleanor drove the entire mile into town—swerved once to avoid a cat and almost hit a child on a bicycle—before she thought of what she should do.

Tessie came running out of the House when she saw Eleanor leading Lily from the car. The bright yellow blouse was spotted with blood. "We'll talk in a minute, Tessie. Let's get her into her room."

Eleanor turned back the bed. Tessie got a bag of ice to put on

Lily's finger. "You just lie down," Eleanor said. I'll go to the sheriff's office. Don't get up, now. You stay right here. I'll ask Tessie to make you a soothing cup of tea. Where's J. J.?"

"J. J.'s off fishing. Eleanor, how can we bear this?"

"They'll catch the animal who did it and put him *under* the jail. I'm going to call Deanie Robart and have him come out and look at that finger, too. And I'll find J. J. You just rest." Eleanor picked up the phone beside Lily's bed and dialed the doctor. Deanie himself answered and promised to stop by Lily's before noon.

"I'm so sorry, Eleanor, but I'm glad you were with me. You know that my feelings about Catherine are mixed-up. I can't help that, but even so, she didn't deserve this." Lily felt about to throw up again.

"No. No one deserves this." Eleanor well knew that Lily always had had an unacknowledged jealousy of monumental proportions toward her sister-in-law. Lily's younger brother, Wills, had seemed to shift all his devotion to Catherine when he married her. Then when he came home exhausted from war, he treated Lily in a fond but distracted way. Since Lily never married, her brother's desertion had wounded her. After the war, he never quite seemed to hear what she said.

AS SOON AS SHERIFF RALPH HUNNICUTT HELPED ELEANOR out to her car, he took the steps back up to his office three at a time, flipped fast through his Rolodex, and dialed. A secretary answered, "Ireland Funeral Home."

"Let me have Alan, please, ma'am."

"He's counseling right now," she answered. "May I have him call you?"

Counseling, my ass, Ralph thought. He's showing some sad sucker around that gloomy room of coffins, advising them to buy the one with the hand-stitched satin lining. "Tell him it's an emergency. This is Sheriff Hunnicutt and he'll need to meet me right fast at the cemetery. He'll see my car at the Mason plot in the old section. I'm leaving right now." With the phone wedged between his ear and shoulder, he buckled on his gun while he talked. He'd only been the county sheriff for three months and he hadn't faced anything other than car wrecks and fistfights.

"Well, Sheriff, what is this in regards to? He's very busy with a client just now."

"Just tell him to come. I'll talk to him there." He grabbed his notebook.

At the entrance to Magnolia, he stopped where Cass Deal was raking pine needles. He looked like a child's stick figure drawing. "How ya doing, Cass? I got a pretty strange visit from Eleanor Whitefield. Have you noticed anything odd this morning?"

"No, what's her gripe?"

"Get in." He repeated what Eleanor had told him.

"That's crazy. She's losing her marbles—you should have seen her drive out here. And look—the two of them left Lily's car just parked haphazardly."

"She always drove like a bat. You know she's sharp as a razorback hog."

Ralph parked behind Lily's car. Everything was exactly as Eleanor had described.

They stood silently, staring. Ralph's ears rang. He thought something had gone wrong with his hearing. He wiped his neck with his handkerchief. Finally, Cass said, "Holy, holy shit. Jesus H. Christ, if this isn't the damndest . . ." He faltered and grabbed onto Ralph's sleeve while the plain of the flat earth tilted upward then steadied. "Sumabitch. Those ladies came upon this."

The two men stood still until Ralph forced himself forward. *He* would have to handle this, he realized. A few bees plied the roses and one buzzed around the face of Catherine Mason. Ralph was not close enough to her to shoo it away but waved his hand in the air anyway. "Have you seen anything, Cass—that is, anything else . . ." He gestured toward the body on the ground. He touched the dry black paint on Big Jim's grave. "Any cars stopping, any people at all?" Any vampires, he wanted to say, but he couldn't bring himself to joke. Cass shook his head no. "That dirt has been rained on," Ralph went on, "and look here, the side of her dress is muddy. She's been lying here at least since that thunderstorm we had two days ago."

"Well, I can't check every damn grave every day."

Evidently, Mrs. Wills Mason had been out in the rain. Ralph looked at her hands and throat for jewelry; there was none. "The only motive I can imagine is grave robbing. Do people get buried with their rings?"

Cass thought not, though come to think of it, he hadn't seen an actual dead person in years, just their sealed coffins.

Her mouth was firmly shut, a faint smile on her lips. Odd, given the way she died. Ralph figured the grave robbers hadn't looked for gold in her tight mouth. Her tongue—was it still shaped around her last word, whatever that was? He stepped nearer. Holy Christ. His stomach flipped as he noticed the fringe of her eyelashes in the sunken sockets. He'd seen worse in Vietnam but this was different. He'd heard that nails keep growing after death but hers were still neat ovals on her dried-up fingers.

The men saw the Ireland limousine approaching and stepped out to warn Alan what he was about to see.

Even he, who handled corpses all the time, lunged backward, then forward, with his arms out as though balancing on a floating log. Crazily, he started to laugh. Ralph noticed that his eyes were odder than Catherine's, like a partially submerged hippo's looking out of the murk. His black suit hung on him as though from a hook. Why is it that morticians look the part? Ralph himself, or so he imagined, could be a lawyer or manager. He had planned to study pharmacology at Georgia State but instead had gone into the army at nineteen, after a year of bad grades from too much partying. His grandfather was sheriff for thirty years, and when he died, the torch passed to Ralph, home after ten years in the army and already sick of working the counter at Walgreen's. He'd been easily elected last year, with an uppity black candidate as his opponent.

"Have you notified the GBI, or are you planning on investigating this yourself?" Alan asked.

Ralph hadn't thought of calling the state Bureau of Investigation yet but quickly covered himself. "Cass, you stay here until I can get back with a guard. I'm going in town to call this in right now. Alan, would you see if you can come up with a tarp to cover her up tonight? I guess we better not touch anything until I get in touch with the GBI fellows." He was sorry he'd said "guess"; he should be more decisive. "I'll call the paper, too. They can send out a photographer for my records."

CASS LEANED AGAINST A TALL HEADSTONE in the plot opposite the Masons. What was he supposed to do if the crazy came back to view his handiwork? The stone cast no shade but felt cool against his back. He was trying to think. What day was it? It was Friday—the rain came on Saturday. He'd arrived in the morning and thought that the Bobcat was not parked exactly in the usual place but closer to the shed wall. He remembered having to sidle to it, but he'd assumed he'd just parked funny. The key was in the ignition, where he always left it. He should have told Ralph but he didn't want any blame for this. I'll remember later, he thought, if I have to.

HATTIE HEARD ELEANOR PULL INTO THE DRIVEWAY, then softly thud into the back wall of the garage. She came in looking wild-eyed, her hair sticking up. "What on earth's the matter, Miz Eleanor? Have you done been in an accident?" That she hadn't so far, Hattie considered a miracle. She and Miss Lily both drove like maniacs. Eleanor walked straight through the kitchen and cranked up the living room and dining room air conditioners. Hattie already had set up the card table. Eleanor thought she never would calm down again or ever shake the image of Catherine from her head. Worse, she felt a new kind of horror over Holt's death. Everybody died, death is a part of life, of course, but she felt hot rage at the thought of how we're squished out like bugs even after—she knew she was being irrational—all the times we've washed our hair, tended to the insurance, wiped grease off the counters, taken in the paper. Daily life was what she passionately loved. It's so easily assumed while we're living it—running downtown when shrimp come in from the coast, taking up a hem, dreaming of floating in a warm pond. She saw the bright blood from Holt's mouth, spurting red on white tile. She was barking mad. She ran her finger over her lower lip, the gesture that calmed her.

"Hattie, pour us a cup of coffee, please, and sit down. I have something to tell you."

Hattie's son, Scott, was the hunting companion of Catherine's son, J. J. Because Scott was black, no one ever would say simply that he and J. J. Mason were friends. J. J. was peculiar, everyone knew. He had few friends of any color, and if seen with any woman, she was bound to be someone beneath him. Since J. J. was notoriously hard to find, Eleanor had told the sheriff that Hattie might know if the two men were fishing. Hattie had shown her a Polaroid last week of J. J. holding up a rockfish he caught—a thirty-five-pound monster, prehistoric-looking with barnacles around its mouth. J. J. had one foot up on a stump. His glistening chest, Eleanor thought, looked barbarian in the sun, and although he was not actually smiling, he had a pleased look. He wore his hair combed straight back, black as a burnt match, just like Catherine's. Just like Catherine's still looked. Eleanor wondered how he could be all that pleased when he had not amounted to much. With all his gifts of superb intelligence and money, all he did was roam around the woods, an outcast. And charm—he could turn the charm off or on. She'd seen him many times looking stormy. Lily had plenty to put up with.

The kitchen table sat under a row of uncurtained, small-paned windows. The air-conditioning tamed the sun pouring through the thin limbs of the mimosa. Eleanor sat down and concentrated on the face-sized blue hydrangeas pushing against the glass. She treated them with sulfur every year to get them to bloom the exact shade her own mother's always had; otherwise, they reverted to the common pink. As she concentrated on Catherine, her vision blurred with tears. It seemed that infant faces, deprived of oxygen, drifted against the glass. She wondered if she should check on Lily. No, later, when Lily—and I—calm down. Lily, she supposed, will have to tell her brother, Wills. Heaven knows what she'll say.

Hattie looked at her expectantly. Eleanor recounted her morning with Lily. "A shame and a disgrace," Eleanor concluded, "Catherine Mason lying out in the rain."

Hattie said, "Lord, Lord," and shook her head. She hadn't talked to Scott since Sunday dinner. As far as she knew, he was out at the grocery store he managed for J. J.

When Eleanor had told her everything, she suddenly remembered the roses. "Hattie, would you mind getting those roses? I think they slid to the floor of my car. I'm too pooped."

"You mean you still intending to have them ladies over? After what you've been through?"

"Yes, I might as well. I might need some company." It never occurred to Eleanor that she could cancel the bridge club, that she could lie flat on her big bed with a washcloth over her eyes until she calmed down.

"Every time you look toward them roses it's going to all come rushing back on you."

"Well, it's a pity for them to go to waste. Life goes on, or should," she finished uncertainly. She suddenly had no idea what to do with herself. She went into the bathroom to change the guest towels and replace the bar of Ivory with a soap shaped like a scallop shell.

She then filled the pitcher, took the roses to the sideboard, and carefully began to arrange them. Her breath still came in shallow puffs. Breathe normally, she told herself, breathe in the fragrance, calm down, be normal, go slowly. But images of Catherine flashed like fast slides. Lily never mentioned her, and Eleanor had not thought of her in months, years. Now she saw her coming down the church steps in a fur coat that dragged, her right eyebrow raised as she made peanut brittle for the Christmas bazaar, her picture in the paper when she caught a blue marlin down in Apalachicola, with Wills holding up forked fingers over her head and looking goony over her shoulder. She brushed her face across the pink rose petals, trying to take in their quietude. Oh, Catherine in her coffin at the funeral home. Eleanor had filed by during visitation, as had everyone in town. She was surprised that there was a viewing, given the circumstances. The room was crowded with wreaths. Little Ginger stood off to the side looking like Orphan Annie. Wills sat on a folding chair with his hands in his hair and wouldn't look up at anyone. Lily fluttered around him, not that he noticed. Not only was Catherine on view—no sign of damage—but she was half propped up. Eleanor stripped leaves off the fleshy roses. She paused, eyes closed, and the image unlocked. She saw Catherine in the coffin at Ireland's, looking not at all as though she were asleep but looking uncomfortable and seriously dead in a bright blue dress.

Irritated with the floppy blossoms, Eleanor haphazardly plopped the Lady Godivas in the gleaming pitcher and they fell perfectly into place. "God damn, what a morning," she murmured.

WHEN RALPH CAME IN FROM THE CEMETERY, Carol, his two-mornings-a-week secretary, was typing carbons on the two arrests from Saturday night's fight at the Gulf station. Her blond hair, teased out a foot this morning, looked more like the explosion of a mushroom cloud than a beehive.

"I've already heard," she announced. "Alan Ireland called to tell you he has a tarp pinned down and told me all about it. Bizarre is not the word! This is going to shake the town to its bare little roots!" She pounded both fists on the typewriter and laughed. "It's like a horror movie that you turn on at three in the morning: matron of prominent family assaulted by ghouls after exhumation."

Ralph didn't know what "exhumation" meant, but he assumed it meant she'd been dug up. Carol was studying to be a court reporter, commuting three mornings a week all the way to Macon. Her wild laugh startled him. He was sickened by the sight he'd seen, but his own impulse had been to joke about vampires. He could still hear Alan's strangled laugh. To outsiders this whole thing would have a grisly humor. "We'll be the laughingstock of south Georgia. It's not six months since all the papers had a big time with that nut out at the mill who was found dead in his garage with eighty birdcages full of squirrels. And no doubt some old-timers who remember way back will say the Masons had something coming."

"Meaning?" She was from Savannah and didn't know the Masons from borscht.

"Old man Mason—Big Jim—was a character of the first order. He organized voting the dead, acted like he'd invented this world. I don't know—you used to hear stories. People danced to his tune around here. And his daddy before him. Then they're some who think Big Jim hung the moon and stars." His own grandfather, for one. Big Jim had given Ralph's grandfather the money to buy the large house, where Ralph grew up with his parents, an aunt, his grandparents, and a cousin. Why Big Jim came up with the cash, Ralph never knew. Other relatives came and went over the years. Now Ralph lived there alone.

"Sounds charming, this Big Jim."

He sat at his desk for a few moments, trying to take notes before he dialed the GBI. Was this even in their jurisdiction? He hoped to hell it was. He dreaded the calls he would have to make. He'd pass on as many as he could to Carol. He would have to call J. J. Mason immediately and, he guessed, then go out to talk to Lily. He'd just as soon Lily go out to the Columns Rest Home to tell Wills Mason.

He rehearsed what he would say. "I have some bad news . . ." "Something you need to know about has come up . . ." "Your mother has been found . . ." For some situations there just are not any words; at those times you just have to make them up on the spot.

"Jesus H., Carol, she's lying out there sprawled in the mud. What the hell is going on? She's been dead forever. A suicide."

"Ugly, ugly. I don't know. The buck stops with you, soldier."

"Hey, lay off." Screw you, he wanted to say. He always blushed when she called him "soldier," a reference to his Vietnam medals and maybe not a flattering one. He would have to look into the stored files later. He swiveled his chair right then left.

When Catherine Mason did herself in, her daughter, Ginger, was in Ralph's seventh-grade class; J. J. was in junior high, two years ahead. When Ginger finally came back to school, they'd all looked at her in awe. Everyone had heard that she discovered her mother dead on the kitchen floor with a hunting rifle beside her. He'd heard endless whispered stories: about Mrs. Mason pulling the trigger with her toe to shoot herself in the heart; about Ginger walking in with her plaid book satchel, expecting the aroma of brownies, and finding her own mother's blood splattered all over the floor; about J. J. disappearing into the woods for days after he heard; and then a couple of years later Dr. Wills Mason having a stroke that left him gaga for good. After that, Ralph wasn't as able to think of his own family as nuts, with their ordinary drinking and shouting in the night, a mother who believed that the end of the world was at hand. He still had dish towels around the house that she'd embroidered with the red word *repent*.

Back in school, Ginger didn't cut up like she used to. Before, she'd been a smart-ass. Now she'd stay in at recess and read at her desk. Everyone was shy around her. Once he and several others had tried to drag her out to play softball—she had been the top choice among the girls before—and she fiercely shook them off and said, "Leave me alone!," emphasizing each word through gritted teeth. Ralph's memory of her after that was fuzzy. When Dr. Mason later took his nosedive, she and J. J. went to live with their daddy's sister, Lily, on Palmetto Road in their old family place. In high school,

Ginger became one of the pretty, popular girls, the model-student type. But no running onto the football field to embrace a hero; not much backseat fun with her. Ralph was, at that time, preoccupied with baseball and working at the Sacred Pig. They'd had the prom on the lawn at old man Mason's. It was a smear of memory. All the beautiful girls, and what stuck for Ralph was the sight of Ginger's Aunt Lily serving punch in a green evening dress. He'd looked down and noticed she had on grass-stained tennis shoes. He remembered making out like crazy with skinny, hot Connie Sims, even though his date was Judith Ann Krasner, privately called Big Dinners among the football team.

SHE LOOKED TOWARD THE TOP OF THE HILL at the Etruscan wall made from stones as big as Fiats. Under the shade of a linden tree, Ginger spread out her work. Planks across the sawhorses so engagingly called *capretti* (little goats) made a good surface for her two boxes of stones from the Melone III site, numbered according to where they were found. These she had selected to look at over the leisurely weekend. She took her coffee out, too, with slices of the unsalted Tuscan bread she was finally used to, piled with tomatoes and chopped basil. She couldn't get enough tomatoes and bought a cascade still attached to the stalk every day. She sat down at the table. Here a breeze stirred even on inferno days like this one.

These pale gold stones all bore some distinctive evidence of carving, perhaps only a ridge or curve that showed the use of a tool against it. They'd come to light next to a long flat stone incised with a spiral. They could be something or nothing. Several smaller stones seemed to have similar flourishes.

She separated those, then began to look at various pieces, turning them from side to side. The damp one-thousand-piece jigsaw puzzles of the White House and the pyramids that she and J. J. used to put together at the cabin always ended up with something the shape of Florida or Montana missing—the crucial tip of the pyramid or the edge of the roof—never just a piece of sky or grass. The puzzles took days; they'd become obsessed to finish, and when she fell asleep in the cot next to J. J.'s, she'd see pieces of the puzzle all night. Somehow the incidents and people in her dreams would also be puzzle pieces. She'd get up the next morning and wander in her shorties back to the card table, where she'd find J. J. already trying a piece, absently eating cereal.

She rubbed the edges of the tufa, consciously pushing out of her mind any thought of J. J. The Philandering Hermit, she'd begun to call him. Although she understood why he kept on treading water, she wished he would change. Unformed, too, was the instinct that if he didn't change, she couldn't either. Together they'd been Romulus and Remus, exposed on the hillside. But Lily was no she-wolf. Lily was a calm, benign presence who allowed them to bring up each other.

After Wills's stroke, their own house in Swan had been sold. A dentist had installed his office in the sunroom and lived with his wife and three bucktoothed children in the rest of the house. They didn't know what happened to the wicker porch furniture, their old toys, the curvy white radio their mother used to play when she made chocolate jetties on the marble-topped kitchen table, or even what happened to the kitchen table. When Wills was taken to the hospital, Lily had driven them to Atlanta to the Ice Follies; they'd stayed in a hotel and ordered ginger ale and hamburgers sent up by room service; they saw the Battle of Atlanta at the Cyclorama. Lily let them order ice cream at midnight. Lily said Wills was going to need a very long rest at the Columns and they should stay with her; after all, the House was their daddy's home and their home, too, and always would be.

Ginger and J. J. had tried not to look when they rode by their old house on their bicycles, not wanting to see the swing still hanging in the pecan tree, their mother's rose garden looking scrawny. They'd survived and each of them began to develop the clever barricades against memory that would become their personalities and characters. They didn't know if Lily loved them. Silently, they had only the knowledge of the solidity of each other. They didn't talk about that either.

The C-shapes on the Etruscan stones could be curls of hair. A head, or maybe the whole body, formed on the lid of a sarcophagus. That's not what she hoped, though she loved the carved likenesses of the departed on Etruscan coffin lids. The museums were full of them, all attesting to the life of the person so long dead. Her favorite was a double statue, a man and a woman raised from reclining, looking off at something in the distance. Ginger found it impossible to see them without almost overhearing their conversation. *Look,* he is saying, *do you see that . . .* They both had those ancient, sweet, archaic smiles of mystery and intimacy, their physical bond clear from the harmonious folds of their gowns, their ease with each other—not easy to find that in this life or the next. She imagined them, not on a sarcophagus, but on a boat, floating toward a large happiness. Something whispered, a secret between them, lasting all these centuries. Her own marriage never hinted toward a voyage into eternity together.

At the site she was working, Marco's team of Italian archaeologists found the first tomb last summer, perhaps seventh century B.C., and of the characteristic half-cantaloupe shape they called *melone.* In the past two decades, several of those had been uncovered outside the town wall. She looked at her photos—the stairway they'd found and a small sphinx. They'd also located another broken section of stairway, after digging through several strata of carbonized sheep dung, the remains of a stone wall, sherd, and ash as hard as lava. One of the old Italian workers was disgusted: "The whole town is a museum. This land is prime for olives."

She sipped her coffee, glancing up at her fragment of wall, as she thought of it. For four months, she had logged the time that every dawn and noon struck the stones. It was easy enough to wake up because the house, six or seven olive terraces below the wall, had the exact same southern orientation, and the sun came blaring into the bedroom as soon as it cleared the low, undulating foothill of the Apennines across the valley. By six in the afternoon, the sun moved over the hill behind her house. She had a theory. The texts said that the wall was part of Monte Sant'Egidio's original town wall. But the angle seemed off, even after studying all the ancient maps. Oddly, not much site work had been done since 1885.

Since college, since divorce, since a stint in San Francisco, where she found the hippie movement revolting, then a dismal year in New York working for an insurance company, she had found nothing to stick to for long. Her attempts to move *out* all ended with several despondent months back at the House, with Lily suggesting various impossible men around Swan. During the last siege, she'd ordered a course catalogue from the University of Georgia. Partly because it was listed first, she read the offerings in archaeology. Immediately, she decided to go. Typical of Ginger. To everyone's astonishment, including her own, she loved her courses. Although everyone in Swan expected her to become bored and drop this work, she had sustained her interest for over three years now. If she could get a Steimleicher grant, she could start to solidify her speculations on the possibility that the wall was a portion of a sun temple. But she would have to go back to graduate school first. She could almost imagine heading her own team.

Privately, she'd had it with how the Etruscans went to their deaths. Her two previous intern digs took place in dank underground tombs tunneled into hillsides, with a director who farted when he walked fast and left all the scut work to the interns. Marco's project was all in the light.

She ran inside to answer the phone. An unmistakable southern voice said, "May I please speak to Ginger Mason? Is that you, Ginger?"

"Yes, I'm here." The drawn-out *Gin-jah* suddenly sounded exotic; she was used to the strain of speaking and understanding in another language. No one from Swan would be casually calling—how's Italy, how's the research, are you travelling, how's what's-his-name, Marco? Negative. She held the phone out from her head as static jagged through the line.

A strange voice but familiar, too, said, "Ginger, hello, I'm sorry to disturb you on your vacation . . ." Long pause. When would they ever accept that she was not on vacation, that she was living here, working? "This is Ralph Hunnicutt—you remember me?"

"Yes, of course, Ralph. How are you? Is something wrong?"

"I'm afraid so. I'm the new sheriff in Swan, guess you've heard that." He paused. Ginger could imagine him looking across the bare courthouse lawn and down at Sister Sissy's Barbecue Shack below. "Ginger—" He stopped, then plunged on. "I'm so sorry . . ."

GINGER WANDERED TO THE FRONT DOOR and looked out. The heavy spring rains had sprouted every summer wildflower possible. Her gaze followed splotches of late red poppies along the edges of the terraces and clumps of irises, long since naturalized, moving in drifts across the long grass. The apples were plumping up, the hard knotted pears still looked bitter green, and a row of plum trees along the edge of the first terrace was breaking into what looked like a bumper crop. What does the *bumper* in bumper crop mean? she wondered, and turned to go look it up in the dictionary. Instead, she ran back to the phone and dialed J. J.'s number.

She tried to imagine the shrill series of rings beginning under her finger ending in that cabin on the river four thousand and some odd miles away, the sound waves hitting the arrowhead collection beside the fireplace, the blue sofa exiled there since her mother bought the curvy Duncan Phyfe one with ivory Napoleonic wreaths woven into the yellow satin. No answer. She held the cool phone against her temple. "Where are you, J. J.?" she said aloud.

She thought of dialing Aunt Lily or the Columns and asking to speak to Daddy, but why waste thirty dollars? He would be hopeless. Lily might be sleeping and right now she couldn't comfort *her*. How horrible that she smashed her finger.

"Two o'clock," she said aloud. What is that white rime on the plums? Seven, eight, nine, must be fifteen trees. Yellow finches darted among the branches. She stared until her eyes teared, and the trees smeared and shifted. She felt jarred, unable to take in what Ralph had told her. Is this what shock feels like? she wondered. Like looking through a twirling kaleidoscope? She loved the ovoid purple plums, known locally as nun's thighs. What will I do with so many plums? Already birds are diving at the green ones. But now I may not be here for the ripe plums. Now I must accomplish thirty things and get myself on a train to Rome, on a plane to Atlanta, in a car to Swan.

For whole weeks she forgot that Swan existed. She was far enough, finally, far in miles but, better, farther in those latitudinal spaces that arc mysteriously and blot out memories of other places and people, as if they have dropped off the flat horizon of the world.

Bumper: unusually full or abundant, a drinking vessel filled to the brim. From *bump, lump,* hence something large. That hardly explains the usage, she thought, slamming the dictionary shut. She circled the yard, and finally her mind wheeled in, coming to rest on the actual, brutal fact she heard from Ralph Hunnicutt, the back of whose white-blond buzz cut she'd stared at in Eleanor Whitefield's math class.

Her mother, exposed. Mother, Mother, Mother. Her stone broken in half. *Mother, Mother, I feel sick.* The jump-rope rhyme whirred by her ear, double-time. *Call for the doctor, quick, quick, quick.* Ginger remembered her red shoes rhythmically striking the gravel playground in fifth grade, the sweep of fear that her mother would die and she would be left to count cars at the funeral. But the rhyme said *Mother, Mother, will I die?* and she had concentrated hard not to trip on the terrible turn of the line *Yes, my child, but do not cry,* each one-syllable word accented with a jump.

Exhumed, he'd said, pronouncing the *h*. Exposed to death. No: exposed *in* death. And what did he say—Lily and Eleanor found her. And the body? Stained with mud. Lily must be shattered. He said her mother was lying in the rain. Something about grave robbers, and did she have on jewelry when she was buried? How could this happen? "No," Ginger had said, looking at the lapis and pearl ring on her own right hand, "no, and the wedding ring is in Daddy's cuff link box in his top drawer." No, no, no, the words had separated from her mouth, risen like smoke rings and faded into space. She saw suddenly how young her mother was, then she saw her open eyes, that blinding yellow kitchen. "No," she repeated.

She knew the rest of her mother's jewelry was locked in a safe-deposit box. Three or four pins, a coral pendant, a square emerald Daddy gave her on their tenth anniversary. Ginger had the string of good pearls from her mother's mother, a few pairs of earrings. She felt the familiar sliver-thin knife cut through her mind—Mother. Mother in the rain. *Mother, Mother, quick quick quick.* And where the hell is J. J.? She dialed again; no answer. She wished he would walk up the path from the road right now. She would like to lie down in the weeds and just cry, but she had not cried in years. Ralph Hunnicutt had been gentle. She knew this news would fly around Swan; he'd be in the eye of a hurricane. "An investigation is under way," he'd said like someone in a play.

Ginger would get the six o'clock train to Rome, spend the night, catch the flight out in the morning. He'd said he would tell Lily she was coming. Ralph Hunnicutt, in his flannel shirts from Sears, his haircuts always razored up the back of his head. Washington, Atlanta, a rented car, hideous trip. Hell.

To get through the night. She must. To get hoisted into the air and flung across the sky in a silver bullet and to come down in another world. To find her father uncomprehending. Sitting in a pressed white shirt as though about to go see patients again. To find Lily crying, her makeup badly applied and her housecoat spotted with cigarette burns. Her mother, exhumed, oh, sickening. Why? She never walked around Swan dripping with jewels—why would anyone think to unearth her after nineteen years? No sense at all. Nothing ever has made any sense. *Life was just starting to make sense*. A box of golden stones. Marco, tanned in his cutoff jeans, pulling out sixth-century B.C. glass beads from a heap of rubble. "Ginger, these would look magnificent on you." Waking with him this morning, his body still so seriously asleep. Touching the black arc of his eyebrows. His eyes the color of the dust-rimed blue plums you clean with your thumb. Tracking the sun across the hills. The long-cooled stones of the Etruscans lay in the fields waiting, the intact jug still with a residue of wine, the bronze votive animals, a coil of rope in the sand. Oh crap, she thought, I haven't even done the laundry.

She packed almost nothing but her cosmetics, some underwear, and her photos of the site to show J. J. She'd wear her navy linen just back from the cleaners, then, at home, go into her old closet and wear what she'd left. She knew she had shorts and good pants and blouses there, hanging in the closet year after year. At home, she'd thought. Was it always to be home? The place that if you go there, blah, blah, blah, they have to take you in, as her father used to say. Swan. She could not imagine Marco there. Her past was a long blank to him, punctuated with occasional pictures she created in the siesta afternoons after they made love. "The land used to be a sea and the rivers still have white sandbars that emerge when the water is low," she'd tell him. "In the summer, the heat makes you feel as though you're walking under water, the heat engulfs you, and as you can in water, you feel currents of heavier and lighter heat when you walk, moving streams and rivulets of coolness in the air. Way in the country, we know—J. J. and I know—deep springs that gush thousands of gallons a minute of the purest water. You can dive straight down and feel icy water pushing up from the bottom."

She had told Marco about her mother's immense rose garden, how they visited country relatives who gave them cuttings of heirloom roses, about the camellia hedge under her window when she was a child, about the bed of pine needles she made for herself in a back corner of the yard, where she took her box of colored pencils and drawing paper. She'd told him little about J. J. and only the briefest information about her mother's suicide and her father's strange history afterward. "America, America," he'd say, and Ginger would think, No, he doesn't get it, but I don't care. He listened as though she were telling him about someone else. She'd seen him take the photo of J. J. on her dresser over to the window and turn it to the light. He'd only said, "He looks like Montgomery Clift in that old movie where the big girl drowned so he could have Elizabeth Taylor." What was important to Marco was the present. Now, today, and the specialized worlds of archaemetallurgy and paleobotany—the work they were doing—and along with it the easy joy between them that seemed to be expanding. He could not even work up a little jealousy when she told him about her college romances, her marriage to Mitchell. Sometimes she felt that her life was a fan she only partially had unfolded for him, but she was willing to let her past go. So what if he saw everything about her family as emblematic of America? She didn't want to think of them. Shed that skin—there's no more to learn from home, she thought, and nothing at all to *do* with it. She loved living in a foreign country where everything was *other*.

Better to lay bare the glass phial, the eroded foundations of a temple, an earring that dangled gently from an ear eight thousand years ago. Much better to go on Sunday to Marco's parents', where ten, fourteen, sometimes twenty gathered around that endless table, and even she felt gently folded into the rhythms of the family. She was kissed and called "bella," she was seated in the middle, urged to eat, eat. Whatever nasty secrets they had, nothing showed. They laughed, laughter rippling around the table with the platters of roast rabbit and potatoes. How would it be to grow up like that? Hence, Marco, she thought, hence Marco.

She wrote a note to him and left it on the kitchen table. He and an archaeologist on the staff of the University of Georgia team had taken the interns to Bologna, a trip she wanted to make because Etruscan remains outside town indicated a sun temple with the same orientation as the one she suspected once crowned Monte

Sant'Egidio. If she had gone, instead of plugging away here, this ludicrous news would not have reached her. Ralph Hunnicutt in his sweltering office over the jail could have worn the skin off his finger dialing her number and she would have been happily sketching foundations, having pasta at a trattoria, talking nonstop with Marco.

Dear Marco, I have to go to Georgia immediately—a family emergency. I don't know the details but will call you tomorrow. Back as soon as possible! Don't forget me. Cold tomato soup in fridge. She tore it up and rewrote it without the pathetic *Don't forget me* and the wifely soup part. He'd find the soup or, more likely, he'd just go to the pizza place on the hill with friends.

As an Italian, she reflected, he might not be as shocked as she at this news. Weren't they always digging up saints, whose uncorrupted bodies filled the towns with mysterious fragrance? Ralph Hunnicutt had said cryptically that her mother didn't look that different. Perhaps she was a saint. But saints didn't blast themselves into oblivion. Suicide—had she ever looked up that word? No need. *Sui*—of oneself—and the ancient suffix *-cide*, appearing in so many awful words. More than a word, to her it was a powerful, hidden, primitive action always forming in her mother's life from the moment of birth. The word itself was totally inadequate to the finger on the trigger.

Ginger found her passport and the envelope of dollars she kept at the bottom of her underwear drawer. Seven or eight months back, she'd had to fly home because her father was taken to the hospital with pneumonia, and the doctor gravely said he probably couldn't survive. By the time she arrived twenty hours later, her father was trying to maneuver a smoke under the oxygen tent. J. J. had not been found until the next morning. He had been miles into the wiregrass over near Retter, hunting bobwhites with Scott. She'd crossed the ocean and driven two hundred miles, while they strung quail on a pine spit and grilled them, lying back in the dry grass drinking awful moonshine out of Mason jars. She was furious. She had not spoken to J. J. for the rest of the week she was there.

Although she had not given up on him, she had trouble imagining J. J. living a normal life, whatever that meant, outside the woods. She held on to the old image of him from a weekend she'd visited him at Emory back in her sophomore, his senior, year of college. He actually invited her down from Virginia to the Spring Ball. He arranged a blind date with his roommate, Mitchell Sloane, and he took Lisa Bowen from Augusta. Ginger remembered the stiff, old-fashioned way he held Lisa, and the slight upward turn of his profile. He'd bought the tuxedo instead of renting it, which was a good sign, Ginger thought. He looked totally natural, as if he'd been born in it. His hair curled over the collar, and as he danced by her he swept his green eyes over her as though she were a stranger, and she felt how wonderful it would be to meet him if he were. They'd learned to dance together at the cabin, awkwardly counting steps out loud and practicing dips in the kitchen. Neither of them seemed to have any innate feel for the music. But that night, she saw his controlled, expressive turns. The sureness of his moves left no room for awkwardness from his partner; Lisa melded into him and they danced under the immense chandelier of the ballroom, twirling, Ginger saw, until the thousands of lights must have streaked into one. She would never forget watching J. J. that night. She had sat at a table with Mitchell, sipping her rum and Coke, probably the third drink of her life, and heard little of what he told her about his contracts class. J. J. was new to her. He would go to med school, marry Lisa, have four children, live in Swan. Maybe she would marry Mitchell. They would have a little girl in a smocked dress, a boy who liked horses. She made the rim of her glass ring, leaned to Mitchell, and gave him her brightest look. The powerful trajectory of their futures—all four together—carried her closer. They would have big family parties at the cabin, cut down a Christmas tree, barbecue ribs, and float on rafts.

Now J. J. disappeared down the river for days, as he always had since their mother's suicide, or he left word with Lily that he was driving down to the Okefenokee, or as far as the Everglades. At the cabin, where he spent four or five days a week, he lavished an inordinate amount of time on cleaning guns and fishing gear, writing in notebooks, reading, or just stalking through the woods looking for arrowheads and bits of pottery.

As children, on a morning after pelting rain, he and Ginger had once found what must have been a Creek target practice area on a sharp incline of new-growth slash pine. Gullies running downhill left dozens of arrowheads perched on alluvial peaks of dissolving red clay. She had picked up two large, crudely cut triangles, which must have been for deer or bear, then they found in one spot a cache of flint bird arrowheads, perfect, smaller than her little fingernail. They'd stuffed their pockets, then J. J. stripped off his shirt and they gathered more, tying them into a bundle. They loved the arrowheads and spent hours lining them up on the coffee table, admiring the ivory and rose veins of the flint and imagining half-naked Indians around a campfire, chipping them expertly with a sharpened stone. They checked out all the books on Indians from the Swan library and spent the winter nights cross-legged on the sofa, passing them back and forth and reading aloud to each other. J. J.'s collection now covered the entire wall around the fireplace.

But Ginger had shifted her allegiance to the Etruscans, far from Swan.

LILY AIRED GINGER'S ROOM and dusted the tops of the picture frames, which Tessie always missed. Deanie Robart had bandaged her finger. She might lose the nail, but with two aspirins the pain had subsided. That Hunnicutt boy had turned out just fine, she thought, despite that awful mother raving about Judgement Day, polite as he could be, and with such terrible news to discuss. Wasn't one of his eyes a little cocked? A war injury, but he was too young for the war. Then she remembered Vietnam was also a war, later and farther away. How thoughtful of him to call Ginger. Lily had told him she'd tell Wills, as best she could. Tessie had tried to keep her in bed, but as soon as Ralph called back and said Ginger would be coming home, she'd jumped up. CoCo rode her shoulder as she moved around Ginger's room.

Most of the dead stay gone, she thought. Yes, her own mother stayed dead. The time of year when they went to White Springs came and went every year and still her mother stayed dead. She remembered when they would sit on the piered porch built around the spring and sip Dixie cups of sulfur water. "This is good for what ails you," her mother always said. They'd worn white spectators, polished every morning, and print voile dresses. In the evenings they'd sat in rockers on the porch of the White Springs Hotel, after suppers of fried chicken and platters of sliced tomatoes.

Lily's mind was still swarming. As if from a distance she watched herself skidding fluidly through the past. She got on her knees and gave a swipe to the feet of the bed with a dust rag. The old days were best. Even tomatoes aren't that good anymore, she thought. Everything had more taste when it was Mama's house and the maid pressed the flounces on their cotton slips. She remembered her mother's lavender ways, her cologne, her hats trimmed with silk flowers, Mama's blue Packard, the drive along the Swanee. And the blowout when that Negro had been kind enough to change the tire. Charleston, too, was very nice on their visit, and once Bermuda, with sunrise-colored bungalows and blooming poinciana, when Lily wrote postcards to her friends Agnes and Eleanor on the balcony and Mama was old and floated her bridge in a glass of water by the bed at night, moonlight combing through the shutter, hitting the three white teeth and the ridge of pink gum. Nothing pointed toward horrible events.

Lily scuffed into the kitchen and poured herself a glass of ice water. Catherine, found again. She noticed that the cigarette she'd been smoking when the sheriff visited had burned into the edge of the table. She blew the ashes onto the floor. Maybe Catherine never died when they thought. Maybe she was alive all the time, yes, teaching school over in Willacoochee. Once Lily thought she'd seen Catherine's face in a train window. The woman waved and suddenly was not Catherine. Or maybe she ran away with a soldier years ago, back in 1945, a crazy time with the Japs and the Germans, and oh, yes, the Italians, though Ginger did not want to hear a word of that. Why Ginger wanted to go live in a foreign country where she has no people, Lily didn't know. Divorced, carrying on with some Italian mackerel-snapper, Marco Polo or some such. She realized her hands were shaking. Get control, she told herself.

She took down the flour and lard, imagining Ginger's big smile tomorrow when she'd open the cookie jar on the counter and reach in for a biscuit. She would be tired after the long trip. Biscuits and gravy. Tessie would bring a fresh hen tomorrow. Lily decided to order the groceries over the telephone. She looked in the refrigerator. A toasted biscuit would be good. What should she do now? There was a little leftover potato salad. Catherine had nothing valuable, those thieves got nothing but the shock of looking at a dead person. And a shock that was. What is in that mouldy bowl? She peeled back the plastic wrap. Squash casserole. Serves them right, the savages, she thought, but why couldn't they just cover her up, at least, and spare us this final humiliation?

She uncovered a plate of cold ladyfinger peas, her favorite summer vegetable, and ate some at the sink. She'd snapped a ton of those peas in her day. My day, she realized, has passed, and what was the meaning of *this* day if a day, all the days, any day, could come to this horror. As if the unforgivable death were not enough, as if leaving those children were not enough, as if causing Wills to have a stroke tragically young were not enough. Lily slipped into her habit of blaming Catherine for everything. As if my life were hers to hand over to raising Ginger and J. J., she thought. As if I had no choice—and I didn't. I had no choice. Now this, Catherine, and how could you? Lily poked out her bottom lip, a gesture since childhood when Mama would say, "I could ride to town on that lip." Fortunately, Mama did not live to see any of this. How quietly Mama left this world, unlike Catherine. Mama would agree that Catherine was still the troublemaker.

Big Jim, her father, all at once loomed in her mind, as though in the doorway wanting his rice pudding. Loose pants held up by sprung black suspenders and hair like boar bristles coming out of his ears. He ruled the roost, ruled many roosts, too many, at least one too many, that house on the edge of the mill village where that floozie Aileen Boyd stood on the porch, her hip jutting out, and Mama wouldn't look right or left when she drove the Packard down Mason Road to the mill office to take a potted plant or a cake to someone sick. Lily remembered once going in her parents' bedroom to say good night. Big Jim was out. At the door she saw her mother lean over the pillow and pick up a long blond hair. Lily had quietly turned and gone back to her room. The next day she and her mother drove to South Carolina to visit Mama's people. Lily felt a wave of rage that her mother had died so soon. She was simply eaten up and no one knew she'd had those pains for years. She and Mama should have had years of freedom. Mama had liked to travel and Lily could go, too, since she'd never married, though she had a few beaux who sat on the front porch in her day. My day, she thought again. She supposed her day was raising those children after their mother . . .

Her mind stopped at the subject of suicide, and as it did she saw a picture of Catherine Phillips when she first came to Swan for Thanksgiving. That was Wills's final year in medical school. As he brought Catherine in the front door, Lily saw her through the glass panels of the foyer and stepped back into the hall to watch until the introductions were over. Catherine—oh, Lily could see her—wore red, which Lily never liked, a red suit with a red print silk blouse under it. Oh, we're very bold, Lily had thought to herself. We have wavy black hair, do we, and surprised-looking blue eyes. A funny blue. Wills never looked away from Catherine. He hovered over her, gawky and smitten, reminding Lily of a heron with folded wings. They were sorry to rush, they said, but the annual Tipton-Swan football game started at two. Mama and Big Jim had greeted Catherine and taken her straight into the dining room, where Lily also slipped into a chair and said how they'd all heard so much from Wills, and how did she like Georgia State College for Women? She herself had gone to Agnes Scott. Catherine did not seem to see the distinction. She'd looked young, young, young. Lily, thirty then, already had a sense that her youth was gone. On trips with Mama she would stock up on henna rinses to cover alarming premature gray hairs. Certainly she would not buy hair dye in Swan. She had been teaching at the mill school for eight years. One by one the local boys had married other girls. She hated the school, especially the children's dirty feet and the days they had to return the specimen canisters for the hookworm tests. Big Jack said she should damn well quit and sit home if the children got on her nerves all that much, but what else would she do while waiting for her life to begin?

"How did y'all meet—I don't think Wills has told us that," Lily had asked, and Catherine's young face seemed now to come close to her own. Those eyes, like looking down into the springs at Glass Lake—the pale aquamarine, blind-looking eyes with irises ringed with a darker blue. Unpleasant to look into, Lily found. But she could find no other fault. Anyone would have to admire her skin, creamy and luminous without a speck of powder. When she turned on that 150-watt smile, you couldn't help but feel pulled toward her. Lily noticed that Catherine's right eyebrow flew up when someone asked her a question.

In the image that rushed over Lily, she experienced a sudden warmth for Catherine that she had not felt that day when Catherine had not particularly noticed Lily's special cornbread dressing and instead talked about the dorm mother who patrolled the date parlors, about deciding to major in design, and asked Big Jim questions about the fabrics produced at the mill. We're confident, too, Lily had thought. The few girls her brother ever brought home usually spoke when spoken to, leaving Wills to do all the talking, while they gulped iced tea and hardly ate at all. None had the gall to address Big Jim familiarly. From this distance, Lily felt the hum of Catherine's energy run through her. Then Wills wrapped Catherine's camel hair coat around her. They had to hurry for the kickoff promptly at two; he wouldn't miss it. His red number 35 jersey still lay folded in a chest in his upstairs bedroom. Big Jim, who usually didn't notice anyone unless they could do something for him, fetched her pocketbook and feigned kissing her hand. Wills kissed his mama but forgot to say good-bye to Lily. The first warning of what was to come. Catherine, however, took her hand and squeezed it. "Wills says you're the real thing. I'm really looking forward to getting to know you better." That megawatt flash.

Lily saw that she had, ever so slightly, a gap between her front teeth. She was so charmed that she forgot to withhold her approval and said, "Do come soon."

The door had barely closed when Big Jim whooped, "That one's a firecracker! Wills will have his hands full there." He snapped his fingers and clapped his hands. "I like her." I do, too, Lily had thought. No, I don't.

Lily jumped, as though her father's clap still jarred the room. Old age has its moments, Lily mused. When she was younger, only dreams gave back faces and sometimes retrieved memories. Now, all of a sudden, full-blown pictures came back whole, with devastating clarity. The memory trailed off with Big Jim sinking into his cracked leather chair. The newspaper rattled and he switched on the radio. Lily and Mama went to Lily's room to take out her winter clothes and adjust hems. They had no interest in the game or in breathing the fumes of the Cuban cigar Big Jim was about to light.

Looking that far back, who could have guessed that she would be called on to raise Catherine's children? She'd never liked children, but their powerful needs, when they came to her, by far outweighed her reluctance to meet them. They were her own kin. Where else could they go? Her life had shaped and continued to shape around what befell her.

Lily opened a drawer and stared for a full minute at the green handle of the biscuit cutter before she recognized it as what she wanted. Wanting company, she rolled CoCo's cage just inside the door. He bit his nails and fixed his yellow eyes on the window. Without having to think, she cut lard into the flour with a fork, rolled out the dough on a board, and cut it expertly into perfect circles. Yes, Ginger would be hungry after such a long trip. CoCo cracked seeds and made a low, purring motor sound. She'd make more biscuits if J. J. stopped by today. J. J. would eat the whole pan.

WHEN THE BRIDGE CLUB—Margaret Alice, Billie, and Ellen—parked out front, Eleanor was regretting her decision, but if she had canceled, later they would have heard she was the one who discovered Catherine with Lily and would have been incensed because she had not confided in them. A part of Eleanor looked forward to the telling; she was ashamed of that. She abhorred small-town gossip. Still, she knew any one of them would have been on the horn immediately, and isn't gossip speculation, whereas this was fact?

Eleanor seated Ellen closest to the air conditioner so her smoke would blow away. Margaret Alice announced right away that storms were expected, so she was a little distracted. The other three dreaded stormy bridge club days. Margaret Alice had a phobia and screamed at each thunderclap. When forked lightning and thunder closed in until they occurred almost simultaneously, she'd weep and have to be led to the sofa and covered with a throw. Eleanor waited for the right time to tell them what happened, but for now, it was too pleasant, just dealing the cards, writing "we" and "they" on the tally, falling into the orderly progression of the game. She was annoyed at how Margaret Alice kept looking out the window as though a burglar were outside. Ellen had never been quite the same after the shock treatments she'd had up in Atlanta years ago. Strange, she was fine with the cards but a bit whiffy on past events, and she lost the French language entirely after two years of study in college. Distant thunder mumbled and she saw Margaret Alice's hand tremble. "Don't worry, it's miles away. There's not a cloud."

After the first rubber, Eleanor asked, "Are you girls ready for lunch?"

As they moved into the dining room, Eleanor was faced with the cascade of roses on the sideboard. "How lovely!" Ellen walked over to the flowers and put her face close. "Lemony scent. Gorgeous. Where did you get them?"

Eleanor motioned everyone to a chair. The table looked fine. She could see that Hattie even had polished the salt cellars. Hattie came in with her ring of tomato aspic and served, carefully including a sprig of parsley for each chilled plate. Only Eleanor noticed the jiggle of the aspic and Hattie's set lips. Eleanor sipped her iced tea and leaned back. "I might as well get this over with. I had a terrible thing happen this morning and I'm still spinning from it. A tragic thing."

Ellen crushed out the cigarette she'd brought to the table and leaned forward, frowning. Margaret Alice was craned around looking out the window. Billie, forty pounds overweight, was eyeing her food. "You know I always go out to visit a spell with Holt every morning," Eleanor began. "This morning I met Lily out there so we could cut some roses." She glanced at the roses and rushed on, describing Lily's glimpse of something blue, then their full view of Catherine tilted out of her coffin and lying in the mud.

"Eleanor, you have lost your mind," Billie shrieked.

"This is impossible. Where was Cass Deal? Why would anyone do such a thing?"

"Obviously, there's a madman at large."

"Nothing like this has ever happened in Swan. The worst thing this year was the sawmill burning down back in October. Remember, it had been a dry month and the fire lit up the night for four hours."

"Ellen, that's beside the point now," Eleanor reminded her. "A macabre event like this is entirely different." Hattie brought in the cold pressed chicken and a basket of rolls, even though no one had eaten their aspic. "Just leave it, Hattie, thank you, we'll serve ourselves."

For the next hour, the four women ate with good appetite and talked. The Masons were one of the old families, after all, and everything was known about them, back to Big Jim's father, John, who had started the cotton mill a hundred years ago, in 1875, when Swan was a railroad crossing, four stores, and a scattering of sad frame houses.

Eleanor and Margaret Alice, both born in Swan, remembered the most. Ellen and Billie had lived there only as adults, about forty years. The Reconstruction years were brutal most places, but Big Jim's father was from England, Eleanor recalled, and didn't particularly hold notions of white superiority, at least in the mill.

"It's a wonder the Klan didn't go after him," Billie remarked.

"This part of Georgia was so empty there wasn't even a Klan back then," Eleanor reminded her. "Besides, he pretty much bought the place. He hired men and women, black and white, if he thought they would work like mules."

"He drove my uncle into the ground my family always claimed," Margaret Alice said.

John's own father, who lived in England, had mills in North Carolina. John worked his youth away learning the business, and when his daddy offered to set him up with a mill of his own, he scoured the South for the right location. Swan not only had two railroad lines, it was close to the steamboat lines on the Altamaha and Ocmulgee rivers. Old John bought land, built square pine houses for tenants, and planted cotton. Margaret Alice said her daddy always remembered John calling cotton his white gold. The second year, he built the mill and started on the mill village. His wife, Mary, from Charlotte finally arrived with the boy, Jim.

"She was said to be horrified, but whether she was or not, she died three years after Calhoun was born," Eleanor recalled.

"That Calhoun . . ." Margaret Alice trailed off.

Twenty workers from North Carolina came when Mary did, lured by John's offer of decent wages. By then, he'd hired an Englishman to lay out the town. In three months, they built the four-chimneyed house out on a low rise of land overlooking the cotton fields. Mary chose the site because of the wild palmettos, two spreading oaks, and the pond choked with water lilies at the base of the slope. "Still the prettiest house in town, especially since Lily took over the garden."

Their conversation started far back in time, not because any answer was located there, not because some clue lay along the hundred-year history of the Masons in Swan—clearly, some nut had escaped from an asylum and had done this horrible thing—but because a suicide reverberates forever and the garish reappearance of the suicide unearthed all they had thought about in the days after Catherine died, leaving no note, no clue at all as to why she would turn violently on herself and leave a legacy of violence to Wills and the two children. How could any mother do that? And how could she just leave everyone in Swan? They moved on through Big Jim's time. "Old coot," Billie pronounced. "No wonder Florence left town all the time."

"What a piece of work is man," Ellen quoted.

They talked about Lily giving up her teaching to raise the children.

"Not that she gave up much. She always thought the mill children were lazy and dumb," Margaret Alice said.

"Well, they probably had pinworms, rickets, a diet of grits. Lily was just not suited for teaching," Eleanor replied. She knew no class of students was lazy and dumb on its own.

"How Lily stuck it out for as long as she did was the wonder," Margaret Alice pitched in. "She was such a spoiled brat herself.

Taking over Catherine's children was the best thing that ever happened to her. She had to think of someone other than herself for once." Margaret Alice had forgotten the storm warnings, but now serious thunderheads gathered outside the windows and pine branches scratched the panes. Her husband once had courted Lily briefly, but said he couldn't look at those bug eyes even if she was the daughter of the richest man in town.

"I wouldn't say spoiled. Imagine growing up under the roof of Big Jim. It wasn't that she didn't care . . ." Eleanor knew that Lily privately had contributed substantial sums to the high school for mill village students' lunches and fees.

Billie said, "When I moved here, Wills was in high school. The golden boy, but I remember there was some problem. He got in trouble for slamming a teacher up against a wall. What was that all about?"

"Who knows."

"Big Jim sent him off to Beauregard Military Academy to teach him some discipline. First thing anyone knew he was the star student in his class at Emory, then got a free ride to medical school." Margaret Alice gazed out the window.

"He was so good-looking before the war." Eleanor was remembering Holt, working his way through school by waiting on tables in the fraternity house.

"He drank, though. I heard he, excuse me, urinated over the stairwell onto his fraternity brothers one night." Billie laughed raucously and reached for another roll.

The women were ready to move into the subject of Wills and Catherine, but a bolt hit nearby and powerful thunder exploded near the house. Margaret Alice felt it in her backbone. The entire sky lighted white. "Sheet lightning," she said. She started to cry a little bit. "Think of Catherine out there in the rain. She was an unusual girl. Who would have thought she had it in her to purely murder herself? They say it runs in families. Thank goodness no one in my family ever did that to me. Those poor children—babes in the woods."

Ellen was dying for a smoke but did not dare light up while Billie was still eating. "It's not raining, so it probably will blow over. The forecast is for continued heat and a hundred percent humidity."

Hattie brought in coffee on a tray, and Eleanor sliced the pound cake. "Hattie, would you please take those roses out of here? I can't stand to look at them another minute."

No one could concentrate on the second rubber. Eleanor decided they could all use a little sherry. She opened Holt's liquor cabinet and poured out generous glasses. Ellen offered cigarettes, and even though the others had stopped smoking, they lit up. Margaret Alice blew a ring toward the ceiling. "They say Big Jim died in a Tipton motel. Second heart attack. Whomever he was with had the good sense to call the sheriff and get him to move the body home so he could be discovered dead properly, in his own bed. Old goat."

"I never heard that. How crude," Eleanor said.

"Yes, honey, they say Florence never knew, just drove herself home with Lily from her people in the Carolinas and put on a state funeral. After that, we didn't see much of her in Swan for weeks. They say she took up with a musician from home, although he was purely doddering. Then she got sick, so quickly, poor thing."

"Well, she didn't live long after that." Eleanor remembered Lily's call on a Thursday, saying she'd just quit teaching at the mill. "I told the children it was a two-day holiday and to go home," she'd told Eleanor. "I figured by Sunday they'd find someone else."

When the girls finally left at five-thirty, Eleanor took the glasses to the kitchen. Hattie had left a note: *I found Scott and asked him to find J. J. This is a bad day.* A bad day, indeed. Eleanor felt ancient. She was dizzy from the sherry and smoke. Her entire hip had gone to sleep around the artificial joint and she could barely move her leg. She realized she had not told Holt Junior what had happened. She dialed her son's number but no one answered.

Hattie had very thoughtfully turned down her covers. Eleanor took a bath with a scoop of mineral salts and went to bed, even though it was too early for sleep and far too late for a nap.

J. J. KEPT ONE FISHING BOAT downriver from the cabin. He took the Jeep along the sandy trail and set off from there when he wanted to fish beyond the sandbars, down where the river started to slow and widen. He'd caught some perch and planned to cook a couple for dinner with some boiled potatoes. As he came around the sandbar with the motor on low, a clean breeze skimmed the water and rose to his face. He loved the sudden silky glide of the river as it straightened out downstream from the cabin.

He cut the motor and bumped into a gnarled cypress knee, the one with his chain on it. The cypress trees growing in the shallows, with long gray moss and their knobby knees protruding, seemed half-human to him, haunting, silent presences in the swampy margin. Some trees have as much being as a person, he thought. The boat nudged the bank and J. J. secured the rope around some roots. No cottonmouth here today. Last week one fell into the boat as he tied up just at nightfall—a right fine specimen, about as big around as a leg. Whose leg, he'd thought, and smiled as he pictured the legs of several women, most recently the strapping gal he'd entertained on his St. Clare fishing trip. Legs like a damn Amazon. The snake had flopped in the end of the boat, quickly straightened out full length, and had given J. J. the benefit of looking into its white, white mouth. J. J. resisted the impulse to step out in the shin-deep water, where for all he knew umpteen relatives swam, and instead scooped his oar underneath its belly and dangled the moccasin in the air—a mean-looking s.o.b.—before tossing it back in the river.

He looked around just to be sure the old boy was not sprawling along an overhead branch today, and hauled his gear up the slippery bank, landing the string of perch on the grass. Ginger had once followed her first impulse and jumped out of the boat when a moccasin fell in. Their father had rammed the moccasin with the oar and jerked Ginger back in the boat all at once. She'd screamed enough to scare every living creature in the vicinity. Of course, it *had* landed on her foot; she usually was not squeamish and squealing. Wills had taught them to respect snakes but not to fear them. "They're more afraid of you than you are of them," he'd always told them. As a child, J. J. wasn't too sure about that old saw. It paralleled "This hurts me more than it does you," which Wills always had barked out when he picked a thorny stick to switch their legs.

J. J.'s first memory of his father was the day his daddy tied two truck inner tubes together and he and J. J. flopped across them and went sweeping downstream. It seemed to J. J. they were almost flying, skimming the surface of the wide river. He had dropped his face in the water to drink because it was the color of Coca-Cola. The taste was plain water. The current fumed and surged. J. J. had felt terrified, exhilarated. His father had held his hand and kept shouting, "Hey, how about it, big buddy!" At Buck's Landing, they picked up some bait and got a ride back to the cabin with Buck. Although Wills at that time often drove the ten miles out of town to the cabin to eat supper, then had to turn around and go back to deliver a baby or fish a button out of someone's throat, leaving Catherine, Ginger, and J. J. alone, J. J.'s memories of the cabin always starred Wills— coming in from duck hunting, fastening cotton bolls to the screens to keep out bugs, unloading a deer from the back of a pickup, building shelves in the pantry. Easier to imagine him back then. The old husk sitting out at the Columns didn't seem like the same human who cooked smothered duck on the outdoor fireplace. As a child, J. J. had been fascinated at how his father could spit out the buckshot while still chewing the duck. He still couldn't do it himself.

He drove slowly. The pines fringed the bottom of the sun, which later would sink toward the river, bending light through the understory scrub oaks and glazing the water. The river, sometimes brown, looked green today, green, he recognized, like the river in his recurrent dream where the water felt like his own element and he was carried—buoyed, tumbled, and lifted—by a swift current. He swam, totally at home in the water, an exultant dream he woke from feeling suddenly beached and abandoned.

The Jeep dipped in and out of low, swampy puddles. With one hand on the wheel, he maneuvered around stumps and fallen logs. This road was as familiar as the lines on the palm of his hand; he could drive it blind.

The trail followed the bluff for about a hundred yards, then swung inland through dryer, higher ground of forest and palmettos for a mile, curving back toward the river near the cabin. He came around the back of the cabin. Scott's VW Bug was parked close to the scuppernong arbor, and as J. J. jumped out, he saw Scott sitting out on the dock sloshing his feet in the river.

Scott had been waiting almost two hours. His mother, Hattie, had told him to find J. J. if it took him all night. He'd left the store in charge of the new clerk, Mindy, who seemed one brick shy of a load. He didn't know why J. J. hired her and hoped he wasn't banging her, but you never could tell with J. J.

Scott stood up, shaking his wet feet, as J. J. took his gear up on the porch, tossed the fish in the sink, then walked down to the dock. "Hey, Scottie, good buddy, what's up?"

"Man oh man. I don't even know how to begin with this one." He was shaking the water off his feet and rolling down his pant leg.

J. J. assumed something had gone wrong at the market. He left all decisions to Scott, except for a few hires. Now and then he'd meet with the salesmen, when Scott had business at the other

Mason market on the east side of Swan to tend to. Some people in Swan had fits when J. J. hired Scott to manage a store in the white part of town. Gradually, the convenient location overcame their hidebound prejudice. Business had even picked up. Scott's friendliness put them at ease and now they thought he was doing fine.

"Let's have a beer, ol' hoss. It can't be all that bad." J. J. could be counted on to take little interest in the stores, or in any of the real estate and other small businesses his grandfather Mason had left. "I plain wore a hole in the river pulling out fish today," he bragged.

"This is serious bidness." Scott sat on the porch swing and J. J. brought out cold Budweisers.

Scott stared at the floor. "My mama was at Miz Eleanor's this morning when she come back from visiting at the cemetery. This is unbelievable but it's true because the sheriff and the undertaker have been out there and seen it, too."

"What the hell are you talking about?"

"Miz Eleanor was taking some roses from your family's graves."

"And they're going to arrest her for that?"

"No sirree, that's not it," Scott almost shouted. "She was with your auntie and they done found your mama lying by side her own grave. Dug up by somebody."

"Hey, wait, wait, stop—is this your crummy new idea of a joke?"

"Hell no, it's the Lord's truth. She's out there right now in the open." He told J. J. everything Hattie had said. "You gotta go on home and see about Miss Lily. You want me to drive you in?" He watched J. J. drain the beer. They both looked out at the green river. A fish leapt out of the water, paused in midair, arched, and neatly disappeared in the water. J. J.'s mouth puckered like a pouting child.

"Nah, no, Scott. You go on back home. I'll head in and call Eleanor and the sheriff, then I'll see about Lily. Thanks for coming out here with the glad tidings."

"You sure you're all right?" Scott knew J. J.'s habit of duck, cover, and hold.

"Peachy." J. J. rubbed his clenched fist against his other hand. He wanted to ram it into the porch post.

He watched the brake lights of Scott's car disappear down the sand road.

ELEANOR'S PHONE RANG EIGHTEEN TIMES. No answer. Maybe the shock had killed her. J. J. reached Ralph Hunnicutt right away and told him he'd heard the news. Ralph had just put down the phone with the GBI, who couldn't come until the next morning. He was going to have to take a turn himself sitting out at Magnolia; his deputy was scheduled to fry catfish at the Rotary celebration and, besides, just plain refused to stand guard at the grave site. Said he wouldn't go near the place. Ralph assured J. J. that he would do everything possible to locate the crazy criminal who had done this. "Right now, we have no idea, not one. The State Patrol has no report of anyone missing from the prison farm or the nuthouse. I've never heard of anything like this in my life. If you come up with a theory, let me know. We assume the motive here must be grave robbing. There had to be at least two involved. No one person could pry off that granite stone."

Sherlock Holmes, J. J. thought.

Personally, Ralph wanted to believe but instinctively doubted the grave-robbing theory. Why wouldn't the thief go for Mrs. Coleman Swift? The Swifts had even more money than the Masons, and so did the Pearlmans, who owned a chain of clothing stores all over south Georgia.

"My mother was never ostentatious. A lot of women lying out there wore big shiny rocks on their hands. This doesn't make sense on any level. Where is she now? Was she—ah, fuck, was she damaged at all?"

Ralph had an uneasy hunch that something even screwier than grave robbing was involved and was disappointed to hear J. J. bring up the same doubt. "No, she's . . . She's . . . Shit, she's, she's lying there like the day she died, more or less." The color of her face flashed yellow through his vision. "I've closed the gates of the cemetery. We can't move anything until the site has been thoroughly inspected. I'm as sorry as I can be about this and I hope you'll convey this to your family. I talked to Ginger over in Italy. She'll be coming in tomorrow. And I'll call you later if anything comes up."

J. J. sat on the porch step, closed his eyes, and imagined himself in his canoe, floating through the Okefenokee. He rubbed his temples, concentrating on skinny palms reflected in water black with rot, a yellow-headed heron in a catalpa tree, and moody cypresses with strands of gray moss lifting like hair. If you were still for a long time, you could see the slow drift of a palm which grew out of an unmoored mound of humus. Land of Trembling Earth. Maybe all the earth is trembling, he thought. We just can't see it. The swamp at dawn with a passel of white egrets rising out of the trees, the floating leaf-mould pillows of pitcher plant, those green vortexes for luring insects. He tried to sense the fecund smell—sometimes he thought he breathed in a touch of the ancient salt sea as his yellow canoe parted the shallow water just over the lowest point of the sea that covered lower Georgia eons before it was Georgia.

If Scott had not come, J. J. would have fried his perch in cornmeal, had a glass of bourbon, spent a serene evening reading the book that had just arrived in the mail and making notes in the margins.

Fight or flight impulses pumped first through the backs of his legs, then all the way through him. What if he disappeared? He'd done it before. Only Ginger had guessed that he'd be in the hut that only the two of them knew about. He'd walked by it recently, hacked branches still leaning sideways, still furnished with the two stumps that had been their seats. The river deepened right there because of a spring, and they could swing out on vines and drop into icy water. She finally told on him before the funeral, and his daddy came to get him. He found J. J. awake, curled in a damp sleeping bag, the remains of a pork-and-beans dinner still in the can. "You have me," his father had said gently, "and Ginger. And Lily. We'll be all right. You've got to trust me on that right now." J. J. had sworn never to enter Swan again, but he crawled out of the bag and walked back to the car behind his father. Whenever the funeral came to mind, he willed it to blur in memory. He moved his mind so fast he could not stop for any detail.

No doubt Ginger is on her way, he thought. What a stinking mess. Seven-thirty in Swan, one-thirty in the morning there. Planes bound for Washington and the Atlanta connection only flew out in the morning. He had all day tomorrow to see about this. She'll roll in around five or six tomorrow, he calculated, if she makes it, if the plane doesn't spiral into the ocean—no, that's stupid—if she has no delays. He picked up his notebook and turned back to the pages on the swamp in April, where he'd sketched a newly hatched alligator sleeping on its mama's back, the finest thing he saw on that trip, except for *Jesus Saves* spelled out in hubcaps on a hillside. He would like to fry his perch, spend the evening with his notebooks, lulled by the chorus of tree frogs outside.

J. J. threw a tarp over his open Jeep and took the Jaguar to town. The cabin was four miles off the main road. He turned toward Swan at the fish hatchery, passing Hunter's Mill, then nothing. He pressed the accelerator. With one curve in ten miles and no human habitation in sight, he let the speedometer needle touch 100, wishing the car would take off into the sky and fly away. He slowed at the black cemetery beside a peeling, boarded-up church. He and Ginger used to shout for their parents to stop there and let them pick wild blackberries. They'd gather handfuls, unmindful that the rampant bushes rooted in graves. The sunken wooden crosses headed each hump of clay and some graves were decorated with jugs and bits of broken, colored glass. Voodoo, their mother said, spirits live in the jugs.

With the top down, J. J. breathed the swells of honeysuckle scent he drove through. He made an effort to relax his grip on the wheel. The sun had finished its raging for the day and no trace remained of the storm that had started brewing in the afternoon. Swan in the dusk he hardly noticed. In the woods not a bird feather or a leaf moved without his attention. Lily thought she raised him but he had raised himself as close to a Creek Indian as he could come. In town he drove over the brick streets, turned at the Four-Story Building, passing the Surprise Store, passing the small unlighted storefronts, where he knew every owner and clerk whether he wanted to or not, and on down Center Avenue with its oval islands planted by the three garden clubs. Clumps of red amaryllis his mother had planted a quarter-century ago still bloomed on cue.

Swan's original layout survived in the broad elliptical road, Whistling Swan Boulevard, circling the town, and in the four inner concentric drives. Other than these curved roads, all planted in 1875 with moss oaks, Swan's streets conformed to the usual American grid, but even streets no wider than pig tracks were lined with dogwood and crape myrtle. Some dreamer, must have been his great-grandmother, named three of the four drives for faraway islands—Minorca, Corsica, Corfu—then in a moment of grim reality, named the fourth for a bloody Civil War battle in the Mississippi River, Island 10.

J. J. swung into Island 10, then took the unpaved road which led to Palmetto House. To all the Masons, it always had been just "the House." The marble block with *Palmetto House, 1877* carved on its face lay hidden under a bramble of Cherokee roses. When the rutted clay road was built, it cut through an old-growth longleaf-pine forest. A wooden bridge crossed Land's End Creek. Through the years, the Masons sold off pieces of property and now people were moving out of the old houses in town to build squat brick ranch-style houses along the road. J. J. glanced at the waterlogged lot he'd just sold to the Covenant Pentecostal Church. A worthless piece of Mason land J. J. never expected to sell. The church members were battling over drinking and dancing, and some loudmouths intended to split off and build their own church where no one could have a lick of fun. May the mosquitoes lift them by the seat of the pants.

From the end of the road he could see Lily standing on the porch looking off into nothing.

J. J. gave her a hug and she began to search her pockets for a tissue. She cried into his shoulder. "I can't stand this. I'm not made of iron. This is beyond the call." He felt her shaking.

"You look bushed." J. J. closed his nose against her bandaged hand's scent of iodine and her sour apron left too long in the washing machine. He led her into the kitchen and poured iced tea. She looked lost in her housedress. Her cowlick poked up and wisps of hair had escaped her twist. J. J. looked at the yellowed whites of her eyes and three layers of circles drooping beneath. He thought, not unkindly, that she looked like an old horse.

She was exhausted, beyond exhausted, depleted after her trip out to the Columns to see Wills. She told J. J. that he had just stared at her with his starved look when she told him the ghastly thing that had happened, then he said, "Catherine, Cat, Cat, how wonderful it will be to see her again." He'd smiled and become agitated trying to stand up. "Get me a comb, Lily. I'm going down to the train." He raised his chin, as though adjusting his tie, showing her his lithic profile.

"There is no train. The train doesn't even run through here anymore. Don't you remember we used to take the train but now we can't? The train station is the Jeff Davis Museum, full of tarnished old uniform buttons and canteens. We can't even take a bus, not that we'd want to."

"Has she had a good trip?"

"Who?"

"That woman you were telling me about."

"Wills, my dear, it was Catherine I was talking about. There was no trip. I'm sorry I had to tell you this, and I know it's hard to understand, but you were going to hear it from somebody. I do not understand how anyone could do this to us."

He shifted in his chair and groaned. His left side was paralyzed except for his huge, twisted hand. She thought his blue veins looked like needlepoint thread. "Turn on the TV. I'd like a Co-Cola and would be much obliged if you'd ask for one. This hotel doesn't have a liquor license, and I've told them they're never going to make it. I've stayed at the finest hotels and they all have room service."

Lily smiled. Sometimes she almost thought he was being ironic. "Wills, you know you're at the Columns. They take good care of you here."

"I'm checking out at noon tomorrow. It hurts right here." He waved his right hand from his shoulder to his knee. "I hurt all over." Usually, he forgot that he'd been a doctor. He complained like a child but seemed to have no expectation that anything could be done for him.

She didn't tell J. J. that she had walked down to the nurses' station. Doors into the rooms along the hall were open and she tried, as usual, not to look at the shriveled bodies with diaper bulge propped in chairs looking out into the hall for some sign of activity. She avoided looking at the woman with fist-sized tumors all over her face and neck, but stopped to speak to Besta Warren, who was from a nice family and had simply fallen apart at fifty and had been making hideous turquoise and blue afghans here ever since. By the time she got to the nurses' station, she had forgotten what her brother wanted.

Now she remembered. "Wills wants so little; it was too bad he didn't get his Co-Cola."

"He'll get over it. He gets over everything else, doesn't he?" J. J. was alarmed at Lily's leaps. She's on the brink, he thought. He'd seen her like this before, when they'd lived through a hurricane warning and she'd feared the House would blow off its foundation and lift into the sky. "I'm going to shower, then let's fix some dinner." In his old room, he flopped backward on the bed. Christ, J. J. thought, I left those perch in the sink.

LILY JUMPED when J. J. came back downstairs. He looked like a pure apparition of Wills when he'd come home from medical school at

Emory. J. J.'s hair was too long. Wet from the shower and slicked back, his hair shone blue-black under the kitchen light. He was tan and barefoot. "Too pretty to be a boy," they'd teased him as a child. He had Wills's speckled green eyes, but his eyelashes were curled and thick. He didn't quite have Wills's height, but he was built solidly, while Wills was lanky and more elegant, Lily thought. He'd changed from what had appeared to be a torn undershirt into a proper white shirt with short sleeves. He never wore anything but white shirts, never cared about clothes a bit, and, on the two or three nights a week he slept at the House, he always put on a spotless one, leaving his fishing or hunting clothes in a heap on the floor for Tessie to pick up. A grown man stepping out of his pants like a four-year-old.

Lily felt like something carved of wax that had started to melt. J. J. heated leftover butterbeans and ham and she sat at the kitchen table. "The day your mama died," Lily began. He popped open a jar of bread-and-butter pickles and fished out some for each plate.

"Lily, we're not going to talk about any of that now. You've had a hell of a day—the worst day of your life. *I've* had a hell of a day. Let's just eat and then you go straight on to bed." He could not take even the idea of any histrionics.

She picked at her beans. This was not the worst day of her life. "Where's Catherine?"

J. J. lowered his fork and shook his head. "Lying on the ground, I guess."

"When's Ginger coming? Where's Ginger now? I made her biscuits."

J. J. went to the biscuit box. "So you did. Let's just have some samples of that major talent of yours. Ginger won't get here until late tomorrow. Maybe you can whip up a fresh batch in the mañana." My God, if she were not so worked up, maybe I could be allowed to be just a tad thrown myself, he thought. "You know it's a long flight, then she has to drive two hundred miles. I wish she'd waited before flying off like that. This may be completely over with tomorrow. Aunt Lily, you've got to keep calm, try not to get overwrought." Hysterical, more like it. J. J. spread a biscuit with butter that had softened in the heat. "They'll catch those idiots. That'll be the end of it. I hope to God, anyway."

Lily burrowed into the concept of traveling and time. "You're right, I'm just spinning. I'm sure Ginger's sound asleep right now—where is she? I've heard they're kidnaping people in Italy or shooting them in the knees."

"Rome. I'm sure she's in a nice hotel. Nobody's going to bother her knees. She flies out of Rome early." And she's probably wide awake, wondering what in God's name is going on here. He lifted his glass. "Whoop-de-do, Ginger, the divine Lily and I are feasting on cracked crab and champagne, discussing the fine points of thoroughbreds. Come on home, down to the heart of Dixie, summertime and the living is easy, fish are jumpin', root hog or die."

"Hush, J. J." Lily smiled even though she didn't want to. With J. J., she sometimes felt that she and Wills were young again, sitting together while their mother snapped the wilted flowers off the centerpiece and their father wandered into the living room to listen to the radio. "She drives too fast. She'll be here for supper. Maybe she'll bring some of that cheese she brought last time. She's thrilled to pieces over this work, digging around in the dirt pulling up little things nobody would want. She had this eentsie clay foot she thought was the prettiest thing."

Lily stared at the back door. "Everyone saw her spirit. You could tell right away that she was somebody. She always lifted her chin when she turned away from you. Like that." Lily looked at him, then at the wall, slowly raising her chin as she turned.

"Who're you talking about?" But he knew.

"Oh, that Catherine—but I was talking about Ginger, too. She has always been the sweetest thing. She used to bring me a tussie-mussie on May Day. But Catherine—hair black as yours, that's where you got it. Wills's hair was a rich brown, like mine, before he went snow white. They stole the show wherever they went. She could be tart-tongued."

"You're talking about Ginger or Mother?" Irritated, he followed her drifting even if he didn't want to. The tall dining room windows opened to the night sounds, the wild chorus not so different from the voice of Lily.

"That Ginger almost won the state debate when she was in high school. The segregation mess, I think they were arguing about even then. Lucky they didn't have guns, those demonstrators. Guns go off. That's what guns are for, to go off." She paused. "And they will keep going off for the rest of our born days. Catherine always wanted her way."

J. J. kept quiet and ate. She was on a tear. Deep shock, probably. Let her river run.

"I'll never forget that day. I felt so sorry for her. Little Gin-Gin shivering and crying like she'd never stop. Holding on to that doll she'd outgrown and yanking at her own hair. That hair's her glory. Like a house afire. You ran off and no one knew where you were, adding to the worry. The mystery I'll never fathom—Catherine was supposed to go to Macon the next day—that red Jaguar she wanted had come in, of course Wills gave her everything she could ever want. I never will understand that; if you'd ordered a car, would you . . ." She trailed off as she dropped three beans in her lap.

"You want a cup of coffee? I'll be glad to make it. I'm going out for a while."

Lily dropped her meandering reverie. "J. J., we must remember to ask the sheriff if she still had the envelope."

"Look, I'm going on out. Let's leave these dishes." Let's sail them out the back door. Hit the fence hard.

"Sugar, there was a note in Catherine's hands before they buried her. I wonder if it was stolen."

"What did it say?" He barely could bring himself to ask, from his long habit of cutting off any memory, any fact, any speculation about his mother.

"I don't know. Maybe it was a good-bye letter, maybe a love letter from Wills. It would be awful if they took it, whatever it was." He didn't ask her who put the letter in Catherine's hand.

"I'll ask the sheriff tomorrow." He always tried not to think about his mother lying in the funeral home in the dress she'd worn on vacation. On Carrie's Island she wore white sandals, which she would kick off in sandy places and dangle from her fingers. When she leaned forward in her bathing suit, he could see a rim of white sand on her breasts and the sheen of suntan oil, which smelled like coconut and sunlight. Her charm bracelet jangled, and holding his and Ginger's hands, sometimes she'd do a little dance step and pull them along. All summer they'd played canasta, Monopoly, Chinese checkers, and Parcheesi. In the hottest part of the day, she made pimento cheese sandwiches, opened big bags of potato chips, and the three of them sat in the breezeway drinking lemonade and playing penny ante poker. He could still hear the waves breaking, then the quick sluicing back into the sea through banks of coquina shells, a sound like breathing in through clenched teeth.

J. J. DROVE OUT TO THE MILL VILLAGE to have a drink with Mindy. Water sprayed as his car crossed the almost-submerged wooden bridge over Cherokee Creek, which marked the entrance to the village. Rains had swollen the creek where he and Ginger used to play when they went to the office with Big Jim. Beyond the creek the rows of workers' houses began. He'd seen Mindy a few times since her divorce. Her husband drove an oil truck and last summer had taken hard to the Holy Rollers, which Mindy thought was all crap. His religious fervor supplied a lot of rules but somehow did not now leave him with the moral obligation to pay child support for Letitia, who was now five. J. J. hired Mindy to work at the store, right now stocking shelves and checking in orders.

Although Big Jim's mill closed ten years back, half the workers' houses were still lived in. J. J. collected the forty-dollar-a-month rent from each whenever he got around to it. He glanced at one house where he never collected rent, just beyond the creek. Ever since he'd heard from Scott that Aileen Boyd, the woman who lived there, had been Big Jim's mistress, he'd figured he would just let her be. And maybe it wasn't true. Scott had heard it through the maids' grapevine when he was a boy. A cat slept on her front steps. Farther on stood three empty houses he had boarded up after the Adventists complained that teenagers were using them to have sex and drink beer. The square street around the mill was lined with board houses set up on blocks, with slanting front porches and generous yards. Lard cans of geraniums, hollyhocks, so tall they arced, cornflowers and weedy larkspurs ornamented some yards. Most were packed dirt with holes where dogs curled. A few big chinaberry trees along the road provided what shade there was.

Mindy had painted her place sea-foam green, as she called it, and grew a potato vine up strings on either side of the porch. He saw her sitting on the steps polishing her toenails, even though it was almost dark. A patch of gold sky remained over the sprawling brick building where his great-grandfather and his grandfather had for decades manufactured cotton drapery material. Mindy's father had been a foreman and her mother worked at the looms, but they were now living in Florida and had moved up. He ran a gas station and she worked inside, selling cold drinks and her own fudge. People came from miles to buy her pecan-studded fudge. They were able to send Mindy a little money, always with a note encouraging her to leave this backwater and move to Denton, where she and Letitia could live in their spare room. They could expand the fudge business easily with an extra pair of hands.

J. J. opened the trunk and took out a bottle of gin. Mindy waved the silver-tipped brush at him and wiggled her toes in the air. "Hey, J. J., I didn't expect to see you. I heard Scott on the phone with his mama and I made him tell me what happened. This just gives me the willies. Are y'all right? You poor thing!"

J. J. realized this was exactly what he'd come to hear. She

brought out ice in tall glasses and a bottle of tonic. Letitia was asleep in the front room. J. J. heard the whirr of a fan blowing back and forth over her. He sat down on the steps and poured. Mindy's toes were the color of dimes. "Silver Fantasy"—she waved the bottle of polish—"that's me." Now that her husband was gone, she spent hours on her skin, hair, nails, clothes. Even after six hours at the store—she couldn't get to work until ten, when she could take Letitia to play at her sister's—there were hours and hours to fill, hours when she'd shell peas, iron, and she didn't know what all. She brought home TV dinners from the store and Letitia loved the sectioned foil trays. She'd boil some corn, maybe, or cook some rice, but dinner now took minutes and then the day still continued. Only around nine-thirty, when dark finally fell, did she feel like the day might actually end. She had rinsed her hair in lemon juice tonight and rolled it on orange juice cans. She could see J. J. looking at her springy blond curls. He handed her a drink and sat down beside her on the steps. She pressed the glass to either cheek for the coolness. She stretched out her legs to admire her shiny toes.

Great legs, he noticed. Nice feet, too. Long and thin like a rabbit's. "My aunt is falling apart. You can imagine. Well, maybe you can't—I can't get a handle on any of this. My sister's flying in tomorrow. They've called in someone from the GBI. I hope they'll solve it soon—tomorrow—and take care of my mother. I'd like to forget this ever happened." He paused. "Fat chance." Bad hair, he thought. Looked like she'd run smack into a tornado. But as she turned her head, he caught the fresh, lemony scent and felt a shock of coolness from the strong drink he'd mixed. She was plain but he liked looking at her. She had a straightforward face with pale freckles, a pert nose, and large dark eyes that always looked sleepy. Her thin-lipped smile almost covered her overlapping bottom teeth. She was stacked. Her breasts looked pointed and full, but somehow she missed being sexy. Or maybe he missed, or something. He wanted company, wanted to feel a grand rush of desire that would land them in the middle of her ugly iron bed. It was not going to happen.

Maybe the nest was still too warm. "For God's sake, let's talk about something else."

"Okay. Have you seen *Jaws*?"

"No."

"Okay. Let's see, we had a delivery today of tomato paste and barbecue sauces. And a little brat kicked loose the electrical plug of the ice cream box and all the Popsicles melted. Letitia colored in the alphabet without going out of the lines. She talked back to me twice today."

J. J. laughed, leaned back against the railing, and watched the stars come out. There, his old friend, the Corona Borealis, pointed out to him by his mother from the porch of the cabin on a summer night like this when she was sitting on the log railing and he and Ginger barely swayed in the swing. Catherine's white hydrangeas grew just up to the porch, moons in wet, shadowy leaves. His mother had taken astronomy in college in order to avoid the math requirement. She remembered the Pleiades, Orion, the Dippers, the Bear. Others she made up. "Look, there's the Anthill, and there's the Train Wreck, and over there's the North Star, just above the Wandering Jew."

He and Ginger had protested. "The Wandering Jew is a plant at Lily's," they'd yelled. "There's no Wandering Jew in the sky." Still, they weren't sure.

"Look, there's his beard, and just follow the imaginary line—his knees, his feet. Of course there's a Wandering Jew constellation. There has to be . . ." Below them, the river plunged through the night. They heard the water surging over a clot of logs along the bank. Their father sat by himself out on the dock. J. J. closed his eyes around the image of his father barely touched by the porch light.

Mindy brought out two peaches. She ate hers, skin and all, letting the juice drip. J. J. leaned over and touched the point of her chin with his tongue. She pressed her breasts forward, then laughed and put her arms around his neck. He felt her hard lips against his, then her driving little tongue parted his mouth and he tasted the juicy sweetness of the fruit when she opened her mouth wider, breathing out into his mouth and deeply in, with his hands in her hair, her hand under his shirt. He knew where this would lead. He was willing now, but something stood apart from him, watching him go into action, and would not go. He leaned back, pulling her head down onto his chest. "You're hard to leave but I've got to get back to the House. This day has gone on into eternity. I'm pretty bushed. Lily's probably wandering the hallowed halls."

She didn't answer. He'd done this once before. The night they danced at Lake T the temperature hovered in the mid-nineties even at ten o'clock. Some guy from Osceola who was dancing alone stumbled and whooped and poured a cold beer over his own head. They'd walked outside, where it was fresh and damp, though not any cooler. He kissed her neck, tickled her bare shoulders with a weed, teased her about stepping on his feet. He was a fine dancer and she thought that men who could dance were good in the sack, at least that's what she'd thought before her marriage. She'd been three years behind J. J. in school and always thought he was gorgeous, nothing like his big old bull of a granddaddy, who'd stand on the back of a truck handing out Thanksgiving turkeys to the mill-workers. Like they were peons. She remembered how thrilled her mother was to cook a bird for the holidays. J. J. didn't have any of the boss man in him. When Scott asked his opinion about a new meat case, he just shrugged and said, "Whatever you think, big chief."

Mindy was just out of a marriage with a taskmaster. Carleton had wanted his undershorts pressed. He straightened the refrigerator every morning. He flew into a devil-minded fit when he came home and found baby Letitia wandering the yard with a dirty diaper. He had sharp yellow incisors which he bared when he ate. He ate dinner with his fork clutched in his right hand and his left hand on the table curled around his plate in a fist. She liked J. J.'s roll-with-the-punches lifestyle, but the taskmaster, at least, had wanted sex almost every night. "Take that thang off," he'd say. "You get on me first." The iron bed had creaked and banged against the wall. She smiled to remember Letitia waking up and calling out, "Mommy, are you all right?" Quick, unromantic, yes, but she was used to the big O on a regular basis. She didn't understand this holding back. She'd heard plenty over the years about J. J. and various women. She was prettier than a lot of them. Much prettier than Wynette Sykes, whose ears stuck out like Dumbo's.

"Why didn't you ever marry?" she'd asked J. J. that night at the lake. Faintly, they heard Jimi Hendrix singing "Purple Haze."

"Darlin', my life's not over. Don't say 'ever' yet."

"Well, why haven't you yet? How could you *avoid* it?"

"You ask a hard question."

"You've been out with so many women."

"You want a long or a short answer?"

"Have you ever had a long relationship?"

"Now, who's counting? No, I guess not. In college once, maybe nine months."

"What happened?"

"What happened to your marriage—things go to hell." He did not say he quickly lost whatever it took to sustain a relationship, would turn viciously critical no matter how lovely, intelligent, suitable the woman. "Maybe I was born in the wrong era."

He knew that she would now say, "Maybe you just haven't met the right person," and she did.

"Could be. Let's exchange life stories some other time. Let's go back and dance." They'd danced and had a couple of beers. She had her car and he had not asked if he could follow her home. He stayed on after she left, waving good-bye with both hands. Her friend who tended bar told her later that J. J. danced with a short skinny girl and finally staggered out alone about two.

Mindy rested her head against his chest. His white shirt looked blue as thin milk in the moonlight. He stared up at the stars and they heard the splash of the creek where the sewage used to be emptied in Big Jim's time. She listened for his heartbeat. Bang. Bang.

ON HER DARK FRONT PORCH, Aileen Boyd rocked and knitted. No need to see. She had a feel for the rhythm of the needles, and the pattern was simple, a white baby blanket for her niece who was expecting in September. Since the mill closed, Aileen had supported herself by knitting and sewing baby clothes for people in town. A twist of fate, since she'd never had any children of her own. She saw J. J. Mason's car pass, saw him glance her way, but she was screened by a piece of lattice.

She liked her work, edging little gowns in lace and threading ribbon through crib sheets. It beat the bejesus out of her old job, sitting at a loom all day. So J. J. was seeing a mill girl. Chip off the old block, although he'd seemed obliging enough the times he'd come for the rent. Then he'd stopped coming and she didn't inquire. People said J. J. didn't care about money. Only those who've got buckets of it can afford not to care. Big Jim would not have wanted her rent. She wondered if J. J. had heard she had been Big Jim's fancy woman, mistress, lover, which was the word she preferred—*lover* made her think of satin sheets. Not likely, they were always careful. In Swan you had to be. And not so fancy, she thought, not a real mistress, but lover, yes, for four years. Dead for twenty years, Big Jim didn't seem as lost as other dead people; even his memory was magnified.

She was nineteen, married to Sonny for two years, when Big Jim first noticed her walking to work. He offered her a ride and she didn't refuse. He was the boss. Suddenly, she was transferred to the office and taught to send out bills and orders and sometimes make fabric sample deliveries in the mill car to nearby towns. Sonny didn't like it from the start, but Aileen was awestruck by her promotion. That first week Sonny shook her by the shoulders, demanding to know if Big Jim pawed her, and she'd screamed that not everyone was as sex mad as he was. Sonny went sour fast for her. She couldn't remember why she'd married him, though he'd dazzled her at sixteen, stopping in front of her house in his pickup. She'd run out when he blew the horn. Elbow out the window, hair blond as hers, he smiled and cracked his gum. He kept a pack of Camels tucked into his rolled-up T-shirt sleeve. They went bowling and to the bush-league ball games. He parked on country roads and rolled out a thin mattress in the bed of the pickup. Aileen had been with enough boys by then to know they weren't supposed to fire off immediately, but Sonny didn't seem to mind twenty-second sex. They hadn't been dating three weeks when he started getting mad if she even talked to another man. Fool that she was, she took his jealousy for love.

She was dying to escape her violent father, the smells and fights of seven people crammed into four small rooms, her mother's hacking and spitting. They were just as glad to see her go. She married Sonny at the Justice of the Peace because it cost only ten dollars. He slapped her on their wedding night because she was too friendly to his own brother. Soon they moved into a mill house. Sonny operated the big machinery at the mill, while she sat at a loom for nine hours a day, wondering what she had *thought* would happen.

When she transferred to the office, Big Jim paid her an extra ten a week in cash, which she instinctively hid for herself in a coffee can under the house at the back of the storage bin. At first she only felt his hard eyes on her, but later that changed. By then, Big Jim told her she was not like other women; he said she was supple like a young peach tree and her long braid was the color of wheat with the sun shining on it. They met at a motel on the other side of Tipton after her deliveries. Sometimes he gave her money, but money was not the point. She had to admit sex was the point for both of them. Sonny's jealousy festered, but he had no proof she was fooling around, and she became a smooth liar. Even though Big Jim was old enough to be her father, he had a vigor and drive Sonny never had. Under Big Jim's body, her own felt shocked and ravished. But she learned to please them both and Big Jim grew to love her. She knew he did, though he never said so. They had a big time together. He was powerful, and when he surrendered to her, she was powerful. His wife had tight, no-color curls. Aileen would unbraid her hair and drag it loose over his body. She'd sass him, too. He liked that.

Sometimes when his wife and daughter were gone, she'd slip into the office at night when Sonny was on late shift at the mill. Big Jim always parked in the porte-cochère on the woods side of the office, so it was easy enough for him to turn out the light and open the car door to let her in without anyone seeing. With her crouched on the floor, they'd drive to the House, where they'd go at it right in the marital bed. Aileen smiled to remember his gratitude. He'd take her foot and press it to his cheek. He'd get on his knees and cover her with kisses, his large hands on her back. And he could go twice. Sonny couldn't; he'd fall dead asleep. She liked the second time better and Big Jim roared his pleasure. She'd be home by eleven. She wouldn't take chances like that now, for anyone. But at forty-three, she wasn't in as much demand for amorous risks.

So J. J. was leaving his calling card in the village. That lynx-faced Mindy no doubt. Well, Mindy need not get her hopes up. J. J. might be his own man, as people said, but he was not going to be waltzing down the aisle with a mill girl. It did not work that way.

ROME NEVER QUITS, Ginger thought. Her hotel window opened above a street too narrow for cars but filled with strolling people even at two, three, four in the morning. As the numbers decreased with the hours, the voices of those remaining seemed to grow louder. Because of the heat, she had to leave the window open. She'd taken off her shirt and lay on top of the sheet in her panties, arms and legs stretched out so no part of her body came in contact with any other.

Marco didn't answer at nine-thirty when she came in from the trattoria down the street. She was surprised to find herself starving and for a whole hour didn't think of what had happened or why she was going, only enjoyed the pasta and wine at a table on a small piazza, where what looked like twelve-year-old boys zipped around on their Vespas and a cat curled in the chair opposite her. Back at the hotel, she showered. At ten he still didn't answer so she gave up. At eleven he called. They were late getting back and he'd just seen her note. Ginger found that she couldn't tell him what had happened. Later, face-to-face, not now. Instead, she said, "There is some crisis and Aunt Lily can't handle it. No one knows where J. J. is at the moment. He must be off fishing somewhere. He's very unpredictable."

"Someone always unpredictable is therefore predictable, no?

You will then count on him not to be around when you want him to be."

"You have a point," she conceded, although she didn't like him disparaging J. J. when he didn't even know him.

"I am sorry you have to go—I will be longing for you and I will miss your face."

Ginger fell asleep reading, then woke up suddenly after an hour and couldn't go back to sleep. She practiced emptying her mind by imagining herself to be a bride doll lying in a long box of green tissue paper, imagining herself on a fast horse galloping across Andalusia, imagining she had levitated from bed and was floating near the ceiling, bumping into corners gently like a helium balloon. Since childhood, she had found dozens of "trips" to take her away. A yellow helium balloon . . .

This is crazy and I'm going to get back to Marco as soon as I can, she told herself. One more flat-out disaster in the family. Hold on, just go through it. How do the Indian mystics walk over a bed of burning coals—empty your mind and just go fast. She imagined her mind as a primitive abacus, like one in Peru she'd read about, a network of knotted strings, with each knot holding a memory. She willed all the knots to be happy ones. While people shouted and laughed below her window, Ginger imagined knot after knot, almost feeling the coarsely-knotted rough twine: the armful of bounding, joyful, curly Tish, a mixture of all the good dogs in the neighborhood, leaping out of a basket on her seventh birthday; walking the beach at Fernandina just at sunrise with her father, picking up sand dollars; riding on the back of a sea turtle scuttling back to the ocean after laying eggs in warm sand. Ginger again let herself balance, arms out all the way to the edge of the water, then leapt off and watched her turtle swim out. For a long time, she followed the turtle into the tide. Then she shifted to her cot at the cabin, with the shelf of orange Twins books beside her bed—*The Polish Twins, The French Twins, The Swedish Twins*—and on the shelf above, her mother's jars of tomatoes and peach and watermelon pickles, their jewel colors crimson, icy green, and the peaches like little rising suns. Ginger went back to herself reading by kerosene lantern, loving the exotic places in the Twins books and realizing, at ten, reading while snuggled under quilts, that she could have that pleasure all her life. No matter what. The knots of memory, so many of them in, she loved the word, a *quipu*. Many cultures had mnemonic systems with beads, ribbons, knots, or pebbles. The word *calculate*, she remembered, comes from the Latin for pebble. She slipped toward the present, Marco's tanned back, her mouth on the hollow of his neck while he slept, the nightingale singing. When she woke him to hear it, he turned and said, "Let's do the nightingale, let's do the moon in the valley, let's do the fox." She had no choice but to love a man who thought like that. Marco—always laughter even in the middle of the night. Laughter—the polar opposite of her expectations. The knots of the present felt small and slippery, while the old ones seemed heavy; maybe they were pebbles after all, or stones, the golden stones she piled into boxes at the Etruscan temple. I'll take those stones into my mind, she thought, and discover something new.

Finally, she slept.

IN HIS OLD ROOM, which was also his father's old room, J. J. ended
the endless day by looking through one of his father's medical textbooks. Oddly, the section on strokes was all marked up with a pen.
Other sections were underlined here and there, but J. J. scanned
"then obstruction in the artery cuts off oxygen to cells," and "when
toxins are released, cells start to die quickly," and "oxygen depletion
will cause the molecular pumps to fade, disrupting the regulation of
sodium, potassium, and . . ." He slammed the book shut. His father,
not many years after studiously noting those passages, had a stroke
himself. He leafed through Wills's senior yearbook, also abandoned
along with old *Life* magazines, then shoved it back in the bookcase.
The short story of his father, downed at forty-four. J. J. thought of
the duck blind at dawn, aiming at a duck flying against the splin-
tered light. The shot, the shock—how the airborne bird would turn
instantly to dead weight and thud heavily onto the water.

J. J. had come to this room when he was sixteen. Lily never had
wanted to change the stiff curtains printed with sailboats or the
table set up with his father's HO model trains permanently stalled
outside a village, with miniature frosted Christmas trees and a little
red post office. J. J.'s old fishing baskets, rods, and archery equipment hung on racks around the big square room, which was identi-

cal to Ginger's, except his looked out toward the woods behind the house, and hers on the front faced the pond, where Lily's two fierce white swans glided on their reflections in the black water.

Lily slept in her parents' old room downstairs, in the bed so high you had to use a step stool to climb in. If she left her door open, J. J. could hear her snore when he came in late and went back to the kitchen for something to eat. The snores were lighter when he was a boy, but often he'd crept out of bed to listen for them, just to assure himself that at least she was still alive, even though she drove him mad with her senseless rules: you can't cut paper on Sunday, it's bad luck to leave a hat on a bed, so-and-so's beneath you, so-and-so's from a nice family, on and on. Fussbox, he and Ginger had called her. Willy-Nilly Lily.

The House itself was a comfort then; he'd had a sense of its immense stability. His grandmother's amber wax grapes still sat on the dining room table, and he always opened the door to the smell of lemon beeswax polish, faint cigar smoke, and something good frying in the kitchen. He found his great-grandmother's yellowed sheet music inside the piano bench. Tomorrow Ginger would be in the room beside his, the head of her bed separated from the head of his by a wall. As he tried to sleep, he kept cycling on Ralph Hunnicutt parked in the county's Ford, slapping mosquitoes, dozing, and jerking awake every time a frog croaked, his mother with a bullet hole in her heart, lying under a tarp. Ginger, yes, three, four, five, six, seven, eight hours, already in the air. Heading out over Europe, coming home, the Atlantic glittering below like hammered pewter. He hated flying over water. The Atlantic, a powerful magnet pulling her plane. No. He would keep that plane up by the force of his will. He only slept by thinking of her already there in her room, her left hand under her head the way she always slept, there, just opposite him but close, the way she'd always been.

July 9

ELEANOR SPENT THE EARLY MORNING reading magazines on her terrace, the only time of the summer day she could enjoy being in the garden. She told Hattie to stay home because there was plenty of food left over from the bridge party, and the day was going to be too sultry to move. She did not visit Holt, had not even considered going, but had surprised herself by considering the possibility of never going again. She'd come out of sleep this morning already thinking. "Catherine would be, let's see, she and Holt Junior were about the same age, she'd be around fifty-five," she'd said aloud. Holt Junior by now had developed a spongy paunch and a bald spot you couldn't miss when he walked down steps in front of you, even though he tried to comb a pale strand of hair over it.

If Ralph or the GBI thought this was a grave robbing, they were whistling "Dixie." Why would a common thief go into a grave after so long? She turned the pages of *House Beautiful*. A woman with a castle in England planted an all-white garden. How dull; did she have dresses all the same color, too? Eleanor ripped out a recipe for turkey with tarragon and bacon. She'd make it when Holt Junior next came to Sunday dinner. Holt Junior—too bad he never married, never found the right girl. She thought of Catherine. What secrets would this drive out? What blessèd thing can we ever know?

What if Catherine had lived? She wondered how Lily would have lived her life.

Catherine would have aged well, Eleanor thought, and Wills, if he had not had the stroke, would be at the height of his powers as a doctor. They would have transformed Palmetto House. Ginger would have shown up on her wedding day instead of locking herself in her room. That poor Mitchell forgave her, although it still didn't work out. She imagined Palmetto House lit up like the *Titanic* at night, music spilling from all the open windows. *When all the things you are, are mine . . .* Holt Junior might have met one of Catherine's friends from Macon. Even J. J. might have been different—put that good brain to use. Lily didn't fit in that picture. Lily would have been forced to invent a different life, but Eleanor could not imagine a life for Lily away from the House.

Eleanor reached for *Holiday*. She'd been nowhere since Holt died. Maybe she and Lily should take a trip together in the fall. It would do Lily good. A cruise to the Caribbean—what a grand idea. They could find bridge partners and stay on board if natives in the ports of call looked unpleasant. On one of her trips with Holt, a lovely lady from upper New York had been hit with a tomato in Barbados.

LILY CALLED ELEANOR but no one answered. She knew Eleanor liked the early morning outside, as she did, and must be out pinching back marigolds or having her coffee in the backyard glider. She knew for sure Eleanor would not be paying her visit to Holt's grave today. Lily was restless. She freed CoCo from his cage and let him fly around the porch. He lighted on her shoulder, fluttering his green wings, and gently pecked her ear. She wished Eleanor would come over for a game of Scrabble while she waited for Ginger. The house was ready. She decided to ride over to visit her other close friend in Swan, Agnes Burkhart. Lily had a raincoat to shorten. Since she wouldn't be long, she let CoCo go in the car with her.

As she drove up Palmetto Road, she passed Wills and Catherine's old house but did not glance in that direction. Catherine had kept Agnes's Singer whirring ninety miles an hour. Once Lily had been at Agnes's getting a linen duster hemmed when Catherine came in with a sketch of a dotted-swiss dress with a fluffy skirt. Agnes, mouth half full of pins, kept squeezing a rubber bulb, marking Lily's hem with a puff of chalk while she mumbled to Catherine about covered buttons and French seams. Lily had greeted Catherine coolly. It was just like her to breeze in wanting what she wanted right then. Catherine wanted Ginger to have the dress for Easter, three weeks away, and Agnes already had a pile of alterations to do for Maggie Everett, who had lost fifty-two pounds on a meat and martini diet. There were complicated inserts of narrow lace on the bodice. Agnes hauled herself off the floor and promised Catherine she'd get the dress made. They say Agnes Burkhart almost went blind from all the hand-sewing she did. She loved Catherine's clothes the most. And Lily, too, had admired Catherine at church with the two children, Ginger in hand-smocked dresses, J. J. in just-pressed sailor suits, and Catherine, oh, she remembered a good-looking navy dress with big buttons, and one winter a lavender-gray cashmere suit with a rolled collar. Lily had combed *Harper's Bazaar* looking for beautiful dresses and skirts, wanting Catherine to envy *her*. Her bond with Agnes came from childhood. They'd gone all through school together; their mutual passion for fabric began with dressing dolls. Often Lily would forget her rivalry with Catherine and buy yardage because she knew Agnes would love it.

"WELL, LILY, I SWAN, come in out of the heat." Agnes flung open the double door. Lily entered Agnes's airless hall fanning herself with a newspaper. This was the house children avoided at Halloween because of Agnes's sister, Evelyn, who hung her hair over the upstairs balcony. Children thought roaches fell from it. Actually, she was only drying it in the sun. Once the sister had called to a child, *"step on a crack break your mother's back,"* and since then children crossed the street and walked on Lard Bascom's side, even though he had a biting dog. Well-dressed women never had compunctions about crossing the broken sidewalk, bringing Agnes a handful of daylilies and plopping down a piece of material bought in Macon. Agnes sewed like an angel.

In what could have been Agnes's living room, Lily found the one chair not covered with clothes and bolts of cloth. Agnes took a seat behind her sewing machine, as though she were about to press the pedal and run the needle down a seam. Lily wondered where Evelyn might be. She used to give foot treatments, trimming yellow corns and scrolling off waxy crescents from calluses. Many times Lily had watched her massage customers' bunions. She worked with a tub of scalding water in the kitchen while Agnes held forth in the living room. It was said that she had her own coffin ready in her bedroom, but who'd ever seen upstairs? The two maiden sisters had lived together their whole lives, inheriting the two-story house, the only stone one in Swan, and so very damp inside. Their father, an electrician, a native of Germany, could not pronounce his *w*'s and *th*'s. Evelyn, who never had cut her hair, was subject to fits, and Agnes often had to rush to her with a spoon so that she did not bite her tongue in two.

Agnes no longer copied dresses. The most anyone could get her to do was a hem or a tuck in a jacket. Her hair, harshly cut like a monk's, shone white under the bare bulb dangling over her machine, and her plucked-to-nothing eyebrows gave her a look of permanent foreignness. In the center of the room stood a worktable stacked with thousands of patterns, spools, pinking shears, scissors, pincushions, and bobbins.

The place was a veritable archive of the dress habits of Swan ladies, if anyone were interested, which, of course, no one ever would be. There was a peculiar, heavy odor. Had a mouse died among the folded tissue-paper coats and prom dresses?

Agnes had not heard about Catherine. She made a little whickering cry and balled her fists to rub her eyes. "My dear, you poor thing. Sometimes I think we are in our last days. These beasts among us . . ." While she recovered from the shock, Lily waited. She cast a glance at the window to see if the jar of Agnes's gallstones still rested on the sill. It did.

"Agnes, I thought of you later yesterday when I kept seeing that blue silk dress," Lily began. "I just wanted to talk to you. I've had quite a setback from all this. You can't imagine. You must have made that dress for Catherine? Doesn't that seem so strange, the dress . . ." Lily couldn't quite articulate what she felt, "that the dress was made for an occasion, no doubt," she continued, "but it played a part in something unbearable later . . ." She shivered.

"Rabbit jump over your grave? I know what you mean." Agnes thoughtfully rubbed the small hump emerging just below her neck. "Catherine's favorite color was blue. Of course, with those eyes. What a shame." She scraped back her chair and turned to take down a ragbag sewn from a U.S. Navy bedspread. "My brother Hugo brought this back from the war. I've kept it for scraps, in case I ever got the desire to make a quilt. I kept a piece of everything pretty." She emptied the contents on the floor. "Hugo's been gone almost as long as Catherine. What shade of blue?"

"Bright blue, marine—with a dollop of turquoise."

Agnes picked through the remnants, passing each one to Lily for the pleasure of the textures. "Here's a burgundy mohair. Little Sarah George wore that suit for seven winters straight." Little Sarah George Godwin, named for her mother's father, was at seventy-something still called Little Sarah George. Agnes stuffed plaid wool and printed cottons back in the bag, then found a scarf of tangerine silk. "This was the prettiest material, so soft it'd tear if you looked at it."

Lily remembered Catherine rising from a table, a sparkling swish of sound like tissue paper crumpling. She'd held a drawstring evening bag in both hands. "Wasn't that Catherine's?"

"Yes, went over one shoulder, cut on the bias, and not everybody can carry that off, believe you me. Catherine out of all the people I ever sewed for had a style—she just knew how cloth would drape."

"You know she studied design those two years she went to college."

"Yes, she could draw just what she wanted. All those notebooks she kept were full of pictures. Not just clothes, which she brought over to me, but I'd see columns drawn out, and notes on how the shadows angled off them, and all that. She drew floor plans like an architect, gates and porches, that sort of thing."

Lily didn't want to discuss Catherine's notebooks. The last thing on earth she wanted to hear about was Catherine's notebooks. A crash—a bed collapsing?—came from upstairs but Agnes ignored it. She fingered dimity stripes of watermelon and sage, rough cotton scrim, and ebony velvet. She rubbed a Scottish tweed between her fingers. "Tsshhh, Libby looked like a strutting peahen in that tweed getup, don't tell her I said so. That was a crying shame about Catherine. I never would have thought she'd do anything like that. After all these years, here's a piece of her pedal pushers, navy denim laced up the side. She wore them with red shoes and a white blouse. I remember as though it were yesterday."

Lily suddenly pictured Catherine on the side of the grave, her face the shade of tea. She buried her own face in the tangerine silk. "I'm sorry, Agnes. I'm upset."

"Of course you are." She brought Lily a cup of coffee with a lot of sugar, the way she knew Lily liked it. "This is good and hot." Agnes sifted through balls of lace the color of clotted cream, a swatch of green-and-yellow-checked taffeta, russet flannel, then she jerked up a piece of blue silk in the shape of a short sleeve. She nodded. "That's from the dress she's buried in."

Lily recognized the intense blue immediately.

"She changed her mind and wanted three-quarter-length sleeves." Agnes held it up to the lightbulb. "She wore a ring of lapis lazuli in those days. Said it was to go with that."

"Remember the funeral, that tragic day?" Lily suddenly realized why she'd come to Agnes. It was to ask that question.

"Yes, who could forget. Ah! I remember her crossed hands. She was not wearing the ring but she was holding an envelope. I wondered if it were her suicide note—you know they say there's always a note left behind. That's how they get back at the living."

So others had noticed it. "No, that was a personal good-bye." Lily did not explain.

In the car Lily saw that the raincoat was still folded on the front seat; she'd forgotten to take it in. CoCo imitated the sound of the car engine. Lily laughed for the first time since her sight had been seared by the vision of Catherine. As she left Agnes's driveway, she scraped her fender against the crape myrtle. She did not see Evelyn on the upstairs porch, hair down and one breast hanging out of her robe. CoCo squawked his best hundred-crashing-hubcaps song.

A MANIACAL ANTLIKE HURRY STARTED at the end of the skyway. The strap of Ginger's carry-on bag dug into her shoulder until she thought her collarbone would snap. Flights delayed by thunderstorms in the Midwest had left hundreds of people lounging in the waiting areas and foraging the bars and food stands.

The arc from Europe to America always disrupted what Ginger thought of as *long time*. To fly across the Atlantic, she felt, was more drastic than simply crossing over miles of ocean. She came down into a present tense where she stepped lightly on the surface, while in the other world, she felt the strata of time below her feet. Even the light came from a more ancient, softened sun.

Outside, the sky looked hazy, whether from pollution or from temperature and humidity, she didn't know. As she headed the rented Pontiac out on I-75 South, she immediately saw the familiar watery, wavering heat lines rising from the highway, just at the far point of her vision. As she came closer, they receded so that where she was going appeared in an agitated state of semi-mirage. The cancerous odor of melting tar flowed up through the vents. She snapped on the air.

Noon, one hour late because of head winds. She'd slept badly in Rome and not at all on the flight. She'd forgotten to bring anything to read and had been able to find only the in-flight magazine and a golf club newsletter someone left in the seat pocket. She'd stared at pictures of an up-and-coming woman golfer for several minutes until the submerged knowledge that her mother had at some point become interested in golf slowly rose in her mind. Ginger remembered red and white socks that fitted over the clubs. She'd wanted them for hats for her dolls. In the returned memory, she saw her mother tee off. Her mother leaned down and pushed the yellow tee in the ground, balancing the shiny ball on top. She hunched forward, poised, and the cutting swoosh of her swing startled Ginger. The ball did not come down on the fairway but hooked in midair and landed in or near a dank little swamp. Then Ginger saw only herself, legs pumping as she ran down the slope to the water, where mud turtles plopped off their logs as she scanned the perimeter for the ball, spotting it, not in the water, but too far out in slimy ooze. Who else was there? Memory shaded a part of the scene. A long-legged crane stepped warily, as though despising to get its feet wet, but did not fly. A man appeared but far away, and by the time Ginger reached her mother again, he was gone. Ginger stared at the beautiful bird, then looked back toward her mother waving to her as she pulled her cart along the grass.

End of glimpse, but Ginger felt a rush of exhilaration. Her mother was young, younger than Ginger now, playing golf alone in her brown tweeds and neat brown and white cleated shoes. The memory widened: Ginger turning flips, sometimes landing wrong and skidding her knees on the frost-burned grass. Frost-burned grass—it must have been late fall.

She was glad to have recaptured this memory and lingered on her mother striding toward the next hole.

GINGER FLIPPED THE AIR DIAL up another notch and stepped on the accelerator, passing three and four straining trucks at a time. The fumes, stale air, and crush of the airport fell away. She felt herself unfurl after the cramped last-row seat on the plane. I-75 cut through the heart of Georgia, running by towns which prospered by its proximity. Millions of transport trucks, plus carloads of Yankees heading for Florida, tanked up at gas stations, pecan candy stores, and Wagon Wheel restaurants, or paused to shop at the cotton mills' outlet stores. The towns I-75 missed languished, their formerly tortured two-lane state roads reverted to country lanes, and most of their downtown Purple Duck and Blue Willow cafés had been boarded up. Who went that way, unless they had to?

At Perry, she turned off and took the slow road through orchards and small towns spared the ugliness of haphazard development. Kudzu-covered tenant farms bordered fields abandoned in the sixties. She slowed, let down the window for the scent of peach and the dusty smell of the pecan groves and corn rows breaking into tassel. One night she'd told Marco the names of towns she liked: Unadilla, Hahira, Osierfield, Lax, Omega, Mystic, Enigma, Headlight, Friendship, Calvary, Lordamercy Cave, Milksick Cove, a litany he countered with Italian places.

Marco always maintained that America must constantly reinvent itself, and she supposed that was true, but maybe not here. The straight road turned dreamy blue in the early afternoon heat. If no oblivious farmer or pulpwood truck pulled out of a side road, she could safely exceed the speed limit, go faster than on I-75, whizzing through rising and falling land soon to be dotted white with cotton bolls, and across all the creeks named by the Indians. The Pontiac moved so quietly on the surface of the road that she might be sailing.

Her earlier thought about the ancient sun in Italy and the present-tenseness of America felt wrong, she realized. She was tunneling through luxuriant blue air in a place profoundly old because it *was* empty. This low dip, this slow hill, were formed by the tides and currents in the warm shallow sea that once rolled over these fields. I'll have to talk about this with J. J., she thought. He'll understand geological time. She and J. J. loved the white sand beaches they found near the cabin. Since a sea flowed, she mused, those who were born here must have a knowledge, a subaqueous, preliterate intelligence. Or maybe it is just the damn heat that makes people look as though they're walking underwater, dreaming with their eyes open. On the windowsill of her room at the cabin, she'd kept her proof of the sea, a line of bleached seashells she and J. J. had found in dried creekbeds, lying there for eons until she'd scooped them up and crammed them in her shorts pockets.

From the crests of the rises, she looked down as she drove into a green sea of expansive longleaf-pine forests. As far as the eye, as if she did not exist. The smell blew through her hair, deeply fresh, one of the scents most basic to her memory. Even public bathrooms scrubbed with harsh, pine-scented disinfectant could make her stop and inhale. The wind in pines, the sound of the human soul, J. J. once said, if the human soul had a sound. No one would say that but J. J. No one has his hot brightness.

Where there's such emptiness, Ginger thought, I feel my mind expand. Italy is everywhere shaped by the human touch—that's why I feel warmed there. But those who worked this land left almost nothing. Unpainted board houses lean for a few decades, turn silvery, then collapse into heaps quickly covered by vines. Even graves with their crude crosses are swallowed by the land itself, which resumes its own contours. All because they built with wood, she thought, like the Etruscans, whose towns have been completely erased by time, except for graves, stone foundations, and mammoth walls.

She stopped to eat at a diner in Hakinston and decided to have coffee with a piece of the lemon pie, even though a fly was trapped under the plastic dome. It seemed more intent on getting out than on burrowing into the meringue. The waitress called her "honey," and Ginger smiled to remember her struggles with the Italian formal "you." In Italy, never in a thousand years would someone address a stranger familiarly. She had heard *"Buon giorno, Contessa"* to a slow old remnant of the nobility making her way to the piazza, and in the bread store, *"Buon giorno, architetto,"* an impossible-in-

America greeting—"good morning, architect"—that happened every day in Italy. Life is untranslatable, she thought; suddenly I'm "honey," but why not, I'm almost home.

Forty miles down the road, she passed the turnoff to the cabin but kept going—J. J. better not be off on some fishing trip. When the profile of Swan appeared in the distance, she finally began to think of what, exactly, she faced. She dreaded, more than the stupid crime and its stupid solution, the fight to keep memories away. She already had felt the thrill of imagining her mother swinging a golf club. The sorrow of her father's life, harder to ignore than her mother's because he still lived, lodged against this hideous event. A push of memories seemed to be pressing somewhere between her shoulder blades, between her breasts. Just in the exact place, she realized, where her mother shot herself.

Glancing east, across the knee-high cotton, she saw slats of gray rain in the distance, moving toward her, racing the car toward some intersection up ahead. Her father used to call it *the walking rain* and she loved the figure of speech. Rain walking across the ground, a change in the weather visible and stalking. Around Swan you always must be alert to nature. Porous limestone suddenly can collapse in a perfect circle, leaving a green sinkhole pond of infinite depth. A tornado can appear on the horizon, a clear conical image imprinted against the vast sky. Or a hurricane, with a secret eye trained on who knows what or where.

After hurtling herself across the ocean, she suddenly was in no hurry to get to Swan. She drummed the steering wheel with her fingers. Let the GBI settle this before I get there, she thought. I can have a quick visit with J. J., cheer up Lily, who must be devastated, and check on Daddy. J. J. and I can go out to the cabin; I'll lie on the dock and listen to the river. She would not get to see Caroline Culpepper, her best friend since nursery school. She'd be at the beach with her children and her sister's family all of July. A wave of affection for Caroline rolled over her. Growing up, they'd played bridge thousands of afternoons. All through high school Ginger slept over at Caroline's on Saturday nights. If only J. J. had married her! Caroline finally gave up on that idea and married Peter Banks, balding even in his late teens, but sweet and number four in his law school class at Florida. During the chaos of Ginger's life the past few years, she always looked forward to seeing Caroline and Peter when she limped back to Swan. Her other close friend from childhood, Braxton Riddell, now bored her. Once she'd thought his azure-blue eyes looked like a Greek statue's. Now he just looked preternaturally blank. I'll see no one, she thought. Only J. J. and Lily and Tessie. I can go back to Rome early next week.

On impulse, she turned toward Magnolia Cemetery. The gates were open. She turned left, then right at the Bryon plot and down the grassy road to her family's graves. The roses, she saw, were innocently abundant, as though nothing had happened. She had expected someone standing guard, but there was only Cass Deal in the distance, working on a new grave. She got out of the car and stepped cautiously toward the gate. The hole in the ground looked newly dug. The broken stones were stacked in a corner and the clay-stained gravel had been hosed clean. Her mother's body and the coffin had been removed. Ginger rubbed her stiff neck. "Once again we failed her," she said out loud. Great-grandparents, Daddy's Uncle Calhoun, Big Jim, and Mama Fan all remained in their appointed places, their Georgia granite markers leached to white by the strong sun, except for Big Jim's, which was smeared black.

Glittering trails left by snails zigzagged across Big Jim's stone. Who would disturb a grave? On the top of the pile of broken stone, she saw her mother's name incised. A clump of clay obscured the letters. Ginger brushed it away and with a marble pebble gouged each letter. *Catherine Phillips Mason.* She went back to the car to get a tissue from her bag and rubbed the name clean. She looked up and saw Cass coming toward her.

"Well, Ginger, I wondered who was snooping here. You haven't changed a bit, pretty as a picture. I cain't tell you how sorry we all are about this crazy nonsense. We got your aunt's car back to her.

Never had a thing like this happen before. Over there in Europe, aren't you? When'd you get in?"

"Just now. I haven't even been out to the House yet. I just came here . . ." She stood with her arms folded, as though she were cold. Could he have done this? Of course not.

"Ralph was here all night, him and his dog. Slept in the car and the mosquitoes about carried him off. The boy from the GBI came out with Ralph a while ago and the officer ordered the remains to be taken to the funeral home for a look. He found some paint scrapes on the gravestone, found out the fellow who did this even used my Bobcat. I remembered when I got here the other day, I noticed it had been moved." He did not add that he had withheld that information until confronted. "So they think a man operating alone could have done it. I'll get Big Jim all cleaned up and I'm hoping we can end this whole thing before long. A shame, a cryin' shame."

"Thank you, Cass, we appreciate that. Everyone has been so kind," she said automatically. "This must have been hard on you, too."

The rain came, immediately pelting hard. Clay rivulets ran red. Cass dashed for his truck. Ginger stood for a moment. Out of old habit, she tipped back her head and opened her mouth for the taste of the warm rain. Then she slid into the Pontiac and headed home.

GINGER FOUND LILY AND TESSIE IN THE KITCHEN, Tessie rolling out shortcake crust and Lily swatting flies with a rolled-up newspaper. "Lord, Lord, we didn't hear you come in, sugar baby, how are you?" Lily dropped the paper. Tessie's hands were up to her wrists in flour. The room smelled like old honey in a hive. They both embraced her, sat her down, and plopped a glass of pineapple tea in front of her. Tessie stuck in a sprig of mint.

"Oh, Lily . . ." Ginger began.

"Let's don't say a thing about what happened. That can wait. I just want to look at you—a sight for sore eyes, sugar, I'm just so glad you're *home*."

Tessie quickly cut the circles of dough with the top of a glass and placed them in a pan. "Yes, sir, strawberry shortcake—I know what you like, and J. J., too."

"Where is J. J.?"

"He's down at the sheriff's office signing some papers. He's been gone about an hour so he should be back soon." Lily opened the screen door and futilely motioned flies out, while others flew inside. Ginger was alarmed at how wild she looked with her hair falling around her face and a dollop of strawberry jam on the front of her blouse. Lily asked her how the flight had been, and how was the drive from Atlanta. Ginger and J. J. always feared they would lose her, too. Ginger drank the cold tea, comforted by the familiar kitchen, with its round table and tall cabinets, whose doors inside were completely papered with handwritten recipes on index cards. Behind the table stood glass-fronted cabinets full of sets of dishes. Her grandmother Fan's collection of glass lemon squeezers still lined the top shelves, and a set of Depression-era ice cream dishes was stacked below. How could green dishes sit there all those years—not one of the twelve broken—and her mother be dumped out of her grave? The flower-sprigged Limoges and the gold-rimmed good dishes occupied the lower shelves. "I think I'll bathe and get ready . . ." Get ready for what? she wondered.

Both Tessie and Lily followed her upstairs, switching on the attic fan in the upstairs hall and opening the door to her high yellow room, where the curtains billowed out with the humid gusts drawn in by the fan. Earlier, they'd turned down the linen spread and placed a handful of zinnias and snaps in a vase by her bed. Ginger very much wanted to lie back in the tub, to be clean, to fall into her own bed, with the whirr of the fan, wanted nothing to be wrong. "Is it painful?" She saw Lily holding her bandaged finger away from her body.

"It smarts. Yesterday it throbbed so I guess it's on the mend."
Lily had a gift for closing off the unpleasant and moving on.

GINGER SLEPT EASILY. She woke as she had many times in her
life—with J. J. tickling the end of her nose with one of CoCo's
feathers. His green eyes startled her. "J. J., you rat!" She sat up and
gave him smacking kisses on both cheeks.

"Italian laziness!" He grabbed her foot hard and began to tickle
the sole. She kicked loose, pushing him back and digging her nails
into his ribs, where she knew he couldn't take it. They rolled
around, shouting laughter. On the stairs with an armful of fresh
towels, Lily thought they'd gone mad. Those two. What could be
funny? Under the circumstances.

J. J. kicked off the espadrilles she'd once brought him. "Are you
okay, gal baby? A loaded question, given the conditions of your tri-
umphal return to the bosom of the family. How's the old country?"
J. J. sat in the window seat and Ginger pushed the pillows behind
her in bed. So many talks began this way, J. J. looking out the window, her with her arms around her knees.

"My work was going well and Italy was heaven for me—I'll tell
you about it—but I already feel like I've come a million miles." She
tried to picture Marco's dense curls, his movie-star look when he
wore sunglasses, and his jacket tossed over his shoulders. "I was all
right until I stopped by Magnolia before I came home . . ."

"Oh God, why, Jesus, Ginger, why would you do such a fool
thing?"

"It didn't seem real. Now it does but I feel numb, kind of sucked
dry. Is it the heat—somebody gone crazy with the heat?"

"Maybe somebody Big Jim suckered. Some fool with something
against the Masons or Mama, at least. Some lunatic after a dia-
mond or gold."

"What if he has something else in mind—torturing Lily with cigarette burns or setting the house on fire . . ."

J. J. smiled. "Or it's our old friend the devil. Pops up, bored with diddling Persephone in the underworld, and thinks, let's see, it's been a long time since I really performed on those Masons. They're always good for a laugh. What little twist can I dream up to knock them into a cocked hat." He threw his baseball cap in the air and socked it.

"No, be serious." At least he was not in his redneck mode, which, as he once explained, he often used for protective coloring.

"All right. Calm down. Think with me. What is this saying? Aside from the jewel-heist theory. Maybe someone wanted to damage her, even after she's been dead such a long time. A crude articulation, but he certainly got my attention."

"This is more and more grisly; I just can't absorb it. Do you suppose someone in love with her for all these years has squirreled away his feelings? But there's rage in this. And that black paint, a primitive marking." Ginger knew of cultures that marked the houses of sinners—maybe this was a throwback to that practice.

"Maybe the whole thing is random craziness. We're forcing an explanation so that it begins to look rational." J. J. bit his knuckle, an old habit. "Our ol' buddy Ralph says the GBI loaded her into a hearse and sent her to Ireland's to examine the body, in case of necrophilia, or God knows what. He said we'll hear something from them tomorrow. The only evidence he's discovered is a dirty handkerchief that Cass Deal found. The GBI took it, too, as part of what they hilariously called suspicious circumstances. How suspicious can we get here? But this suspicious handkerchief was wadded-up nice linen, not a cheap three-to-a-package number. This fruitcake apparently had wiped his hands, hadn't even jacked off. No, Miss Nancy Drew, no monogram and no store label. A zero. No chance for *The Case of the Dropped Handkerchief*."

"J. J., stop, stop. When she died . . ."

"Let's don't put each other through a conversation about her. Lily said that Dad probably left a letter in her hand, but Ralph said nothing like that turned up. I have no memory of any letter."

"Me neither."

J. J. stood up. "Let's zip out to the cabin. We can pick up some beer and take a swim."

"Lily has planned dinner. They were making shortcake when I got here and I could smell Tessie's pepper chicken." Her chicken always was known as pepper chicken because she tipped the pepper jar generously when she smothered the pieces in cream. "I hope she fixes mashed potatoes." Ginger was suddenly famished. "I wonder what he wrote. And if he possibly could remember? Do I have a suit at the cabin?"

"Lily seemed vague, said maybe he wrote a love letter, who knows? Your chest of drawers hasn't been touched, except once when a winsome young thang needed to borrow a sweater."

"Who was it? I bet it doesn't bear repeating."

"No one you know."

"I can well imagine."

TWO YEARS AGO Alan Ireland had outfitted the two-car garage behind his funeral home with a drain in the concrete floor, a sink, and
a long table. He did not want to taint his main mortuary when a
grisly murder occurred in Swan, or to crowd it when he had an over-
flow from a collision or a flu epidemic that snuffed out three or four
old folks. Most of the embalming took place inside the house,
which for fifty years was his family's home, a grand, columned
brick house rising out of banks of azaleas, a place of pride for the
Irelands. Then his father had started the mortuary, exiling the family forever afterward to living upstairs. Even now, Alan often was
startled as he entered his grandmother's front parlors, the now heavily draped rooms choked with fragrances of the standing sprays and
wreaths surrounding the viewing alcoves, where the mourners and
the curious came to pay their last respects.

No one ever had mentioned it, not even his wife, but he thought
he smelled something beneath the cloying gardenias and roses. The
smell of iron lingered, the ferrous red smell of blood. Perhaps it was
his imagination. He didn't mind his eight-year-old daughter, Janie
Belle, playing hide-and-seek in the coffin-selection room or seeing
the peaceful dead laid out in the front parlor. She'd even seen him

arranging hair and brushing makeup on corpses. She had not witnessed other preparations, or so he thought.

Janie Belle called from the back steps of the house, "Daddy, Mama made coffee." She carried a paper sack trepidly down the steep steps and handed Alan the thermos and cups.

"You go play, angel. Daddy's got business to do." He called her "angel" because she looked like one, a plump dumpling with pale corkscrew curls and a face so little occupied by its features that it gave the impression of a painted egg. He feared she'd inherited the Irelands' physical neutrality. Strangers always forgot they'd met him. Only in old age, when the skin became etched with lines, did Irelands acquire character.

Janie Belle posted herself on the back porch and watched the arrival of a man she didn't know in a black car. She gouged her fingernail under the last chicken pox scab on her cheek. Janie Belle wouldn't stop scratching even though her mama told her she'd have ugly pox scars on her face and no one would want to marry her. Her mama even threatened Janie Belle by saying she was going to call the police on her if she didn't stop scratching. Her heart quickened as she saw the sheriff's car turn in behind the stranger. She swung over the rail and hid under the porch.

GBI investigator Gray Hinckle, who'd followed from the cemetery into Swan behind Alan, stepped out of his car. He and Ralph wheeled out the stretcher and Alan jerked down the cord on the garage door, which fell hard on the concrete floor. "Alan, you tryin' to wake the dead?" Ralph asked. The air conditioner near the ceiling churned and dripped.

Gray pulled off the tarp from Catherine's body. "Let's whip through this. She's not exactly my idea of a party girl," he said.

"It just makes you wonder at human nature. Who could want a ring or necklace enough to face this in the dead of night?" Alan passed around rubber gloves, tied on an apron, stepped aside. Gray cut the dress up the right side, then the left. He sliced through her stiff slip and partially disintegrated underwear. The folded-back fabric revealed the bony torso, the navel like an olive pit, the blackened edges of the rib cage, and a delta of hair like a matted rat nest. "No recent discoloration or foreign substance such as urine or semen," Gray said. "No evidence indicates necrophilic activities."

Ralph, standing by with a Styrofoam cup of coffee, tried to control the expression on his face. He'd seen plenty of dead bodies. The soldiers he'd dragged to medic stations still had looked like themselves, like they could resume their lives, if the doctors somehow could have saved them. Mrs. Mason's skin looked like the punching bag swinging from the rafters in his attic.

Because the wound almost in the center of her chest was covered by gauze and tape, she had not been buried in a bra. When Ralph saw the wing-shaped brown stain, a last seepage of heart blood on the gauze, his throat seized, and he coughed as he swallowed, spraying coffee drops onto the white shirtsleeve of Gray Hinckle. "I am so sorry."

Gray was irritated. This shirt was made of Sea Island cotton. He laid the scissors on Catherine's stomach, went to the sink, and delicately dabbed at his sleeve with a wet paper towel.

Not from a sense of thoroughness, but out of embarrassment at snorting coffee and fear of losing face with Gray, Ralph pulled on gloves, picked up the scissors, and cut away the yellowed bandage. Bull's-eye, he thought. He pulled the sheet, rolling her over. The exit wound was small, too, indicating a low-caliber rifle.

"She shot herself with a .22?" Gray asked.

"Yeah, must have been a shorter barrel." Ralph backed up, away from her ancient young breasts with blackened nipples and the hole that had ended her life. Alan clutched the end of the table. He felt woozy. He didn't remember whether or not he'd had chicken pox as a child. Could this be the start? Would his face cover over with pustules? Mesmerized by the sight of this body his father must have embalmed, he did not see openmouthed shock on the ovate face of Janie Belle at the side window, where she stood tiptoe on an upsidedown flower pot for a full view.

"No sign of any recent interference anywhere. Our work is finished. She can go back to where she came from. She's all yours, Alan." Gray looked as if he were about to say more. Ralph thought he almost made a joke, but did not want to appear tasteless.

Ralph squeezed the bridge of his nose. He was going to sneeze. Gray unfolded a large muslin sheet, slid it under the body, and wrapped her like a swaddling baby. Alan turned up the air conditioner. At least he would make the sale of another coffin, and the Masons always went for the bronze.

Ralph excused himself for a moment and went inside the house to check in with Carol at the office. After he hung up, he stood by the window looking out into a cement pond with a fountain oozing a trickle of water through moss. Janie Belle kneeled in the crotch of a hog-pear tree, about to jump. Goldfish hung in the green slime without moving. A young tom jumped up onto the stone side and peered intently at the fish. Ralph, fingering the Vietnam medal he always carried in his pocket, felt his mind trawling, but for what?

The cat pawed the water and still the fish did not move. Balanced on the side of the fishpond, the cat extended his skinny front legs, arched his back, and looked down with disinterest at the swollen fish, then nimbly leapt into the azaleas. The perfectly round, cat-sized hole he made in the leaves remained open a moment, then closed.

Ralph stared after him and shook his head. *Suicide.* Oh boy, oh boy, how could we not have seen that? he thought. He rushed back to the garage, where Gray was writing in a notebook. "Hey, we missed something. If she pulled the trigger herself, that exit wound wouldn't be even with the front wound. It would be higher because of the way she had to hold the gun. There's something rotten in the state of Denmark."

"We're looking into necrophilia here—diddling with the dead—not into the intricacies of a suicide that happened years ago," Gray said. But he frowned hard at Ralph. "You know, you are right, son of a bitch! Let's take another look-see."

"I'm sorry as I can be, boys, but I've got to get back to the house." Alan felt ill. Surely this was beyond his services as a mortician. He stood at the door. His shirt clung to his chest and back.

Shoulders round like a girl's, Gray thought. "That's fine, Alan, my boy, we sure do appreciate you taking the time to help us out. We'll just add this as an addendum. It'll probably turn out to be nothing." They shook hands. "We'll close up. And she's sure as hell not going anywhere. Just hold her in your deepfreeze until Monday."

With Gray's calipers, they measured the wound. "We'll be able to determine range, I believe. Given that skin has shrunken away from the original hole, given that she would have had to pull the trigger with her toe from a sitting position, with the gun barrel against her chest, given all this, we can't tell shit for sure right now. Ralph, if you hadn't got coffee all over my shirt, we might never have noticed this."

What Ralph noticed was Gray's "we." "If I'm not mistaken, it was an 'I' what noticed this." When he was nervous, he sometimes lapsed into grammar he'd struggled to overcome.

"Okay, okay, just keeping up the teamwork, pal. I'll get an exact angle on that exit wound. If she did pull the trigger, it sure wouldn't be dead level with the front wound." Gray rolled the body over again. "It would be, say, three or four inches higher, right? I'll take a roll of film and meet you at your office to go over the records."

"I'm starving. Let's meet at the Three Sisters right in the middle of town."

"Now we're cookin' with gas, coach."

CATHERINE IS COMING TODAY. The thought was clear in his head, but he wanted to tell the woman with the food on the tray. "Sss . . ."

"What is it, Dr. Mason? Do you want something else?" Mary June was on double shift, trying to save enough money to take her boys to the beach for a week. She had run from one bed to another for nine hours. Flu going around in the heat of summer.

He shook his head, disgusted. "I want . . ." She waited. "If you see her, I want . . ."

He seemed to doze, he jumped from a plane, the checkered, war-ravaged German countryside rose toward him, then his head snapped up with a myclonic jerk.

"Who? Ginger? I heard she's coming to see you. Won't that be nice? She's coming from a long way."

Something roared, the silk parachute collapsing in his ears. "I don't care about that . . ." Who is coming? Catherine—what was Lily saying about Catherine?

"Now, you don't mean that, I know." She wondered if he'd suffered another small stroke. His language abilities seemed more impaired today. "How are you feeling?" She usually paid less attention to him than to other patients. He looked perfectly all right, maybe a little vacant like some old god left out in the rain. After all, he was only sixty-one years old. She remembered him from childhood, pressing her tongue down to look in her throat, then giving her the wooden depressor, which she took home and painted with a face and glued to it a paper evening gown with a hem of sparkles. Later, he took the Brownies on an overnight camping trip when she and Ginger were in the same troop. He'd cooked hot dogs over a campfire, taught them to sing in rounds, "There was a desperado from the wild and woolly West . . ." She had wished he were her daddy, instead of the mean hired-out drunk who twisted her mother's wrist until the bone popped in two.

"Take two aspirin, drink plenty of liquids, and go to bed," he answered. She had once teased him about doctors always prescribing that, and it was one of the few things he remembered about her. His brain worked peculiarly, as though water started down the chute, then shunted off into a side trough. He recognized everyone, knew who they were to him, sister, son, friend—it just didn't seem to matter. She guessed his neocortex was plain fried. Sometimes tears would well up when J. J. or Ginger started to leave, but the instant they were gone, he forgot. He could go from one to two, but when three came he was lost, like he'd say he wanted a newspaper, and if you said okay, you'll go get it, he'd say go get what? His recurrent demand, "Give those starving people something to eat," she never followed. Mary June knew that the occasional eruptions of some trace of his former self were devastating for his children. She'd seen Ginger leaning against her car door with her face in her hands after he'd suddenly come out with some ripple of vitality she recognized as his. "It's the first of the month. Did you say rabbit first thing? You could use the good luck." How did he know the time of day, much less the day of the month? Another time he said, "Give me some sugar before you go," which Ginger said was his old way for asking for a good-night kiss before she went to bed. He'd never inquired about his health, or why he was sitting at the Columns these many years instead of living at home. "The lights are on but no one's home," Mary June would explain to people in Swan who asked after him.

"Dr. Mason, I was sorry to hear about what happened." She half wanted to say so and half wanted to see what he'd say.

He poked at the fried ham on his plate. He sighed. "What is this crispy critter? Dada doesn't like this one bit."

GINGER IMAGINED THE RIVER on nights when she couldn't sleep. She hadn't been there in a year and a half—during her daddy's last emergency she was home so briefly—but even thousands of miles away she could picture driving herself down the sandy white road through the woods, taking the turn at the big oak, glimpsing the stone chimney through the trees, then emerging into the sudden light of the clearing. J. J. pulled up beside his muddy Jeep. "Backy-home-againy," she said, repeating J. J.'s baby phrase.

The river in the twentieth century never rose more than fifteen feet above its banks, but the year before the cabin was built in 1898, it flooded the entire palmetto plain for two weeks. Because of that, John Mason was able to buy five hundred acres, sixty of them fronting the river, for fifteen dollars an acre. On the high point of the land, he built this pine log cabin that always had been, at metabolic level, home to Ginger and J. J.

Ginger thought of the cabin as a way their lives were manifest in another form. "Here we are," Ginger said quietly, biting in her bottom lip. "Isn't this close to heaven?"

"Maybe not at the moment. You might want to walk down to the dock until the place airs out for a few minutes. After Scott told me,

I left in a hurry yesterday and forgot to take a string of perch out of the sink. I'm sure they're high."

Ginger went inside anyway, holding her nose. "Not too bad."

J. J. threw open the back door and ran to the woods with the fish. Ginger walked from room to room. Even though J. J. lived here most of the time, little had changed. When they were children, Catherine had cleared out the canvas cots and rusted fishing tackle of the previous two generations. Big Jim never used the cabin after his children were grown because Mama Fan hated the place. One mouse jumping out of the flour bin, leaving tiny white tracks across the floor, was enough, but then a snake was found coiled at the foot of little Lily's bed while she slept. Mama Fan drove home in the middle of the night and never returned. Her old rotted chairs and mildewed tick mattresses had made a lovely bonfire one Saturday, when Catherine had three men help her empty the place. The cabin then became Catherine's retreat, a place she made for Wills to escape constant calls, a place where the children could "run wild," and a place where she turned up the music, read, worked in her sketch books, and wandered in the woods looking for wild azaleas, Cherokee roses, and violets to transplant around the house. Ginger and J. J. loved, and their parents had loved, the long porch stretching all across the front of the house, the double screen doors opening into an enormous, almost-two-story log room with a stone fireplace. The kitchen and three bedrooms opened off the main room. Catherine had found a country man to make beds from pine logs and branches. She scoured the countryside for Wedding Ring and Tree of Life quilts—no one in her family or Wills's knew how to sew a stitch—and rustic local furniture, her prize find being two walnut eighteenth-century huntboards, still standing on either side of the door.

Ginger peered into what she still thought of as her parents' room, although J. J. had moved in long ago. From his desk in front of the window, she looked down at the C-curve of the river. J. J.'s journals—twenty or twenty-five identical black-and-white-mottled school notebooks—stood along the back of the desk, the recent one, pen beside it, opened facedown. Ginger always had wanted to read J. J.'s journals but had caught only glimpses, even though she used to grab one from him and run until he caught her and snatched it back. She hadn't wanted to pry, merely to understand the hidden brother behind the wisecracking, womanizing, hunter-gatherer man of the woods. But her quick stolen looks yielded only notes on Indian initiation rites, birdcalls, lists of books read, and precisely written descriptions of things he'd seen in nature, with colored-pencil drawings of a dogwood blooming in a tenant farmer's yard, a ragged blue heron posed on one leg in Yellow Jacket Creek, a flimsy mint-green moth that landed on his hand, a bluish stone on its shadow. Even this glimpse—such delicacy and exactness—made her scared of reading further. He'd had a bookcase built in the corner by the bed and had moved the leather chair from their daddy's old office into the angle. The books were all history, mythology, books on birds, fish, geology. She imagined J. J. there, reading and writing through the morning, while she was thousands of miles away. The flip side, the other world.

Otherwise, the room remained the same. Ginger looked at her mother's clunky marble-topped chest of drawers, taken from Catherine's childhood room. She moved a book to see an oval scar on top. Long ago, her mother had marred the marble with a wet bottle of fingernail polish remover. Ginger ran her finger around the faint ring. Her mother had let her polish her nails when she was very small, even though Mama Fan said it was quite tacky for children to wear polish.

The door to Ginger's room was stuck. She pushed it open with her shoulder and pulled apart the blue-and-white-striped curtains. The room looked out on the scuppernong arbor, the stone grill beside it, where her family used to have almost all their summer dinners. Tomorrow, she told herself, tomorrow I will lie on my back in this bed and listen to the bees in the grapes. I'll put on some old records and make brownies. I'll walk all the way to the hideout—

there will be perfect arrowheads on the path. She put on her suit and ran past J. J. washing his hands in the kitchen.

"I'm coming," he yelled after her. She paused at the end of the dock, bracing herself for the cold. Holding her nose and shouting, she jumped in. She swam upstream for the pleasure of floating back. Beyond the cleared banks near the cabin began dense growths of gallberry, palmetto, and vine-draped pines. Where the river narrowed, oak branches from either bank intertwined overhead. Through half-closed eyes Ginger saw bolts of light through leaves; she drifted, then turned and kicked her way back upstream toward the boils. J. J. cannonballed off the dock and swam up to her. They crawled out on a sand crescent and, hoisting themselves up by tree roots, climbed up a slick clay bank to a ledge of grassy land.

"All right, O Hisagita Immisee." Ginger ran up the slope to the springs. The rope was yellow, made of some kind of plastic. They used to swing into the water on vines, later a hemp rope, but now J. J. had attached this new thing, which probably was guaranteed not to break. "You first—I'm not sure I can take the cold."

As children they had elaborate rituals improvised from their reading about the Creeks. Hisagita Immisee, the god of the tribe, translated as "Breath Holder." They thought the name must have come from a great swimmer who could hold his breath long enough to swim down into the roiling water at the bottom of the spring. When J. J. first made it to the bottom and stuck his fist into the blue source, he became O Great Hisagita Immisee.

J. J. took the rope back for a running start, swung out, and dropped. He surfaced and flipped downward. She watched his clear body, stippled with light, turn mazarine as he propelled downward through colder and colder levels of water until near the bottom he became a fishy shadow. Down there, she knew, the cold sensation turned hot, because to feel any colder you'd turn to ice. Her own lungs felt the pressure of his held breath. She grabbed the rope with a stick, swung out, her feet on the big knot, once, twice, finally letting go. She came up gasping from the hard shock of cold. As she flipped down and swam with open eyes, she passed J. J. shooting upward and their eyes met, his starved or scared wide, his torso white marble, legs working like some primitive amphibian, but the eyes, suddenly unknowable, someone in a dream, a statue hauled up from an ancient shipwreck. She thought she could not go all the way, but she pulled at the water as though opening heavy velvet curtains, kicking with deliberate strength and *there,* she was at the cleft of white sand and the three dark blue openings they had longed to enter as children, imagining a kingdom where the furniture was made of driftwood, pearls, and shells, where the real Hisagita Immisee lived with fabulous extinct river creatures with no eyes, where the fiery cold water spurted pure and sacred out of the earth. They'd heard, too, that dead slaves lived in a realm under rivers. She held the palms of her hands against the surging water for the push of energy she used to feel move into her arms and down her spine, a thrill then and now, even as the hard bulbs of her lungs tightened and she pushed up and climbed toward the bend of light, the surface of the spring.

Lying in the grass breathing hard, J. J. felt a pain rip through his head, a sharp letter opener through a thin envelope. Migraine. An aura of jagged light appeared to the left in his peripheral vision. Ginger was over him, shaking drops of water from her hair onto his chest. He sat up. "Whoa," he said, "we'd better get moving. The sun's going down." She looked restored to herself, her normal self, jumping on one foot and hitting her head to force the ringing water out of her ear, running her fingers through her hair their mother always had called lucky strawberry blond. Underwater, she had looked as though she could swim forever, like a nymph who returned to earth once a year, her trailing hair coral in the sun-pierced water, mouth an O, as though water ran through her, her eyes flashing flat and quick, all that as they passed, him swimming up, emerging, so much easier than her descent, her parting the waters with the small arrows of her hands, tiny bubbles flowing from her nose, the albuminous spray of her hard kicking, then she was past, and he burst into air. He squinted up at her as a large silence swelled in his head.

RALPH AND GRAY WASHED THEIR FACES, soaped their hands and all the way up to their elbows in the bathroom at the Three Sisters. It was late, but Martha still had plenty of meat loaf in the oven.

The three sisters who owned the café looked alike and always dressed identically, although in different colors. Angela wore yellow and ran the cash register; Emily wore red and waited tables; Martha wore green and cooked. They all had caps of curls, a color called Bronze Aura, and wore blue eyeliner that made them look round-eyed like dolls. They'd grown up in Swan with a widowed father. As far as anyone knew, not one of them ever had seen the need for any relationship beyond their own tight circle.

Ralph opened his granddaddy's report on Catherine Mason's death while they ate. The report was typed on the old Remington still sitting on a desk in the office.

CASE 802
SEPTEMBER 3, 1956
Catherine Phillips Mason, dead of self-inflicted gunshot wound to the heart. No attempt to resuscitate. She was discovered at the home address by her daughter, Virginia, 12, at 3:30 P.M. She died at approximately 1:00 P.M., according to

Dr. Dare. She was found on the kitchen floor, beside a turned-over chair (Exhibit 1).

Ralph glanced at the small photo, a snapshot attached to the page with cracked tape, of Catherine in a pool of black blood. She was barefoot, indicating that she pulled the trigger with her toe. She was wearing a white sundress with black dots on it. God, what a sight for Ginger. ("She was expecting warm gingerbread and that's what she found," he remembered hearing over and over through the years.) The gun lay beside her, almost cradled in her arm.

Emily brought a basket of cornsticks. She glanced at the page in front of Ralph. "God in heaven," she said. Even a glimpse and she recognized the noble forehead and unforgettable eyes of Catherine Mason. The report continued:

This office was notified by Carla Rowen, the nearest neigh-bor, who found Virginia (Ginger) Mason in the middle of Palmetto Road near her house. According to the statement made by Dr. Wills Mason, his wife had occasional spells of depression, but no previous signs of self-destruction. He re-called that before the birth of their daughter, Virginia, she had been withdrawn, but in recent years there were no known aggravating circumstances. Weapon was a .22-caliber automatic Savage rifle owned by Dr. Mason. The bullet was recovered from the wall. He stated that he kept the gun in an unlocked cabinet, along with three other more powerful deer-hunting guns. He was not sure if the gun in question had been loaded. The maid, Tessie Mae Cartwright, was at her own residence on West Orange. She stated that on her day off she shopped at Dixie Market and McMillan's Five-and-Ten between 11:00 and 12:00, then visited her cousins Sally and Precious Cartwright on East Oconee for the noon meal. This was verified by the Cartwright cousins. The Mason children were in school. Dr. Mason left his office at

10:00 A.M., made rounds at the hospital until 11:00, then stated that he drove out to the cabin, where he expected to meet his family in the afternoon. Mrs. Mason had no known enemies. No sign of forced entry or struggle. She left no suicide note.

Ralph handed the page to Gray. He read on:

SEPTEMBER 4, 1956
Further interviews with the nearest neighbors and with friends and relatives of the Mason family produced no further cause for investigation. The entire town is shocked and repelled by this act against God.

Two of the last entries in the file were handwritten. His grandfather seldom wrote letters, even when Ralph was in Vietnam on his last assignment before he resigned. He recognized the hand mainly from his grandfather's old-fashioned flourishing signature on birthday cards.

SEPTEMBER 6, 1956
This sad case ended at the funeral yesterday (clipping from *The Swan Flyover* enclosed). A fine family broken up, resulting from a selfish act. How someone could do that to her children, I don't understand. The minister said a troubled soul is at peace, but she left some troubled souls behind her.

SEPTEMBER 7, 1956
Telephone call from Mrs. Mayhew (Charlotte Anne) Crowder, Macon, Georgia. She demanded further investigation. Stated that as a former college roommate and friend she knew without a doubt that Mrs. Mason would not commit suicide. I explained that there was no evidence to the contrary. She became hysterical and said to find some. She in-

sisted that Catherine must have been trying to defend herself with the weapon. She demanded that I look at notebooks kept by Mrs. Mason. My search of the house on the morning after the death revealed four boxes of bullets and ten of shotgun shells in the gun cabinet. One of the remaining three guns, a Winchester .30-06, was loaded. I saw no notebooks. After Mrs. Crowder's call, I called Dr. Mason with great reluctance. He said his wife sometimes wrote in diaries, but he had not seen them.

Gray held up the photo. "Look, would you, that gun—she's still holding it after dropping out of a chair? Is that the position of someone who just sent themselves to hell? She looks like she's taking a nap—except for the mess. Whatever happened to the two children?"

"They're around Swan. They must have pleasant dreams." Ralph read the last entry:

SEPTEMBER 16, 1956
Fingerprint analysis shows the prints of Catherine Mason. Smeared prints reveal that others handled the gun but these are deemed inconclusive. All evidence points to death by suicide. Case closed.

As Ralph handed the last sheet to Gray, he noticed the back of the folder. A doodle. And in his grandfather's hand, scrawled along the edge, he read, ——Big Jim, R.I.P. Under that he made out the scratched-out initials S and what could have been a D or a B. Then Rotary Club 12:30.

Gray pounced on each page. He rather relished the turn this case had taken. Ralph felt a wave of defensiveness for his grandfather, who probably simply could not imagine that a Mason could murder, or be murdered, for no reason, although searching the house the day *after* the suicide seemed dumb. He and Gray had figured out in one morning what seemed to have escaped his grand-father, who was on the scene. He felt a blaze of pride. "Hotshot," Granddaddy had called him when he was a child.

An early scene zigzagged up into his consciousness. When Ralph was very young, his granddaddy used to take Big Jim quail and dove hunting near Tallahassee. His granddaddy in his uniform hauling and totin', and Big Jim, with his gleaming shotguns, outfit-ted in a suede hunting jacket with dozens of pockets inside. From somewhere, somehow, Ralph remembered Big Jim expansively opening the jacket. The pockets held doves with their heads poked out, looking as if they'd nodded off briefly and might wake and fly.

Ralph's grandmother would be mad the whole time her husband was gone. As she washed up, she clattered the plates so hard Ralph thought they'd break. "That old rooster. If I told your granddaddy once, I've told him a hundred times that Big Jim gave him the mill vote, got us this house, and now he owns him. Big Jim says *jump*, and your granddaddy says *how high?* He'll drop everything! And bring home doves for me to pluck." Even then Ralph knew his grandfather usually operated a speed trap on Sundays out on the road to Osceola, stopping Yankee snowbirds' cars and charging them twenty-five dollars on the spot. This wasn't graft; every southern sheriff was entitled to that little bonus. His grandmother didn't like him losing out on this part of his income.

Ralph scooped up the red gravy with a cornstick, while Gray fin-ished reading. He hoped Gray didn't ridicule the investigation of the house taking place the day after the death.

Gray put down the file and concentrated on his plate. Without them ordering dessert, Emily brought over two generous slices of devil's food cake. "Last customers of the day get a prize."

"You are beautiful." Gray flashed a smile.

Ralph felt obliged to point out the note on the back sheet of the file. "My granddaddy was the sheriff," he confessed.

"Well, don't be too hard on him. Back then they couldn't access range with the exactitude we can now. I'm ninety percent sure she didn't pull the trigger. I'll check everything with my boss. Easiest crime on God's green, husband shoots wife and either he says he didn't know the gun was loaded or he arranges a suicide scene, which he 'discovers' and is all torn up over. Oh, yeah, there's usually a lover boy in the wings. Hard to prove, even now. The husbands will jump all over the place with lie detectors and not a court will look at them because these aren't your hardened criminals. Or"—he pointed his finger at Ralph—"or *maybe* it was disappointed lover boy who stepped in. And who wants to open that can? Suicide becomes the easy way out of the investigation. And then there's the third choice—someone out of the blue."

But why would his granddaddy not follow up? Ralph wondered. Even if he owed his sheriff's election and his home to Big Jim, he was dead by then. The small-town rich man. Did his power triumph over death? And yet his granddaddy had not pushed, had in fact botched the case. "My granddaddy probably thought too much of the family ever to think in those directions. The Masons planned the whole town." Lame, he knew. He knew, too, that his grand-daddy was loyal as a dog.

"Maybe he was protecting someone. Look, we're not looking to understand it at this point," Gray said. "What we'll have to go on is who dug up the grave. By the way, since that red paint residue on some of the stones matches that old coot's Bobcat, our man obviously knew how to operate it. What about that gravedigger, Deal—any chance he's a weird one? I had the feeling he knew his machine had been moved."

"Jesus, no. He's old. He just forgot. Long as I've known, he's worked there."

"Talk to the children, see what they remember, and any other individuals you can think of. If the doctor's really cuckoo, no use in going after him at this point." Gray picked up the check. "You got some cases in Swan, coach. I remember that codger who lived over a garage and saved his urine in jugs. We were called in after an explosion . . ." Gray slapped his leg and whooped. "He was—he was all cut up. Even in the hospital the nurses found out he was peeing in the bedside pitcher." He socked Ralph softly on the shoulder. "What'chall got in the water over here in Swan?"

BACK AT HIS OFFICE, Ralph called the House. He told Lily he needed to meet with J. J. and Ginger in the morning, that he had some news of possible interest from the GBI.

"What is it—did they find the criminals?" she asked.

"No, ma'am, I'm afraid not. They've got an alert out to all the counties though, and they'll probably solve this pretty fast. I'd like to go over a few things tomorrow morning with J. J. and Ginger."

"I'm expecting them any minute. I'll tell them."

LILY SNAPPED DOWN THE CARDS. She was in her third try against Old Sol. Tessie's smothered pepper chicken waited on the stove, the table was all set, and she even had filled the fireplace with saucer magnolias after her Scrabble game with Eleanor.

Lily didn't care if Ginger and J. J. were late coming home from the cabin; they always were, and she needed a while to calm down. She sipped a tall, iced Dubonnet. The phone had been ringing all day; now the tree frogs were starting their annoying yammering. People were calling just like they did when someone died. The Rowens from down the road had even brought over a lime Jell-O and cream cheese salad, which she knew those children wouldn't touch. They were picky, both of them, prince and princess from the day they were born, and she supposed she had contributed to that. J. J. wouldn't eat the white of the fried egg and Ginger wouldn't eat the yellow. She wouldn't eat dark meat; he wouldn't eat the light, though they fought over the wishbone without ever, as far as she knew, making a single wish. Never knowing exactly how to be a mother, she just tried to please them with food and whatever she thought they wanted. She gathered up the cards. What didn't sit right was Ralph Hunnicutt's call. He'd held something back from her.

Lily saw the lights bumping along the driveway illuminating the trees. She could tell from the way Ginger slouched her shoulders that she was low. J. J. came up the steps like a sleepwalker. When he kept his mouth open like a panting dog, it meant one thing: headache. "What have y'all gone and done, just worn yourselves out?"

"We stopped by to see Daddy. It was no fun. He looked through us like somebody looking in a store window. I said, 'Daddy, it's me, Ginger,' and he said, 'I know that. It's disgraceful that you haven't been to see me.' I said, 'Daddy, I've been thousands of miles away, but I'm home now,' and he said, 'Blood is thicker than blood.'"

"He made a list of things he wanted, totally ignoring Ginger. He wrote down eyedrops, chocolate wafers, socks—stuff he doesn't need. I got the same things for him not two weeks ago." J. J. brought out ice water, which he felt like dipping his face into. "Let's eat and get it over with. I'm not going to last."

"I'm going to find you one of your pills right now," Lily insisted. "You just sit here in the cool and rest for a few minutes and let it take effect. That sheriff wants to see you both first thing in the morning."

"What for? Did they find out who did it?" Ginger kicked off her shoes.

"No, something about the GBI. He didn't say. Acted real vague, I thought."

You should know vague, J. J. thought.

What Ginger and J. J. both wanted to do was go to their rooms and close the doors. The jagged light still flashed at the edge of J. J.'s vision. Ginger began to feel disoriented. The connection with her work and Marco had been too easily broken. A few hours home and she always felt this way—her real life sloughed off and the old life asserted itself. No one ever asked about what she did. She picked up *their* tempo, *their* concerns, fell into the stream of living that went on here, with or without her. "When are you coming home, chile?" she was asked over and over. Too polite to say, "Never," she always demurred with "I'm home right now."

The air conditioner in the corner window of the dining room labored like a crop duster about to take off. Lily heated the dinner Tessie had left, and opened a jar of watermelon pickles. The familiar starched linen mats monogrammed with Mama Fan's scrolling FML, the sedating scent of magnolias in the fireplace, and the impossible smells of the House merged—how could Mama Fan's Fleur de Rocaille perfume and Big Jim's leaden cigar smoke linger this long? Ginger felt suddenly exhausted beyond exhaustion. Nightmare. How could she have forgotten and fallen into the spring with joy this afternoon?

Lily served the plates and passed them. J. J. thought he should help; Lily must be dead about now, but his own head was pounding to the rhythm of "Take Me Out to the Ball Game." The idiotic lyrics cycled with each surge of blood in his temples. "Thanks, Lily, for going to all this trouble. I'm sorry we're not in top form, either of us." As Lily passed the sauceboat, Ginger and J. J. exchanged a smile. Lily's flotsam and jetsam gravy, they recognized.

"Tell me if the potatoes are not hot enough. These pickles Tessie put up last summer are absolutely delicious. It is too bad Wills is not here with his family. I know he would want to be. It breaks my heart to have him sitting out there year in and year out. If your mother hadn't . . ." It was a sentence she never finished. "I don't think this would have happened to him."

J. J. put down his fork. He pressed his temples, where the pain seesawed. Everything that ever happened was his mother's fault. Ginger wouldn't have choked at the finals of the state debate tournament; he would have gone to medical school in his father's footsteps; his father never would have taken a drink. Stroke they called it, and stroke it was, but massive quantities of alcohol and a fall in the bathroom with a clunk of the skull on porcelain hadn't ever come up in Lily's equations. Was it Mother's fault, too, J. J. thought, that someone has broken into her death? Her fault that the potatoes aren't hot? All he said was, "We're all real tired."

Ginger and J. J. never crossed Lily. For one thing, it just wasn't worth it. For another, she was all they'd had for so many years. She was who she was, and they felt protective toward her no matter what. That no real conversation would occur, they seemed to sense from childhood and never had attempted one. "Don't talk in front of the help" blurred into don't talk about anything that matters at all. As if Tessie didn't know everything about them anyway. Lily had opinions but refused to examine them. In her thinking, ambiguity did not exist; the first conclusion drawn remained conclusive. During their early years with her, all they wanted to do was forget what their mother had done, forget the months after that when their father came home from the office and poured large glasses of bourbon, forget his "accident." Landing at the house with Lily had delivered them. They were safe with Lily in their daddy's childhood home, Big Jim's place. Instead of dying right after Big Jim, Mama Fan seemed more to have faded away. Big Jim they remembered as someone in rough brown who swooped them in the air and then gave them gumdrops. J. J. remembered that Big Jim ate the licorice ones himself. When they were older, he'd let them select pads, red pencils, and staple guns from the office supply cabinet. They remembered his toenails curved down like an owl's beak as he clicked across the floor. And his funeral in the rain when Lily had hysterics after finding a twine-bound bouquet with a card that said *Always and all ways* near the grave.

"Food on the table," Lily mused. "Always food on the table. Not everybody can say that. No matter what, you must eat. You might as well eat well." She herself pushed back from the table, lighting a cigarette. "Our president promised that the national nightmare was over when they locked up half the government last year. And all those boys looked so nice—not Nixon, of course; he looked like he was carved out of a potato."

"What does that have to do with the price of tea in China?" J. J. asked.

"Oh, I just wish *our* nightmare would end. It reminds me that the criminal could be someone in a nice suit, someone you'd never imagine."

Only Ginger fell onto the food, helping herself to more mashed potatoes, a second piece of chicken, another biscuit. "Peach cobbler—just tell me Tessie will make peach cobbler for dessert tomorrow." She was remembering the shortcakes that were under way when she arrived.

"You know Tessie—she's bringing white peaches tomorrow morning."

"I cannot wait." Ginger, buttering the biscuit, felt her words cut off in the air, her hand disconnected from the knife she held. "This is surreal," she added. "Mother is back in the funeral home. *Impossible.*"

"Sugar, just enjoy your dinner."

"Daddy could at least unzip himself from that fake Daddy suit, step out as real and *do* something." An old fantasy. A black-faced doll she once had became a blond doll when you turned her upside down. Another doll unscrewed, revealing smaller and smaller dolls inside each other. A panda unbuttoned and inside were pajamas and a robe. He was *in there* somewhere.

J. J. knew he had about five minutes left in him. He poured a shot of bourbon to help his head. It scorched right through his stomach. He swayed to the bathroom and threw up. Usually his head felt better after that. He sipped ice water while Ginger ate a revolting mound of whipped cream and red, red strawberries. "I'm gone, you girls. Would you excuse me? Thank you for an enchanting day, another of many enchanting days in the annals of the Mason family."

Ginger helped Lily stack the dishes in the sink and rinse them so Tessie wouldn't face a huge mess in the morning. She made a cup of coffee for Lily, as she had every night when she lived there, and brought it to Lily's room. Lily undid her hair, changed into her nightgown, and propped up in her parents' bed with her coffee. The day had lasted a week. She wanted to say something to Ginger about how none of them deserved this, but she felt emptied. Ginger sat at the foot of the bed. Lily remembered her hanging on the end of the tester like a monkey until Lily thought the wood would break. Ginger loved her grandparents' room, the organdy canopy over the bed, the dressing table's pretty silver combs and mirrors and crystal perfume bottles, even the closed-off fireplace with pictures of the dead great-aunts, uncles, and great-grandparents on the mantel. Rogues' gallery, Mama Fan had called it. Lily had replaced her parents' heavy green damask with a yellow-flowered chintz, replaced their musty Oriental rug with yellow wall-to-wall, but the ornate gold mirror and the blue velvet slipper chair, worn on the arms, were the same. "Take your brother a pitcher of water. He suffers when those migraines hit him. You don't know how often he comes in just flattened. I think they're caused by chocolate. They say chocolate and cheese bring them on. But Catherine had them, too. Maybe he inherited them from her." She wished she hadn't said that.

Ginger did not answer.

EVEN THE WEDGE OF HALL LIGHT was a fist in the eye. Swallowing hurt and he had the sensation of riding a horse under a constantly expanding and contracting tent of gauze. He willed the two pills to dissolve in his bloodstream and flow up into the bony faults and branching rivers in his head. Canaliculus, canaliculi, streaming with fire. He tasted blood. Always, he was afraid of his father's stroke. A bubble of blood breaks—you're lost. Peace, he said to himself. Peace, let it go, let it be. The distant clinks of cutlery and dishes amplified in his ears, then bathwater running seemed to roar through him. Ginger used to sing "Blue Hawaii" in the bathtub. Tonight she was silent, although J. J. imagined he could hear the soap fall into the water, then slip through him. He felt the glare of the overhead light flash in the steamed mirror in the back of his skull. Pressure in his throat, spine, the backs of his heels.

He vomited again, into the pan he'd brought up, then he fell back into what he knew as the blackout, the unendurable crest of pain, the electrical sawing, buzzing, drilling pain that must come from outside himself because it would be impossible for the mere cranium to erupt with such force. For an hour he lay without opening his eyes to the pain of light, unable to call out for Ginger to close the door, unable to kick off his shoes. The feathers in the pillow bothered him with their rustling, as though they wanted to fly again. His own heartbeat, too loud, a tom-tom on a high mesa.

He lost himself, to sleep, to a hard wash of watery tide, and he thought or dreamed he was going in for brain surgery, dingy hospital walls, iron beds like a malaria ward in the tropics, and then he knew it was the Swan hospital before his father transformed it; he saw it at three and four years old and recognized it now, where he was about to go under the big light, big as a sun, his father striding down the long hall with sunlight at the end of it, blinding, his father in his early manhood—maybe thirty-three, the age of perfection, J. J.'s age, the age Ginger was approaching—when he was the angular man in the photo, leaning against the curved hood of his convertible with a horn that played the first few notes of "Darktown Strutters' Ball," *I'll be down to get you in a taxi, honey . . .* , but Swan never had a taxi. J. J. felt a rise of happiness at seeing his father, all power and energy, even coming toward him for surgery. He had no memory of moving from the Emory apartment, when Wills finished his residency, to one of Big Jim's houses in Swan, which Catherine always referred to as the honeymoon cottage. Now he saw his father, restored to himself. A glorious man. Brain surgery, but why? "What is wrong?" he asked the nurse. "Stunted pineal gland," she said, and J. J. wanted to laugh but his stomach wrenched. "What's that?" he shouted to her myopic eyes. "That's the little pine tree in your head, son." Who said that? He was being rolled fast down a wide hallway, the way it was before Daddy went up against old Dr. Dare and had the ward turned into private rooms. Big Jim was mayor and he had seen to that. Anything his son wanted he got. "You can have anything in the world you want," Big Jim was fond of telling his children and grandchildren. When Daddy had just started his practice and was about to deliver his first baby in Swan, he'd rushed into the operating room to find Dr. Dare repairing the fractured leg of his dog. Wills was brushing dog hair off the operating table as the completely dilated woman was wheeled in. The dream slid away fast. J. J. felt as though he were sinking through layers of rain, of sifted earth, but there was no bottom. Only the sight of his father stayed, moving toward him, that rangy body, now listless by a window at the Columns, energy prolapsed from the hopeless waste of two lives, his mother's high-wire act throwing his father into a spiral of anguish. Was there anguish before? From where, the war? Wills never would discuss the war. And none of them spoke of Catherine afterward, shame folded them inward, too tender a spot, her love that must now be invalid forever.

They referred to "before the accident," when Wills beelined to the sunroom after work, letting down the matchstick blinds and opening the liquor cupboard. From the door, J. J. had seen him drink straight out of the bottle before he even put down his bag. Tessie was left to feed them. Kindly she said, "Just don't pay him no mind," the only point of view that made sense. When Wills dropped them at Sunday School, afterward they waited on the sidewalk until he came for them. Sometimes he forgot. The Bible lessons were about a woman who looked back and turned to salt, about a father who would sacrifice his son, a brother who killed his only brother. They were sent in summer to a long session of camp in North Carolina, then for a visit to Mema, their Phillips grandmother in Vidalia. She was blind and a hypochondriac, who raved alternately about how spoiled Catherine was by her father and about how Catherine would never have done this if she hadn't married into the shameless Mason clan. She'd railed against Wills's breakdown, calling him selfish. J. J. and Ginger had fled and played all day in the limestone caves behind her house. They were old for it by then, but they fashioned horses from the red clay floor and baked them in the sun. The last of the dream switched into the creek behind Mema's and they went searching again for treasure until J. J. scooped his hands into a pool and brought up a cache of perfect quartz crystals, clear as the water dripping through his cupped hands. The dream made another shift, and he was still as a trout in clear water. Still.

———

HE APPEARED TO BE SLEEPING. Ginger came in quietly with a pitcher of water and a glass. "Are you okay? I brought a wet washcloth." As she had in high school, she wrapped the cloth around ice cubes and placed it across his forehead. She rinsed out the pan in the bathroom. Gently, she pulled off his shoes.

"God, I'm on the slope of it now. Cut the light . . ." His fingers gestured toward the hall.

"Call me if you need anything. I'll leave the doors open." Ginger turned off all the lights and felt her way to her room. Big Jim's clock struck eleven. Westminster bells, Lily once had explained, and Ginger as a child always thought of foggy London, with concentric circles of chimes spreading over the rooftops. She knew the striking chimes hit J. J. like stones. You *had* to count with them every hour of the day—the little dings at the quarter and half hour, marking how hours grow and accumulate and then diminish and start over again. The big hours sounded so solemn, counting off in the dark. The sad *one,* the clipped *two,* the tic-tac-toe of *three,* the neat and hopeful *four,* the swelling insistence of *five,* the alarming now-now-now of *six,* the heavy import of *seven,* the rising hour for school, worker-bee *eight, nine,* somehow magic, *ten* like jackstones thrown, *eleven,* a growing confusion, too many, then *twelve* hard gongs, transformation time, the glass slipper turns to wood. In the dark, Ginger felt the wide board floors, spread her hand for the spool bed just as she reached it, and flung off the bedspread.

Number games, number dreams, how many nights had she used them—they must have come from her first years at the House, falling asleep to Big Ben chimes, waking in the night with the fear that she was the last person left alive on the planet. Relentlessly, she used to multiply—any number, the cost of a candy bar or a sweater or a friend's father's car, she'd multiply by 2, 4, 6, 8, 10, on and on, then start back with 1, 3, 5. Eleanor Whitehead, her math teacher, had been startled by her ability to calculate almost automatically. Everybody knew Big Jim could add a column of three-digit numbers in his head; the skill must have cropped up in the granddaughter. Ginger learned to fall asleep with numbers filling her mind. They spilled into dreams, burgeoning and speeding beyond her ability to fix them. What was 582993 x 93886? Crazily, she would start to count on her fingers, but the numbers receded in space, and she woke up anguishing after them. She hated the number nightmares, and it was then that she trained herself in other ways, the happy memories recalled, the animals she'd loved, the most beautiful places, and, most recently, the favorite Etruscan paintings and votives.

She wanted to think of her project and of Marco, to somehow find him in all this. The scents of orange, grass, and iris would not be summoned. Lately, she'd felt more peaceful and often had not depended on her rituals to sleep. Her mind felt bright and fixed on her work. She'd not had to fight the irrational sense of hopelessness that dogged her, or the moments of shyness, almost shame, that few would suspect she felt. Marco. She tried to bring his face into her vision but kept seeing the joyous flute player painted in the dim Etruscan tomb at Tarquinia, his happy step and curly hair. She let herself imagine the song he played. Reedy, shrill, otherworldly. How very strange, just as she was beginning—at last—to taste the freedom of being adult, her mother violently rising from the ground. Ginger knew that her elaborate games began when she could not, could not think of her mother, when her anger and helplessness had nowhere to go. She knew she had to get through, she knew that at twelve years old, even then on the road, thrashing and crying after finding her mother, her face untouched, blood Ginger skidded into, blood, the scream Ginger still heard in her entire body, bits of her mother's burned raw flesh on her dress, the sharp slam of the door, running, heat pouring over her, flailing, dust, then Mrs. Rowen saying, "Honey, honey, what's wrong?" and holding her, Ginger crazy, fighting, finally saying someone had shot her mother and she was dead. She knew in many small moments since, such as in a restaurant bathroom, when she felt a surge of panic that she'd been left on the roadside, her friends driving off, and when her brain sometimes just locked and she couldn't think at all—she knew she must get through.

She started to relive it. Her usual gymnastic maneuvers could not keep it away. The same strobe-beating colors, the scream in her head, was this J. J.'s migraine in another form?

She tried to see the box of Etruscan stones, what about the golden stones, some with spiral designs broken in fragments? Twenty-five centuries under the ground and now brought into the light by her own hands. The excitement of brushing away the dirt. Marco beside her in a stringed-off area, the other interns, Cynthia and Jessica, in their lanes, all coming up with these fragments. But her mind veered to cleaning her mother's name on the dirty stone that morning. She had to force herself to search her memory, which required thinking of her mother. Her entire training was against that. The question she cycled around was why, why hadn't they known? To kill yourself must take planning, perhaps months of options considered and discarded. That her mother could pick up any gun was unimaginable.

As though it were recorded, she replayed, in the weeks after her mother's death, over and over to the last conversation they'd had. School had just started.

She was in the seventh grade. Her mother had made waffles for breakfast and Ginger didn't want any. She wanted cinnamon toast and orange juice. Tessie always made toast the way she liked it, but Tessie had the day off. Ginger had sat on the kitchen counter beating her heels into the cabinet door.

"Don't do that. You'll chip the paint. Get down and have some breakfast so you won't be late. Daddy has to go." Her mother was slicing the skin off cucumbers at the sink. She wrapped them with carrots and celery in waxed paper and put them in Ginger's lunch sack with her sandwich. Her daddy came in and poured himself coffee. He glanced at the front page of the newspaper, which was already unfolded on the table, and sat down beside J. J.

"Hey, buddyboy, got your report?" He'd helped J. J. with research on the Seminoles for Georgia history class.

J. J. nodded. "Can I have your waffle, Gin?" J. J. asked. His hair was wet. He looked like a little otter. He was wearing a new plaid shirt and had made neat covers from brown bags for his schoolbooks. He was in the ninth grade. Already, girls were looking at him, even sophomore girls.

"Y'all be good! We're going to the cabin tonight." Her mother handed her two pieces of cinnamon toast to eat on the way to school. Her daddy held the door and the three of them walked out. It still felt like summer. A white clematis vine threaded around the columns at the end of the porch. From the driveway, Ginger looked back. Her mother in a yellow dress with dots of blue and green leaned in the doorway as they got in the car and drove away. Her hand on the screen door handle. They drove away. They drove away and left her. Her hand on the door handle. Ginger could recall the exact feel of that door, its black iron latch. Then she lifted her hand in an ordinary wave good-bye. The door swung shut; her mother a shape, disappearing. They drove away and left her and she shot herself. No, she went back inside the cool kitchen for several hours and then she shot. What did she do for those hours, what did she think? Did she think of the days when J. J. and Ginger were born, the heads with soft fuzz cradled in her arms? Eyelids like moonflowers. Or of her own father, lifting her on his shoulders. Ginger had the old photo, Catherine with scrolling curls pulled up in a ribbon, holding her little spotted dog named Pansy, its wet button nose against her cheek. Did she think of the lace bow around the dog's neck?

Ginger leapt out of bed. She wanted to enter that kitchen with a different role, one that stopped the action, made it run another way. The utter ordinariness and banality of the scene made no sense. Why would you peel cucumbers and read the paper if you planned to kill yourself? Her mother was bright and funny. After so much time, Ginger barely could remember her being funny, just remembered that she was. She remembered more clearly the peeling paint on the kitchen door, the rotation of the latch, the two-note screech as she pulled it open, all those more clearly than she remembered her mother's wit. How barbarian memory is.

J. J. FLICKED ON THE BATHROOM LIGHT and reached in to close the door on Ginger's side. "Are you back among the living?" Ginger asked. He emerged in a few minutes.

"It's an empty freight train now, just the cars jangling." He'd brushed his teeth and washed his face and neck, run the wet washcloth all over him.

"I was just thinking about the morning Mother died."

"Well, let me not interrupt a stroll down memory lane."

"If we could understand it . . ."

"We had a pair of doozies for parents, that's all." J. J. took his usual post in the window seat.

"You don't think that."

"I don't? Suicide for a mother? Drooler for a father? Poor Lily as force-fed model adult in the tender years?"

"It's the happiness when we were little that seems so brutal. If we'd always been miserable, it would have been easier. At least we'd have known what to expect."

"Good solid misery. It came soon enough."

"You've never told me. How did you feel when you found out? Somebody came to football practice and told you, and then I didn't see you for a long time. Why didn't you take me to the hideout? I was left with the Rowens. Mrs. Rowen kept trying to give me oatmeal." How to say, she wondered, that it was as if life broke off that day and I balanced, moving fast, on the smallest piece?

"No guilt, now, please. But oddly enough, guilt was what I felt then. We hadn't made her happy. We were trouble. Afterward, when Tessie would take us out to the cabin for the day before I could drive, I'd go to the rack and see what it was like to touch the triggers on all the guns. When I was about fifteen, I used to sleep with that little Beretta pistol of Big Jim's under my pillow. It wasn't loaded but I liked to run my hand under the pillow and find that cold trigger. Mama hated the sound of a gun going off. You couldn't drag her on a duck hunt."

Ginger was quiet, hoping he'd continue talking, but he didn't say anything more. She couldn't remember when she'd last talked to J. J. without his sarcastic or ironic remarks keeping her away from him. And she hated when he assumed his redneck pose. "I think we've never trusted a human since then. Well, Lily, as far as that goes, and friends"—she thought of Marco—"but that down-deep, intimate, everything kind of trust is hard for me to come by."

No response. Then J. J. said, "Mitchell, for prime example. I thought with Mitchell you'd stumble into happiness. A good man."

"I developed an allergy toward him. I couldn't help it. He was like feverweed to me. I think I always felt close to you because you were the only one who could know. I just can't help but wonder how it would have been different, a plain old normal life. I'm off digging up sherds thousands of miles away and you're out there in the woods—you're almost a hermit—reading about reptiles and Indians. If you think about it, we're just magnified children." I *was* like that, she told herself. I'm not as stunted as he is. Now I'm starting to live like anyone else.

"Yeah, well, this reappearance doesn't do much for my interrupted joie de vivre." There he goes again.

"I always thought you'd be a writer. Faulkner, Eudora Welty, Carson McCullers, Flannery O'Connor, James Agee, like them."

"I write all the time. Just not books. No 'Song of the South' ambitions. No 'I-don't-hate-it-I-don't' monologue in a Yankee dormitory. No one's ever explained the South—you *know* that? But too many have died trying."

"The South is like the ancient Greek plays. Things happen in Idaho and Michigan but they don't happen the way they do here. It's different."

"Ah, yes. All that old murky stuff, the archetypal swamp mud abides, abides. Something affects little-bitty babies when they are born—the shadow of the hanging tree, Robert E. Lee on Traveler, riding off into the gauzy air. And all of us narcotized by the scent of magnolia."

"Don't mock, it's true. What about Mother? Do we remotely think this is just a gruesome mess without a trail of tears?" She couldn't explain how when she left Swan each time it was more than leaving.

J. J. didn't answer, so she continued. "Even the Jews who escaped from Hitler and, God knows how, came here—before long they're adding columns to the front porch and standing up for 'Dixie' at the football games. The place moves inside you. Even that New Jersey science teacher who came here was yes-ma'aming and talking at half-speed after a year. Really, J. J., admit!"

"Okay. This is the truth. See, I don't really think the first cause of that is the War Between the States or slavery or the lure of the old plantation. The first cause lies closer to that narcotizing scent of magnolia. In a way it's stronger than anything, stronger than evolution. Foreskins persist in covering the penis despite generations of circumcision. Nature's not swayed a bit. But the Feldenkreisses naming their daughter Lee Ann, calling her 'Missy,' and pouring juleps, that's just what they do with the spell they fell into. What we *think* of as South is only what is culturally available. But the land itself holds us in a thrall—the forests, the heat, the waters. I'm waiting to catch one of those eyeless fish we know are down there. If I were to write, a big *if*, I'd like to write something plain and real about the land. But you have to have a story, too. All the ones I know, I don't want."

Ginger wanted to throw her arms around him or a big Mary-blue cloak to shelter him. She waited to see if he would continue. "Unfortunately, all I know about, other than nature, is freaks and funda-mentalists and a family that can't win for losing, and signs for Judgement Day. I wouldn't touch it."

"But I would like to read what you could write. No one has seen anything from your notebooks. Forget the old writers, our family, nooses swinging from the hanging tree, or fanatics wrapping barbed wire around themselves. Thoreau is beautiful—you've lived in the woods a lot longer than he did." They loved *Walden* in high school, used to sprawl in front of the fireplace at the cabin in winter, Ginger under a blanket on the sofa, him with his legs slung over the arm-chair, each with a copy, reading aloud and eating pickles. "You could go travelling in the Amazon and find unknown medicinal plants, or orchids they think are extinct. Maybe you're the Bartram or Darwin of our time."

"Maybe not." He couldn't explain why he didn't write. It was not just his instinct that living in south Georgia trumped fiction any day—more doodley-squat events, violence, and craziness than any square mile in the world. There was more—the feeling of immense silence that words pulled out of, and the lack, the big white space around words once they were written down. He loved Ginger; she was the person he would face all his life. He decided to try to ex-plain himself to her. "You know how a fish sounds when it leaps out of water? If I could write that in a word, I'd know how to be a writer. Or like the bee, that sizzling sound when it goes back to the swarm. Words are all you have to write with and most things don't go into words."

She had an inkling of what he meant. "You mean you can't spell an owl's call or a watermelon splitting open?"

"Yes. They teach you that the alphabet covers all the sounds but it just covers *words*. And words . . ." He floundered now. "The body, how we live in the body. Migraine. Sex. Fear. Power. Can you write the sound of a gunshot that you didn't even hear but fires off in your body every day?" *There.* He felt weak, the God damned migraine had left him empty. He leaned toward the window, his hand on the screen, listening to all the night sounds together, tree frogs and night birds and bullfrogs and mosquitoes and the grace notes of the spring falling into the pond, a nocturne he knew by heart. "Listen." He saw the faint blur of Lily's two swans at the edge of the pond.

"J. J., just try. Write what you want. No one can transcribe a blue jay or that water sound—but isn't that what music is for? Because we can't? You have to make substitutions."

"Ginger, my good girl, always winding in the kite. I could sail off if you didn't keep that string taut."

"You'd better not, mister. How can you even say that?"

They both feared suicide was catching. Now she knew J. J.'s spiraling mistrust of the work she thought he was born to do. She would have to think about what he said. Was it true? In Italy, she often thought something similar. The land, beautifully tamed by eons of farmers, seemed so human in scale, so friendly. Perhaps even the rampaging Visigoths someday found themselves turning Italian. "J. J., you're the best brother. Of all the brothers I could have had, you are the best."

From the dark window, J. J. saw headlights and switched off the lamp to get a better view. A car drove slowly by the house, seemed to stop, then turned around down the road at the dead end. As it passed a second time, the headlights were off. J. J. could see only a black form moving by.

"What was that?"

"Probably someone wanting to see the house where the bizarre Masons roost."

"I'm gone, J. J. Call me when you get up."

July 10

TESSIE'S KITCHEN FILLED with the fragrance of ripe peaches. She squeezed each one in the row above her sink for firmness. Her uncle had brought over a bushel basket from his grove near Perry because she liked to put up peach pickles every year. She picked out six perfect ones for the cobbler she intended to make. Ginger even liked it for breakfast. Those children, as she still thought of them, had downright peculiar eating habits; she reckoned that came from having no mother. Sometimes she had arrived at work and found them eating bowls of ice cream for breakfast, their daddy too, so what could she say but "Mercy on us, wouldn't you rather have biscuits and syrup or some ham and eggs?" Later, Lily couldn't do a thing with them either. They just did what they pleased, but they were always polite about it.

Tessie sat down at the kitchen table and drank her mug of coffee. The house was quiet. She thought she'd miss her two children, who'd moved up North, and Robert, her husband, who'd died, but in truth, she enjoyed the house that stayed clean. She liked the small pile of laundry she gathered on Saturday. Wash it, dry it on the line, iron by nightfall. Her rows of pole beans and a dozen tomato plants she found easy to manage. She liked her cold suppers on a tray on the back porch, with the gospel station turned on low so it wouldn't bother the neighbors, not that much could bother Miss Jetta next door, crazy as a loon. When Ginger drove Tessie home from the House, she'd park across the street just to watch Miss Jetta obsessively sweeping her dirt yard and calling on the devil. Tessie steered clear of Miss Jetta; maybe she really was possessed by a devil. She wore a bracelet of dimes, old conjure, Tessie knew. How she stayed that crazy and alive no one understood. At night when her house was quiet, neighbors left sacks of sweet potatoes and onions, or a wrapped-up piece of cake, on her porch. From her few frizzle chickens running around, she had sense enough to gather eggs. Catherine used to bring her a handful of roses. Everyone else was afraid to go into the yard because Jetta waved her broom like a witch, but when Catherine put down the dog roses or sunflowers on her step, Jetta would stand behind the chinaberry tree and peer around like a shy child.

Tessie walked to work in the mornings before it was too hot. Late in the afternoons, after she got dinner together, Lily would drive her home. From the branch off the paved road onto the road to the House, Tessie walked slowly. She passed the dentist's, Catherine and Wills's old place, where she used to turn in to find Ginger and J. J. already playing in the sandbox or making a mess in the kitchen, Catherine clipping the dead roses, Dr. Mason already gone for the day. Now as she passed, she always closed one eye and said a prayer because the house still was marked by the evil eye, an electrical force she could feel along her spine. She passed the Rowens' house, then down the road, almost to the end. Rain had done its work on the clay road and she walked the shoulder, brushing through the purple vetch to avoid squishing in red mud. At the turn into the driveway, the mailbox door was open and she pulled out a small parcel wrapped in crumpled white tissue paper and tied with twine. Didn't look like much of a present. She carried it up to the house and put it down on the back porch with the sack of peaches.

AFTER A MIGRAINE, J. J. often woke with a sense of immense well-being. He was not sure whether a real chemical effect swept through with the cessation of pain, or if it was the body simply feeling the psyche's complementary afterimage of pain. Ginger, too, revived overnight. They dipped doughnuts into their coffees at the Three Sisters Café and Ginger read the paper, not commenting on the small article about their mother on page one.

They'd stopped in early to see their father while he ate cereal and toast from a tray. "Don't come in," they'd been greeted.

"Fine, Daddy, that's fine, you just enjoy your breakfast and we'll stop by later."

"No, that won't be convenient."

Ginger had brought a jar of Tessie's blackberry preserves. "Would you like some of this on your toast?" She spread the jam while he watched sullenly. He caught sight of his own face in the mirror and gestured with the toast. "Who is that and why doesn't he ever say anything?"

J. J. and Ginger had stared at each other. "Who?" J. J. finally asked. But Wills had forgotten his question. "That will be all," he said imperiously.

"Sure thing, Your Majesty, the least your nearest and dearest can do." J. J. was not inclined to humor him when he got in these moods. "Old stuffed goat," he'd muttered. "Old bastard."

Ginger had tried again. "Would you like these pillows fluffed?" His reflection in the mirror suddenly looked spooky to her.

"Where have you been? What took you so long? I've waited and waited." Wills looked up at Ginger. Through the blinds, soft morning light raked across his bony knees protruding from his robe like stunted skulls. His sad, stringy calves looked withered, his feet . . . But she stopped, concentrated on his knife-edge nose, his cocked head where she could see a shade of him as he was when he was her father; she even saw the twelve-year-old boy holding a fish on a string in the photograph on Lily's dresser.

"We got up early and came right out."

"Well, you can tote yourselves back where you came from. You've made your bed, now lie in it."

GINGER REFILLED THEIR CUPS. She loved the blue tables and the crazy collection of salt and peppers. Their table's were a puss and a boot. Martha, the sister who cooked, made the best doughnuts in the world, lightly fried and dusted with powdered sugar. Ginger had three. J. J. never had more than two. "If your butterfly metabolism ever leaves you, you are going to be one fat pig."

"Ah, sugar and grease—that's what I like about the South. I feel my arteries hardening with every bite."

Cy Berkhalter sat in one of the booths along the wall. He nodded gravely and stared into his coffee. His son, also his law partner, was another suicide. Gun in the mouth in the back storeroom. The Masons always recoiled from him, and he from them. Ginger went back to the kitchen. "Martha, it was worth the trip home just to taste your doughnuts."

"Hey, sugar." Martha scooped up two handfuls from a mound of fried holes and put them in a bag. "We're just so sorry to hear about your family's trouble. You let us know if there's anything we can do."

"Just let us know if you decide to make some Brunswick stew."

"We don't make that in the dead of summer. We'd die ourselves." Martha regretted her word choice. "But I could make you some fried catfish with hush puppies, that's good anytime of year." Ginger would have liked to rest her head on Martha's big broody bosom and weep. She would like to be fed by the sisters and listen all day to Emily's banter and jokes with customers.

The screen door of Three Sisters banged behind them. The Jaguar seats were already hot. J. J. made a U-turn on Corsica Street and swung around Oasis Park in the middle of the street, which was the exact center of town. A red Lab, paws on the marble side of the fountain, lapped at the water, and a small boy—looked like Ray Evans's youngest—splashed water at the dog. The Oasis centered on a tall broken column ringed with marigolds, zinnias, and yellowing grass. The falling notes of water gave the illusion of coolness to the tiny park. Marianne Shustoff got out of her car at the cleaners with an armful of laundry. Someone yelled, "Six o'clock, Edna Kay. Don't forget." J. J. took a right on Magnolia, passing Mrs. Woods, who managed the insurance office, slowly walking along the sidewalk with Wilton, her grown son whose tongue lolled and feet dragged. Over the street, sycamore branches met and intertwined. Ginger and J. J. tunneled through the watery green shade where only jagged swatches of sunlight shone, hitting a windshield here, a patch of brick street there. In the Nifty Shop window, Gladys draped a naked mannequin with butcher paper while she unbuttoned a crinkly yellow dress. Maud Richards knocked on the glass and pointed to a handbag Gladys had already arranged with matching scarf near the front. Neither one noticed Aileen Boyd's hip-length braid of blond hair swaying as she jaywalked toward the Nifty Shop carrying a shopping bag of baby clothes to sell on consignment.

"Oh, there's Skeeter Brooks, sexiest boy who ever went to Swan High." Ginger waved but Skeeter was loading croker sacks into the back of a pickup. "Too bad he knocked up that girl from the county and had to get married."

The small shops slipped by the window, the feedstore that smelled of alfalfa and dusty seeds, Uncle Remus Hardware, Hellman's grocery where Jackie Hellman hoisted a dripping side of beef into the front door, Grossman's Mercantile with bins of cheap shoes piled outside. She glimpsed Ann-Scott Williams putting the diamonds and watches back on display in Teebow's Jewelry. Ginger's own wedding ring had come from there. Inside it was engraved one word: *forever.*

CHARLOTTE CROWDER POURED TEA from on high. She liked to watch the steamy stream splash into her flowered cup. She slipped off the rubber band from the morning paper. Jasmine jumped down from the windowsill and twined between her feet. Charlotte pulled her up by the tail, which Jasmine liked, into her lap. "Wild thing." She ran her hand through the cat's mottled fur—she must have inherited the coats of a hundred strays—then rubbed her head with her knuckles, and Jasmine turned and gently bit her wrist. "You bad cat," she admonished, tapping her on the nose, but she liked it that the kitten she'd found at the dump never had become truly domesticated. When she'd finally trimmed back the Confederate jasmine ruling the back garden last spring, the cuttings piled over her head. Rather than waiting for the yardman, she loaded the car and took them to the Macon city dump herself. Typical, of course: Charlotte liked instant results. The kitten had come pouncing over to her from smoking pits of garbage. She could not just leave it for wharf rats to attack. She pulled out the woody, dusty jasmine branches from her trunk, flinging them toward a mound of tires. The kitten began to lunge at the flowers. Hence the name Jasmine, for a kitten who already had done battle with enough rodents that she was formed for combat—affectionate but likely to turn fierce at the slightest provocation, rather like Charlotte herself, so they got along fine. On the way back from the dump, Jasmine leapt from the back seat onto the top of Charlotte's head, digging in just enough to stay perched all the way home.

Charlotte's husband, Mayhew, had felt Jasmine's claws one time too many and steered clear of her. Secretly, he feared Jasmine would jump on his face in the night and scratch his eyes out. He made sure she was closed in the kitchen when they went to bed.

Mayhew surprised Charlotte with two pieces of toasted pound cake, her favorite breakfast. He felt buoyant with a fat contract in his briefcase, ready to be signed at the bank at 10:00 A.M. "Oh, you angel brains." Charlotte broke a slice in two and offered him a bite.

"No, I'm off to see the wizard, my love." He liked Charlotte in the mornings, calm before the day seized her. He drove away thinking of her as a ship in full sail, carving a spuming wake as she moved forward, driven by whatever wind was blowing. Charlotte always *trailed* things, nickels, lipsticks, Kleenex, postcards, sunglasses. Mayhew himself was compact and neat. When he came home from his real estate deals, laden with details of listings and the minutiae of pest inspections, she found him picking up, one by one, all the leaves that had fallen that day from the rubber plant onto the patio. As she emerged from her painting studio every afternoon, she threw her arms around him, her fingernails rimmed with paints, hair practically on end with, he thought, excitement. Or maybe she'd just cut her own hair again. Shot with gray now, she still wore her cropped blond curls as they looked in the photo of her at five years old, when she stood on a dining room chair and blew out the candles on her cake. "To be out of there! Away from that sour household!" she shrieked when he asked what she had wished. She smelled of linseed oil, tossed her head back and forth as she sang *Let's twist again like we did last summer,* scuffed into the house on mules she decorated with fake flowers and sequins. Mayhew, wary by habit, awed by her life force, would follow her into the kitchen, bracing himself for whatever she might be concocting for their dinner. She was fond of coconut and might use it in unsuspected ways.

He smiled to himself as he turned into the opening in the box-wood hedge surrounding Macon Properties. He was crazy about her. She'd never bored him once, though he'd wished many times that she would not always, exhaustingly, surprise him. Charlotte had the biggest laugh he'd ever heard, raucous, unfeminine, making him uncomfortable in a group of his friends, but simply to be in the room with that laugh compensated for whatever he had to put up with from spoiled clients of Macon Properties, who thought they should all inhabit plantations draped in moss dripping she-oaks.

At the most rudimentary level, when you heard a laugh like that, you were pulled in, you rolled into laughter that rocked you in the joy you lost and found and looked for throughout your life but mostly lost.

Charlotte let Jasmine lick butter off her fingers. She read the first page last because that's where all the bad news began. She preferred the recipe page, and the wedding write-ups were good for a laugh. She usually just skipped the news, but today she looked to see if Mayhew's deal for the golf course land was mentioned. She gasped, "No!" as she recognized the photograph on the far right side of the page. Catherine! Those dead-level eyes sizing you up, the tender mouth.

SPECIAL FROM *THE SWAN FLYOVER*

BY RAINEY GROVER

DECEASED WOMAN EXPOSED IN SWAN

The body of Catherine Phillips Mason was found unearthed in the family plot at Magnolia Cemetery on July 8. The grave of another family member, James J. (Big Jim) Mason, was defaced with black paint. Officials are investigating motives for this bizarre crime. Sheriff Ralph Hunnicutt of Swan stated that grave robbery was the likely motive. The body was discovered at 9:00 A.M. by the victim's sister-in-law, Miss Lillian Elizabeth Mason, who was visiting the family plot, and Mrs. Eleanor Whitefield, former mathematics teacher at Swan High, when she visited the grave of her husband, the late Holt White-field. Cass Deal, cemetery caretaker, stated that he had seen no un-usual activity. Mrs. Mason died in 1956 by her own hand. Formerly of Vidalia, she was married to Dr. Wills Mason, whose ancestors were early settlers of Swan. She is survived by Dr. Mason, who resides at the Columns Rest Home, and by two grown children.

Catherine! Charlotte banged her cup on the saucer. How impossible. How loathsome, poor Catherine. As she stood up, the paper slipped down, and Jasmine spilled to the floor. Shock rushed down her back. The sleeve of Charlotte's robe caught the teaspoon, which splattered rusty tea spots onto the chair cushion.

Charlotte's robe fell open. Underneath she wore a pair of Mayhew's striped boxer shorts. She walked barefoot on the herringbone walk around the side of the house. She turned on the hose full force, blasting the drooping cosmos she'd seen from the kitchen window, then sprayed the yellow dahlias, forgetting that their leaves do not like to be wet and in this humidity would surely mildew. Crossing the lawn, her memory swerved back to Catherine—yes, she'd suggested the arbor leading down to the creek. In another life, it seemed. Since Catherine's death, there'd been trumpet vine, wisteria, what else? Now Mayhew had planted that pink pea vine she hoped would die. Though they were in their twenties by then, she and Catherine turned cartwheels on the lawn when Mayhew bought her the brick house right in the middle of two acres of dogwoods and camellias.

Now Catherine, brought back into the light of day. In life, she'd belonged in the light. All that passion and fun, all that sharp beauty and tenderness, snuffed out. Charlotte had missed her with a cold fury. She missed the lips peaked like the towers of the Golden Gate Bridge. Missed the way Catherine stepped like a deer through brush. Out of everyone she'd ever met, only Catherine's sense of life lived up to her own expectations. Most people are so tamped down. Catherine was, how to put it, *ready*. She missed the years they would have had renting beach houses together and going crabbing with the children, turning up Bobby Short tinkling at the faraway Carlyle Hotel in the kitchen, while they made huge pots of shrimp Creole, or, who knows, taking off to Paris, saturating themselves in art and writing postcards at a little iron table. She never tasted my recipe for chicken, coconut, and lime soup, she thought. She imagined Catherine taking a sip, closing her eyes in order to taste more privately. "Hey, Mambo, what *is* the secret?" she'd ask. The secret was that Charlotte had lived, had been to the Yucatán peninsula and tasted spicy soup, while Catherine lay in the ground.

Charlotte no longer recalled why Catherine called her Mambo; the name came from their first days at Georgia State College for Women, where they'd been assigned to the corner room of Fall Hall. She and Catherine simply linked. They'd painted the beige room lavender, without permission, with clusters of grapes at the corners. Even so small a rebellion marked them. Of course there was precious little acting-up back then. Both girls had studied art. Charlotte loved oil painting then, though she'd since turned to watercolors, which suited her spontaneous, some would say slapdash, style. When they took art history, Catherine went mad for Matisse and decided she wanted to make pottery with bold colors, then she wanted to design patterns on silk, influenced by his blues and yellows. All year they'd lived for art. Charlotte must have drawn the blue-rimmed plate with two oranges a hundred times. Catherine wanted to make things with her hands. She embroidered bees and lizards on their pillowcases, she knitted big wool scarves with chevron designs. Pad after pad she filled with sketches of architectural details taken from photographs of French cathedrals—arches, gargoyles, tracery. Then early sophomore year she met Austin, then right away, she met Wills. Charlotte became active in theatrical productions, then interested in dance, and although she loved Catherine as a friend for life, she was not much interested in the late night discussions about whether it was possible to love two men. Often she fell asleep while Catherine held forth about Wills's brilliance and Austin's daredevil personality. Suddenly, too suddenly, when Catherine came back from Swan after Thanksgiving, she was engaged to Wills.

Charlotte lost touch with Catherine's children after her death. That idiot sheriff acted like she committed some breach of etiquette when she called. "Listen, sheriff man," she'd shouted, "Catherine Phillips would not *do* this, do you understand me? I know, I know she never, ever would kill herself." Until she read the article, she had forgotten that when she asked, he said no notebooks had been found at the scene, and she shouted, "Do you think they'd be laid out for you on the kitchen counter?" She remembered that she'd called him a "donkey turd" for his poor investigation. Where the archaic *donkey turd* had come from, she couldn't imagine. Her letter to the county judge demanding an investigation was not even answered. Wills refused to talk to anyone. The grief he plunged into was harrowing. Even after weeks of notes and messages, he did not respond. She had driven to Swan several afternoons, hoping to see the children, but Tessie said they were at the cabin. Intrepid as she was, she wouldn't intrude on Wills when he so obviously did not want to see her. Perhaps she just reminded him too much of Catherine. After Wills's grand-slam failure, she'd never seen him again. For a few years, she sent birthday and Christmas presents to Ginger and J. J., for which they wrote short notes of thanks, then the tumult of her own three adolescents took over and she stopped.

Now this many years later, watching the play of rainbows in the spray, she wondered about Catherine's death. She suspected that Catherine had a—she wouldn't say lover because she did not think Catherine actually would betray Wills—an affair, probably platonic, going on in Macon. Or maybe she would. Those were war years. Her college love, Austin, lived outside town then. There was a time, she couldn't remember exactly when, that Catherine suddenly had started to visit Charlotte in Macon more but she wouldn't stay long. A coffee, a quick lunch at Davison's, then she'd fly off. Once Wills called—oh yes, it was during the war because he was on leave—and asked to speak to her when Charlotte hadn't seen her. Out of instinct, she said, "She ran out to do a little shopping for the children." Catherine never mentioned the call.

Charlotte waved the hose, wondering what had happened to Austin, driving Mayhew's new alyssum plants into the dirt.

HAVE YOU SEEN THE PAPER?" Aileen's customer, Mrs. Shad Williams, called to order a set of yellow bootees for a baby shower. "The most awful thing happened."

She related the news about Catherine.

"How sick." Aileen felt her stomach lurch.

"Black paint on ol' man Mason's grave. Sounds like an ancient curse or something." Mrs. Williams read the article. "Honey, take your time with those bootees. The shower is August the first. Now, come see me soon."

Since Big Jim's death, Aileen didn't want to hear about the Masons. She'd been transferred back to the looms immediately when new management took over. Gradually, she'd built up her own business, and by the time the mill went under, she was already supporting herself. Big Jim would have taken care of her, if he'd lived. With her income and the money she'd stashed over the four years of their affair, she lived comfortably.

She still went all over funny every time she thought of the night at the motel when she'd gone back in the bedroom after taking a shower—a shower was a luxury since she only had a small tub with intermittent hot water at home—and Big Jim in his undershirt and shorts was toppled sideways on the bed. She thought he was joking and poked him in the ribs. Then she saw pink spittle running out of his mouth. She felt for his pulse, calling to him *wake up, wake up, no, no, no.* He'd had a previous heart attack, she knew, but he'd always boasted that his mended heart was stronger where it had broken. She'd shoved on his pants and shirt. She called Sheriff Hunnicutt and in a lowered voice told him to come get Big Jim and take him home. She fled. Before leaving the room, she saw his wallet on the bedside table and took all the cash in it, almost nine hundred dollars. She'd read later that Big Jim was found at the House, dead in his bed, by the maid when she went to work at seven the next morning. Apparently, the paper said, he'd died of a heart attack in his sleep. Hunnicutt always had nodded to her whenever she saw him, but never said a word. She knew his loyalty to Big Jim was unswerving but she didn't know why. Big Jim would only say that he'd been able to do Hunnicutt some favors.

Aileen frowned as she stared out her kitchen window. Black paint. Plenty of people hated the Masons, mostly out of jealousy. No one ever hated them as much as her former husband, Sonny, had years ago. But years and years had passed. Good thing he was living out in Arizona now. Even his mama had moved out there. Aileen hoped they were baking. Ever since the day he'd discovered her affair, she had prayed never to see his ugly face in this lifetime or the next.

She had never known whether Big Jim had arranged for Sonny to be drafted or if it happened by chance. Shortly after he was called up, Sonny came home—unexpectedly—on a weekend pass from Fort Benning before being transferred overseas. She'd hated the idea of going with him to Germany, although she'd told him out of fear that she'd follow in a couple of months. As soon as he left the country, Big Jim was going to tell her how to get a divorce. Then Sonny would be stuck overseas. Big Jim laughed about that. Aileen had hoped that by the time he was discharged he would have found someone else. Or maybe, she'd dreamed, she and Big Jim could run away together, and even marry. Big Jim often spoke of Bath, England, where his ancestors had lived.

Aileen was at the mill office when Sonny arrived that weekend. Since she had not known he was coming, she'd left an aqua peignoir on the bed. Big Jim had brought it back from New York. Next time, he'd said, he would take her. She'd left a wad of cash in her jewelry box, which Sonny found, along with an amethyst pendant she only wore inside her blouse because it was too fine and would call attention.

She'd gone to work to catch up on bills, and fortunately Big Jim was at the House. She sorted papers, feeling proud to be there. Maybe she could take secretarial courses over at the ag college in Tipton; she could be promoted again. As she sat at a desk in her corner of the anteroom to Big Jim's office, Sonny's face, dripping with sweat, appeared in the glass of the side door. Before she could get up, he stormed in shouting *whore, bitch.*

"Get out, you're going to get me fired," she'd shouted back. He pushed her to the floor and kicked her in the stomach. Then he went wild and turned over Big Jim's desk in the next room. Said he was going to kill that piss-ant if it was the last thing he ever did. "Screwing that bastard, you low-down slut." He kicked the desk chair, tore papers and piled them in the wastebasket, then set them on fire with a cigarette lighter. The blaze shot up, scorching the ceiling, then burned out as Aileen crawled into the outer office, slammed the door, and locked it. Through the wall she shouted that she wanted out of the marriage, it was no marriage anyway. She dialed the sheriff. Big Jim had told her if she ever needed anything, to call Hunnicutt. Sonny battered the door with a chair and broke through. He grabbed the phone and hit her on the head. As she fell, she saw him running out.

Sheriff Hunnicutt, sensing ugly gossip for Big Jim, had driven out to the mill village in his wife's inconspicuous old Ford. He'd found Sonny back at their house and locked him up overnight, though he wrote no report. The next day he'd taken him in the county car back to Fort Benning.

Aileen assumed Big Jim had pulled strings, because Sonny was shipped overseas the next week. "The little freak is gone." Big Jim had laughed. "I threw him to the alligators." You can't say that, she'd thought. If you do, the Lord will punish you. Fear had flushed her entire body, fear for Sonny, who, when they were first married, would sing doo-wop in the bathtub when she ladled pots of warm water over his scrawny body. He was only nineteen, a hothead. Then fear for herself had swamped her first fear. Sonny might come back and strangle her or set the house on fire. He might go after Big Jim. Like in the Old Testament, some prideful person was always getting back in spades what they'd caused to start in the first place. The fear had settled into her bone marrow. There was no one to tell, of course, or her affair would be discovered. Big Jim bought her a living room set and said, "Good riddance." His delight in her seemed to increase. She and Big Jim had three more good years. Aileen had begun to enjoy the rest of her life—her work, sewing, a church Bible study group.

While Sonny was overseas, she divorced him and dumped all his things on his mama's porch in Osceola. His mama probably didn't want him back there either. He'd been a hellion growing up.

Aileen checked her basket to see if she had enough silky cotton yarn for the yellow bootees. She would have to fill this day. She opened her Bible to the lesson for Sunday, but her eyes fell upon the words *sin, iniquity, wicked, wrath*. She put on an old record by the Soul Searchers. She would make a pan of brownies from scratch.

CAROL WAS ALREADY AT HER DESK when Ralph arrived. "Mrs. Whitefield called before I could unlock the door. She said to tell you that Catherine Mason was buried holding a letter. She said she remembered it and had asked Lily, who remembered it, too."

"And the letter reveals the naked truth?" A letter, he'd seen no letter but maybe it blew away. He'd have to comb the cemetery. In the school yard across the street, boys were gathering for a baseball game, oblivious to everything except the crack of the ball against the bat. They knew nothing of broken-into graves or burned villages in Vietnam. We should play more ball, he thought. He would organize two teams this summer, when all this blew over. He saw J. J. pull up and park in the jail loading spot.

Ginger gave Ralph a quick hug and pulled the doughnut holes out of her bag. "From the Sisters. Have some." Ralph grabbed a chair from Carol's office and they sat down. "Well, how grown-up— the sheriff. How does it feel to sit at your granddaddy's desk?"

Ralph grinned at Ginger. "You're sure looking good. Long time no see." J. J. stood behind her chair. Ginger was capable of all the niceties; he wasn't.

"Take a load off." Ralph gestured to the empty chair, but J. J. said he'd stand.

Ralph asked about the fishing at the river. "I heard Ralph Rogers got a forty-pound rockfish out of Resurrection Creek last Friday."

J. J. nodded. "Must of been there since the Stone Age. I hate seeing those suckers come up. They do look like something that oughta be extinct. Kinda pretty though, those jaws, some of them with four or five pieces of line hanging off." Ginger rolled her eyes at his ol'-boy role coming on this early in the day.

They fell silent and Ralph pulled out the folder marked *Catherine Phillips Mason.* "I know you've had a shock and y'all know I'm mighty sorry this has happened. I don't understand it yet and I wonder if we ever will. It falls to me to tell you something else. Something entirely unforeseen. I don't know what the verdict will be, but we performed an examination—Gray Hinckle from the GBI and I—and we've gone over the evidence—this record here and, well, of course"—his voice dropped—"the body. It's beginning to look like . . . because of various measurements we've made and all . . ." He looked down at the floor because Ginger and J. J. were both staring at him as if a tidal wave were about to break over them. "This is preliminary. All the evidence has to be rechecked." Ginger and J. J. watched his mouth form words, expecting to hear that their mother's body had been violated, watched his mouth while he said, "But we think that your mother did not kill herself. That is, she herself did not pull the trigger . . ." He stopped.

He had no idea of the import of his words. The words seemed to sift through the air from a great distance.

Neither of them said anything. J. J. moved his hand to Ginger's shoulder and she covered his hand with hers.

"Because the exit angle of the wound"—he looked down at the notes he took from Gray's call—"is incommensurate with what would result from a gun held by the victim. I hate to burden you with details, but sometimes the .22 doesn't go all the way through a body. You know, it's basically a rabbit gun. But Mrs. Mason—your mother—must have been thin. I've read the report written back when it happened. That was when my granddaddy was sheriff, I guess you know. They didn't have the fancy equipment we have now. Those GBI boys have other tricks of the trade these days. She's been checked for gunpowder residue in her nose and on her hands. They've got some kind of dust that picks up microscopic particles."

"What are you saying?" Ginger pressed her elbows into her knees and stared at the floor. J. J. shielded his eyes as though he were looking into the sun.

Ralph's words formed a distant hum. "The size and angle of the wound point toward the conclusion that she couldn't have aimed at herself." Ralph thought even back then somebody could have noticed that, but maybe that was because he'd been in Vietnam, where men were shot every which-a-way, whereas his granddaddy mostly saw blacks cut up on Saturday night. "I'm going to ask you to read the report and see if there's anything you can add, from your memory of the event. I know this is damn strange for y'all. In Gray's call, he'd said his boss, the expert, thought she'd had the rifle put in her hand after she'd been shot. Maybe someone had taken it away from her as she tried to defend herself. She might have first grabbed the gun in self-defense. They'll try to test for powder burn, but after this long they might not come up with anything definitive. Looked to Gray and his boss like she'd been shot from six to eight feet away."

I'll think this through later, Ginger thought. She was the first to speak. "When will they know for sure? How can they tell after so long? She was shot by someone? But that can't be. Who? Who?"

Ralph shrugged and shook his head. "About that letter, do you know the contents?"

"No. Lily doesn't know. She thought it might be a note of love from Daddy."

Ralph said nothing, stared at her, unable to admit his suspicion that it might have been a confession and apology. Now it was lost or taken. What a sheriff. What was that old verse, *the fathers have tasted bitter grapes and the sons' teeth are set on edge.* That about said it. Damnation.

J. J. picked up the file. A surge of elation pushed against his skin. The post-migraine delight—or was it that what Ralph just said was what he'd wanted to hear ever since he first heard the word *suicide*? He read quickly. He did not look at the photograph of his mother sprawled on the floor, but he saw it anyway, saw what he'd seen over and over although he did not in actuality ever see her, only Ginger had. Only Ginger had taken the full impact into her body.

Ginger reached for the report. The photo must have been taken an hour or so after Mrs. Rowen found Ginger on the road. Ginger stared. She heard again her own strangled cry. But if her mother did not pull the trigger, she must look at the picture again. Cabinet door ajar, her legs splayed, one shoe off, the peeling screen door in the background. Surely, something showed that Catherine did not do it. The *something*, if someone had noticed, that would have changed their lives. She forced her memory: Again, she reaches for the screen door and slowly it swings open, the sight of her mother blasts her out again, the indelible, searing blood, the bang of the door. She looked at every detail. She was feeling her way, the way she felt her way to bed in the dark. She had the impulse to drive to their old house, the dentist's, ask to see the kitchen. She'd heard they ripped it out, replaced everything, even extended the kitchen and added a patio so that the hideous event would be obliterated.

She tried to re-create it exactly: the round table by the windows, the shelf of cookbooks, the glass cabinet for hunting guns, the curvy white appliances. Her memory and the photo were the same.

"See anything new to you?" Ralph let them read. He wondered if they'd thought yet that Wills could have pulled the trigger.

J. J. spotted the gun cabinet part in an instant. He kept his own cabinet locked. Back then, no one did. He and Ginger were raised around guns and knew not to touch them. He read the report to Ginger, who was tearing off her thumbnail in her teeth. "Hell, there's some explanation." He looked at Ralph's quizzical expression. Son of a bitch, he thinks Daddy did it. "My dad couldn't have raised a hand against her. Is that what that fuckup said? You don't believe that. That's crap. All these years we've had a suicide. Now we have a father who's a murderer? Do we get to choose?"

As he spoke, J. J. knew without hesitation which he would choose. Nothing could be worse than his mother shooting her heart out.

"Nobody's saying that. Nobody's accusing anyone. Yeah, the agent brought it up as a possibility. He doesn't know your daddy from Adam. We don't have a lot to go on, do we? Can I get you some coffee? Carol always makes a strong pot."

Neither answered. "Also, Daddy is like a big baby now. He's slumped over in a stupor half the time. He certainly doesn't have the I.Q. at this point to break into her grave. It's preposterous even to think of that. If there were any conceivable reason anyway." She dismissed the question of Wills's guilt from her mind as soon as J. J. raised it. Odd to think of Daddy's I.Q. Once he was an idealistic young doctor, who'd refused to step into the family business. For as long as he'd been gone, Ginger had felt an irritated knot of anger toward him. He brought this on himself. But what happened to him went way beyond the bounds of just deserts. Other people had bouts of madness or drunkenness, recovered and went on with normal lives. It shouldn't have happened to a dog. Ginger felt the same stunned glimmer of elation as J. J. A random crime was a whole different grief.

In the folded memory, Ginger still has her hand out, the immense calm of childhood about to be ended, she's about to open the door but the memory cracks—she always called first, "Mama, hey, I'm home, let me in."

Let me in! Always, always, her mother kept the screen door latched, ever since gypsies came through town and stole her underwear off the line. Almost everyone in Swan left their doors unlocked, even at night. Catherine locked hers. But the door swung open in Ginger's hand. Her mother had unlatched the door for someone, a friend, a repairman, a neighbor. She blurted this out.

"Someone she knew. Or maybe she just left the door open this time." Ralph was taking notes. Good. He would have some things to tell Gray.

"J. J., how could I not have remembered this?"

"Because of what was on the other side of the door."

She could never remember her walk home from school that day. In memory, she left the playground, and then she was hit by the sight of her mother. She ran, she's running still down the white road, Mrs. Rowen's floury hands around her, then nothing else until the funeral. When she remembered the dark circle of blood, she was always twelve, wanting to bang her head on the floor.

J. J. kept reading. "Look here, Charlotte Crowder, Mama's old friend, called up," he read on, his finger following the words, "but there's no follow-through here? What did she know?" Wills had cut off everyone after Catherine's death, J. J. remembered. Charlotte sent notes and called at first, then she stopped. J. J. hadn't thought of her in years. "I wonder if she confronted Dad, if Lily knew she'd called the sheriff."

Ginger wandered into the outer office and came back with a mug of coffee. J. J. stared at the doodle in Ralph's grandfather's hand, something scratched over—he made out an S.

"We can speculate all day. Sorry to say so, but it's the easiest crime in the world," Ralph smoothly echoed Gray. "Husband goes after the wife and it's your word against his. Nobody can prove a thing."

"But how could he have *thought* Daddy could do such a thing?" Ginger became outraged. "Oh, Ralph, I know you can't speak for him, but do you have any idea?"

Ralph didn't want to continue Gray's speculation about a lover in the wings, or to go into how his grandfather was indebted to Big Jim for swinging the sheriff's election. "I'll just be blunt. Your dad's the only lead out there—it's based on statistics, not on anything real. Why didn't my granddad do a better investigation? I think he was in Big Jim's pocket his whole life. He might have been grateful for certain things. There's the possibility that he was protecting your family. Women, you know, they get unhappy, don't see any way out—they kill themselves. A murder might have stirred up some old shame. God only knows." Could his grandfather have been lame enough to think it just wasn't *polite* to inquire too closely?

He shook his head. "We can go two ways—start investigating a murder or depend on solving this by finding out who, uh, violated the grave. From my point of view, I've got to follow up on the latter. I'm sure you'd want to pursue both," or maybe not, he thought, "but the GBI agent says there's no way to trace the killer, short of a confession, after this long. He said when a trail is this cold, finding the killer usually happens only if a surprise confession pops up, some old guilt working its way out. That may be years from now. Maybe never. Let's just get her back in the ground, when she's finally released on Monday, and hope to close the case."

Ginger looked at the obituary from the local paper, with her mother's photograph above it. She recognized it as her mother's engagement picture, which used to sit on Wills's desk at his office. She had an impressive forehead and direct eyes. Her lips formed the perfect cupid's bow of her era. Around her neck was the flat gold necklace her father gave her when she was eighteen, against her mother's wishes. Ginger could hear Mema, *He spoiled her. She wants too much*. Her mother always loved that necklace. Her gaze was serene; nothing ever could go wrong. She looked out from thirty-five years ago into a future that did not include her two puzzled children huddled in the sheriff's office going over her file, her husband propped into a chair by a window overlooking the weedy tennis court of a nursing home.

HOLT WHITEFIELD USUALLY VISITED the cemetery with his mother on Thursday mornings. It was something for them to do together. Today she refused to go and considering the shock she'd had out there, he was relieved. Instead, he took her to the Three Sisters, so crowded this morning that they had to sit by the door. He read the Macon paper while she chatted with everyone coming and going. Catherine Mason was in the news, page one, a small article about the exhumation, but what, really, was there to say? No one had a single clue. Emily brought a platter of bacon and grits with a side order of limp toast that not even the homemade pear preserves could redeem. "Eleanor, bless your heart, what an *awful* thing to happen to you and Lily. Those children were in here this morning, J. J. scowling as usual and Ginger sweet as she can be." On his way out, Father Tim Tyson leaned over to pat Eleanor's back, and Holt saw his mother straighten her shoulders as though shrugging him off. The priest worked a toothpick between his molars, and a gray food fleck landed on the table.

Holt lowered the paper and stared at it, his top lip rising in disgust. Holt was no friend of the Episcopal church anyway, and he barely nodded to Father Tyson as he passed on by, with "Don't be a stranger."

"I double-dog-dare you to give him the finger, Mama."

"Oh, Holt." Then Eleanor was clasping hands with Rainey Grover, whose bulbous buttocks in pink stuck out so far you could rest a glass on them.

"I don't know how you'll ever sleep again." Journalist or not, Rainey wouldn't think of asking questions that might upset Eleanor. Rainey in her belle-hood had men from three counties swarming around her, a regular Duchess Hotspur. She worked for her husband's Swan newspaper now; who would have guessed she'd end up with Johnny Grover? But who'd have guessed that Holt, with his I.Q. off the charts, would end up as local high school principal? Rainey's small face, polished like a just-dried bowl, rose out of the body of an ancient fertility goddess. Holt remembered hearing years ago Buddy Perrin say a night with her would kill the weak and cripple the mighty.

Rainey looked down at Holt with God-given blue eyes. Holt had helped her boy get a scholarship to Mercer College. He's not *that* old, she thought, and just look at those old-man suspenders and the way he combs that lick of hair over his pate. She smiled good-bye to Eleanor, showing wide white Chiclets, Holt noticed, smiling a tight smile to cover his own slightly back-sloping teeth.

"Would you like to ride around?"

Eleanor thought she would. "Ride by Billie's. Let's see the row of pines she planted down her driveway. Then we'll stop in to check on Lily."

"Mama, what do you think is going on with this Mason mess?"

"If they find the letter out there, then I think it's probably a random piece of work by someone crazy. If they don't, maybe someone wanted it—or something. We'll just have to wait and see."

"What if Wills isn't as damaged as he seems?"

"Lily would know if that were true, and even if it were, I doubt if he could have engineered this from the Columns. And why on earth would he?"

She did not ask what he thought. Just as well. Holt, after years and years, still was not about to erode Catherine's trust. She never had betrayed his secret.

FATHER TIM TYSON DROVE the three blocks from the Three Sisters to the post office to mail his request for a new parish. Swan was a constant ordeal, especially after the two years in Newman over in Meacham County, where the people were more gracious and the rectory considerably nicer for his wife, Rosemary. Every month she complained when the Circle met for New Testament study. At least two members had to sit on straight chairs in the hall, barely able to hear, because the living room was too small. Five years here and he still didn't feel accepted. Just now Eleanor Whitefield pure snubbed him and ditto that queer son of hers; everybody said he defied the teachings of Jesus and practiced sodomy. For a moment, he concentrated on what sodomy might be, exactly. Buggering, yes, he knew that, but he saw only biblical hordes led by Charlton Heston, pillaging and looting. Now he had to think about this disgrace with the Masons. He'd been told that Big Jim donated the chandeliers in the church years back and had his men build the pierced-brick serpentine wall around the Memory Garden, but the current clan donated a few hundred dollars a year, if they remembered at all. Lily still brought flowers for the altar on her parents' birthdays, enormous sloppy bunches from her garden. J. J. never darkened the door, and when, as the new priest, he'd made his rounds, calling on the members, J. J. had offered him a drink of whiskey and told him not to expect him, as Sunday was sacred fishing time. Tim Tyson's lips twitched in anger as he recalled J. J.'s cruel little smile. Had his own way of praying, he had said; that old excuse. As if we were meant to be solitary. As if the church were not about holding the community together, as this sinful one needed.

He stopped at the Pappas fruit stand and surveyed the bushels of corn and baskets of plums and peaches lined up along the sidewalk outside the shop.

"Mighty fine peaches, Father Tyson. Would you like a sample?" Tony Pappas seemed to smile all over his face. His large black eyes made him look like an icon painting from centuries ago. Everyone in Swan came to Tony. He lavished his attention on mounds of lemons and polished apples on his green apron.

"I'll take your word. Give me a sack of those, please, Tony." He pointed to the yellow plums Tony had picked earlier from along the roadside toward Osceola. Father Tyson had other things on his mind besides fruit for Rosemary's pie and stared off into the middle distance as Tony examined each plum for bugs or bruises. The letter had dropped to the bottom of the mailbox with a thin *plink*. Maybe the bishop would send a young man just out of seminary to Swan. Trial by fire, he'd find. Highest suicide rate in the state, highest incidence of intestinal pinworms, and quite a few plain loonies. God help me, he thought, I've dealt with arson and stealing from the collection basket and pregnant twelve-year-olds. No wonder I could not face the uproar of finding that piece of paper on the ground. I did the sensible thing. I'm going to pray for them all, but I have enough on my plate.

Tony whistled as he bagged the plums. He threw in a couple of peaches for good luck and touched the blue eyeball he wore around his neck. According to his grandmother, priests sometimes cast the evil eye. Today Father Tyson looked hot enough to pop.

Yesterday, Father Tyson had just settled Mattie Tucker in the front seat, after helping her take a vase of glads to poor Ham's grave.

As he went around to his side of the car, an envelope lay at his feet. Small, dirty. In typed letters he saw the word *Catherine*. Under it, *The last day*. Around town they'd been saying Catherine Mason was buried with a letter in her hand. Here it was, blown to his feet, blown to the priest of the church to which she had belonged. Was that not auspicious, was not God sending him a message? He slipped it into his pocket and drove Mattie to her sagging house with several cats waiting on the porch. She was one of his saviors in Swan. She and four other women tended to the needs of the church as if it were their own home. Mattie, always immaculate in her brown or gray anonymous dresses, ironed the altar linen, baked cookies for the Episcopal Youth Fellowship, and sat in the third pew every time the doors of the church opened. She did not deserve for Ham to up and die like that, washing the car on a Saturday afternoon. Father Tyson did not mention to Mattie the envelope secretly shoved in his pocket.

When he got back to the church office, he took out the fragile envelope and pulled out what appeared to be a blackened-edge page ripped from a spiral notebook. In handwriting different from the envelope's he read:

> *Beauty is a thing beyond the grave.*
> *That perfect bright experience*
> *Will never fall to nothing*
> *And time will dim the [blurred spot] sooner*
> *Than our full consummation [blurred spot]*
> *In this brief life will tarnish or pass away.*

He held the lined page up to the light. The paper was soft, speckled with mildew. A hard shudder ran through him as he realized it had been held in the hand of a dead woman under the ground for all these years. Beneath the watery blurs he made out *moon* and *here*. He dropped the page on his desk and wiped his hands on his pant legs. *Time will dim the moon. Our full consumma-*

tion here. Could they find fingerprints on something this damaged? He thought not. Since he was a man of the cloth and had no fingerprints on file anywhere, he knew he was exempt from the law. He wrapped the letter in crumbled tissue paper he pulled out of the wastebasket. *Full consummation, that sounds sexual.* His mouth turned downward. *I will not speculate on the meaning of this,* he decided. *I do not want to be involved.* He put the page under his sermon notes. *I do not want to know.* Yes, her life was brief, but killing oneself is surely to be condemned. Shame. Her family had to walk out of Eden, covering themselves. And look what they've become. More than any visitation, he dreaded the monthly call he made on Wills Mason, who looked at him as though he were a cockroach on the wall. He had trouble enough in the present. To meddle in the past was beyond the call.

That night, reading under a circle of lamplight in the corner of the bedroom, he waited until Rosemary fell asleep, her hair wound in tight sausages secured with rubber bands, a mask of pale green cold cream on her face. He felt more serene after reading the Book of Job. Rosemary's eyes fluttered when he picked up the keys and he waited until she snorted and rolled on her side. He drove out Island 10, and on out to the Mason house, killed the lights, and stuck the letter in the mailbox.

When he coasted into his driveway, Rosemary was waiting at the back door. "Tim . . . at this time of night?" she was almost shouting. With the dim garage light shining on her green face, she looked frightening.

There was no lie to tell, nothing he could invent that she would not know was untrue by tomorrow or the next day. Any accident, death, emergency in Swan would be hers by noon. He told her the truth. "I just did not want to be pulled into their lives."

She looked at him blankly. "But you could have *offered* them . . ." The night freight rumbled by two blocks back, muffling her words. Then she said something else and went back to bed.

He thought she said *shame.*

GINGER TURNED THE AIR VENT toward her face as J. J. raised a cloud of dust between them and Ralph's office. She saw a lone figure in blue looking out at them from the upstairs barred window of the jail. She had an impulse to wave but did not. "If we just spring it on Daddy, maybe he will react in some revealing way."

"You think this kind of news goes straight to the reptilian brain stem?"

"It felt that way to me." Even going as far as to speculate that they might stun Wills into a reaction made her need air. Her throat felt too tight to breathe. She conjured the face of Marco, but his look, she realized, would be incredulous. Marco, she feared, could not follow this. Who could?—J. J. and I are the ones swallowed by the whale. Or do I underestimate Marco, automatically shut down? *Easiest crime in the world,* Ralph had said. "There's a rational world to live in, isn't there?" she asked, but J. J. only sighed and shook his head. I've been feeling my way toward one, she thought, and if this news is true, maybe we can reach around the past years back to the earliest world, where Daddy let me put his stethoscope to the hearts of my dolls and taught me to bandage their legs. At the very rim of her consciousness, she knew his warmth—he is running from rain, holding her, a red plaid umbrella over them, and he is laughing. Her small arm crooks around his neck and his face is next to hers. She hears and against her chest also feels his laughter. Not an ounce of her believes that her father could be a murderer. What colossal bad luck he'd had. "You look miles away, J. J., a stone on the moon, come down."

"What strikes my brain stem is all we don't know about what we know. You want to try talking to him, I'll take you." He turned in at the Gold Star Drive-In and ordered a beer brought out to the car, though it was only eleven o'clock. The Gold Star was a Mason building, but he almost never went in, just occasionally stopped to brace himself there en route to the Columns.

"Sun's not over the yardarm, J. J."

"Well, it's dark under the house."

Ginger ordered a lemonade. It was cold and sour. She thought she was getting a sore throat. She pressed the cold glass to her forehead, then emptied it on the ground.

J. J. and Ginger differed over the mental state of their father. Ginger often saw flashes of the real Wills. She saw his mind as a film exposed many times. He found fractured and layered images but couldn't put together a scene. When she probed, asking him about the cabin when he was a child, about medical school, about Big Jim and Mama Fan, at times a power came back to his face. "Your grandmother," he said, "loved the smell of a gardenia. She had a big bush of them eight feet tall."

"Where?" Ginger knew, because it still bloomed outside Lily's bedroom window, under her own.

"I don't know." But he said *grandmother*, Ginger would think; he has enough reason to know that his mother was my grandmother.

The possibility that he would come back never really left her. The chemical levels would separate or purify, leach through to the dried areas, the damaged neurons would knit again into a pattern, synapses reconnect. She willed them to stitch together. "What in the name of God are we supposed to do? For Christ's sake, turn up the air." Now she sounded like J. J. If she lived here, she'd probably become like J. J. A Chamber of Commerce sign on the outskirts of

town said in foot-high letters *If you lived here, you'd be home now.*
Wills's two years of drinking (decline, Lily called it) after Catherine's
death Ginger and J. J., too, attributed to his grief, which moved
Ginger to a pity J. J. could not allow. *A pity beyond all telling,* she'd
underlined in her copy of Yeats's poems, *is hid in the heart of love.*

J. J. considered Wills a total goner. He judged his father's character: weak. And his indulgent weakness had lowered him and
Ginger to orphans. Wards of the Lily. If you love someone, if you
have a choice, you don't let them down. Ever since they'd been let
down, down, a free-fall down, J. J. had smoldered with a double-
edged fury. All three of them were fingered by Catherine's death,
and he could forgive only Ginger. He was able to see her innocence
but not his own and certainly not his father's. He remembered feeling as if he were turning into wood when Lily, swinging into the
drive at the House, suddenly announced, "You're home, this is
home." Their own house was left closed for months before Lily decided to sell. He and Ginger would take the key off the nail on the
trellis and let themselves in to find a game or a jacket. Some of their
clothes still hung in the closet. Everything of Catherine's was gone.
A dirt dauber built a four-chambered nest on the leg of a pair of
J. J.'s jeans. No one had unplugged the refrigerator. They escaped
the quiet house covered by a layer of dust and ran toward home, as
they now knew it. They'd had to invent themselves after Wills
flaked on them. Bird girl, J. J. thought, bird boy, mismatched socks,
swingers of ropes, searchers for petroglyphs, snapping turtles, back-
of-the-classroom, moon-howlers, pick a card, any card, X marks the
spot. Long after they were too old, they tore through the woods
yelling like Indians on the warpath in the Saturday movies. They developed with all the subtlety of kerosene-soaked rags.

At best, he attenuated his rage toward his father by seeming to
humor him like a spoiled-rotten child. At worst, he went for weeks
without visiting at all, then would arrive one afternoon to find Wills
in a snit because he'd had to wait in his bath for help, or someone
had stolen the dollar bills he kept for cigarettes. News of a car crash

killing seven and a spilled glass of water received equally bland stares. J. J.'s absence troubled him not at all. J. J. would lean against the air conditioner—it diffused the smells of diapers, bandages, IV bags, pissed mattresses, fried food, and hell-bent misery absorbed in the walls of the Columns by years of dying patients—not making conversation, his lips set in a curl, sometimes wondering if he would be caught if he held a pillow over Wills's face and put him out of his misery. Whose misery? J. J.'s. His father's arrogance and imperialism he found so unbearable that in the few moments when Wills turned vulnerable, looked straight at him with the eyes of a bagged hare, or reached out a shaky hand for balance, J. J. exited as soon as possible. Driving toward the Columns, he briefly considered whether or not subconsciously he'd suspected his father. But the idea, dropped on them by Ralph, was preposterous.

There were no columns at the Columns, only squat porch posts along a low two-story building made of cinder blocks painted beige. Patients propped in rocking chairs sat silently facing the parking lot, like Easter Island carvings facing the sea. One or two fanned with cardboard Jesus fans, the rest slumped over in the trance of heat and near-death. A young man with no arms or legs was trussed into a lawn chair. "There but for the grace of God . . ." J. J. pushed Ginger's elbow forward.

"Don't," she said, "just don't."

"Let's run the gauntlet." All through high school, they dreaded the journey from car to corridor to Wills's room. All through their twenties, they'd never become inured. "Last one in is a rotten egg."

Turn left at the entrance and you faced the crazy ward; turn right and you faced the old people's area. Though he was a little bit of both now, Wills lived among the old. Most rooms were shared by two, but he had his own, with his leather reclining chair, an antique chest lined with photos, and fresh ferns Lily brought each time one curled and dried, not that he noticed. His old gabardine and linen suits hung in the closet, his *summa cum laude* medical diploma above the mirror. The institutional iron bed Lily had covered with a blue comforter. From the window he looked out onto a tennis court, absurdly constructed, with federal grants, for those who could barely stand, much less swing a racket. The net sagged and weeds sprouted through the baking clay.

Doors along the hall stood open, the occupants hoping for a passing greeting or a visit, but Ginger and J. J., familiar with the cast of characters, today looked neither right nor left. Wills kept his door closed. Ginger tapped. "Daddy, it's us." She peeped in, then opened the door wider. Wills lay on his side, his feet under the covers. His hands, pressed together as if in prayer, rested under his head. They came in quietly but he sat up.

"Who, what?" He looked wildly around the room, then recognized them. "Oh, I must have been dreaming."

"What were you dreaming?" Ginger asked.

"Dreaming of dreaming."

Ginger could be blunt, but J. J. was startled when she cut short the usual banter. "Daddy, we have learned something serious and very surprising. You know that mother was taken out of her grave? Lily told you."

He stared at her, then at J. J. "Catherine, she was a lovely woman."

"Yes, well, something even stranger has happened. The GBI examined her body and now say that she did not shoot herself."

"No? What are you talking about? J. J., speak up, what is she saying about my wife?"

"Dad, she's saying what she's saying. The police have new techniques. Mother was murdered." He said it brutally, although he was not yet sure he believed it himself.

Wills reared back as though water had been thrown in his face. He made an animal grunt, flung himself off the bed, and teetered over to the leather chair, where J. J. sat. He leaned into J. J.'s face. "Where's that rifle of mine? I know my gun went off. She went *bang*." He held his finger to his temple.

J. J. spun toward Ginger and shouted, "She went *bang*. Did you hear that? She went bang. This is fucking unbelievable. What did we do in another life to deserve this?"

"Quit it, J. J.!" Ginger tried to lead Wills to a chair. "Daddy, listen. No, she didn't use the gun. That's the point. She did not pull the trigger." Wills sagged down, his knees flopped open. "Try to remember. Who would have shot her? Did anyone hate her?"

"I hated when she was gone." He reached over and turned on the TV. Lawrence Welk appeared and Wills smiled.

J. J. stood up and snapped off the TV. "I have to ask you this. Did you, did you kill her, kill Catherine?" He wanted to grab him by the throat, shake him until he spoke an intelligent sentence.

Wills raised his chin and looked defiant. "Don't be ridiculous."

"Who could have, goddammit, think for once. Who could have?" Wills stared at the empty screen.

"What is wrong with you? It's time for my programs."

"It's dawning on me that nothing is wrong with me or Ginger after all. What happened to her notebooks? She used to write in spiral notebooks. There were lots of them." He could see the cutout paintings and paper-covered cardboard Catherine glued on the covers, each one different.

"I don't know." Wills looked alarmed, as though something were expected but he did not know what.

"Why wouldn't you talk to Mother's friend Charlotte?" J. J. pushed on.

"I always talked to Charlotte. Charlotte. She was real nice." Wills smiled sweetly and patted Ginger on the leg. "Sugar, you're so pretty."

"Daddy, can't you come in from somewhere and react to this news? Are you stunned to hear that what we always assumed is not true?"

"I'm tuckered out. Ring for a drink, will you, sugar? Scotch and soda. Jigger of gin."

"You can have some juice, if you want." Ginger gave up. She washed her face in Wills's bathroom. "Cold water, J. J. Splash your face and cool off. If the news reached him, I can't tell. When was the last time he helped with anything?"

"You'd have to go on one of your archaeological expeditions to find that fact."

A tiny man on a cane opened the door. "Howdy, Doc, you want to play slapjack?" His smile exposed glistening bare gums. Ginger recognized him as Gene, the desk clerk at the Oglethorpe Hotel when she was a child. He still had cornflower-blue eyes bright with life.

"No."

"So nice to see you, Gene." Ginger quickly covered her father's rudeness. "Why don't you come in and visit? We're going to love you and leave you, Daddy. J. J. wants to go fishing and I'm going to visit with Lily." She wanted to call Marco, wake him up if necessary, just to hear the timbre of his voice, ignorant of all this chaos, still thinking that they existed together just as they had three days ago.

"Hey, Dad, do you need anything? We can swing by later if you do." J. J. walked out, reaching for his keys, without waiting for an answer. Ginger kissed Wills's cheek, a gesture she had to force herself to perform. Gene took the cards out of his bathrobe pocket anyway and Wills looked interested.

"Now, Doc, when I turn up a jack, you slap it. That's all there is to it."

GINGER RETURNED TO THE HOUSE with a mission, although she didn't mention it to J. J. He obviously was in his fish-out-of-water mode, almost flailing with anger and impatience. Though the drivers of cars they passed waved, he waved to no one, just slung the car around corners, then gunned it at Island 10. She felt at least twenty kinds of tiredness. At the House, she barely closed the car door before he scratched off. "Come out to the cabin later. I'll cook some birds. *Arrivederci, Roma.*" He practically fishtailed out of the driveway. Ginger was annoyed. He always did that: he went along *together,* but at a point—and she could feel that point coming—split off on his own.

One sole of the old loafers she'd found in her closet peeled back, letting dust into her shoes. She stopped in the driveway and took them off, shook out the fine silt, and walked barefoot across the grass. *JJJJJJJJJJ,* the cicadas chattered in the oaks, *JJJJJJJJJJ.* Enough to drive a person mad. She flung a rock into a tree and the racket stopped, as though switched off. How can they make that much noise? What bow do they use across what strings? They started again. She would look them up in the old *Britannica* in the downstairs hall. When she travelled to the ruins on Crete, the cicadas were ten times as loud. There she'd had a memory of home, of these moss oaks vibrating in July heat, of herself in her yellow room, the noise sawing through her head as she pulled a comb through her wet hair, driving out thought, driving out everything but the grinding heat, and there on Crete she had felt simultaneously the yammering song of those cicadas in the acacias at Knossos drop back through time, a Greek chorus, a fricative beat to accompany the Minoan builders as they stacked mud bricks and swilled sour wine from amphoras cooled in underground rooms—*that,* she thought, archaeology never can uncover, that pitch and relent-lessness of the cicada on summer afternoons, sounding through epochs, but memory can bring back the sweat dripping down my backbone, my young face in a foxed mirror, the eyelet dress, already limp hanging on the closet door, memory can do that when the ci-cada suddenly stops then starts again, that awful vibrato, memory—for as long as it lasts—then everything is archaeology, sifting layers and layers, covering the site for the winter, uncovering and starting again. Seventeen years the cicada incubates, then bursts into, not song, but raucous noise, making up for all their years underground. Mother's hideous emergence. Could I think of this in archaeologi-cal terms? What does a wrapped mummy say about those who buried her? Ancient bodies found in peat bogs say nothing good—their heads split open by an ax, so long ago that you only could ask, not why the deed, but what sort of ax? How was the stone worked? Where was it quarried? Ancillary questions.

She opened the door to the wide hall, the round table in the middle with keys, mail, and a bunch of Lily's orange nasturtiums in the blue vase with crackled glaze made by Catherine in a college pottery class. Ginger had known that vase as long as anything, as long as she'd known the splash of light at the back of the hallway way back when she played Mother, May I? with J. J. on rainy Sun-day afternoons when she was very small. After the noon dinner, her mother went upstairs with Lily and Mama Fan to look at pattern books in Lily's room. After coffee, Big Jim napped and her daddy read the paper.

In the game, you were given an instruction by the "mother": take three giant steps, or take three butterfly twirls, or take two baby steps. The goal was the French door at the end of the hall. To progress, they had to remember to ask before twirling or jumping, *Mother, may I?* Are we always going to be asking *may I, may I?* she wondered. J. J. always won because he never forgot the mythic instruction, but Ginger, anxious to perform her cartwheel, scissors step, or three somersaults, forever went back over and over to the front-door starting line.

Big Jim's clock struck one. The appalling horror of her mother being undressed, examined. Her body the subject of ghoulish jokes. The mummy at Zagreb, she remembered, that mummy wrapped in linen strips turned out to be a young girl, perhaps from Egypt, but on the linen swaddling, when they looked closely, they found faint markings that partially unlocked the Etruscan language. Her mother, unwrapped, was found innocent of the crime of self-murder. *Mother, may I, may I take two grasshopper leaps?*

MARCO PICKED UP on the first ring. *"Cara, cara,* where are you? Should I take a plane, I could come to you tomorrow. Will you tell me now what is the problem? I know you have found something serious there." Ginger told him, emphasizing that there was nothing anyone could do, she just needed to stay through the week until, she hoped, everything would be solved, her mother safe in the ground again. It was less embarrassing than she'd thought; perhaps this event finally had inured her to something as everyday as embarrassment. Maybe now she could learn to say the word *suicide* without her tongue sticking to the roof of her mouth.

"Tell me about work, tell me everything." She wanted to hear his voice, let his voice wrap around her, his voice from a place that had nothing to do with this place, a place all its own, more humane, more beautiful. Not more beautiful, she corrected herself. He had found a baby owl, still covered with down. His sisters-in-law were feeding it soup with an eyedropper and chopping up bits of meat. The owl sat with them at dinner on the back of a chair, letting the children pet its back. The project was going well, but the heat made everyone silly. They were making up work songs with dirty words. Ginger's eyes burned and her throat went taut. She never really cried, but tears formed, spilled over. "I miss you." She tried to say it lightly but heard her voice hit a note of panic. She missed the whole world she knew because of him. "We'll talk later. More later."

In the dining room, Lily was pinning swatches of cloth to the draperies, a coral pink, a yellow cotton damask, and a hideous gold and rose stripe. "Nix that stripe, Lily. It's heavy, don't you think?" Ginger was relieved to see Lily quite put together again in a navy suit with polka-dot blouse, her glasses hanging on a beaded chain, and her hair nicely swept up in a twist. Depend on Lily to take the brunt, then roll over and move on.

"Yes, you're right. But how can I ever decide between this gorgeous pale yellow and the pure persimmon pink?" She laid larger samples on the seats of the chairs, stepping back to admire them. "Agnes would like the pink."

"Isn't this blue still fairly new?" Ginger remembered swatches from her last visit, but maybe that was in the den. Lily was always recovering, repapering, repainting, repotting. Her handbag was stuffed with color chips, bits of tile, fringe, pages torn from magazines showing bedrooms literally festooned in English chintz and foyers decorated with French bread racks and enormous turtle shells.

Let J. J. tell her. Why was she always the one? She was going to keep quiet about what Ralph had told them. She lacked the energy to handle Lily's reaction, and what if it later turned out to be false? Lily and Ginger sat down at the table, with J. J.'s empty place still set. As Tessie served chicken-fried steak and mashed potatoes, made just for Ginger, she tried to imagine Marco facing her across this table. Lily rambled on about Bonny Vinson winning a scholarship to music camp even though she faltered at high C in the high school choir, about wallpaper and the coarse tung shan material she had not chosen. Ginger was not going to bring up anything unpleasant. Enough is enough, she thought.

Lily had spent the morning at the Mill Store, which still operated, although the Mason mill was long closed. Bennie Ames had turned what had been a place to sell flawed goods and overruns into a drapery and upholstery store. She and Agnes often went together, but in times of crisis, Lily always headed there alone. Because she'd spent good childhood afternoons with Big Jim, walking behind him as he checked the women at the looms, watching the corded backs of the black men as they hoisted three-hundred-pound bales on their shoulders, and diving from the giant scale into bins of bolls, she was comforted all her life by the pure smell of flax and cotton. She liked to run fabrics through her fingers, finding the warp and weft, thinking of her mother doing the same, her closet full of flowered bolts and folded aqua linen and a dreamy green silk that Mama called "water of the Nile." Mama said, "We're fabric people, like others are Sioux people or mountain people." Her family, too, had been in the cotton business. At the Mill Store, Lily could slip closer to her parents. The shelves of watered silk and embroidered organdy, the rack of colored spools of thread, the cutting table with its precise ruler glued to the end and the *thump-thump* of the bolt unfurling across it—no trouble could accumulate there. No grotesque memory, no brutal acts, just beauty, the possibility of transforming a bed or chair, as Mama always did.

Ginger was saying something. ". . . the barn key."

"What, sugar? I'm in a heat daze today."

"I want to go look through the boxes in the barn, the boxes from our old house. You know, I never have looked at one thing from there. Not even at my character dolls or the dollhouse Daddy made for me." She stopped. She didn't mean to fall into the family habit of dissembling. "But that's not the point. What I want to see is if there are things that belonged to my mother." She wanted to search for her mother's notebooks that she'd seen mentioned in the report.

She wanted to call Charlotte Crowder, who'd thrown a fit to the sheriff.

"I don't see any point in dwelling on this ghastly situation. Just let the sheriff handle it, try to enjoy your time here without riffling through old mouldy blankets and yearbooks. Let's don't be morbid." Lily held the swatches to the light. "I think I'll order the persimmon since I have yellow in my bedroom. Do you want anything else, sugar?"

"No thanks. Good choice. I like the persimmon. I'll stay until heatstroke sets in, just a few minutes."

"The key is where it has always been, hanging on the back porch. Ask Tessie. She's out there shelling butterbeans for supper."

Tessie already had gone through a colander full. "Butterbeans, Tessie, I love them."

Two of Lily's cream-colored Lincolns, a 1950 and a 1960, were still parked in the barn. In the face of her reasoning, J. J. had given up on trying to get her to sell or junk them. When asked to do so, her explanation for keeping them was simply, "Darlin', I *loved* those cars." Ginger rather liked them, too. In high school she had a few times sneaked into the '50 one with Tony Pappas to make out in the backseat.

She opened the barn's back room door, formerly a maid's room. Though it had been several years since she'd been in here—she saw boxes of wedding gifts she had not wanted—nothing had moved: Lily's headless dress mannequin, trunks with rusted locks, softened cardboard boxes, the standing wicker cornucopias Mama Fan had used for garden parties, upholstered chairs Lily rejected, a bookcase of medical journals, house magazines Lily might someday look at again, and a mildewed four-volume history of Georgia with, Ginger knew, a large photograph of Big Jim's father with bushy eyebrows, a lugubrious mustache, and fierce, staring, daring eyes that would follow you if you propped up the book.

In the first boxes she opened, she found her tin tea sets and dollhouse furniture wrapped in newspapers, a coat of J. J.'s, and

Mama Fan's fine monogrammed sheets, which she decided she would take back to Italy with her. She went through old tax forms, deeds, and bank statements. Large white checks fell out with her mother's and father's handwriting. Pay to the order of Swan Water Company, seven dollars and 10/100. Under that, folded tablecloths and a jar of Bakelite and mother-of-pearl buttons. She poured them in her lap. She had loved the button jar as a child. She sifted her hand through them now as she had then. Her mother had sewn yellow curtains for Ginger's room and covered them with bright buttons. Who had packed up the house? The boxes had no order, no labels. She had brought no tape to reseal the cartons and, with her plundering, she caused more disorder. But who cared about this kitchen midden? It should all be burned. One box she opened was packed with baby clothes, her own batiste dresses, rompers with food stains on the front, bibs embroidered with bears and geese. Wrapped in a baby blanket, she found the family christening gown, with trailing skirt inserted with circles of lace. She put it with the sheets to take with her. Perhaps she would marry Marco, have a baby who would be baptized far from here. Where were her mother's things? Were her college textbooks thrown out, her letters and baby pictures, and those notebooks, so like the ones J. J. kept?

She saw a labeled box, different from the others, a red-striped box from Rich's in Atlanta. In her mother's familiar slanted handwriting, it was labeled *Maternity Clothes*. So, a box sealed prior to the packing of the house, and well sealed. In the cleaning of the house, it probably was stacked along with other packed boxes. Ginger split the crackling tape and shook out a rose velvet jumper and the satin blouse that went under it. Slacks with a stretch placket in front, a black dress with black grosgrain ribbon woven around the skirt. Beneath the clothes, she saw two sketch books and a notebook. Ginger breathed out a long sigh. It was a moment she knew. The moment the second step of the Etruscan staircase came clear under their brushes, they knew they'd found something major. Beneath the books she uncovered a reel of film and a few letters tied with ribbon. They were not addressed or stamped. In neat capitals on blue envelopes, each said *Catherine*. Clearly, she had found something Catherine had wanted to conceal long before her death. Conceal from whom?

She slid Catherine's secret things into a pillowcase and wrapped a sheet around it. Her mother, so long the arrow shot into the center of the back, now a mysterious presence completely open to revision. The remaining five boxes revealed little, although Ginger was happy to find her mother's recipe box, the red and white cookbook she remembered her mother consulting, and two church and garden club recipe collections from local women. She would lug these inside, too. Someday she would try homemade mayonnaise and icebox cookies. She imagined Marco working at the site, stripped down to his undershirt in the heat. What a miracle, a dig. That we find things still there after three *thousand* years, when even these boxes seem old. Ginger walked along the azalea border hoping for a cool current through the garden to the house. What if this were a thousand years from now and someone were searching for clues about Swan? The peculiar habits of a people who raised square white houses, procreated, and lived their short spans in the pine barrens of a place once called Georgia. The Etruscans called themselves *Rasenna*. Now they are only Etruscans, their own name almost lost. *Catherine*, the letters said. *Summer, 1943*, the notebook said. So, ready or not, I will see something of Catherine as she was to herself, she thought. She pushed her lead body through air that seemed to be turning solid. One foot, then another. She climbed the twenty-six steps to her room, turned on the fan, and closed the door.

J. J. SAT UNDER THE ARBOR. Everything sticks to everything, he thought. His back stuck to the back of the chair. He'd ripped off his T-shirt, so sweated through that a salt rim had formed a cloud on the back. His arms felt glued to the table, his fingers tacky on the drawing pencil, and his hair lapped to the back of his neck. The Dr

Pepper thermometer nailed to the house read 98 in the shade, heat close to 10 x 10. He might spontaneously combust, leave a grease spot in the dirt for Ginger to find when she came out later in the afternoon. No, no, no, no, nothing more for Ginger to find. He would always care for himself, primarily because he didn't want Ginger hurt again. He was drawing small shells he'd found in a sand-shelf outcropping by the clay road to the cabin. Bivalves that once breathed in sea-wet sand? Or just something dropped by a bird riding a long draft from the coast? He felt he had eaten heat. Since he'd eaten little of the feasts Tessie prepared for Ginger's nontriumphal return, why not eat heat? A plate of heat, a sack of heat, a glass of heat.

Last night in his room, after he'd spilled his guts to Ginger, he tried to sleep with a wet washcloth over his eyes. At four, he leapt from bed and stood under a cold shower, going back to bed wet. Lying on the damp sheet, he thought this must be what it was like to be unborn, eyes closed, heart pumping, turning in a salty undertow, awake but *not there,* twisting, jabbing against a soft wall, the sheet coiled like a rope down his stomach, between his legs, and he tried lying so still, willing sleep, but just as sleep approached, his whole body jerked and he was awake, floating in heat again.

He slapped gnats away from his eyes. The drawing was distorted. He ripped it in two, then from top to bottom. How long until Ginger arrived? He decided to go down to the bend. He had already placed himself, leaning back in the rowboat under the willow at the clear pool formed from an old half-washed-away beaver dam. Fish might be biting in that shoal. Trout. He would see clear through the water to the coarse sand and pebbled bottom.

LILY FOUND that she couldn't lie down for a rest. The back of her head seemed to broil on the pillow. A trapped butterfly battered against the screen. None of the Masons liked air-conditioning in a house, and usually the attic fan kept them cool enough, but today the fan sucked in hot air. She wandered into the kitchen for a glass of tea. Tessie was having one, too, half dozing and looking at a magazine. "Is Ginger still out in that hot barn?"

Tessie jumped. "She's up in her room. Had a armful of stuff. Sleeping now, I imagine." Tessie gestured to a wrinkled package. "Miss Lily, this was in the mailbox this morning. I forgot about it. It sure is a poor-looking gift."

Lily unwrapped the tissue. The envelope. Speckled with age, yellowed, the envelope had found its way back into her hands.

"What is that?" Tessie looked up.

"A note. Just a note of sympathy. Thank you, Tessie."

She took a long drink of tea, then went back to her room. Inside the envelope, she found, as she knew she would, the page torn from one of Catherine's notebooks. She, not Wills, had lifted that cold hand and laid the envelope on Catherine's other hand. A gift, a good-bye, placed partly out of shame, shame Lily still felt, because the very day of the suicide, after Tessie's friends cleaned the house, when Wills was incoherent with grief, and shock and rage, crying and cursing Catherine at the same time, finally leaving the house to look for J. J., she had tried to give Ginger a sandwich but her teeth clenched and she would only lie on the bed shaking, and when she finally slept, Lily, in a rage herself—how could that bitch do this to her brother!—had gone to Catherine's sewing room. She'd filled the wastebasket with all the loose paper on the desk, pulled the half-finished skirt from the sewing machine and torn it to pieces. She ripped off the drawings tacked around the window, scooped up the row of notebooks between bookends, sketch books, the fabric-covered boxes of letters and photographs. All this she'd piled onto a blanket and dragged to the garbage beyond the garage. *Catherine had everything.* Lily had bitten her lip hard. *She had everything I wanted and she threw it away.*

In her bedroom, Lily put the page under the inside flap of a book jacket. Who had left this? The insane person who dug up the grave? An unaccustomed streak of adrenaline coursed through her body. The violator of the grave was still free.

After her rampage through Catherine's private room, she'd moved to the bedroom, jerking armfuls of clothes from the closet and throwing them out the window on the garage side. Catherine was vain, no doubt about it. Lily had begun to lose a bit of her zeal by then, but still she made a pile and set everything on fire. A fitting end to the day. Still Wills did not come home. By the time the fire had cooled, she wondered if she, too, had gone crazy, like Catherine must have. She saw the edge of one notebook in the ashes and shoved it with her foot. Who cared about her egotistic ramblings, her drawings of doors? Mostly burned, the black book still smoked.

Because Ginger had kicked and lashed out with her fingernails when Lily tried to rouse her, Lily had spent the night in J. J.'s bed—not that she slept, not in that house where someone had committed a crime against nature. Early in the morning, she went out to the fire and picked up the last notebook, cooled now and wet with dew. The pile of ashes was almost all that remained of Catherine Mason, née Phillips, late of Vidalia, survived by destroyed children, destroyed husband. Ashes to ashes. Her at the morgue with a hole for a heart. Lily opened the book and read. There was some gibberish about how cashmere was made and goats and combing. She turned over pages of drawings of a chair. She recognized the chair at the cabin, a rough thing with steer-hide seat and leather thongs tying the rungs. Catherine had drawn it forty times, at least. Then she came to the page she tore out. She resisted Catherine always, but always there came a moment when Catherine won and Lily reluctantly loved her. As violently as she hated Catherine that day, she was moved by the poem, which she assumed Catherine had written, and moved more by thinking of Catherine at the cabin, out on the dock in white shorts and a halter printed with watermelons, looking at her art books, writing in her notebook, saying the poem aloud. Someone so alive—just gone. She'd dumped the charred notebook in the trash.

Ginger wouldn't go in the kitchen for orange juice. Lily had left a note for Wills saying she'd started to clean out Catherine's things.

The sooner they're gone, the better for you, she'd written. She'd packed an overnight bag, took Ginger, sullen and silent, out the front door, and drove her to the House, where they had to face Catherine's mother and several distant relatives.

LILY ANSWERED THE PHONE in the hall. "Miss Lily, this is Ralph Hunnicutt."

"Why, yes, Sheriff." Who knows someone found the envelope? she wondered. Should I tell him about it? No.

"I just got a call from the GBI. I wanted to let you know that the tests confirmed what I told Ginger and J. J. this morning. Their mother definitely was murdered. The agent said that at this late date, of course, there's no evidence at all as to who killed her."

Lily, stunned, repeated, "Murdered." Yes, she was murdered by herself. "Do you mean *again?* She was murdered *again?*" What was he talking about?

"No, ma'am." Was he not speaking the king's English? "The first time. The death. She was murdered by someone."

Silence.

"As I explained this morning . . ." Shit, they hadn't told her. "I'm sorry, Miss Lily, but J. J. and Ginger can explain everything. They must have been too upset to tell you yet. It wasn't definite," he added.

Lily held the phone without saying anything, then hung up. She went back to the kitchen. Tessie was ironing her aprons. "That was the sheriff. He said that Catherine did not kill herself, she was murdered. The GBI said so." She sat down and lighted a cigarette.

"Sweet Jesus. Is this good news or bad? I think it's good but depending on who shot her it's bad." Tessie's iron sizzled a black triangle onto the white apron. "Lord have mercy on us." Who? she thought but did not say. She carried with her the image of that kitchen she and her two friends had scrubbed down. Wiping up blood with the sponge mop, squeezing it out in the sink, the steaming-hot water swirling with blood and soap. She'd thrown out those rolled logs of Catherine's peanut butter cookies in the refrigerator, too. Who'd want to bake them with her dead? Now they were saying murder. Her friend Rosa had speculated about that while they cleaned that day, but she'd told her to hush. It couldn't be Dr. Mason, but—but who else? "What do you think, Miss Lily?"

"I think I want to tear my hair out." But instead, she put her head in her hands and cried. "A murder case. At least the suicide was . . . oh, contained. Now everyone will gossip for years." She could not bear the prospect. Wills would be drawn into this, a crime of passion? The idea of suicide flashed across Lily's mind, a handful of pills, an obliterating blast, like Catherine. But no, not now. We all can forget her suicide as something infectious that might spread.

"Can't J. J. hush it up?" Tessie asked. "Mr. Big Jim sure could. Mr. Big Jim, he called the shots around these parts."

"Those days are gone." Lily felt a surprising surge of hatred for Big Jim. "Where *is* J. J.?"

"He hightailed it to the woods, same as always."

Lily heaved herself up. Lily loved Wills. With all her strength, she said, "Tessie, please tell Ginger that I know. I'm going out to the Columns to visit my poor brother. Let me take him some of those butterbeans. He'll enjoy them so much."

It would have been nice if'n J. J. was here to drive her, Tessie thought, but she said nothing. A hundred times her husband had told her not to mind Mason business. *You don't have a dog in that fight,* he'd remind her.

HOLT WAITED UNTIL ELEANOR NODDED OFF. They'd had a cold lunch at her house after their drive around Swan. She was settling down after her shocking experience, but the reappearance of Catherine had stirred up memories of her husband's death. She kept bringing up details of his illness until Holt Junior suggested that when something unpleasant occurred to her, she might instead search for a moment of happiness. She'd then had a nice lunch, telling him about the drive they took up the California coast when Holt Junior was six. She'd warmed to the subject of baby seals for rather a long time. Now she was comfortable in her husband's easy chair with her feet up on the ottoman.

Holt tipped out without disturbing her and drove to his cottage opposite the high school, where he served as principal. He never tired of looking at the U-shaped rose-brick school with many small-paned windows. From the first class he took there in the ninth grade, he'd felt just right among the airy rooms and the oiled heart-pine hallways. He liked the students, the well-brought-up, sassy town girls and the earnest boys in from the surrounding farms. His teachers pleased him, too, with the exception of one drinker who sipped vile vodka and milk from a flask while trying to conjugate Latin verbs. Swan High won state one-act play competitions, debate matches, and track meets. The choir placed every year in the regionals, and he thanked Muffy Starns for holding practice three afternoons a week. The same Board of Education was voted in every three years, all friends of Holt, so the school ran with harmony. On a wall of his office hung photographs of retired teachers, including both of his parents, looking young and vibrant.

From his breakfast room window, he glanced at the school. Living so close, he kept the building under his protection. He found it a pleasure to walk across the street to work, then to go home at noon for a sandwich and a quick nap.

In truth, Catherine's reappearance had stirred memories for him, too. He had once encountered her in a situation almost as shocking for them both as Eleanor's graveside nightmare must have been. But no, he mused, I exaggerate. Nevertheless, he'd had an illusion of a successful secret life until that encounter. A moment of change arrives and you want to go behind it, make another turn, take another road, but there it is, the marker known as before and after. He replayed the small slice of time all the intervening years had not dimmed or edited, the scenes always current.

In the parking lot of Miss Bibba's Dine and Dance on the outskirts of Macon, a hundred miles from home and not a likely place for either him or Catherine to be, he'd pulled over under the billboards, the darkest edge of the lot, and slouched down. The doors of Miss Bibba's swung open and he saw a woman come out with a man about her own height, a man with medals shining on his navy pilot's uniform. As they came nearer, he recognized Catherine Mason. He caught the man's profile. Even now he would recognize that straight nose, unbridged, coming down sharply from his forehead, the sensual big lips. The way they walked in step suggested intimacy, not just a casual evening between friends. They were close, smiling, and Holt saw the man brush his lips through her hair. How curious: In memory, he saw this in black and white. Wills was off serving his air force time in North Carolina, his medical unit waiting for emergency relief orders to Europe.

Holt stretched his legs under the table. His knee sounded like a rusty zipper opening. He'd been 4F because of his football injury. He opened a beer and walked to the living room. Because he never bothered to accumulate much, his house stayed neat. Eleanor had seen to the selection of furniture and duly had things hauled away when they became too grotty.

He wished the memory ended there. They'd laughed their laugh, had their fling, that's that. He tried to conjure Catherine's face—a small dimple in the middle of her chin, pale skin, yes, she had curly hair—but he couldn't see her clearly; years had erased the whole image. He remembered better an air of, not disdain, but aloofness. J. J. must have gotten a double gene for that. She'd lived for thirteen more years, Wills building his reputation in Swan, Catherine growing all those roses. Children, trips, the whole thing—before the suicide. Who knows what goes on between people? They seemed among the blessed. But Holt always wondered if the suicide had something to do with the sharp-looking officer with the full lips. If the memory ended there, Holt thought, life would have been simpler. But the moment, instead of slipping away, exploded.

What luck. Catherine and her man were parked next to his car. As the man opened the door for her, she glanced Holt's way. At that exact moment in their fates, Lucy Waters, rushing out the side door of Bibba's, an enormous smile of anticipation lighting her face, reached Holt's car, her hand out to open the door. Catherine took in at one glance Holt's startled face. She looked at him, then at Lucy. Lucy's faltering voice quavered, "Oh, hey," over the top of the car. The navy man stepped back, quick and wary, as Catherine and Holt locked eyes. Holt saw the confusion in hers. They both were caught. Then she raised her shoulders, adjusted her coat, slid into the car, and they drove away.

As far as he knew, Catherine never told anyone that he was seeing Lucy. If she had, Holt would not be looking out at the double white door of the high school, where he loved his job as principal. Far more heinous a crime than Catherine's wartime fling, the scandal of Holt Whitefield seen at midnight in the far corner of a parking lot beside a sleazy supper club, seen slouched in the front seat, waiting for the light-skinned eighteen-year-old, niece of Hattie, recently hired to work in the kitchen at Bibba's, to peel onions and potatoes as her mother and grandmother had done for years in Swan white folks' kitchens, that scandal would be reverberating yet in the annals of Swan. *Domino, domino.* If anyone had known, if it ever came out that he'd paid her rent on the apartment over a garage in colored town in Macon, that he drove in late, out early . . .

Often when he watched the girls' gymnastic classes, he thought of Lucy's gracile body. He could write a book, if he were so inclined, about first seeing her helping her Aunt Hattie in the kitchen when his mother was having a party. He'd come in from college. She was laughing, her head thrown back, and she stopped as he came in. How narrow she was, built thin as a pencil, with, he thought, such capable-looking hands. Of course, he noted her skin, dusky, like a pale person standing in deep shadow. In another time, he thought, she would have been a dancer. In another time, we could have walked down Corfu Street together, but not in this lifetime.

Two weeks later he had seen Catherine at a wedding reception. They took cups of punch off the same serving tray and Catherine raised hers and toasted him, saying no more than what a beautiful bride Camille Stevenson was. Neither of them ever mentioned the night in Macon. We run on what's not said, he thought, at least in Swan we do. For all the talk, talk, talk we do, the crucial subjects are swallowed without a sound.

Holt had kept no pictures of Lucy. If he were run down by a watermelon truck, he didn't want his mother to find that face among his effects. Because he had crossed the color barrier, he never could separate his cultural fear and self-censorship from his feelings for Lucy. Even his memories were cauterized. For her part, she had been terrified. Finally, it was she who broke away, moved to Washington, D.C., and found a job with a political family. She never married either. If he ventured a casual "How's Lucy doing?" to Hattie, all she ever gave him was, "She's doing fine up there in the North, just fine."

Once at 3:00 A.M. he'd answered the phone to hear a heavy breather. At first he feared someone had found out about Lucy, but the voice finally said, "You should be ashamed teaching young people when you're queer as a two-dollar bill," and hung up. Let them think queer, let them think anything, but not the real truth.

THE BLINDS WERE CLOSED in Wills's room. In the dim blue TV light, he stared at the game show without looking up when Lily came in holding a covered dish. "Are you all right?" She kissed him on the forehead. He nodded but didn't look her way. She thought she'd come to comfort her brother, but, she realized, she needed comfort herself. "It's hot out there. You're lucky to be in such a cool spot." She sat down beside him and took off her shoes. The air conditioner blew directly on her legs. Together they watched. She was grateful for the idiotic buzzes and shrieks from the contestants. She could rest awhile, quiet, her hand on her brother's arm, and forget the chaos at the House. She could close her eyes and imagine that she and Wills, young again, sat in his old room listening to *The Lone Ranger* on the radio. She glanced at him. Lord, he was handsome then, best-looking boy in Georgia. Who was this old stump?

Lily drove slowly home. She thought she must have worn ruts in the road, so many times had she gone back and forth to the Columns. All of Swan languished in the afternoon heat. The gardens, lush in June, were beginning to fade, the hydrangeas visibly shriveling, the hibiscuses dropping buds before they bloomed. Tessie watered Lily's pots of trailing yellow nasturtiums twice a day, but they looked puny by three o'clock.

In backyards all over town, children ran in and out of sprinklers and pushed each other down on the wet grass. The luckier ones had talked their mothers into loading the car with friends and driving out to Lake T. For years the town pool had been closed because of segregation, and the nearest place to swim was ten miles away, where from the anchored raft, you could dive deep enough to find a layer of cold water. The mothers sat in brightly painted metal chairs under the pines, talking and dispensing change for ice cream sandwiches and Paydays.

The one-legged postmaster, Ollie Fowler, drove slowly with the window down, collecting mail dropped in the five boxes around Swan. Back at the post office he sat behind the pulled-down grates and sorted the thirty or so letters going out of town. Father Tyson, he saw, had written to the bishop again. Mildly curious, he held up the envelope to the light and made out the words *be of service*. The marble post office, closed for the afternoon, smelled of dust and brass spittoons and glue.

Eleanor, napping in her chair, woke up suddenly. Holt Junior had left. She would bake something special for him. He seemed distracted. A lemon pound cake that he loved. Later she'd drop it by his house on the way to her hair appointment with Ronnie, followed by a manicure and pedicure—she could no longer reach her toes— with his wife, Tina. She dreaded and anticipated the talk about the Masons.

Several teenagers drank milk shakes at the Sacred Pig. One was Francie Lachlan, daughter of the mayor, who had a head of blond curls the angels would envy. She was tanned after a month at Carrie's Island and wore a tight orange top which stopped above her waist, revealing just how delectable a young body could be. Her father called the boys who were always around her "flies." He had plenty to worry about—Francie was wild about Richard Rooker, who set up pins in the adjacent bowling alley. Wrong side of the tracks and full of testosterone.

Swan's tobacco warehouses rivaled the hottest places on earth.

The sun bore down on the corrugated tin roofs, reflecting shimmering waves of light that could be seen from Mars. In the lighted doors at either end floated gilded particles of dust from the pungent, drying leaves stacked in long rows. For an instant you could think you were walking into a temple where gold swirled, a magic chamber where the unintelligible, musical cry of the auctioneer could herald a miracle. But a few steps inside, a biting, parched, sour stink burned your nose and cut into your lungs, the heat clamped down onto your head like a hawk onto prey. Absurdly, the auctioneers smoked. All afternoon farmers hauled in pallets for tomorrow's auction. Buyers down from North Carolina cigarette factories moved in droves across the street to Scott's store for cold drinks. Usually, they upended the first one, then drank the second one slowly. Twelve teaspoons of sugar, twenty-four. Mindy and Scott kept the coolers full and still ran out every day. They stocked plenty of ice in the freezer, though, and Mindy popped open bottles while Scott poured. Mindy liked the men. They flirted and asked her to go juking, but she knew they were all married, and just laughed. Every night she was hoping to see J. J.'s Jaguar pull up in front of her house.

The streets of Swan, once brick, but now paved over, softened, going back to their liquid petroleum origins deep in the earth's core. A small girl, running to a neighbor's house to play dolls, was half across the street before she felt the bubbling tar blistering her bare feet.

Rosemary Tyson sat at her dining room table writing, *Dear Daddy, I was thinking of you this morning, how you polished my patent-leather shoes with Vaseline before Sunday School when I was little. Remember?* When the weather turned cool, he could visit. They would take walks and come back to the kitchen and drink coffee together and eat oatmeal cookie sandwiches with sweetened cream cheese inside. If her husband had passed by, he might have noticed her lovely neck reflected in the mirror. With her hair up and her head bent over her letter, the mirror caught the creamy light falling on her. He might have leaned over to kiss that delicate curve and felt a surge of happiness from her beauty. He might have whispered, *I'm sorry.*

All down Central on the island parks, just-hatched chicks rolled in the dirt and pecked under the palm trees. Years ago a local poultry farm experimented with raising a type of Burmese chicken, an exotic rust-colored bird with fluffy legs and a blue crown. When they refused to fatten for the frying pan, they were simply released. No one foresaw how quickly they could multiply. Some people liked their plumage or presence—what town other than Swan boasted of such wildlife? Sick of chasing them from their tomato patches and flower beds, both Billie and Margaret Alice set out poisoned corn. The birds even migrated downtown, where they perched on the edge of the Oasis fountain.

The three sisters finished scrubbing down the counters. Four o'clock. Time to go home. They packed a grocery bag for supper, ham and potato salad they would enjoy with a pitcher of tea on the screened porch while they worked on crossword puzzles in the long twilight. Among the three of them, they could finish the dailies easily and even the Sunday ones in twenty minutes. By nine they'd be talking softly, listening to the crickets. They drove home, harmonizing "In the Sweet Bye and Bye." Martha pointed to high clouds blowing in from the east, possibly a squall over the Atlantic, moving in, bringing relief.

GINGER LEFT A NOTE for Lily propped on the dining room table. *We're reeling from the latest news from Ralph and know you are too. Sorry I didn't tell you. I think I'll spend the night at the cabin and leave you to a peaceful evening.* She hoped Lily would sit on the porch with her needlepoint, complete a few more stitches toward her lifetime project of twelve chair bottoms. Maybe she would take one of her pink pills that helped her sleep.

Ginger opened all four doors of the rented car; it would have to air out before she could touch the steering wheel. Because the House was sited on a rise, she could see across corn and cotton fields to the west. Already farmers were plowing under spent crops, sending dust into billows that faceted the beams of sunset, striating the sky lurid flamingo and purple. She took the long loop to the cabin, around Swan, passing the turnoff to the woods where Jefferson Davis finally was captured by the 1st Wisconsin and the 4th Michigan cavalries, who immortalized themselves in southern history by approaching from different directions and firing on each other. *What can you expect, damn fool Yankees?* She drove through the old-growth pines, calming herself with the scent. Will there be a third drama, one every decade or two, pulling me limb from limb, from wherever I have managed to go? she wondered. Maybe this is my path of enlightenment. Five acts with long intermissions. Just when I thought there was nothing more my parents could do to me. In the front of her mind still jangled the sound of the telephone as she sorted her boxes of stones in Monte Sant'Egidio. Ralph's call. *Squillare,* "to ring" in Italian, the shrill squeal built right into the word. Only now were the subsequent events beginning to swamp that first trauma of his gentle voice.

All afternoon at the House, she'd looked at the sketch books her mother had packed and sealed with her maternity dresses, the clothes she'd worn when pregnant with Ginger. If she lived to be a famous archaeologist, a discoverer of the Etruscans' origins or a lost city, lost continent, the *Argo,* anything, no discovery ever would mean more to her than today's. Yesterday existed, then today. Yesterday she did not know about them, and now they would be cherished. Out of long habit, she tried to attenuate her reaction. Just wait, she kept whispering. Wait for J. J. But she had sat cross-legged on her bed, turning the pages, gazing on each pencil drawing, each word in the margins, *cardinal, aquamarine, charcoal,* and *paint a wall with a green circle.* Her mother, she discovered, was a list maker:

Goals: research French antique roses
check into beach rental for July
Mother's recipes—Lane Cake, Wills's Nut Cake,
    Besta's Lemon Pie, her brown sugar muffins
call Charlotte about pastels
hedge along back?
bias tape—yellow, black

Bits of fabric were glued onto the pages beside drawings of sundresses and evening capes. She listed words she must have liked: *susurrous, prelapsarian.* Ginger had no idea what they meant, and then easier ones, *fluvial, dithyrambic.* She experienced waves of pleasure, recognizing a younger Tessie, hand on hip, drawn in colored pencils, the dining room window in their house with vines around the edges, her father's profile, the House seen from a distance, several pages of roses (not so well done), her mother's friend Charlotte in some costume with a plumed hat.

Looking, she recaptured her real mother, not just the mother from her official registry of memories. The last page of the first sketch book would be her joy. In the year of Ginger's birth, Catherine had drawn a self-portrait, quite pregnant, in profile. The face, smiling—there, the tiny gap between her front teeth—is turned to the viewer, and inside the silhouette of the orange maternity dress, she sketched the coiled baby. The baby who was Ginger.

The second sketch book, she knew, would become a treasure for J. J. She would give it to him and see his face as he looked at page after page of drawings of himself from the week of his birth until his twenty-third month, when Ginger was born. J. J. in Big Jim's arms. J. J. in a basket. J. J. in a high chair with his arms over his head. J. J. on a pony. A gift, a tremendous gift of love, a bliss, not mixed with the article about Catherine in the paper, the constant blaming from Lily, the corpse, the blankness of the father, but actual pages, pristine love, drawn out of fascination with the little boy who was Catherine's firstborn child, her son. The last page had her name, Virginia Mason, lettered in red, with her birth date. Underneath, Catherine sketched J. J. holding the new baby.

Ginger had closed the book and fallen back on her pillows to sleep. A door had slammed shut downstairs, jerking her awake with the sudden feeling, on that day, of reaching for the handle of the screen door into her mother's kitchen. But it was only Tessie.

SHE PASSED THE OUTSKIRTS OF SWAN, low brick liquor stores, the drive-in theater, and the road to the mill, then hit the open road through virgin timber, wavy up ahead, with black-water swamps on either side. Beside her on the front seat were the sketch books, the film, the notebook, the packet of letters she would share with J. J.

Music on the radio, sky growing more spectacular by the second, the images of the sketch books flashing in her mind, the new knowledge, scary and liberating—all enjambed, sending a rush of excitement through her body. She felt good. *Dithyrambic* was one of her mother's margin words, yes. A turkey buzzard—hideous creature—swooped down to feed on roadkill. She hit the horn and slowed, then as she sped up, she reached over to push back the sketch books on the seat.

In the moment she looked down, a pulpwood truck passing another oncoming truck pulled out into her lane, the chrome grille magnifying, heading straight at her. She slammed on the brake and swerved off the road, held on to the steering wheel as she careened along a ditch, humped over gullies, slashed through saw palmettos, and stopped. The truck pulled over down the road, and the driver jumped out. When he saw her get out of the car, saw that she had not rolled down an embankment and broken her neck, that she had not landed in six feet of swamp water and drowned, he simply waved and jumped back in his truck. She ran to the road shouting, "Stop, wait, you son of a bitch, stop!" But he already was inching his load of pine trees back onto the road. "Bastard," she shouted. "You stupid hick idiot." He drove on, tossing out a can. "You . . . What an asshole jerk."

She again felt the truck roaring toward her. She would have been instantly dead if that logjam had jammed her. The red flag on the longest log flapped in the wind, grew smaller, disappeared. J. J. would have been summoned by the State Patrol. *I'm afraid there's been an accident.* He never would have left the woods after that. Marco, *Marco.* Lily, Tessie. Doomsday, just like the signs nailed on trees always said. Day of reckoning. God, damn, damn, damn. She stamped in the road. Wouldn't that just round it out, her own luck as bad as her mother's, her father's. The sketch books would have burned and J. J. never would have known. J. J. would have buried her and her mother at the same time. She tried to swallow her rage but turned and beat her fists on the hood. Shaking all over, she let out a scream that spiraled into the air, hanging there after she closed her mouth. Life is too accidental, I can't take it. J. J. would have been lost. One moment "Moon River" on the radio, the next oblivion. She sat down against the car and thought she'd like to strangle that idiot with a wire. Slowly, until his eyes popped. She closed her eyes. In the complete silence, she could feel her heart about to explode, hear the blood rasping in her ears. The road was empty. There was nothing to do but get back in the car.

The Pontiac wheels spun in the sandy soil but torqued and the car spurted back onto the road. As though nothing had happened.

I saved myself, Ginger thought.

J. J. HAD CAUGHT THREE TROUT. He was standing at the sink cleaning them when he saw Ginger round the white curve and stop. She arrived at the cabin at that late hour of the evening when the languescent river darkened to green-black satin, shimmed with gold. A faint mist rose from the water, staining the air blue under the trees.

The water looked miraculously joyous and beautiful after her scare down to the bones. Her father used to imitate Paul Robeson singing "Ol' Man River" as he put away the boat and tackle. Keeps on rolling. She stood and stared. The ebullience she felt earlier returned. Her rented stone farmhouse by the stream in Italy existed in a floating soap bubble, which might land miraculously without bursting. She imagined Marco standing behind her, her back along his body, his arms around her. What would he say?

"Hey, gal baby." J. J. was rinsing his fishy hands. His two-day beard shadowed his face. "What's all that?"

"I am bearing gifts. I am a sorceress who grants wishes. A conjure woman with voodoo to ward off gypsies, grave robbers, and family hexes. Also, I am returned from the dead. J. J., I was almost smeared into the pavement like a jackrabbit." She described what happened.

"Did you get his plate number, or the company?"

"No, I was about to ram head-on into trees. The ass looked back like a goofball and drove on. The truck was green like all the trees they're destroying."

J. J. was, after all, Big Jim's grandson. There were not that many pulpwood crews. Tomorrow J. J. would track the driver down. They were probably culling Mason land; he seemed to remember selling off rights. It would be the last time the bastard pulled a stunt like that. His boss would chew him up and spit him out. "Chivalry is dead."

"No joke. Are we having grilled trout?"

"Yes, but first we are going to swim. We're going to wash away all your fear."

"I'm fine, really. I want to tell you about what I found in the barn."

"A chapter for *The Secret in the Old Barn?*" He rolled a dish towel and snapped it at her.

"You write it, Mr. Faulkner. What happened to all Mother's things, do you suppose?"

"Sands of time."

AFTER DINNER, Ginger sat J. J. down on the sofa and just handed him the sketch books. She wanted him to look at them alone. "I'm going to take a bath. Then there's more I haven't looked at. Is that old movie projector still here?"

"Yeah, I can find it." He rubbed his rough face. Usually, you see your fate from behind, much later, not speeding toward you like a turpentine truck, he thought. The sketch books leaned against his chest. Volatile oil, he knew, flash point. But after what Ralph told them, he was ready, finally, to look at the past.

GINGER CAME BACK in a pair of cotton pajamas that smelled fusty. They'd been damp and dried many times in her bottom drawer.

J. J. looked up at her. "This is amazing. I can't say how amazing. This is what *I* do." He gestured to the margin words, the drawing of three walnuts on a piece of flowered fabric. "Like mine. Mother's process—like mine, or mine so like hers. I never knew that I absorbed her daily practice by osmosis when I was nine, eleven. You think she read like I do, fell onto a book and didn't look up until the last line?" He remembered her notebooks sticking out the top of her handbag or lying on the backseat of the car. He remembered her room under the eaves of the house painted in wide blue stripes. But he must have pored over her drawings, he must have been allowed. The pages and pages of his baby face and the pregnant profile with the nascent Ginger—he could say nothing. He looked up at Ginger leaning over his shoulder. "I was one ugly white child."

"You look very jolly. I bet you were a good, good *bambino*."

In his life that stopped the day Catherine died, shunted off, and resumed on different terms later, nothing had picked him up by the back of the neck like this. "Gin, I don't think I can take in anything else for a while. Let's go out on the dock."

She put her arm around his shoulder. "Southern nights, give me a southern night anytime. Nothing like it on God's green Ping-Pong ball. Smell the honeysuckle? Connects me directly—do not pass Go—to my first kiss out on one of these county roads with Tony Pappas in his father's fruit truck. He picked a sprig and put it behind my ear, then kissed me with his luscious Greek lips. He smelled like lemons."

"A defining moment, no doubt. He implanted you with the desire to meet foreign men."

"He was born in Swan. Daddy delivered him."

"Still." The Pappas family always would be *the Greeks* in Swan.

"J. J., do you feel that we got Mother back?"

"We did." J. J. hauled up a net. Earlier, he'd lowered a watermelon into the cool current. He split a side with his pocketknife, then pulled it open with his hands. He and Ginger only ate the heart. "Your favorite taste, after Pappas lips." He handed her a chunk. They rinsed their hands in the river, then leaned on the pilings, looking up at the Milky Way, a broad sweep of pavé diamonds.

"It looks like a sequined train on the bride of heaven's dress. If you look in the same place for eleven minutes, you'll see a falling star, guaranteed." She didn't mention Monte Sant'Egidio, where on San Lorenzo's day in August everyone came out together, walking in the hills on the night of the shooting stars, and the stars seemed intimate, maybe because they were associated with a particular saint. They're his largesse, his fireworks for his friends below. Here the barbed stars tore holes in the sky.

"If I look in the same place for twenty minutes, my neck will snap." J. J. lay back on the dock. "I come down here all the time. Just visiting with the stars, nice and immense, keeps me out of trouble. Lying here, you can unhook, drift. Let's go back."

J. J. set up the projector on the sofa table and Ginger hung a white sheet over the fireplace. The brittle film broke as soon as the reel turned. J. J. wound several turns around the reel and started again. For seconds, nothing, then trees and sky slid onto the screen. A white building they recognized as the Marshes Hotel at Carrie's Island.

"But who is that man?" Ginger wondered. Coming down the steps laughing, a man in a white suit, his face shaded by the tropical garden palms. The film cut to a fair, the World's Fair in New York, shiny exhibit booths and in the distance the New York skyline. Then Catherine came on, the film fluttery. She wore a large straw hat which she held in a breeze. She sat on the porch railing of a yellow house, and beside her a swing moved back and forth. Someone had just risen. The camera panned to the right, a white door, then swung back, closer to Catherine. Ginger and J. J. watched her young face break into a smile. She raised her hand and waved her palm back and forth, a little wave like the queen gives when passing in a motorcade. The screen went blank, flashed a moment of a cocker spaniel with his tongue out, then the film flew off the reel.

"When we were little, I don't think I knew how pretty she was. She was just Mother." Ginger was dazzled by the smile, the *soft* look of her face.

"I knew." He rewound and played the film again. "Odd that this is one of the things she sealed in the box. I don't think it was because of the World's Fair. She must have wanted to keep the shots of the man at Carrie's Island. Or herself at that moment, wherever she was."

J. J. poured Ginger some orange juice and himself a glass of Scotch.

"They both were laughing."

The five letters, undated, were from someone named Austin. They were a mixture of quite desperate and poetic love letters and descriptions of his travels. Apparently, he was a navy pilot who lived outside Macon. He thought of her in Philadelphia, he missed her in New York, he longed for her back at the farm, where there was a new foal he named Cathy. He wanted her the previous night on the terrace when the half moon rose and the band played "How High the Moon" and everyone was dancing. *Somewhere there's music, Cath, it's where you are.*

"What a romancer. Listen to this. *When I think of how I most want to spend my days, you are all I see. Catherine morning, Catherine noon, Catherine night.*"

"Looks like she was having an affair."

"Why do you think that? I don't see any dates. He must have been pre-Daddy."

Then Ginger opened the notebook. "Shall I read? The first sentence says, *I write in purple today, like the menus in Paris.* She never went to Paris." Ginger paged through. Quotes, doodles, drawings, and poems were interspersed with a few pages of written diary entries. She and J. J. faced each other from opposite ends of the sofa, her knees up, his feet on the coffee table, just as they'd sat for all the years they'd taken turns reading the Sunday funnies or books about the Creek Indians, *The Swiss Family Robinson*, the discovery of Troy, and *Green Mansions*.

The House has many cool big rooms. Floors smooth to the foot have been waxed and walked on and waxed until they shine like water. The screen doors bang in the afternoons when the rain gusts. When the rain starts, I jump up from my nap, from the wide bed of thick old sheets edged with crochet intricate as filigree, and run all over the house latching doors. The house is old and melancholy—smells of Big Jim's hair oil, cloves, the toast Lily burns every morning, and something dense— Florence's fruitcakes soaked in bourbon? The sofa cushions give off the heavy scent of Lily's Shalimar. I'd like to fling open all the windows and let the rain lash in. Big Jim hates staying in bed, hates being dependent on Florence, Lily, and me. He squeezes my hand and looks up mournfully from bed like a faithful bird dog locked in a pen. In his illness, he has turned sweet. I guess he was always courageous—he stared down the strikers and beat down the union. How many times have I heard that story? Visitors come and go. I spell Lily and Florence every afternoon so they can go to their bridge clubs. The baby sleeps and I write to Wills or lie down in the room where we've set up a crib. I open a drawer in this farthest bedroom and pick up an engraved yellowed card inviting me to a christening that took place sixty-four years ago. Just underneath is a photograph of that same baby, Big Jim's dead brother, Calhoun, at thirty or so, already balding and paunchy. He's long gone with the wind and rain. I can't help but balk. Feel the cutting scissors of Time, capital T.

The liquor cabinet in the sideboard has a box of nightclub swizzle sticks from the thirties. The Bartender's Guide, published in '28, tells me how to make a Biffy, a Barking Dog, Mississippi Mule, and a Diki-Diki. But we drink only gin. I take Big Jim a big glass with lime every afternoon as the day starts to grate on his nerves, when he has nothing to do but wait for supper. Of course, he's not supposed to have alcohol after a heart attack but who can tell him anything? In the sideboard drawer, *a stack of old photos. In them the now abundant garden—Florence keeps planting plumbago this year—wild with tangled vines and tumbling roses and a patch of nettles that erupt my skin—becomes almost bare—orderly, clipped, planted, and edged—a background for the young wife Mary holding one, then two boys, Big Jim—James then— and Calhoun. Mary is skinnier and more serious with each child. She died young. A row of trees along the wall is now gone. Time. Mary, that whole family—dead except for Big Jim. But in the photo, Mary smiles at someone, me, she never knew. Someone who uses her hand-painted platters and monogrammed towels and recipes.*

It's as if I fall through trapdoors, into old books and clippings, letters. Mary, John, and the two heirs apparent wish you a Merry Christmas before you were born. The boys, Big Jim and Calhoun, with straight arms and knee socks. A husband who likes his Yorkshire pudding and bubble-and-squeak too much. The last photos in the drawer are newer; black and white instead of brown and white with ripple-cut edges. Florence and Big Jim at Manatee Springs, pushing off in a boat. Ah, once he travelled with her! And the two of them gazing down through the water—what were they thinking? (What to think of the hulking bodies of those almost-lost manatees roaming deep-black water?) Lily and Florence in Bermuda on a pink beach, Lily in an awful woolly bathing suit. Lily in college, Wills leaning against a car, me, my arms around Florence and Big Jim. Weddings. Faces, smiling into the future, full of life, looking trustfully at the camera—and at me in the closed dining room, looking for a cocktail napkin for a sick man. Oh, here we are.

"Look, she's drawn a glass full of swizzle sticks. You got your love of writing from her, too." Ginger passed J. J. the notebook. "J. J.— we never knew anything."

"Pretty cool. I like what she wrote. It's good. Keep on."

Big Jim worsened. Wills got leave. Now Big Jim has revived. I admire him although I know he can be mean as a snake—and that he always runs around with other women. Lily thinks he will ascend into heaven to sit on the right hand of J.C. Wills could stay only four days. In uniform he seems older. The serious war in his face. When he appears in a doorway, I always feel an expansion. A light. He likes the dining room since I painted the walls bright peach. The word he used was flamingo. Am I as real to him as a rock or wave or storm or bread? I'm going over to the House less. The baby has a rash. Lily comes for supper often but does not offer to take the baby for a walk or to stay during the day. She is lost but does not know it. She thinks the sun rises and sets for the House. I will take Baby with me to Macon.

At home again I talk to my notebook. A. L. His last gift was a pearl pendant in the shape of two crescent moons back-to-back. Baby and I go to the cabin. I love the humidity, the afternoon rain in sheets, and the passionate creeks. I run errands for Florence. We've started to call her Mama Fan for Baby. She does not like "grandmother," "grammy"—names for the old. Big Jim wants this or that. Wants to boss. I go to the office, too, and settle orders, meet payroll for him. I—or Lily—could run the mill. Florence resents him but keeps the stiff upper lip. Stiff everything. The House full of fits and starts. Many silences.

Big Jim sits on the porch in a rocker. He is allowed to walk around the yard, to the corner and back. He uses a cane. "To beat the women away," he brags. Charlotte is coming for the day. I miss her. We really talk. Chicken salad with pecans.

Wills's letters are all about the camp—the rumors, the wounded flown back from abroad. Blown-off faces and legs.

Our life in Swan seems too remote to comment on. Wills, all present tense, like all the Mason men I've heard about. Yesterday is as over as the Wars of the Roses. People like that eternally renew, empty, renew. I am adored when I am present. A dis-ease the doctor cannot cure. Does he have pangs for us? Or is it business at hand? I am fascinated by this, envious, scornful. These people are too terrible, righteous as angels. They live in a flat world when clearly it is round and turning.

The leopard has come back to my dreams. I lie along his muscled back, my mouth against the hot fur. He has been running. I don't move because I'm afraid to wake him. Who is this? I am afraid to wake up.

My face in his hand felt like a cat's. I am restless. Sometimes afraid. But of what? Sometimes the repairman at the door is a strangler in green. But it's only sullen Clovis with his little sullen Sonny, sent by Big Jim to fix the fence. I can't make them smile and don't try. Big Jim's men worship or hate. The pearl crescents lie back-to-back on their bed of cotton. My favorite moon, the thinnest crescent. Wills may spot the waning gibbous from the officers' barracks tonight, lifting over the line of planes on the runway ready to go. The pearl crescents. Like two people in bed not sleeping.

Beneath love, inside sex, the climax like sheet lightning, the cry of the body flying away.

"That's steamy." Ginger looked up. "What do you make of this?"
Clovis, he thought, one of Big Jim's men who used to fix things. "Let's wait to talk. There's something she's not saying."

Like the alligators sunk up to their eyeballs, I lower myself into the cool river every afternoon. Baby likes to be dunked. He shrieks and smiles.

"Hey, you liked the river even then. Little J. J. baby, baptized by the waters. Here's a drawing of a baby foot—yours."

Leftovers, scraps, crumbs.

I won't be one of the broken. Keep right, keep the rules, don't walk on the grass, don't tread on me. If you leave the sheaf on the rib, the removed bone grows back. If the sheaf is stripped, no renewal . . . Baby crying. He's good and is beginning to want to skip his morning nap.

Took the baby to see Mother. I never knew her grandmother was named Sarah America Gray. I like each part of that name. A tiny girl named America.

If I come to you, it will only be to borrow a cup of salt.

"Am I missing something? Could you open the back door? There's not a puff of air coming in the windows. A cup of salt? This is pretty elliptical."

J. J. didn't think so. "Well, there's sadness. A cup of salt is not something you would borrow, so it's about tears. See, it's like a poem in one line. That's a big *if* she starts with." He recognized the method. A way to hide. He had many. Even if you don't think anyone will read your notebooks, you write, not what you meant, but what reminds you of what you meant.

"Not much left." Ginger flicked through the pages. Blue, purple, black, crimson, dark green inks. She had a faint memory of reaching for small bottles on the desk and hearing *no*. As she read, she felt a spreading sorrow for her mother—obviously full of ideas and art—stuck in Swan, a war going on far away, no husband, annoying in-laws. She remembered long headache days, when her mother would not get up. Were those migraines like J. J.'s, or was she depressed? This she thought over but tactfully did not voice, since J. J., too, was, by her lights, stuck in Swan. She wondered if he saw it that way. "I always felt sorry for *us*. Mostly mad at her. Too unable to understand how that act could come out of all our lives. Now she is not a suicide; she didn't throw that blanket over our heads. Finding the sketch books, even the strange notebook—seems like this whole ordeal is a labyrinth."

"It is a labyrinth."

"You know I went to Crete last year. I was studying Knossos. The cicadas blared like maniacs and I stumbled through the ruins in hundred-degree heat. I didn't see any real labyrinth for the bull, just an added-onto, stacked, sprawled house of a thousand rooms that anyone could get lost in. Still, I love the story of Icarus flying out of there on wax wings. The moral we've been spoon-fed is 'don't fly too close to the sun,' but the real moral must be 'attach wings to your back and fly.' I like to imagine him soaring out over the island."

J. J. lifted his glass of Scotch. "Here's to Icarus, who drowned in the sea."

"Even if we don't solve every single mystery from our family, I think we have a whole history to rewrite. Mother's tragedy—ours— is shifting, turning inside out. And at least we've had all these years in the light: hers went dark so soon."

J. J. had been gripped by every word in the notebook, ever since he heard *here we are*. He felt with every word what Catherine meant. "And here's to Mother, Gin," he added in a low voice. "She was something. We don't have any idea how much silence there was between one page and the next."

"Here's the rest."

My days should be natural, like drawing a bath. Oh, to be natural. Can I be baked by the sun, moved by the wind, washed by the rain? Should I keep bees? In early morning light they are gold sparks. So many in the catalpa—they purr.

A rose the color of a massive bruise.

Big thunder. The kind that loosens the fillings of your teeth! Tree frogs and roving clouds. Hollyhocks and Queen Anne's lace keep Baby and me company at the table. I hope my life will use all of me.

Lily green. Lampblack. Almond green. Comb of light.

Segments, particles, patches, splinters, remnants.

The gift pearls are gone. When I last opened the box, the gleam of a galaxy streaked out. Hammer this home. I am as real as bread or moss. Soon my baby will quicken. The avalanche of life force begins, sending us all forward into a new world. Wills's world. When he comes marching home. Austin's world. Blown roses. Baby's world. His toes in the river. Little X in the flux of the womb. Swimmer. Mine. The color wheel, spinning fast.

She, Allegra, Alexandra, Miss X, she, the soles of her feet smaller than grains of rice. She's in the hidden envelope at the bottom of the drawer. Little thorn. Little almond. Little finger. The briar rose.

"That means she's pregnant with me?"
"I'd say so."

It's true—I am going to have a baby. Already it has gill slits, a primitive tiny blob of a creature who will become someone. How ordinary to have a baby—to squat in the fields, drop the child, and keep on picking. But what a miracle. I have to think—this is my baby. I didn't tell Mother. Will only tell myself for now.

country captain chicken
tarragon green beans

brown sugar muffins
butterscotch pie

"What an ending. I wish we had some." Ginger closed the notebook and slid it onto the coffee table. Neither of them spoke. A
green lizard squeezed under the window screen and darted sideways across the fireplace stones. "Do you know it's two-thirty?"

"Austin. The big romancer. Do you think the pearl gift was from
him? I don't remember any pearl crescents among her jewelry."

"Must have been." J. J. wanted to read the journal to himself. As
Ginger had read, he was flashing on the unsaid. The *tone* of secrecy.
The past was stripping down, like those clear overlays you peel back
to reveal muscle, then circulation, then bone. Was his mother pregnant by Austin?

Late, as Ginger slept, J. J. sat at the kitchen table with the notebook, the same table where years ago Catherine sat writing late at
night, a cricket creeping across the floor, the kitchen quiet, the
washed dishes draining by the sink. The notebook made his mother
live. He was again beside her in church when her gold beads broke,
rolling out of reach on the floor, the choir screeching "Jerusalem."
Memory, he thought, cuts and comes again. He sees the half-moons
of sweat under her arms, Ginger squirming, Dad's hands on his
knees, solid as a sphinx. We all rise. Young again. The benediction.
The scent of his bay lime cologne and the fetid water of the church
flowers, then, soon after, we clamor for the wishbone, ask what's for
dessert. Back to our coloring books, he thought, connecting the
dots. The finished pictures never had resembled what was intended. He still saw the constellation of dots. He opened his own
notebook. *River on Fire,* he wrote on the last blank page in the book.

GINGER, wide-eyed in the night, started going over every resem-
blance to her father ever mentioned. She was sure J. J. had picked
up the dropped crumbs through the forest but neither of them

could absorb the possibility quickly enough to talk about it. Their lifetime habits of mutual protection stalled them even now, after the knockout shocks of the week. Usually, she heard that she was the spitting image of her mother and, turning the pillow over to its cool side, she remembered, *this is my baby* in the notebook. She had her mother's rather thin lips and the same expressive shoulder gestures. But she had Wills's square fingernails and flat tight butt— surely those were identifying genes. She and J. J. called him "sackbutt," among other attempts to render him harmless. She imagined her profile in the mirror, her rear a bare curve. She ran her forefingers around her thumbnails. I'll have to look at J. J.'s nails tomorrow. Her hair, pale silky red, had come from nowhere. Big Jim, Florence, Lily with hair the color of steel wool, Catherine's parents—all dark. J. J. with hair black as a crow. There must have been an ancestor, perhaps that Sarah America Gray, with her hair. How many more questions could arise?

Along with blunt shock ran a current of joy. She kept thinking of the word *redeem*. To redeem, meaning "to take back, to buy back." We paid. We will not, she tried to form the words, have the cicatrix *suicide* carved across our faces. We need not have practiced jungle survival for all those years, learning to make sun hats from palmetto fronds, drinking by touching our tongues to the ends of wet pine needles. Out of the staggering, stupefying horror of what happened, J. J. had found out that the deepest part of him came directly from his mother. He was, she thought, saved. Mother had managed to hand him her finest heirlooms. Was there something she handed me? Ginger, who never cried, began to cry, turning her face into the pillow. She gave in to a sense of release, complicated now, but whatever came next, her mother was freed from suicide, free to love her in the past. *My* baby. The knowledge of her mother that Ginger had as a child was true.

A few days before Catherine's death she had been sewing a circle skirt printed with sombreros. Ginger had sat cross-legged on the daybed, playing with her character dolls, probably the last day she'd ever opened the shoe box and taken out the Polish twins with their red, rickrack-trimmed skirts, their velvet ribbons, and their black aprons over their skirts. Catherine had pressed hard on the pedal and zoomed along the seams. Ginger still could feel the hard bodies of the two dolls she'd dressed, see the unnatural orangy tint of their faces and their empty eyes. Really, she'd preferred the Dutch twins.

This speck of memory—something to hold. She had been simply with her mother on a quiet afternoon at home. While she'd read the notebook aloud, she had glanced now and then at J. J., frowning slightly, looking into the fireplace or at his feet. He was so concentrated that he appeared to be in a trance.

Ginger flung back the sheet and went into the kitchen. J. J. jumped, dropped the notebook. "You remember the recipe for that grainy fudge? Want to make some?"

July 11

MAYHEW, always up early, saw the article in the paper and took it into the bedroom. "Charily, Charily, wake up. This is something." She swam up from a dream of driving a race car, skirting the edge of an abyss, woke to see Mayhew leaning over her. Irrationally, she thought he looked like a boiled pig, then she focused, saw dear Mayhew, and reached for her glasses.

SPECIAL FROM *THE SWAN FLYOVER*

BY RAINEY GROVER

TWIST OF EVENTS IN SWAN CEMETERY CASE

SWAN, GEORGIA—GBI investigator Gray Hinckle and J. E. B. Stuart County Sheriff Ralph Hunnicutt, investigating the recent exhumation of a body buried for nineteen years in Swan, Georgia, have come to the extraordinary conclusion that the original cause of death, previously presumed to be suicide, was murder. The alert officer and Swan sheriff concluded that because of the entrance angle of the bullet wound near the woman's heart, she could not have pulled the trigger of the .22-caliber automatic rifle found next to her body. Other advanced forensic techniques have supported their theory. The body is that of Catherine Phillips Mason, wife of Dr. Wills Mason, long a resident of Swan. Her disheveled body was discovered beside her grave in the family plot by her sister-in-law, Lillian Mason, and Mrs. Eleanor Whitefield, neither of whom were available for comment. Sheriff Ralph Hunnicutt says his office is pursuing all leads and he expects to capture the culprits. When asked about the unexpected turn of events, he said it is too soon to comment.

Charlotte leapt out of bed. "God Almighty, Jesus, Joseph, and Mary, this is hideous. But, Mayhew, I've waited nineteen years to read that! I *knew* Catherine would not commit suicide. Remember, I *knew*. She just would not."

"Well, it's pretty strange that someone would kill her, then years later someone *else* would dig her up. Would you say the two might be related?"

"But how, who, *who*? I never thought that anyone who knew her was involved in her death. Who knows? It's absurd. Someone broke in, broke in both times; that's the only answer."

"If it's two random crimes, I say she had shit for luck." Mayhew smoothed back her hair hard, as if he were petting a dog. "Try to keep your head screwed on." He knew she'd be spinning way out over this news.

CHARLOTTE DIALED O. "Operator, may I have information in Swan, the number for Lillian Mason?" But what would she say to Lily after all these years? Those Masons squelched the investigation because they were ashamed. Charlotte never liked Lily, wanted, in fact, to kick her in the pants. So proprietary. So controlling. A saint, though, to raise those children.

"Well, I can give you that number, honey, but I can tell you Lily is not home 'cause I just saw her drive off from the drugstore with Eleanor Whitefield."

"Thank you, I'll try calling later." Charlotte shrieked, "Gawd that town!" If Catherine hadn't married into that poky fiefdom. If she had chosen Austin. Charlotte pulled out the Macon phone book. Austin. Austin Larkin. His thin blue letters had arrived at the dorm daily. She could still see a stack on Catherine's dresser in their dorm room, held down with an ivory-backed mirror. Catherine lying back in bed with a textbook on her chest, kicking her legs in the air. "He says I should float down the Nile on a flower-covered barge." Catherine lined the window ledge with conch shells and amethyst geodes and ambrotypes of nineteenth-century children—all gifts he pulled from his pockets on the weekends. When she came back from that Thanksgiving wearing Wills's square emerald ring, Austin had backed down the dorm steps shaking his head. Never said a word. As far as Charlotte knew, Catherine never heard from him again, except for the event of the roses. One winter afternoon, he flew his tiny plane low over the campus, scattering roses for Catherine, thousands of roses.

Charlotte wondered if he still lived somewhere near. Despite whatever had happened in his life, he'd want to know that Catherine had not killed herself. Charlotte was sure of that. He'd been brought up forty-five minutes away, in Stonefield. She called the operator; no Larkin was listed. She would go there and try to find him. Austin, what a hunk. "Hubba hubba," Catherine used to say. Could she paint roses falling out of the sky? She had not seen them fall, only the quad after he flew over, strewn with petals, buds, full-blown blooms. To each stem was tied a thread with a small white flag attached. In black calligraphy, *CRP* was written on each. Rose—Catherine's middle name. Catherine had picked up only one. It was as if she picked up a bolt of lightning, Charlotte thought. She could see the bloodred rose against Catherine's pink angora sweater. In memory, the moments form so oddly, she thought, like a swan sculpted in ice floating in my bloodstream.

AILEEN WAS OUT EARLY. She had to drive over to Tipton to the Singer store because her last needle had snapped off. She needed more tiny pearl buttons and some ready-made tatting for edging the baby blankets of her less particular customers.

A sign on the door said *Back in fifteen minutes.* Since she didn't know when the fifteen minutes had started, she walked across the street to the Main Street Café to have coffee and wait. Someone had left the Macon paper on the table. As she slid into the booth, the story on Catherine Mason jumped off the page at her.

Not a suicide.

She read the article twice, ignoring the waitress who poured her coffee. When she tried to pick up the cup, it rattled against the saucer. She put both shaking hands on her lap and pretended to blow the hot coffee. Across the street, a woman was unlocking the Singer store. But what could now raise her from her seat and send her among the buttons and zippers?

The information in the paper, she feared, was the truth, even though she'd told herself a different version ever since Catherine Mason died. That day, when news of the death had flown through the mill village, she had been completely relieved to hear that Catherine was dead by suicide, not by murder. She'd been desperately afraid at first that Sonny had tried to rape her and then killed her. He'd often railed on about Big Jim deserving for *his* family women to get fucked, tortured. He said he'd stick knives up them and see how horny Big Jim felt then. Sonny was *always* blowing up, but Aileen was scared of him. He'd gone into details that made her fear he'd do those things to her. But Catherine's death had been simply suicide. No evidence to the contrary. No torn-up house. The sheriff knew how Catherine died, she'd thought. The sheriff could tell by how she was found, what gun was fired. They said she was holding the gun. Who knew what she was going through? Maybe her own husband screwed around. The sheriff knew those things. Sonny, she'd quickly concluded, didn't do it; he simply left, the way he said he was going to.

Aileen always felt that she walked with Sonny's shadow covering her. The preacher might explain that as her knowledge of her own sins, but Aileen never had told the preacher—or anyone, not even her sister. At work, when she'd looked at the office door, she was afraid Sonny's pointed face and fish eyes would appear in the glass. His violence would sometimes scare her during sex with Big Jim at the motel. Even when she could take her time for the luxury of a shower afterward, she feared he might burst in and rip back the curtain. Sonny could find them. Alone at home, she had dreamed over and over that he was breathing outside the door.

After Big Jim up and died, even a branch scratching against the window made Aileen gasp. Then one morning, Sonny had appeared at her door, opened the screen, and walked in. All her fears during his four-year absence suddenly took the form of his real shape. It was as if his raid on the office were continuing. She was terrified by his bushy white run-together eyebrows, the distant look in his eyes. By then Big Jim was dead a year, the wife was dead, too. But Sonny, just out of the army, had come home still ranting about revenge. He yanked her hair back and spit in her face. "You pussy bitch. You stinking whore. He's dead but he deserves to be drawn and quartered. *His* father fucked my grandmother. Who do they think they are? You're not worth killing. But I'm going to get that family, all of them, those sorry motherfuckers. That puffed-up doctor, I'll see how he likes somebody doing his woman."

Out of fear, she lied. "It was never how you thought. Big Jim wanted me but I *didn't*. Those things you found were because he was trying to get me. You never trusted me, ever. Now he's dead. And we're divorced, for God's sake. You were dead wrong. Leave me alone. Forget it." She wanted to kick and spit at him but remained still and controlled.

Sonny sat down. To hear the name Big Jim still enraged him. He banged his fist on the kitchen table. He looked at her, wide-eyed, grinding his teeth. He slung his arm across the table, sweeping the jelly and salt and pepper onto the floor.

"Please. Go. Please leave, go. Leave those people alone—they never did anything to you. It's over, he's dead." She put her head on the table and cried.

He laughed. His eyes darted and he blinked over and over. His top lip raised like a dog about to snarl. Suddenly he slammed out of the house "Okay. Okay. You win, you slut. I'm going out West to Arizona, and you're not ever going to see me again." He said it like a threat, emphasizing each word. He jabbed the air with his middle finger.

Aileen breathed out. To placate him, she said, "Well, I hope your life goes better now. I never meant you no harm." She rubbed her head where he'd pulled her braid. She closed the door and slid the bolt. She wished he were dead. She imagined slashing him with the turkey knife.

A month later, the night when she'd heard of Catherine Mason's suicide, she got in the car and drove forty miles to her sister's. Sometimes in the years after that, she'd imagined Catherine Mason wondering what had brought Sonny, a millworker who was sometimes sent there for repairs, to her door. Aileen imagined his attack, Catherine grabbing a gun, and Sonny turning it on her and firing, pausing only to arrange the gun in her hand while her life dripped out on the floor. But Catherine was a suicide. Sonny was long gone. Over time, her memory of Sonny receded. She began to leave her doors unlocked, like everyone else in Swan. She had not seen him since that day—nineteen years. After that long, can something still fester? Had he done this trick at the cemetery? Her mind would not stop whirling. Remembering his vacant eyes, she would not put it past him.

Aileen glanced at her face in the window's reflection. "I'm plain gaunt," she said to herself. When her face and lips had been kissed and kissed by Big Jim, she looked full and rosy in the motel mirror. Twenty years had sculpted her so that now her high cheekbones stuck out, concaving her face. Her lips looked pinched. I look like I suck lemons, she thought. Her hair remained thick and lustrous. She managed to sip the coffee, managed to light a cigarette and blow out smoke toward her own face in the glass. She looked at herself again. Her eyes looked wild. She saw a fox face, something on the edge of the woods with shining eyes—she could be Sonny's twin.

She decided she would just drive on over to her sister's in Tyler. She would have to figure out how she could go to the sheriff, Hunnicutt's grandson. She knew she should, but should, would, could, blended together in her mind. Could she think of how not to tell the whole story? She did not want her carefully hidden life to be more shamefully exposed than Catherine Mason's rotten body. And Big Jim, the bank president, mayor, owner of the mill. She would just wait and see what came to light.

Her sister, a widow now, would be glad for her company. They could make blue plum jelly, and Jeannie could help her sew. She could buy the few things she needed. If Sonny paid a visit to the mill village, there'd be no one for him to hit. Then she thought of the other Mason women—if Sonny was that crazy. But she didn't really believe he had come back after all these years. Maybe she *would* talk to someone. She liked the preacher in her sister's Primitive Baptist church. He spoke the gospel while looking at the sky, then would lower his head and bear down on the congregation with burning eyes. Aileen liked his unruly brown curls and the ropy cords in his neck. She imagined sweeping her hair over his sinless body. Last time she heard him, she'd gone to the verge of feeling saved.

I'll go, she thought. I'll get up from this booth and go. She left the newspaper on the table, Catherine Mason's photo faceup for the next reader. She walked across the street and bought the lace and pearl buttons she needed.

RALPH'S PHONE AT HOME and at the office would not stop ringing. With the news hitting the morning papers, reporters from all over the state and as far away as Tallahassee and Mobile kept calling for information. Gray, with backup from the GBI staff, was conducting his own investigation. He'd walked out of the Columns after interviewing Wills convinced he had nothing to do with the exhumation. "Old fart could barely brush his teeth. Now, whether he pulled the trigger years ago, we're just not going to find out unless something breaks open from an unexpected quarter," Gray said. Ralph had combed the cemetery and had found no letter. Nothing. Gray had asked him to check up on J. J. Embarrassed that he would have to phone and ask J. J. where he was last week, he stopped in Scott's store to verify their fishing trip to St. Clare's.

Scott was wiping down the sweating sides of the ice cream freezer. He was hoping J. J. would stop in to go over some orders he wanted to make. "Yes," he told Ralph, "we chartered a boat down there, fishing for marlin." Scott gave him names and numbers, without mentioning that he'd slept on deck both nights because J. J. picked up a twenty-year-old girl named Gay Nix at the tackle shop, and they were rocking the cabin. That was nobody's bidness. A big girl, who'd brought on board a sack of fried catfish and hushpuppies from her mama's fish fry stand next to her daddy's tackle and bait place. She'd kept up a shrieking laugh, and Scott had concentrated on the slap of waves against the bow. Usually, J. J. didn't spin off like that on their trips. Had to be mighty hard up to go after that big-kneed gal. Far as he knew, she never asked them their names. J. J. kept calling her Sunshine. No need to tell the sheriff any of that.

Somebody down in St. Clare's was mounting two fish they'd caught. Scott showed Ralph the receipt. Plenty of contacts. A relief. Ralph had no reason not to believe him, but for God's sake somebody had to have dug up that body and maybe it was J. J. and this loyal buck. He didn't want to be like his grandfather, who let the Masons slide by. He had to admit, however, that no motive presented itself, aside from pure craziness. Whatever he was, J. J. was not one drop crazy.

Mindy up at the register cut her eyes at Ralph. He is cute, plenty cute, she thought. That slash of scar all down his arm is from Vietnam. Who was it said he'd been left for dead and had to walk at night through war zones to get back to his troop?

Ralph picked up a bottle of Dr Pepper and some peanuts. "Well, Miss Mindy, how's everything?" She wore a scoop-necked lavender T-shirt and he gazed down the great divide between her pushed-up breasts. She saw his look and reached to pin her hair, the gesture of raising her arms lifting her breasts. Ralph pulled on his earlobe and looked down at the change on the counter.

"I'm just fine and dandy, Ralph."

"You sure are. Hey, you want to go out to the Shack tomorrow night? They've got a band." He hadn't danced in years. This Mason mess made him want to hit balls, run, dance, fuck, drive fast. Anything to remind him that the world was not going crazy again. He looked into her pert face. She wouldn't have any idea about war or the horror of corpses. Ever since the war he'd been amazed by people's innocence. He looked over at the rows of dish soap and detergent to block the sudden vision of Tommy Melton crawling beside him one moment, his head blown to bits the next, blood spurting from what had been his neck, his face like a run-over cantaloupe in the mud. Mindy's old husband, Holy Roller now, with one leg two inches shorter than the other, never got drafted, like so many others—like J. J., come to think of it. Some said Mason contacts had fixed that, but Ralph didn't see how he could, with the military offices way over in Dannon.

"Let me see if my sister will keep my little girl. I think she will. You know where I live—the sea-foam-colored house in the mill village." She kept looking right into his eyes. He imagined rolling that T-shirt right off, the explosion of her flesh into his hands.

"Mindy," he said. "What's that short for?"

"Just Mindy. Mindy Marie." She would wear her low-cut white eyelet that buttoned up the front. With her Saturday paycheck, she'd buy those fuchsia sandals with wedge heels in the window of Buster's Shoes. She liked his square teeth and his golden chest hair in the V of his shirt. She hoped he didn't have furry hair on his back like her ex-husband. Who would wait around for J. J. Mason to turn up? Not her. "Mama named me after her mama, Sugar Marie, and her granny, Mindy Lou."

"That's right nice. And much better than 'Sugar Lou.' Although, come to think of it, that's a good name, too. Around eight tomorrow?"

He is damn cute, Mindy thought. Sugar Lou, who would have thought of that?

RAINEY GROVER PUSHED BACK HER CHAIR from her desk at *The Swan Flyover*. The famous doctor's diet promised that she wouldn't feel hungry between meals, but her stomach was roaring, as if it were trying to digest itself. After two weeks of starvation, she hadn't lost but one pound. She'd expected five by now, hoped for eight. She opened a drawer and took out a package of cheese crackers with peanut butter, 125 calories apiece. She closed her eyes and ate one of the little sandwiches slowly, throwing the rest in the wastebasket. She had forty pounds to lose. At the conservative estimate according to the diet book, she would be down to her slinky best by February. Immediately, she wished she had not eaten the poisonous-looking orange crackers spread with evil peanut butter. At lunch she would skip the allowed piece of fruit.

She'd spent the morning calling people she met last March at the newspaper conference in Atlanta. She was bone-sure that no Mason had disrupted a grave. When, since the fabled Big Jim, had they ever shown enough energy for such an exploit? Her husband, Johnny, agreed. She wanted to be the investigative force for the case. That Lily or Wills could engineer a grave-opening was ludicrous. J. J.? But why? And besides, he was off fishing, playing the nature boy as usual, with that muscle-bound black stud who worked for him. J. J.—Swan's answer to Tarzan. Only Ginger was on the move, and she went from pillar to post, without ever settling on anything. The news that their mother didn't shoot herself must have rocked them all the way back to the cradle. When her own mother simply died of sugar diabetes, Rainey had been outraged. For years she half expected her mother to call or write.

Her colleagues scattered around Georgia were wildly curious about the case in Swan but had nothing to add, no similar activities in their towns. "Must be Martians," the editor of *The Cleveland Ledger* said. "I wish something exciting would happen here," others lamented. Rainey walked over to the long windows looking out onto the sidewalk and Main Street. Passing clouds reflected on the glass. Cliff Bryant, walking his two spaniels, Stevie and Clarkie, made her smile. His own doggish muzzle made him look as though he, too, might yap instead of speak. Agnes Burkhart, who with her cropped hair and laced, square-heeled shoes looked as though she'd been picked up by the wind from a street in old Europe and set down in Swan, came out of the drugstore with a little bag, probably medication for her sister's fits. Francie Lachlan slammed on brakes and got out of her new yellow convertible with three boys. Pied Piper of, where? Hamlin? Watch out, Francie, she thought. Rainey had been the honeypot of her day, though she'd never had the pleasure of a daddy who bribed good behavior with fancy wheels.

Such a normal day. Cusetta Fletcher, new-rich in town, swaggered into the furniture store. She waved to Bunky, her neighbor, who caught her eye as she drove by. The slow flow of cars seemed to move through a dream. Rainey loved Swan. All her life it had seemed the best place on earth to live. Even as a girl, she'd felt she never could leave. She liked working downtown with Johnny, her desk looking out at the Oasis, the noon walk over to the Three Sisters, where she picked up most of her news. She even liked the tentacular gossip, rampant in any place where no news is no news.

She looked at her watch. Another hour until her carrot, chicken soup, and small salad. The sisters would commiserate as they plunked their coconut pies onto the sideboard. She pushed in the basketball bulge of her stomach, despising herself for fantasizing a slice of that tall, creamy pie sliding onto a plate. Now she and Johnny never made love with her on top. Too tactful to say so, he felt squished, she knew, when not many years ago, Johnny could span her waist with his fingers.

J. J. SLEPT IN, for once. It was almost nine by the time he lowered himself into the river. Four turtles, one a pretty substantial snapping turtle, sunned on a log the current had wedged against the dock. They regarded him without interest. He would let Ginger sleep as late as she could. She'd polished off the fudge at five in the morning. When she got up, they would call Charlotte Crowder in Macon. He'd already called Scott and found out that green pulpwood trucks belonged to Tall Pine Company thirty miles down the road in Flanders. That was the company to whom J. J. had sold cutting rights. He'd called Andy Foster to let him know he'd never get another tree from J. E. B. Stuart County unless they dealt with the bastard who almost ran down his sister yesterday. "Squirrelly little guy, we just hired him last week. I'll sure see about it," Andy Foster told him.

J. J. swam out to the sandbar and back, then lay flat back on the dock, his feet in the water, and looked at the sundogs and rainbows between his wet eyelashes until he fell asleep again under a clean sky.

STONEFIELD'S ONE AND ONLY MAIN DRAG, thought Charlotte, looked like one of those dreary WPA pictures from the Depression. Leaning, tin-roofed stores with throwback names like Bunny's Dry Goods. As opposed to wet? The wide street accommodated a sleeping hound in the middle, which the few passing cars swerved around. Now that she was here, she wasn't sure what to do. She went inside a small dime store on the corner. It smelled of stale popcorn and parakeet cages. Charlotte thought purgatory, if it existed, would be something like a dime store in a small town. Her eye was caught by the wall of embroidery threads, the skeins in figure eights silky and bright. She picked out damson, scarlet, spring green, rust. As she paid, she asked the clerk, "Do you know of a Larkin here in Stonefield?"

"I wouldn't know. I'm not from around here. I'm from Lux." Lux was all of eight miles away.

Charlotte walked down one side of the street, crossed, and started back up the other. Three codgers sat outside the barbershop, chairs tilted back, their cheeks puffed with snuff. She glimpsed a soda fountain in the drugstore. She ordered a milk shake and the boy who made it whistled, to her joy, the Academic Festival Overture. "Do you know of any Larkins in town?" she asked.

"Yes, ma'am. Mr. Austin Larkin still owns a place off the highway out east of town, but he doesn't live here. Hasn't for a hundred years. Comes back now and then. He lives out West somewheres. Place is falling apart."

"Where's his house? Is it far? I want to leave something for him." What a lie. What could she leave, skeins of thread?

"You go out to the red light"—he pointed—"then go about a mile and you'll come to two big pines. Turn in there, and the road, nothing more than a pig track now, leads up to the house."

Charlotte found the pines, with a leaning mailbox underneath. She opened it from the car window and saw only a clutch of leaves and a thick spiderweb.

Branches and palmettos slashed the sides of the car. She crept forward, the car bottom scraping, and stopped under a pecan tree. Austin's house was a sprawling two-story farmhouse with wraparound porch and a round turret. Flaking white paint revealed a yellow coat underneath, probably from a happier time. Charlotte thought those who painted their houses yellow were optimists. From an open door on the right side's lower wing, a tall black woman looked out. "Hello," Charlotte called. "I'm an old friend of Austin Larkin. Is he here?" She walked up to the woman, who held strips of willow in her hand.

"Nome. He ain't here. He done been gone a long time." She gestured Charlotte in out of the heat. The table was covered with stripped willow branches. Charlotte introduced herself and the woman responded, "I'm Edwina, living here to take care of Mr. Austin's home while he be gone out West."

"You're weaving?" Charlotte looked on the benches around the table and saw a fine egg basket and several small round ones, perfect for bread—no, for her collection of old marbles. You could dip in your hand and let them run through your fingers. "How beautiful."

"Yes'm. I pass the time. It's lonesome out here. My husband's gone all day."

"I'm sorry. At least it's peaceful." Charlotte waved her hand at the window, a neglected garden with some half-dead geraniums around a birdbath, weed trees, an overgrown field swaying with grasses and black-eyed Susans. "Do you sell them?" She lifted a basket.

"Oh, no, just give them to my chirrun. They use them for this and that. Nobody would pay good money for a little ol' basket like this." She waved a taut oval basket woven from osier. "It's just a old habit I got from my granddaddy." Her long fingers looked as supple as the willow wands she wove.

"I'd like to call Mr. Larkin. We were in college at the same time, then we lost touch. Do you have his number out West?"

"Nome, I sure don't. We don't have no phone. He just turns up here now and then. I don't think he plans on coming back home to live."

"When was he here last? Did I just miss him?"

"I reckon it was last November. He came back for some bird huntin'. Would you like a glass of tea? I made some fresh this morning."

"Why, thank you." Charlotte examined the egg basket. Her church craft fair could sell these like hotcakes at Christmas. Austin or not, she'd be back to talk to Edwina later about making three dozen of these. Would she be interested? Edwina walked like a queen, stately in her big shoes. Slowly, she poured and, as though she were transporting communion wine, set down the glass in front of Charlotte. Her two bare rooms were immaculate. Through a door she saw her bed made up without a wrinkle, the white curtains (from old flour sacks?) crisp at the window. Charlotte felt a stab of admiration for her reclusive life far in the country, the practice of an art that sprang so naturally from the ground. Weaving baskets seemed a felicitous life. She imagined Edwina gathering her materials along the wet spots where willows grew. One could rest here, she thought. Her own life crowded her head—too many people, exhibits, the children, dinners, Mayhew's business, clubs, commitments. Sometimes she felt like a monkey swinging from tree to tree. And her painting squeezed in around the edges. This egg basket with its ridge up the middle to keep the eggs from knocking against each other—what a piece of necessity and beauty. If Catherine were here, she would want to stay all afternoon and learn how Edwina worked. Sometimes she thought Catherine knew everything. But how? She sprang from a tight Protestant family, just as intent on saying no as Charlotte's family had been. *The paintings, don't they tie you to them so you never want to get away?* They had looked furiously at the Matisse book, dazzled. *So divine, they rush all the way through you.* No wonder Austin had worshiped her. Or do we project on the dead a knowledge of life unchallenged by their silence? Charlotte always wondered what she would have said, what she would have been, how they would have gone forward . . . Dead, Catherine became a never-opened safe-deposit box for the imagination.

Charlotte thanked Edwina and said she must be going. She was dying to look in the windows of the main house but waved and headed for her car. Edwina again stood in the doorway. "Wait a minute." She turned back into the dark house and emerged holding the egg basket. "Take this. I'm glad you like it. Everybody's got some eggs."

AS CHARLOTTE PASSED THE POST OFFICE SIGN, she had an inspiration. Austin would have left a forwarding address. Obtaining it turned out to be easy. She simply said she was an old friend, had been to his house looking for him, and now wanted to write. The postmistress looked in her pigeonholes, took out an envelope, and copied his address. "He doesn't get any mail anymore. He's been gone too long. I think even the tax office forgot him."

"How long has he been gone?" Charlotte glanced down: 1518 Whitman St., Palo Alto, California.

"Ah, he left during the war. He warn't a plain soldier like everybody else. He flew some big planes. Then I heard he went out near San Francisco, something else to do with airplanes. So I heard. Comes back here every so often. He's still a good-looking man."

"Thank you so much." So he'd left the South long before Catherine's death. "Oh, what did he do when he lived here? I lost touch with him after college."

"I believe he used to travel in sales, equipment for cotton mills. Then all the mills went bust 'cause of the Japanese, so I guess he made other plans."

"Thanks again." Amazing what you can find out, Charlotte thought, quite pleased with her detective work. What she would do with the information she had no idea. Regardless of the span of time, she just knew that Austin should know the news about Catherine. Maybe she would call him. No, too awkward. She would write, say she remembered him well, and since they both had loved Catherine, she wanted him to know.

Seeing Edwina made Charlotte want to get back to her studio over the garage, to sit under the skylight in front of the A-shaped window looking out at expanses of trees and a big sky. She would paint not the cunning basket filled with eggs, but Edwina herself, long and big-boned, outlined by the sun in the doorway, her eyes black as asbestos, something in her hand, something to give.

IN THE LONG SUMMER TWILIGHTS Marco walked in the fields around his archaeological site. Although the current excavation surely had more to reveal at the most conservative estimate, his guess was that the site was potentially on a vast scale. He hoped to extend funding so that he could start preliminary surveys of surrounding terrain even while his team's work continued. He wanted to begin with one group carefully walking the transects along the contours, bag whatever turned up, then pinpoint a few places for trial digs. Already Marco had picked up a few scattered sherds, probably Roman. With endless land spreading around them, it was always fascinating that the ancients built right on top of what was there before. Many local Christian churches rested on Etruscan stone foundations; below that, probably something from the earlier Umbrians. The artesian springs in this area guaranteed long habitation.

The farmer would not be pleased. A neighboring farmer last year turned up a bronze cup incised with Etruscan writing. For months he had hidden it in his hay barn but had not been able to keep quiet about it in the piazza. The police eventually made a visit and he handed it over. If Marco found funding, and the Italian ministry granted him permission, the farmer would lose his tobacco crop.

Even though he would be compensated, such invasion didn't sit right with local farmers who feared for their land becoming tourist attractions.

This particular gently terraced hillside would have been appealing in any era. Wide swaths of olive trees interspersed by rangy old grapevines stepped down to flat cultivation. Marco skirted the tobacco plants, keeping to the field's edge, where the plow had left a ridge. He walked to unkink after a day at the site and to pass time until he could meet friends for dinner. Ginger had just called him at his mother's. Midday there and she was just getting up. She told him about finding the film and her mother's drawings and notebook. She and J. J. had made candy and drunk some icy vodka, then gone in the river late at night. "Don't worry, we've done it all our lives," she had said.

He missed her. During the day he was too busy, but he missed seeing her concentrating on her work, her startled look when he called to her, her hair falling around her face until she reached back, swirled it around, and pinned it up. He'd moved two interns to the area she'd been working and half hoped they would not find anything. When she returned, she would unearth a gold bee or a pot handle with datable glaze. Mostly, he found that he wanted to reach for her. Her physical absence felt solid, almost like a presence. Her life over there in the South was another world for him. The brother sounded dangerous, a man cut off like that. He unbuttoned his shirt to catch some of the breeze. That Ginger had knocked around in San Francisco, New York, had been married, all this seemed more inert as facts than the old chronology of sequential settlements on this land. He sensed her damage. He'd known her five months before she'd made love with him. Other American girls were stepping out of their clothes after coffee in a bar. Sometimes her eyes fixed somewhere beyond him—she travelled, he thought, *over there,* or she would turn silent in a group. But he felt her slowly changing, loving her work, quick to retreat but trusting him. Over time, he thought, she would simply walk away from the past, close the book on the dark story of her parents. His love would be a light to flood her bones.

"Should I go there to Georgia?" he'd asked. She insisted that she was fine. Her voice sounded remote. She would be back soon, maybe next week. The site would be closed for August, a reprieve for him to catch up on paperwork and for the team to go off on holiday. He and Ginger could go to Elba for a few days and lie in the healing sun. This made sense, but something was gnawing at him. She was the only woman he'd ever wanted to dance with in the kitchen, the pasta water coming to a boil, steaming the windows, his old albums, Johnny Mathis, Dominico Modugno, the Platters, the big crooners, a green-checked tablecloth, a bowl of sliced tomatoes, his uncle's wine in a yellow pitcher. Laughing, speculating about the dig, Ginger licking sauce on her thumb. I haven't loved her enough, he thought. What is life but this? Choices made early in a relationship determine the course. To wait for her, as she asked, is that the right choice?

WHEN GINGER WOKE UP, J. J. remembered to show her the bone fish spear. "I found this the day before I came home and saw Scott sitting on the dock looking hangdog, the bearer of bad tidings, which he sure as hell was." Ginger sipped the scalding-hot coffee that had sat too long while she slept an exhausted sleep. He held the tiny spear. "Isn't this something?"

Ginger jumped up. Immediately, he saw the joy in her face. "Oh, *beautiful!*" She held it in the palm of her hand. "It's so precise, so gorgeous. Where did you find it?"

"Near the dock. This is the best thing I've found since that shark's tooth on the sandbar." J. J. even showed her his drawings of the spear.

Ginger knew that since sharks regrow their teeth many times, they are the fossil most frequently found from the ancient Eocene sea, though this far south, not many turned up. The pointed shark tooth sat on the mantel, almost as big as the palm of a hand. She picked it up, held it beside her jaw. "As old as it gets. Imagine him trolling that warm sea eons ago. Chomping on something finny. I find that incomprehensible, like black holes in space, and other galaxies."

"Incomprehensible that we can pick it up on a sandbar." Ginger is the only person who can travel with me, he thought, travel around an object, travel back and forth in time. "Gin, I think we should take a ride."

"Where? I know—to Charlotte Crowder. Let's call her."

CHARLOTTE'S NEIGHBORHOOD LOOKED FAMILIAR, though they barely remembered going there. J. J. recalled a Thanksgiving, when the turkey was burned outside and raw inside. Ginger remembered the Crowder children's huge white dog.

When they got out of the car, Charlotte ran to them, hugging and exclaiming. She was breathless and immediately began telling them that her cat had been caught in a mulberry tree all morning while she'd been gone, and she came home and had to climb a ladder which slipped and sent her, one hand on the cat, sliding sideways. "I am so glad to see you. We have a lot to talk about—years to talk about." She put her hand to her throat, hoping they did not hear the catch in her voice. They had not come to see her cry. She led them into her sunroom piled with books and newspapers. The cat slept soundly on the flowered cushion of a wicker rocker. "That's Jasmine, the culprit." She brought in a tray with tea and cookies. "Ginger, when you were little, you used to drink only ice water with a spoon of cane syrup in it."

"I did? I don't remember that."

"And J. J., I still have a letter you wrote me when you were seven. You asked for two books for Christmas. You said, 'Please, may I have two this year?' I remember so many things." Again her eyes smarted as she bent over the tea glasses. Parents remember the ten thousand things a child says and does. Ginger and J. J. had no one to restore the fragments of their early days to them. "How proud your mother—and your father, I must say—would be to see you! You're both fabulously beautiful and I can still see your tiny faces—both so bright—in your faces right now. Some people lose their youngest faces . . ." She realized she was starting to chatter.

J. J. told her about seeing her name in the sheriff's report. "You were the only one who doubted the suicide. We read that you insisted that he investigate. Of course, we never knew that. What did you think at the time?"

"You *know* I never thought Wills would have done something like that in a million years, but I thought *someone* had stepped into the house, picked up the gun. Maybe a robber, a gypsy, some crazed goon or half-wit. Your mother, I knew then, never would have destroyed herself and, I imagine, a hunk of your lives."

"Understatement," J. J. said.

"Your mother, if you'd like to hear, was an extraordinary person. In all my life, I never met anyone like her. I feel I've been looking for her in my friends ever since and they all come up short."

"We would like to hear," Ginger said. "We found one of her notebooks and two sketch books yesterday and read them last night. We are just getting to know her again. It's so strange, how suicide cut her off from our memories." Ginger loved looking at Charlotte. Mother's age, this is how she would be. Welcoming us in a sunny room, telling us some anecdotes about ourselves, pouring tea.

Charlotte told them about college days at GSCW, their passions for art nouveau, modern dance, clothes, and clay soul jugs. Catherine, they learned, had collected folk pottery. She told them about Catherine's toast-colored coat with a lynx collar, which made her face look wild and fresh. "Sophomore year," she told them, "Catherine was elected the Kappa Alpha Rose at Emory. She wore a sleek white evening dress and was serenaded by the entire fraternity dressed to kill in Confederate uniforms. Your daddy, a glamorous med student, was her date. She snowed him." The cat woke up and climbed onto Charlotte's lap. "Oh, and Catherine was a daddy's girl. That man doted on her, spoiled her, your grandmother thought." She wondered how she could convey what it was like to spend a simple hour in Catherine's company.

J. J. picked up the egg basket from the coffee table. He held it up for Ginger to see. "Look, this is real fine." Ginger leaned to him and together they looked intently as J. J. slowly turned the basket. Charlotte saw the look of familiar connection that passed between them. That rare, wordless bond that spoke more clearly than words. As she saw this, she felt less sad. They had lost so much of their mother, lost so much of their own childhoods. And Wills's downfall, what an H-bomb that must have been. But irrefutably Ginger and J. J. had each other. Who knows, the choice relationship of their lives. And maybe it would not have been so if their parents had been able to raise them. She wondered if they ever had realized that. Something taken, but something given.

Charlotte heard Mayhew come into the kitchen. He peered in the sunroom. "I'll be damned. I am so glad to see you children—of course you're not children." He embraced them and clapped his hands. "You're staying for dinner. I insist. I've got steaks to throw on the grill and Charlotte is a master of the baked potato." He disappeared into the pantry.

Charlotte heard herself launch into the awkward subject. "There was someone else—Austin Larkin, who went to Tech—mad for her. This may seem like a myth or a dream, but once he flew over the campus and scattered thousands of roses for Catherine. This was right after her engagement to Wills our sophomore year. I always wondered if Austin overwhelmed her, while Wills seemed more like someone to build a life around."

"Austin," Ginger faltered. "What a fabulous, fabulous gesture. I'd run away with anyone who scattered roses from an airplane for me." Marco, she thought, he's that tender, too. Ginger rubbed her lapis ring over her lips. A flash of insight hit her. Marco was *her* inheritance from her mother, maybe she now could let herself have a big love. She smiled at Charlotte.

How lovely she is, Charlotte thought. That silky hair and natural, sort of bony elegance. Ginger saw the admiration in Charlotte's eyes and felt expansive. "This Austin comes up in her notebook, which was written during the war. I wish you would read it and tell us what you think." She didn't speculate. She took the sketch books and notebook out of her bag, along with the film reel. "And this was in the box, too. Do you have a projector?"

"We do, and miles of film of the children. Let's look when it gets dark."

"We should call Lily."

"Sugar, you go up to my room and call her, and, J. J., if you would give Mayhew a hand, then I'll sit here and finish my tea and read."

From the first page of the sketch books, Charlotte was mesmerized by the prolific drawings. She grasped with firsthand knowledge Catherine's hard, joyful work. By the time she started the notebook, she was so jittery she wanted to jump out of her skin from the shock of seeing her own name, reading the chronicle of that elusive time, plunging into Catherine's delicate, reserved emotional terrain, and more, imagining J. J. and Ginger discovering the notebook lying on top of all the years of silence.

OVER DINNER, Ginger, swamped with fatigue, leaned her elbows on the table. Mayhew's steak, doused with his own Ol' Hoss sauce, was delicious, and she didn't know how much she'd missed big baked potatoes piled with sour cream, butter, and chives. She would have to make them for Marco someday, she thought distractedly, if she ever could find sour cream in Italy. Tired, she ate slowly but with her usual relish. Charlotte seemed to forget about the plate in front of her as she described trips she and Catherine made up to Tech for dances, her plans for her garden, and the antics of her three grandchildren. Gently, she asked about Wills, not knowing whether the children had conceived of him as a possible murderer, an idea hardly to be avoided now.

J. J. said, "He's like a big, bad baby in a high chair, banging his cup. It's hard to explain. Who was he back then? What was he capable of? Maybe you'd know more than we do."

Charlotte nodded. "He never . . . He saved people. I remember many times when he got up from the table to rush out to someone passing a kidney stone or someone who'd fallen off a ladder. He ignored Big Jim's business—not many men would—in order to help people." She didn't say that in her experience she'd often found that someone's strongest characteristic has an equal and opposite component. She simply did not know how far Wills could be driven. Under the wrong circumstances, couldn't almost anyone turn murderous or cruel?

Mayhew set up the projector on the end of the table, and Charlotte pulled the draperies, closing out the night gathering on the garden. Ah, there was Austin as she remembered him, against the pink oleanders at Carrie's Island, where she and Mayhew had spent many weekends with their three children. The World's Fair footage passed, then the film abruptly shifted. When the yellow house appeared on her dining room wall, she recalled immediately the peeling paint on Austin's farmhouse. "Austin's porch," she said. Mayhew looked at her, frowning. She remembered that she had not had a chance to tell him about going to Stonefield. "I'll explain in a minute." She fell silent, they all did, when Catherine loomed on the wall, filling the space between the windows, her face incandescent in slashes of sunlight.

Charlotte brought in for dessert a plate of barely thawed lemon squares, and Mayhew put on a pot of coffee. "I went to Stonefield—only this morning, seems like a week ago. She described the house and Edwina, then her inspiration to stop at the post office. "Austin lives in California, has for umpteen years, the same town as Stanford."

"You know what they say." Mayhew pushed back his chair. "God tilted America at the Rockies and everything loose rolled west."

Ginger wondered if, twenty years from now, she would have the confidence in her instinct to pick up an action on someone's behalf the way Charlotte had this morning, when she acted on her understanding of a friend from way back in college.

J. J. was admiring Charlotte, too. No logic, he thought. Plain blood knowledge.

Reading the notebook had confirmed everything Charlotte had not fully suspected. Catherine had met no mysterious stranger; she was seeing Austin during the war. But why? Charlotte knew she was devoted to Wills. Now this new, gaping question was opening before all their eyes. Mayhew and probably 99 percent of the people she knew would disagree, but Charlotte thought Austin as a father might be not so bad a discovery, considering the fate of Wills. If a family secret were brought into the light, which is surely a strong congenital abhorrence of all southerners, no matter how old or insignificant the secret, there might be an unexpected way forward.

Privately, in college she had longed for Austin herself, but since he already loved Catherine the possibility was totally unrealistic. She had hardly articulated her infatuation to herself. Senior year, she'd met Mayhew. They were instant friends, a friendship that strengthened on her part. On his, he'd been drawn to Charlotte with a migratory pull, the way sea turtles guide themselves back across the ocean toward their island of origin.

Charlotte opened her handbag and found the address the postmistress had written on a forwarding slip. She handed it to J. J., insisting that they spend the night, but Ginger said they must get back to Lily. When Ginger called from upstairs earlier, Lily was having dinner with Eleanor. Then she let it slip that Tessie had spent last night at the House. Ginger and J. J., so caught up with their own emotions, hardly had considered Lily beyond her initial shock and injured hand, nor had they thought that she might be frightened to stay alone. "I feel so guilty," Ginger said as they got in the car. "She said she and Tessie sat up in their bathrobes last night watching *Wuthering Heights*. Is there something we can take her?"

"At this time of night? A fifth of Southern Comfort? Let's think about it tomorrow, Scarlett, my dear."

"J. J., the idea of Lily and Tessie drinking cocoa in the den and watching a movie. I never thought of them like that."

"Best of friends. They just don't know it."

July 12

IN THE NIGHT GINGER WOKE UP. A fox barked in the distance, a high repetitive yap, answered by another fox. She lay awake, watching a cottony light begin to streak the windows. She heard J. J. moving around in his room. Vaguely, she heard something slide, then the shower running. Nothing on earth felt as comfortable as her bed in her room. The four pillows were right. She went from one to another for coolness. In the course of the night the two firm ones were flung to the floor, leaving the flat, down ones. She concentrated on Marco. If he were here, listening to the young foxes. If his leg weighed on her hips. If he woke up in the night and said *what are you dreaming now?* She fell asleep and when she woke again, full sun struck the mirror in her room and the house was quiet.

When Ginger trailed into the dining room, Lily was reading a magazine. The remains of a platter of scrambled eggs and bacon were still warm. Tessie brought in buttered toast. "Sugar, I was so worried. You two were away so long, and now J. J. has gone again."

"What? Where is he—the cabin?" Ginger reached for the jam.

Lily folded sections of the paper. "He left this note. I don't know where he is."

Top o' the morning, the note said. *I will be back in a couple of days.*

"That's it? I don't believe this."

"He probably went off fishing with Scott. You know he can only take so much."

"What about us?" Ginger kept staring at the note. Surely, surely not. She remembered that when Charlotte found Austin's address, J. J. had stuck it in his shirt pocket. She wanted to believe that J. J. had been hit too hard by the notebook and sketch books to run off downriver in his usual fashion now. But she found it difficult to believe otherwise, since he only left the county for occasional hunting and fishing forays, once with her former husband, Mitchell, to Nicaragua to hunt ducks, twice to a college friend's cabin in Colorado to hunt elk. Travel that involved only camouflage pants tucked into high boots. When she thought of what *she* would have done if the notebook had raised the possibility that Austin was J. J.'s father, she knew that J. J. had gone to California. He would be almost to Atlanta by now if he left around five. He'd take the first plane smoking on the runway, fly to California, and what? As the idea began to seem feasible, Ginger was thrilled. He'd gone for her. "Lily, what if we take a little jaunt, too?"

"What a good idea. Where could we go?"

"We could go visit the Culpeppers at the island, but I'd really like to drive up to Athens and talk to Professor Schmitt about my graduate work. I need to go over all the requirements with him and see how much I have left—in case I decide to finish my degree. We can spend the night at the Inn on the Park, have a nice dinner." She wanted to make amends for deserting Lily during all the fracas. She was embarrassed to see how thrilled Lily was. "You can take your needlepoint to work on, and I want to show you Mother's sketch books that I found in the barn yesterday. It seems like a miracle." She did not mention the notebook. Lily had no need to know about Austin or any of that. For her own protection, Ginger thought. And for ours. If Mother had a lover, we'd never hear the end of poor Wills in this lifetime or the next. Secrets are being revealed, she realized, but we keep folding others inside them. She sighed. There must be another way to live, but we don't know how.

Lily gathered her cup and plate. "Would you like more bacon, sugar?" She was thinking of the envelope someone had brought to the mailbox. Would she ever know who had found it at the cemetery? She thought it was not the criminal who had dug up the grave but someone she knew, someone who now knew something, not much, but knew that Catherine's hand had not held a confession. She did not want to discuss the contents with anyone, ever. And especially now that Catherine was no longer the weak suicide. The memory of her own act of arson burned her enough. When the graves were restored, she intended to take flowers to Catherine every week. Previously, she'd driven out to Magnolia with two vases on Saturdays, one for her mother and one for Big Jim. Nothing for Catherine, who had disgraced the Mason name. Lily had another idea, another way to make amends. She would give Holt Junior whatever money it took to send a local girl to college every year. He could name the scholarship after Catherine. But she would never tell about her burning of Catherine's private things. She did not want to hurt J. J. and Ginger with the knowledge of her crime against their mother. She could not stand it if they thought of her as someone who would do such a thing.

RAIN BEGAN AN HOUR OUT OF TOWN and pursued them, now sprinkling, now blinding the windshield, all the way to Athens. Ginger kept letting down the window for the black dirt scent, the waves of oak and pine spicing the steamy air, the scorched ozone smell of lightning, the dusty odor of wet fields and fertilizer. Lily looked through the sketch books without comment. Finally, Ginger asked, "What do you think? Didn't she have a gift?" Come on, Lily, she thought. Give her *something,* after all we've learned.

"Oh, I remember well. She was devoted to those books she

kept." The rage that fueled the fire that burned the notebooks, obliterating Catherine from memory, had remained the strongest emotion Lily had felt in her life up until the news that her sister-in-law was not a suicide. All the years of vitriol and indignation she'd felt. What a waste. All the poisonous remarks she'd made because she thought Catherine had destroyed her brother. "What we are capable of, we never can gauge," she said cryptically.

Ginger drove. *Capable,* she thought. What a nice, solid word. It must come from *capere.* To hold. If you're capable, you hold on to something. I want to think of myself as capable. I have to take charge. I was the screw-up who couldn't get downstairs for my wedding. The temp in San Francisco living in a studio I barely could stand up in, dating another screw-up who worked as a bicycle messenger after graduating from college. The mole in the basement apartment in New York, trudging to the insurance office like a drudge, calling in sick so many days that they fired me without paying my final check. All the bad attempts at romance and sex. See Jane run. Run, Jane, run. What floundering, what a colossal waste.

During the past two days, as their turn of fate sank in, Ginger had begun to have an inkling of herself as someone with a mother to admire. Catherine would have been like Charlotte, vital, connected, warm. She would have developed in fascinating directions. So what if she had a love affair? She was passionate. Perhaps Wills had been like her husband, Mitchell, and Austin resembled Marco. Catherine had married at twenty, far too young.

Looking back a few years, Ginger could see how wrong she had been about herself at every step. When she went to college, she refused to study out of fear of failing, even though she'd scored well on the SATs and had made straight As effortlessly in high school. Going back to school after the divorce, she saw how easy the courses had been all along. Anytime she looked though photo albums, she was shocked to see that she had been thin and pretty. She often looked awkward—a hand in motion, her eyes closed, knees too close to the camera—but pretty, definitely, when she had not felt pretty. Other girls always seemed more put together, ready to take their chances with men. When Ginger heard, "You have the most beautiful eyes I've ever seen," or "You're the most interesting girl I've ever met," she assumed southern hyperbole. She'd hardly ever noticed that although she had money to buy clothes and have her hair done, she wore the same things over and over and just let her hair hang. Luck and chance, if it had been luck and chance, finally led her to that first classroom in Athens, where Dr. Schmitt's lectures not only engaged her mind but seemed like codes for unlocking the lost secrets of the world. She loved her tiny Athens apartment with a waist-high fridge and a mattress platform on concrete blocks, a door on filing cabinets for a desk. She was in love with her textbooks and professors as she never had been in love with any man, until she went to Italy for the internship and met Marco. Propped in bed, surrounded by books, she ate saltines with mayonnaise, devouring at the same time the whole history of archaeology.

Athens, where she had lived in passive desperation with Mitchell, became a haven as soon as she was in school. She walked her landlady's dog across campus, feeling a charge from the mellow brick buildings.

As she drove into town now, she turned off on Ridge Street and pointed out to Lily the side entrance to the antebellum house where she'd lived. They had a bite in the Bide Awhile, then checked into the Inn. Dr. Schmitt agreed to meet her at his office midafternoon. Lily decided to rest while Ginger went to the university. Later she would walk to the needlepoint shop Ginger had pointed out down the street as they drove in. She'd spotted a handsome bargello pattern in the window, which would be magnificent on a wing chair.

Ginger had an hour before Dr. Schmitt would be in his office. She looped back around the university, turned down Cane Street, where she'd lived with Mitchell. Oh, glory, there he was. She stopped a hundred feet from the house and flipped down the sun visor. Mitchell was opening the door to a blue car. He looked exactly the same, except that his hair was longer and brushed back. Without a glance her way, he drove off. She exhaled, realizing that her breath had stopped while he flung his suit jacket on the backseat, closed the door, and got in the front. Ginger knew he was returning after lunch to his office downtown. Working on Saturday. How typical. At a distance, behind sunglasses and the visor, she followed him. On impulse, when he swung into his office parking lot, she followed and pulled up beside him. Still, he didn't look her way. She observed his eyes crinkle in the heat as he stepped out of the car. He reached down and pulled a weed from the sole of his shoe, his shoe polished every morning, she knew, his nails buffed, his crisp shirt unfolded from cardboard. And as he is outside, so he is inside, she knew. Clean and right. Ginger opened her door without knowing exactly why. "Mitchell, hey, Mitchell."

He looked at her blankly only for an instant, then bucked back his head in overreactive surprise. "Well, hey, Mason. Knock me over with a feather." She was the last person he expected to encounter on his way to take a Saturday deposition from a student who claimed a teacher had raped her. There Ginger was, smiling at him. Of course, he had heard from a dozen people about the exhumation and had wanted to call her and his old roommate, J. J. He had not yet summoned the courage, after not speaking to either of them in four years.

"I had to come up to see about my degree status. I decided to ride by our house. I saw you coming out."

"I've heard about your mother. My God, what in the devil do they think happened?"

"Let's get out of the sun."

Mitchell checked his watch. The deposition was scheduled in ten minutes. Let them wait. "Get in my car and I'll crank up the air. I have to go into a meeting in a minute. Maybe we could meet later?"

"Oh, I don't think so. Lily is with me." She got in the front seat. "I just wanted to say something. I'm not sure what, but something overdue. Maybe it's as simple as 'I'm sorry.' I am. I don't even know if you're married or what, or if you care to hear anything at all from me, but I've felt really terrible for you, for who I was when we were together. In hindsight—the one hundred percent clear vision of hindsight—I was a walking disaster. You didn't deserve that."

She looked to him like a child confessing a theft from her mother's handbag. "Guess what, Mason. I have figured out a lot of things over the past few years myself. I know I didn't reach out far enough for you. Sometimes I think you were unreachable, but other times I can see that you were right there, waiting for something. That something just was not me. At the time." He wondered about the circuitous journey from the news of the exhumation to this confessional in the parking lot. "Aren't you living in Italy?"

"I was. I am. But I had to come home because of all the craziness. Mitchell, you look so good. I hope everything is going well?"

"Yes, yes. I'm a partner in the firm. I have a girlfriend with a three-year-old boy. He's a pistol."

"You heard that Mother was not a suicide?"

"Yes. I can't imagine how all this must feel."

"Overall, good. For J. J., too." She told him about the sketch books and notebook, but nothing about Austin. "They probably can't find out after this long who shot her. They don't even seem able to find out who violated the grave."

He saw the other lawyer entering the office. "Speaking of violating, I've got to go inside for a bizarre case right now. Look . . ."

"This is not the last time. I'll call you next time I'm here. I'm glad we ran into each other."

"We didn't. You followed me, you crazy nut!" He kissed her on the cheek. She did not reel back. "How's your dad taking all this?" He figured Wills must be a suspect but didn't want to say so.

"He's oblivious mostly. Helpless. Still has his mean streak. He didn't always."

Mitchell remembered the chilling visits when they'd haul Wills out to the car for a Sunday ride, and he'd sit in the backseat lunging for the ashtray and burning the leather upholstery with his cigarette. Old wreck. No wonder Ginger dragged a ball and chain. J. J., too. After the divorce, Mitchell told no one, because he did not want to damage his law practice, but he'd consulted a psychiatrist in Atlanta—far enough away—for three months. He'd come to understand, looking out on Dr. Patton's walled garden with a moss-covered nymph trickling water from a basket, that because of the suicide, Ginger might not have been able to love him. She feared the surrender of a part of herself to someone. Without her knowing it, marriage reenacted a possibility of self-obliteration, her greatest fear. She would *have* to escape an intense relationship. "Witness," Dr. Patton had pointed out, "the wedding day." Sex was crucible and fire for that fear. Dr. Patton had led him by the hand from bitterness and a crushed heart, and from his jural black and white thinking, to a place where he could look at Ginger and himself and sympathize with both. He had reached around the crumbled marriage, back to the Masons as he knew them in college, when he'd gone to the cabin with J. J. and they'd swum in the river, hunted wild hogs, and played poker all night. Then J. J. asked his little sister down from college in Virginia to be his date. She wore a champagne net dress with sequins around the hem. Her hair formed a short, red-gold halo. By the end of the evening, he'd asked if he could go up to Virginia to see her. The next day he took her three of his favorite albums and walked across campus with her under the yellow sycamore trees, their feet scuffing through wet leaves.

Mitchell not only was happy to have retrieved their earlier selves, he then was able to resume his life.

His mother, however, never got beyond her fierce dislike of Ginger and berated her still whenever she was reminded of her existence. "Unnatural," she called her. "Scattered. And she cut her fingernails with clippers. I've never known a woman to cut her nails with clippers." Any little memory spurred her. "Couldn't boil water." "What a brat. She wanted to be the bride at the wedding and the corpse at the funeral at the same time." Mitchell didn't really mind the criticism. He had been hurt, and even if he'd managed forgiveness, he thought his side deserved to get in a few licks. He watched her drive away.

GINGER LEFT MITCHELL with a sense of happiness coursing through her. She'd expected never to see him again after that January afternoon in the courthouse. He'd sat in a raincoat with his arms crossed, never looking her way.

Now she'd simply appeared, spoken, he'd kissed her, welcomed her, obviously had forgiven her, even without her apology. She'd felt like a hit-and-run driver. But clearly he was on down the road, as she was.

The thousand images of him that ran through her mind did not now have to be mentioned. She held on to one for a moment— Mitchell trying to stem the gush from a broken toilet pipe when they'd come in late and found a flood in the hall. The mighty push of the water he tried to plug with one hand, while fumbling for the shutoff valve with the other, his bright pink sweater drenched, his feet skidding, and then as he managed to turn the valve, he plopped down in a pool of water. She froze in the hall in the instant before he turned to her and laughed. She laughed, too, and could hear their laughter still.

DR. SCHMITT ROSE FROM HIS CHAIR and embraced Ginger. "Ah, Pupil Number One!" He, too, had read the news. Had everyone in the state of Georgia heard? He pushed back from his desk and listened to her story.

"And at the end of this saga, I've decided, I *think* I've decided, that I do want to finish my Ph.D. Coming back to school was the best move I made in my very long series of false starts. And the work in Italy—I could stay there forever."

"Yes, I've heard things are going brilliantly." He hoped she bloody well had the sense to continue. He totted up her course work. They reviewed the possibilities for independent study and looked at the catalogue listings from the University of Perugia, where she could take some on-site courses and transfer the credit. "Looks like two more quarters here will do it. The rest can be done from Italy."

"Not bad. I'll be Dr. Mason! If I finish—ah, my father!" She'd never thought of taking over his title. "My father was a doctor in Swan before his stroke." Her plans were surging forward. She'd not known she could transfer units from Perugia. I'll go back to Italy for August, she calculated, then Athens for the fall. Marco can come here for a month at Christmas, then I'll stay for winter quarter. Then I'm hatched, sprung, born again, baptized in the river.

She wanted to give Dr. Schmitt something but had forgotten to buy a nice bottle of wine or a bunch of flowers. She opened her handbag and felt the bottom until her fingers touched cool flint. She held out her favorite arrowhead, found when she was nine, a medium-sized ocher beauty chipped by a master. "Here's something from Swan."

LILY WAS WAITING IN THE LOBBY with a Dubonnet. She'd met another lady in the needlepoint shop. They'd ended up having a pot of tea together. She was elated and opened her shopping bag to show Ginger the natural yarns in blue, pale orange, and caramel wool. Ginger joined her with a Dubonnet, a drink she found too sweet but she wanted to second Lily's choice. Lily looked transformed from the fright she'd been when Ginger arrived from Italy. She leaned back in the flowered armchair, relaxed. Her shoes looked rather stylish.

Lily saw her glance and laughed. "I bought shoes." She held out her feet for Ginger's approval.

"Very nice." There is something infrangible about Lily, Ginger thought. She manages to *right* herself. Maybe it's a talent to re-arrange reality so that the ugly is isolated like an infection, while the good red cells move on it. She's unlike Daddy, who went belly-up. No matter what devastates us, in a few hours she has loaves of banana bread cooling on the rack. I'll invite her to Athens for a weekend. I'll insist that she come visit me in Italy.

Ginger found herself telling Lily about seeing Mitchell, which led them to a second Dubonnet and a reminiscence of the wedding. This time they could joke a little. "Tessie turned two shades darker," Lily said. Then she said, into her drink, "I've always regretted that I said you were as bad as your mother that day. You know, sugar," she added lightly, "I was a little jealous of your mother."

But Ginger was still talking about her aborted wedding. She remembered the back of Mitchell's mother as she bustled to the car. She looked as though she might burst. "Old biddy. How she brought forth someone as nice as Mitchell is a mystery."

As far as Lily knew, J. J. was rounding the bend of some river, casting a line at this moment, passing Scott a beer. Ginger wished she could call him tonight but she had no idea where he was. He *could* be on the river. Her father, on a mercy mission during the war, had once parachuted behind enemy lines into Germany. If J. J. did go to California, he was on a dangerous mission, too.

She took Lily to her favorite restaurant, the Cue-T, a barbecue shack on the edge of town. They both ordered the chipped pork doused in extra hot sauce, fried sweet potatoes, and coleslaw. Pecan pie for dessert. Ginger ate like a famine victim.

WITH THE TIME DIFFERENCE, J. J. had lost only two hours when he landed. The sun was still high overhead, but so obscured by fog that it looked like the moon. He stepped out into what could not quite be called rain.

Cold, don't they know it's July? He studied a map at the rental car desk. Palo Alto was straight south, San Francisco straight north. In less than an hour he'd checked in at the first place he saw, a small, functional hotel in downtown Palo Alto. He looked up Whitman Street on the map and saw that it was only one street over. To unkink and decide what to do, he walked. Here the air felt balmy, the way California should. How long since he'd been in a town outside south Georgia? He'd driven up to Athens to see Ginger during her divorce. He went to the dentist in Atlanta last year to have an impacted wisdom tooth pulled, then had driven back to the cabin still numb.

He liked the streets he crossed, an old neighborhood of close-together houses with hummingbirds buzzing the fuchsias. He stopped in a place filled with the warm roasted aroma of coffee beans and sat down to have a cup. He wanted to stay there a few minutes and watch the street scene. A revival cinema that looked like a wedding cake was playing *Gone With the Wind*. If they knew the half of it, he thought. Students, professorial types, bicyclists, women in tight tops with no bras, long Indian-print skirts. The libbers, he supposed. Sexy as hell. He avoided women who were waiting to relinquish their souls to a husband. No one said hey, and hardly anyone glanced at him, though out of habit he looked at each person he passed. The custom of anonymity was new to him and he liked it. In Swan, he knew everyone and what they were thinking before they even knew it, as they did with him. He walked across the street to a stationery store and bought a new notebook and a pen. Later, he would write everything so he'd remember to tell Ginger. Maybe I should take trips to New Orleans, Richmond, Charleston, he mused. Drop in and observe and go. The places that came to mind were all southern. London, he thought. Someone had taken Indians there once and displayed them in a cage. He'd probably feel like that in a foreign country. A dancing bear. What must it have been like for Ginger, he wondered, to land in Italy and start up living a life? Start collecting the things that allow you to exist there. He imagined Ginger looking up the word *towel* in the Italian dictionary. He'd bought a notebook and pen. Sheets, frying pan, a life begins. Who are you when you know no one? Palo Alto seemed foreign enough to him. Men with shaved heads and yellow robes shaking tambourines and dancing on the corner, Indian, Chinese, Japanese restaurants, health food stores, whose vile aromas gusted out onto the sidewalk as he passed. Who was Austin Larkin here? So far from Stonefield. He doubled back to Whitman Street. 1518 would be ten blocks down. He decided to walk by Austin's house. He quickly entered a different neighborhood of Spanish-style houses mixed with a few barny Victorians and boxy houses which looked like Mondrian paintings. He walked past streets named for writers—Cowper, Melville, Byron, Hawthorne. The quaint names seemed soothing here on the last edge of the country.

At a corner house, he stopped at a row of cherry trees where jays dove for the last fruit. The perfume of star jasmine along the garden wall fused with sprawling pink trumpet vine and the raucous cries of the birds. He stood and let the sensations gather. The color of the shuttered house reminded him of the light that rocks out of a cantaloupe when you split it open. What if he lived there instead of Swan? Stepped out to clip the ferns that hung along an upstairs balcony. Far inside the house, he could see a child in the kitchen. *Their lives in a place I don't know.* Then the moment broke. He walked on. Some houses seemed to be mostly garage. This squashed together, you could hear your neighbor fart, he thought. At 1518 he stopped. A gray house, contemporary, blank across the front, with a peaked roof. 15 and 18 equals 33, his age, a calculation Ginger would make. Lemons, and what he later found out to be loquats, grew up over the windows. The two-car garage facing the street dominated the house. He stared, thinking that he had no context for this sort of house. He felt suddenly large and strange, a cardboard giant standing on the sidewalk outside the house of a man his mother had lusted for dozens of years ago. How many choices of theirs brought me here? he wondered. Austin. Someone Mother loved, though not enough to leave Dad. So is he a candidate for murder? Not likely, that many years after a short affair ended. Maybe Dad finally heard about the affair. Charlotte said Austin had moved to California during the war.

J. J. wanted a face-to-face look at Austin. He wanted a gut reaction. He wanted a no or yes to tell Ginger. That's why he was here. No time like the present, he told himself.

He stood at the front door only a moment, then lifted the knocker. Austin must be in his mid-fifties. Not the lover boy he was. J. J. braced for a puffy man with turkey-gobble neck and glasses. A young woman slipping on a shirt over her bathing suit answered the door. She was small, with dark straight hair cut in a wedge so that when she moved her head, her hair seemed to follow a second later. She buttoned one button, looking at him with raised eyebrows. He took in her thin wrists and pretty legs, her aura of self-containment. "Hi. Did you come about the pool sweep?" she asked.

"No. My name's Mason, J. J. Mason. I'd like to speak to Austin Larkin. Is this his house?"

"Yes. Daddy's not here."

"Do you expect him soon? I should explain. I'm J. J. Mason from Swan, Georgia, not far from Stonefield, where your daddy grew up. He knew my mother in college, Catherine Mason."

"Mason," she said. "I don't remember Daddy mentioning Mason, but I do remember him mentioning Swan. Who could forget that name?"

"Well, my mother was Phillips then."

"Oh! Catherine Phillips! Oh, yes. His college love. He thought she dangled the stars from the heavens. He's talked about her."

She put out her hand. "I'm Georgia Larkin. Named for you-know-where by a loyal son of the state. Come in." Her smile went all the way back to her molars. She had perfect, movie-star teeth. Good dentist, he thought.

The front door actually opened into a courtyard. The anonymous exterior had nothing to do with the lush and blooming tropical yard with a circular pool. The U-shaped house was entirely glass on its private side. From outside, he caught a glimpse of a book-lined dining room, a bedroom with bright yellow walls. She had been lying on a mat. "It's getting late. Would you like a glass of wine?"

"Thank you, but you don't need to go to any trouble for me." She went to the kitchen and came back with a tray holding a chilled white wine, glasses, and a bunch of grapes. She'd thrown on a loose white dress down to her ankles.

"I'm afraid the grapes are hot. They sat in the backseat of my car." She poured the wine and dropped one plump grape into his glass. "Daddy won't be back until late tomorrow afternoon. Will you still be here then?"

J. J. nodded. "I have some things to do here." Just let me sit here and look at you, darlin', he thought. Georgia. Neat ankles and small feet. But her face, was she beautiful? She looked—intrinsically herself. What would she do if he reached over and touched the side of his forefinger to her thick eyelashes? So this was what they meant by California girls. She's just God damned something, he thought. "Are you an only child?" Feature by feature she didn't look anything like Ginger. But one thing about her reminded him of Ginger—how still she was.

"Yes, does it show? My mother died when I was a senior in college. Daddy hasn't remarried but maybe he's about to. He's traveling with a woman he's been seeing for a while. She sells real estate here in Palo Alto. A grown-up, thank God. My friends' fathers are always marrying people our age."

"Well, I'm looking forward to meeting your father. Sorry about your mother. I lost mine, too." He pinched his chin. "If I could call him tomorrow . . . what would be a good time?"

"I'd say around four. What are you doing tonight? Would you like to see the sights of Palo Alto? Actually, I have to go do a little work at the store around nine but you could come if you'd like to."

"Sure. My pleasure. Where do you work?"

"I don't work there. I help sometimes. Daddy owns three bookstores in the Bay Area. Stonefield's—you recognize the name? There's an event tonight and I have to introduce the readers. Actually, right now I teach riding and train horses. I taught fourth grade for two years and I'm taking a year off to figure out what I want to do."

"May I take you to dinner first?" In all his brooding on the flight out, J. J. never suspected that the trip could take such an upturn. "You're my introduction to California so I want it to make the best impression."

THEY MET AT ST. MICHAEL'S ALLEY. He'd changed into his other white shirt and thought he might look wrong in jeans, but instead he seemed overdressed among the men in dashikis, Greek striped shirts, and T-shirts. A few men wore khaki suits and rep ties. Many women had a lot of hair and wore gauzy cotton dresses and tribal beads, though some were well dressed like the women in Swan.

Georgia was already at a table. Half turned around, she was talking to a group who had books on the table and were passing around pieces of paper. She held out her hand to him. First touch. "Hi, hi. These are all the people who're reading their work at the store tonight." She pointed. Ron, Suze, Abby, Dickie, Cady, Herbert. They waved, smiled. "This is J. J. Mason. He's out here from Swan, Georgia, down near where my dad's from."

J. J. nodded at everyone. When he sat down, he asked, "What are they, all writers?" The waiter introduced himself, to J. J.'s amusement, and took their order for wine and beef bourguignon.

"Yes, a big group of friends. There are more, you'll see. They're all older than I am. Most of them went through the writing program here or the one in the city. They're in their thirties and get together all the time to criticize each other's work and drink wine. They have a grand time."

"Any good?"

"Yes. Well, mixed. Some have published books. Herbert, I think he's the best writer in Palo Alto, never sends out anything. Kind of hangs on the edges."

"Why not? If he's that good . . ." The waiter, Kipper, brought a small loaf of warm bread and their wine.

"I don't know. Maybe he's afraid. What do you do down in Swan?"

J. J. took a sip of wine and shook his head. "Not any one thing. You could say I'm kind of a property manager. But here's to you." He raised his glass. "Thanks for coming out with me. I didn't expect to be so lucky."

"Too bad Daddy is down in L.A. What brings you out here?"

J. J. looked at her. He wasn't ready to say. But he also did not want to dissemble with her. By this point in an evening, he realized, he was used to thinking of how he could slip free. He was puzzled. Friendly as she had been, he hadn't detected a trace of flirting. She flashed the same smile on the table of writers and on the waiter and on the slice of bread she buttered and handed to him. "I love their bread. They bake every afternoon." J. J. watched her chew. Usually, he didn't like to see people eat. She was neat as a cat. Probably doted on by her daddy all her life. A little princess. And usually, he didn't go for brown eyes. He thought of Mindy, Julianne, how any little thing set him off. He felt himself veering toward his critical mode, but nothing occurred to him.

He risked one of his moves. "Your eyes—I'm trying to think what color they are. Brown, but I see flecks of gold. Like looking at the bottom of the river."

"That's so nice. My dad says they're the color of good sherry. Yours are the color of the wet agates we pick up over at Pebble Beach. They're so beautiful when they're wet but fade and powder over with salt when they dry."

"Back to your question. The answer is complicated. I've knocked on your door out of nowhere. My family has a complicated history. I thought your father might shed some light on a situation that has just come up at home." Immediately, the exhumation scene rose in his mind. He went silent.

The waiter brought their salads and ceremoniously ground pepper from on high. Georgia regarded J. J. with curiosity. She liked him. His face, chiseled, seemed tight but softened when he talked. He looked, she decided, the way marble can look, both hard and caressable. He was not saying something, and, how odd, that something had to do with her father.

J. J. poured more wine. "Let's talk about you right now. The past certainly can wait another day." In the background the writers laughed and read lines aloud. He heard several toasts. The small jammed restaurant became a swirling background for the face of Georgia, right across from him, a flush to her cheeks, her bare shoulders in shadow. I'd like to drink pure water from those delicate cups in her collarbones, he thought.

"Quick subject," she said, laughing. "I went to Stanford, moved home when Mother died. I didn't want to leave my father alone. I majored in poly sci—it was the times more than an intrinsic interest. Mostly, I majored in horses. I've always kept a horse at the Stanford Barn, ever since I was eight. I liked teaching but I'd rather be outside. I'm wild about my work at the stables, although everyone says it's a girl's passion—I shouldn't consider horses a life's occupation. But I don't want to manage one of the bookstores. I love to read but selling doesn't thrill me. So I'm searching around, I guess, but not with any urgency. I may go to vet school. I want to be sure. I'm having a good time."

He kept losing his train of thought. She roadblocked his usual habits. Because he found nothing to criticize, he turned on himself. This glimpse of another way of life, even a brief glimpse, turned the telescoping lens on his solitary existence and his own knock-headedness. I'm stalking the woods wooing perch when she's living her life three thousand miles away, he thought. If I don't get out, I'm going to turn into one of those grizzled old guys hanging around the bait shop. Not that he wanted to sit at a table and read drafts aloud while eating.

"How do you like the bourguignon? It's rich, isn't it? Tell me about you."

"I'm older than you. Jesus's age, thirty-three. They call it the age of perfection." He raised his glass in a mock toast. "I have a sister two years younger. Ginger. Let's see. I graduated, what, ten years back from Emory. I was *supposed* to study medicine like my dad but took to such useful things as literature and philosophy. Never married. Never came close." College seemed a lifetime ago. He could be describing someone else. "We've got a place out on a river, a place"—he paused—"that's special. I spend a lot of time there."

"What do you like to do?"

He started to talk about fishing and quail hunting but said, "I do some writing myself. And drawing." He motioned with his head toward the table behind her, where a fat woman with stand-up black hair stabbed the air with her fork and kept repeating, "Lousy metaphor, lousy." J. J. thought, with her heavily outlined eyes, that she looked arboreal.

Georgia had imagined him in an office going over leases, although he didn't look the part. "That's a long way from property management. Isn't that what you said you do? The South has so many great writers. Why is that?"

They talked. All through dinner, dessert, coffee. Suddenly, Georgia saw that the writers had gone. She and J. J. were going to be late, not that anyone cared. They walked the couple of blocks to Stonefield's. In the back room, huge foam cushions were scattered around the floor. The store manager already had introduced the reading, and the hefty woman was in full swing. They sank into the cushions against the back wall. J. J., who'd never been to a reading, quickly became entranced. Georgia, who'd been taken to readings all her life, had a chance to sit back and think about J. J. She glanced at his profile, his white shirt with rolled-up sleeves, wondering what he thought of her. He had certainly looked her over. She'd never felt so exposed by a simple dinner in a restaurant. His eyes were never still. They roamed over her, hungry, though now he looked remote. Just then he threw his arm along the back of her cushion, winked at her. Winked. Did people still do that? Herbert started his reading and she tried to listen. Something about J. J. seemed from another zone entirely. Unwillingly, unwittingly, a thought kept trying to break through as she struggled to sort out her reactions to him. What she felt was not even attraction, though he was gorgeous—more that her instinct was aroused. She stared at their parallel legs, almost touching, their feet. She jerked.

He smiled at her.

She smiled back and their eyes locked. "Are you liking the reading?"

"He's good. He's got it. I think he knows it." He gave the thumbs-up gesture.

THE WRITERS WERE GOING to Abby's house to continue their argument about the use of metaphor. Ron was proclaiming it dead, Abby said he was full of shit from his year in France and metaphor was how language grew. J. J. was attracted by the heat and light of active, living writers but declined. "I'm on eastern time. It's three A.M. Thanks, though."

"In California it's always earlier and later at the same time," Herbert added.

Georgia and J. J. walked back to J. J.'s car and drove down an alley of tall palms, parking at the end. They crossed the Stanford quad, where gold tesserae in the mosaicked front of the chapel picked up the sheen of moonlight. J. J. and Georgia stood in the deserted quad. His mouth was close to her hair. He breathed in her scents. "You smell like vanilla ice cream."

"You're wild! You southern gentleman."

His eyes followed the dark rhythm of the arches enclosing the courtyard. "This seems like a place Don Quixote might ride into on his horse." They sat on the edge of a fountain. "Distinctly un-American." The impact of the California landscape, as much as he'd seen so far, hit him hard. "The hills on the way from the airport were gold. Summer in the South is green, green, a thousand shades of green. Not a criticism." The palms rattled overhead in a slight breeze. "I've been in one place so long. This is surreal."

"Someone's vision. The founders lost their son, so they built a memorial. I love it here. I love all the palms. I was born at the campus medical center, so it has to be home for me. When I go South with Dad, that lush vegetation feels exotic—vines could crawl in the window overnight. When I was little, I thought the farm was Jack and the Beanstalk land." She smiled. Their shoulders touched. "I like being here with you," she said simply. This was her navel of the world, this stone folly in a dry land. She loved it that J. J. thought of Don Quixote here. He'd touched her own sense of this place. The indistinct thought that had been swimming through her all evening turned into words. *I recognize him,* she thought.

Six hours with him—preposterous. As if he heard her thought, he turned to her, inclining his head to hers.

They drove back to her car under leafy branches arching over Hamilton, University, Whitman, the leaves already turning rusty, the white globe streetlights like a string of moons under the sycamores. They both were quiet. The empty streets seemed like streams, easily taking him toward a river. "Call me tomorrow if you'd like to see the stables. Or just come." She wrote her number on a gas receipt and jumped out. He got out on his side, starting to say something, but she waved and opened her car door in a way that did not allow him to speak.

A grand magnolia loomed over the lot where he parked. The creamy blossoms took him directly back to Big Jim's. How can they thrive in this dry air? he wondered. Betray the humid South so easily? He raised his arms and flexed. His body was carrying a tension. He wanted to lie down in his plain hotel room and go over each minute since he landed. Not a tension, he thought. The good feeling of a 110-volt current charging all the synapses. He resisted the thought that he'd like to live here, but he felt the vitality and health of the place. Ginger would like it here. Lily would find it appalling, he imagined. He looked down the street at a row of shingle cottages with lamplit, lambent windows and shadows of giant ferns. I could rent one with a squat little garden and grow two tomatoes in wine vats. I could sit outside without mosquitoes dive-bombing me. Maybe here I'd write a long, layered novel about the South. Big Jim. Top of the heap. Wills. Wonder boy, the slow explosion into bits. Hell, write it there, he thought. Dip the pen into the pools of my sweat forming on the ground. He remembered a line from one of the poets. *Change me, change me into something I am.*

July 13

RAINEY LEFT JOHNNY at the breakfast table reading the Sunday Atlanta paper. She did not now like to linger at the table after any meal. The last piece of toast, the three slices of ham, no. The scale showed that she'd lost another half pound, though if she drank a glass of water, the needle would flap back to its stuck position. She needed time alone to write a column she had in mind. In fact, she had the inspiration for a weekly column that would get her away from the society page entirely. What we lack, she had told Johnny, is a local perspective on the national news. She did not say *feminine* perspective because she did not want to hear him groan. If she didn't mention that, she spared them both: he would not have to take a wearisome, predictable stand, and she would not have to invent tangential reasons for what she wanted.

Increasingly, the news of women changing their lives was sifting down South as far as Swan. She, for one, welcomed every missive from marching women, women starting magazines, women taking over the helm. She thought, however, that her own voice was outside politics. She would write a purely personal weekly opinion that happened to be that of a woman.

She'd left on a fan at her desk. Her papers lifted and fell, lifted and fell—the write-up of a wedding and a recipe for sour cream muffins mixed in with her investigation of hospital conditions. Last week a cockroach was served along with the salad on a patient's dinner tray. She swung her chair around to the typewriter. What should she call the column? "Rainey at Large." No, that reminded her of her weight. She thought of a newspaper colleague in Tipton's column "Pats and Pans." Horrid. The phone rang. *"Swan Flyover,"* she answered.

"Rainey, hey, this is Angela Kinsella in Simmonsville. We met last year at the conference."

"Yes, Angela, how nice to hear your voice."

"You, too. Y'all doing okay down there? I heard about what happened in Swan, and Peter Drew over in Knightsborough told me you'd called him about it, wanting to know if anything like that had happened there."

"Yes, I did. The GBI and the sheriff here haven't found a lead." Rainey picked up her pen.

"It's nothing as bad as what happened to that lady in Swan who was dumped out in the rain and all, but I wanted to let you know that last night here in Simmonsville, somebody broke down some crosses and turned over an urn on a grave. The worst was they broke the door into one of the mausoleum-type graves—you know the kind aboveground in the shape of a cedar chest?"

"Yes, I know those. Do they know who did it?"

"No, maybe some hoodlum, some fruitcake, or Saturday night drunk who'd read about Swan. But maybe the same person that came to Swan. This sort of thing doesn't happen every day."

"Thank you, Angela." This was small potatoes, but on the chance there might be a connection, she said, "Let me get all these details straight . . ."

RALPH HAD JUST STOPPED by the office after church. The bells still pealed two blocks away, a joyful noise over the whole town. Father Tyson had asked the congregation to pray for Catherine

Mason and for the entire community that had to experience the sorrow of such a crime in their midst. Amen, brother, Ralph had thought. He picked up Rainey's call. "Good. This is good news. It's *something* rather than nothing." He dialed Gray at home.

"Well, sounds like a fetishist on our hands. We'll look into it. Don't worry about this on Sunday; sooner or later we'll find him."

Ralph would look up *fetishist*. He thought it had to do with someone who liked feet too much. He poured coffee, forgetting it was yesterday's cold leftover. He decided to walk over to the Three Sisters. Like most of Swan, on Sunday morning, he thought nothing better on earth existed than hot doughnuts. Let the GBI track this loony tune roaming the state of Georgia.

Ralph remembered the Goat Man, who used to pass through Swan when he was a child. Maybe the grave-visitor was someone like that. The Goat Man walked alongside a wooden cart, tinkling with hanging pots and scissors. His herd of goats walked companionably along with him, each with a bell. Sometimes he stopped outside town in a field, and a few people ventured near to have their knives sharpened. Ralph went once with his grandfather, who was suspicious of the Goat Man. He could still see his bony frame, Father Time beard, and rheumy, faraway eyes. The Goat Man was clearly a character. This swine-face grave-opener was probably some oily puke holding down a job, paying taxes, passing for normal.

As Ralph crossed the street, he saw a woman waving to him. She stepped out of her car and leaned against the door. He recognized her as that woman from the mill village who sewed baby clothes. He saw her pull in her lips and cross her arms over her chest. She looked cold, which was impossible in the heat. But maybe she was sick. "Is something wrong, ma'am? Are you all right?" He recrossed the street.

"Could I talk to you? It's important. Your granddaddy helped me a couple of times. My name's Aileen Boyd."

"I'm glad to hear he was of help. Now, what can I do for you?" She was right pretty in a hardscrabble way.

"It's real private."

"Let's go to the office." He took her elbow and guided her upstairs and into the small interview room in the back. Aileen sank back into the sofa cushion, resting her head, her eyes closed. "Now, what's wrong?" Ralph asked.

"Everything. It's about Catherine Mason," Aileen said. "Where do I begin? I guess with Sonny. Sonny was my husband."

Ever since Ralph read his granddaddy's report on the suicide, the doodle on the folder kept snagging in his mind. S, his grandfather had written, and B or D. Sonny Boyd. He'd suspected him. Bingo, bingo.

GINGER AND LILY LEFT ATHENS AROUND TEN, driving back to Swan through Matteson Junction, where Lily's Agnes Scott roommate came from, and where Lily once met a man at a tea dance who seemed to like her, though she never heard from him again. They looked at the street lined with old houses Sherman did not burn on his march to the sea. Then Ginger sped through the country-side snarled with kudzu to Milledgeville, where her mother and Charlotte met, where Austin scattered the roses over the campus. She kept trying to shake the dream that woke her up in the night. She had been standing on her mother's shoulders in the river, her face barely breaking the surface of the water, her breathing possible only because her submerged mother held her up. She sat up drenched, about to scream.

When they got out of the car for lunch, the smothering humidity from yesterday's rain enveloped them. Downtown Milledgeville felt like a just-drained swamp. One minute outside town, they entered deep country again—roosters running underneath board houses perched on stones, Repent signs, telephone poles strung with gourds for birdhouses, geraniums planted in tires, wash flapping on the line, whitetail deer bounding across the road. By late afternoon they entered Swan, gleaming after another rain and bathed in blond light. As they approached the House, they saw Tessie on the porch watering the ferns and a man in the doorway. "Oh, J. J.'s back," Lily said.

Ginger squinted in the glare on the bug-glazed windshield. "That's Marco!" she shouted. "That's not J. J.—that's Marco!" She slid to a stop and leapt out.

"Oh, the Italian," Lily said aloud. "So the Italian has come to Swan." Able was I ere I saw Elba, she remembered, and Caesar crossing the Rubicon. She saw his bear hug, Ginger jumping up and down, his smile over her shoulder.

He waved to Lily as she walked up the steps. "I am made very happy," he said to her. The way he said *very* made it sound almost like *furry*. He kissed her hand like a count in an old movie.

Lily, too, felt a fine shiver of happiness. "We're so happy to have you in Swan. So you've met Tessie and CoCo?"

PALO ALTO ON SUNDAY MORNING reverted to the sleepy town it had always been before the invasion of hip. Bicyclists picked up the paper at Dan's, the owner of the yogurt shop turned up the jazz station and swept the sidewalk.

J. J. went back to the coffee shop he'd stopped in yesterday. He sat at a window, staring into the blank pages of the notebook he'd bought. He intended to see Austin, then catch the 9:00 P.M. flight back to Atlanta. He'd arrive at dawn, be in Swan by ten. Plenty of time to deal with the reburial.

The waitress beamed at him, definitely checking him out, as she brought his coffee and croissant. As she bent down, she smelled like fruit. He lifted his face to her entirely, smiling and looking into her eyes. Full benefit. "You're not a regular here," she said. "I'm Ariel. This is my aunt's place. I work here to support my habits." Crystal prisms hung from her ears. She wore a patchwork Indian skirt and Birkenstocks.

"What habits?"

"Oh, books and shoes. Nothing lethal. Want anything else?"

He resisted a come-on remark. He liked the blunt openness of California women. "Thanks, I'm just fine." Although he wanted to call Georgia, he held back. She probably does not want to be awakened by some cracker she went out of her way to entertain, he thought. No, I know she liked me. He was shaken by the kind of ease he felt with her. Same comfort he felt with Ginger without the tiger instinct for protection. Georgia seemed able to take care of herself. Praise the Lord. He strolled around town. In a shop window he saw women's fall clothes. On impulse he went in. The long green turtleneck would look good on Ginger. The price tag stopped him for a moment, but he bought it anyway. He held up a pale yellow cardigan, cashmere, and bought that for Lily. He saw a pink terry robe and had that wrapped for Tessie. He had suffered the agony of buying Christmas and birthday presents but never spontaneously had bought a gift before. He looked at the displays, wondering what Georgia would like. He picked up a scarf, handwoven in plum and blackberry from something soft. He bought it.

Stonefield's was opening across the street. No blue laws here. At home, his books had to be ordered. He didn't mind the wait, really. When the box arrived, opening it was one of his exquisite pleasures. He left his bulky gifts at the desk and browsed, picking up more than a dozen books that appealed to him. Even the bookstore had a coffee bar. He took his stack to a table and sat with another coffee for an hour. He was happy to find the letters of Van Gogh. The powerful colors and images in his paintings talked back to J. J.'s big argument with the act of writing, which he'd tried to explain to Ginger the night she got home. Between what he wanted to write and what appeared on paper when he did, an abyss opened. Van Gogh's yellow chair, blazing out as itself, radiant with its own ability to be *chair,* did not acknowledge that gap. Maybe the letters would tell J. J. why. He leafed through, briefly wishing he were at the cabin, at his own desk, the river outside the window. He glanced up. A couple, students he guessed, kissed on the sidewalk, oblivious to passing people who smiled and stared. They were in their own floating world. He returned to Van Gogh. *Now we see the Dutch paint things just as they are, apparently without reasoning,* he read. He thought of his mother's sketch books. He glanced down the page: *we can paint an atom of the chaos, a horse, a portrait, your grandmother, apples, a landscape.* What he liked was *we can.*

He picked out a few novels for Ginger and a book on English gardens for Lily. With the gifts he'd bought, he was shocked that he'd spent almost a thousand dollars. He almost never bought anything, but when he did, he thought of Big Jim, all his wheeling, dealing, gusto, his whoring, bombasting. Thanks for the Van Gogh, Big Jim.

He asked directions to the stables and drove through the campus, past the medical center where Georgia must have first been shown to the light. Down a lane where girls in hard hats rode thoroughbreds, he came to a great red barn. He walked toward a covered ring, smelling the good scents of leather, horse manure, alfalfa, and sawdust.

He spotted Georgia up on a large gelding, bearing down on a substantial jump. She *must* have done this before, he thought, but still he frowned and held his breath as she approached, leaning stiffly forward, and the horse seemed to elongate as he left the ground and arced over the pole. "Damn," he said aloud. He was able to watch her without her knowing. She continued on course, her horse meeting each jump but not, J. J. thought, with ease. Each approach seemed tense. She saw him and trotted over.

"This is Winkie. Calm down, Wink." Her hair in back dripped with sweat under the velvet hat. In her sleeveless riding shirt buttoned up to her neck, she looked ravishing. He took in every inch of her bare arms, her tall black boots.

"That horse has some fierce eyes. He looks like he's ready to tear out of here and never stop. I knew you were beautiful, but I didn't know you were brave. I wouldn't get on him for love nor money."

"He's a dream. We bought him off the track. That's why he's antsy." *Beautiful,* he'd said. When she went South, everyone constantly told her she was beautiful.

They walked slowly along a path while she cooled down her horse. "Want to have lunch?"

"I'd like that."

"Let me brush him and take a quick shower. I have to be back to teach the intermediate class."

SHE DIRECTED HIM TO THE ROUNDUP, a place near the stables. They sat at a wooden table outdoors and ordered hamburgers. Above them the craggy limbs of giant oaks squiggled against blue sky. "Do you come here every day?"

"No. I try to take my lunch. The three instructors usually eat together."

He told her about his morning. "I think I spurred the cash flow at Stonefield's today. You know there's not a bookstore within a hundred miles of Swan. And that one bookcase in the department store in Macon is going to have Charles Dickens and Kahlil Gibran."

"You're so literary. Why do you stay there?"

He felt she'd poked him with a cattle prod. "No, I'm not. I'm basically a fisherman. Do a little hunting, too. I wouldn't know what to do with myself without the river a stone's throw away."

"My dad misses the South. I left him a note saying that you are in town."

"I probably won't see you again, unless you're home then."

"My last lessons end at six today. Sunday is actually my long day. The kids are free on the weekends."

"Call in sick. Food poisoning at the Roundup. We could drive over to the coast."

He's awfully cocky, she thought. Southern women are probably all over him. I'm not like that. If he stayed long, would I become like that? His arrogance, a quality she usually hated, didn't irritate her, because she sensed that his confidence with women was skin-deep, literally. Every time his life or his past came up he ran for cover.

THEY DROVE THE LONG WAY, through the somber sequoias and hills, the road gloomy in sunlight sieved through long branches. As they turned north onto the coast road, J. J. stopped talking. The Atlantic was one thing, the Pacific another, he saw. The cupped hills, tawny as lion's fur, dipped to beaches where swags of foam scalloped the sand. Georgia pointed. "Pull in at San Gregorio. We can see seals."

They walked, hardly talking, through wild roses. In the distance J. J. saw islands, as clear cut as pieces in a jigsaw puzzle. Finally, Georgia said, "I need to get back. Cindy could only take two of my classes." The waves breaking on rocks sent fine spray over them. He would have liked to stay all day. Walking back along the trail, Georgia was ahead of him. *I have always had the coarse lusts of a beast,* he'd read in Van Gogh's letters. No, he thought, I'd like to press my lips softly to every part of her. I'd like to lick her face. In the wind, her aqua riding jacket smelled loamy, and J. J. was sure her face like his had a rime of fine salt. He touched her elbow. "Georgia." She turned and he put his hands on her shoulders. "May I?" he asked so quietly she barely heard him. With great care, he kissed her, then gently pulled her close to him.

J. J. CALLED THE HOUSE before he checked out of the hotel. Tessie put down the phone for a good five minutes before anyone bothered to pick up. Lily, out of breath, didn't even ask where he was. "We've had a grand surprise! When we drove in from Athens, Marco was here, Ginger's beau from Italy."

"You went to Athens?"

"Yes, we had a lovely trip. Now we're making dinner. Will you be here in time?"

"In time for what?"

"The burial, J. J. At eleven tomorrow. Are you at the cabin?"

"I'll be back in the morning. I just called to tell you. Y'all all right?"

"Yes. Marco is showing Tessie how to make something out of potatoes. You drop little balls in the water, and I forgot to tell you the big news. Ralph just called. He's the nicest young man. He said he has some new information but he can't discuss it yet. He also said there was a minor grave disturbance in Simmonsville, which might be related. Ginger is so happy she's fit to be tied, but she's anxious, too, you know her. I tried calling the cabin but you weren't there. And Dr. Schmitt says Ginger can finish that Ph.D. degree pretty easily. We shall see. I'll make some biscuits. She saw Mitchell, too. We'll tell you every little thing. I always said he's as nice as they come. Not that Marco isn't. See you tomorrow."

Lily. That Lily. They only made one of her.

J. J. drove down Whitman. Four-thirty. Austin should be there. He still saw Georgia growing smaller in the rearview mirror. He had not said that she affected him with a ferocity he'd never felt. He had not said he'd call. The kiss had to say what he did not. He'd forgotten to give her the plum-colored scarf.

He wanted to face Austin and go home. He craved empty days at the cabin, where he could sort through this journey to the other side. A block away he parked by a dry creek and looked down at the pattern of the current sculpted in the sand. Georgia said that every afternoon around four, an ocean breeze came in. He lifted his head for salt wind but instead inhaled the fusty, herbal smell of eucalyptus. Dread similar to what he felt when he entered the Columns slowed him. Coming from a place where every house and street was animated by a story, he thought the neighborhood of low houses with closed facades looked barren. But Georgia had opened the door of one of those houses yesterday. Twenty-four hours ago.

Austin opened the door before J. J. knocked.

J. J. faced a man who looked younger than his years. Charlotte had said he was two years ahead of them in college, so he'd be maybe fifty-seven, fifty-eight. Under his loose silk shirt and linen pants, he was obviously fit. His combed-back silver hair accentuated his modeled face. Large lips for a white guy, was J. J.'s first thought. He took in the rigorous profile and the tan. Austin, J. J.

thought, Georgia's daddy. "Mr. Larkin." J. J. held out his hand. "I'm J. J. Mason, Catherine's son. Proverbial voice from the past. I'm sorry to interrupt when you're just home."

"No, no, I'm happy to meet you. Come in, come in. Georgia left me a note saying you'd stop by this afternoon." He had only a trace of his accent left.

"I had the pleasure of dinner with your daughter. She made me feel right at home in Palo Alto." He looked around at the living room, which he'd glimpsed through the windows yesterday. Austin gestured him to a chair. Two contemporary sofas in okra-green linen around a fireplace and bright abstract paintings. The walls were covered in pale grass cloth. So this is where Georgia lives, he thought, imagining her curled on the sofa reading by the fire, rain streaking the long glass wall.

"Can I get you a drink? Whiskey, soda, wine?"

"Thanks, Scotch, that would be great." The back wall was booklined. While Austin was in the kitchen, he looked at titles. Along the front of the shelves, rocks and gems, along with a few shells, were arranged. J. J. picked up a geode darkly sparkling with amethysts.

Austin came back holding a tray. "I'm a rock hound. Most of my collection is at the office." He looked at the books. "I've also collected signed editions over the years. With all the authors coming through, and owning bookstores, it's been an easy collection." He took the tray to the coffee table. "What brings you to *me*, J. J.?"

"Long story. Thirty years long, or longer. But let me tell you what has happened this week. Believe me, I would not barge in like this if it were not important. I haven't left Swan in several years," he admitted. Terse and factual, he told Austin about the exhumation and the subsequent conclusion of the GBI that Catherine had not died by suicide.

Austin leaned forward, his hands in the gesture of prayer, silently parting and closing them. His eyes never left J. J.'s. "Your mother, Catherine—I met her when she was nineteen. A lovelier woman never walked. Everyone who knew her felt somehow defeated when we heard she'd killed herself. I was living out here at the time. Someone from Tech sent me the article. I couldn't take it in, but I hadn't seen her by then in several years and had no idea of the circumstances that might have provoked her."

J. J. explained that the GBI thought they could not find the murderer by now, unless someone up and confessed. "My family is convinced it was a random crime."

"You'd have thought, if you'd known her when I did, that she'd be among the lucky ones. She went forward with a kind of simple belief that the world is a curious, wondrous place. I see the same faith in my daughter."

"This is the hardest part to say. We found some of Mother's belongings in the barn. She'd apparently sealed a box after Ginger was born. It had been stashed in the attic, otherwise it would have been thrown out with all her other things after she died. Ginger went through all the stuff that was transferred to my granddaddy's house when we moved there. She found a box of maternity clothes, a reel of film, two sketch books, and a notebook. And four or five letters from you, all undated. Mother's friend Charlotte—remember her?"

"Of course. A considerable person, too."

"We ran the film at Charlotte's house and she recognized you. Then the notebook brought up an entirely new issue, and basically I've come because of that." He told Austin about the pearl crescents, the elliptical prose, the tension, and finally his concern that Austin might be the father of Ginger. "I'm sorry—you must feel like the Martians have landed."

"This is stupendous. All of it. Are you sure I can't get you another drink? Let's talk this through."

J. J. followed him into the kitchen. On the mantel, he saw a photo of Georgia on horseback holding up a first-place ribbon, another of a woman who looked like an older version of Georgia. "Georgia's mother?" he asked.

"Yes. She died five years ago." His eyes narrowed with hurt. "I met her on leave toward the end of the war. I was flying Wildcats in the South Pacific. Air force pilot. I didn't think I'd lose her so early. She was only fifty-two. Bone marrow disorder hit her and she was weak one month and dead the next. Let's sit outside."

Austin continued to lean forward in his chair. Behind him the aquamarine pool rippled. A white cat J. J. had not seen yesterday touched its tongue to the water, then settled at Austin's feet. "I can't explain Catherine, I know that. She was an unlikely person to have an affair—and I didn't think of it that way. I was crazy about her. The very first time I saw her, I was down from Tech for the weekend. She was acting in a Greek play. The girls all had on these toga things and were dancing. She looked like she was having fun. I know these days the idea of love at first sight is an archaic concept. But that was what happened. She had me in the palm of her hand. I was happy and miserable, miserable when she went out with other men and didn't seem to notice that I was left on the sidelines. When we were together, the main thing I remember is that we laughed at the same moments. She practically destroyed me when she got engaged to Wills."

"Charlotte told us about you scattering the roses over the campus."

"I always hoped the big romantic gestures would sway her. I was calling her even on her wedding day, begging her not to marry him. She felt terrible, she said, but said it was the right thing, she knew it." As Austin talked, more of his southern accent, neutralized by years in California, returned to his voice. "Speaking of suicide—the day after she married him, I tore off on a car trip to Carrie's Island and seriously considered ramming into the intercoastal bridge. I didn't. Gradually, I got myself together again and life moved on."

"But how . . ."

"I didn't see Catherine until about three years later. I literally ran into her at the Georgia-Alabama football game. I was on leave, recovering from an appendectomy. You were a toddler. I guess left at home. Wills was in uniform. He always looked through me as though I were made of glass. Cordial, never friendly. The next week I called Catherine. She was going to Macon and we met for lunch. After that we met several times. Everything rekindled for me. I can't say what she felt. Maybe you know from the notebook. Lonely. You know women had different lives then and your mother was meant to do something with hers. She came to the farm. Four times. I'll just say it. We slept together there. In my parents' lumpy Victorian bed. She didn't seem to feel guilty. Wills got home when he could. You mentioned the pearl crescents. They were my mother's. I gave them to Catherine the first time she came to the farm. One day she mailed them back to me. She never mentioned birth control or pregnancy. *Not to worry*, she said. Of course, I heard later that she'd had another baby.

"Ginger. My sister is thirty-one. When were you and Mother together?"

"Summer of '43. In fact, around this time. First part of July. I remember being alone almost all that big July-August heat wave at the farm. I had a few weeks to recover before seeing action again."

"Ginger was born May 1, 1944."

"So"—he counted back—"highly unlikely but remotely possible." Austin lowered his face into his hands. "I only saw Catherine once after that. I had a drink with a man named Paul, who worked for your granddaddy. I briefly went back to my old job after the war. I sold spindles and did a little business with the mill. We were at the bar at the country club in Swan, and I saw Catherine alone, about to tee off. I ran out and we talked for a few minutes. Her little girl was playing. I was over her by then. This was 1950. I'd met Clare at the end of the war and was about to move permanently out here to be with her. I can't say for sure, though, if Catherine had faintly suggested it, that I wouldn't have taken her away in my car that day. She seemed the same, but I think your dad's war experience had made her more solemn."

"His war experience? He was a medic, mostly in North Carolina."

"Surely you know he was in a unit that treated the prisoners after the liberation of Dachau?"

"No." J. J. swallowed the gut-burning Scotch.

"They never told you?"

"No. A family not known for mentioning the unpleasant. I knew he once parachuted into Germany—I've always imagined him floating down."

"I'm sorry. He treated those emaciated, brutalized people for weeks. Sorry, son. A Tech friend of mine was in his unit. He's been messed up ever since."

"I'm God damned." J. J. told him about Wills's desperate drinking and the resultant stroke.

"That's a hell of a fate. He had nothing but promise before the war."

"Yeah, well. He was a good father up until. Just curious. What's your blood type?"

"A."

"That doesn't help. My dad is A, too."

"I'm ready to do whatever you think best."

"I don't know of anything to do. I'll tell Ginger there's a remote chance that you're her father. Maybe I can find out from Lily if Ginger's birth was early or late. That would seem to be definitive."

"Refill?"

"No thanks, I'm going to the airport. I may drink a few on the flight. This Dachau news is hard to take. And they're reburying tomorrow."

"So, no one told you about Wills. That's so typical, isn't it? But those guys never liked to talk about the war, those who witnessed big-time horrors. I was in the air. Midway Island—that was bad enough."

They walked through the yard. The sun had fallen behind the lacy Chinese elms and olives. "California light," J. J. said. "It's different. The outlines of things are sharper here. I want to thank you. I apologize for all this digging in the past. Seemed important for Ginger."

"Yes. And I'm somehow unburdened to hear that Catherine did not take her own life. The other parts, I'll have to absorb. Your dad. Do they suspect him of murder?"

"I think so. Lacking anyone else. He wouldn't have, not for the world." The GBI would check on Austin if J. J. mentioned the notebook, which he would not. Austin was running bookstores, raising a family, when Catherine died. He had nothing in his eyes but honesty. J. J. could understand easily his mother's attraction to Austin. And back when they all were in college he must have been what Charlotte called him—a dreamboat. "They've got to be suspicious but the likelihood is nil."

"I'd doubt their suspicion with all my heart, son. Innocent or guilty, he's serving a life sentence, from what you've told me." J. J. felt a prick of pain. Second time Austin had said *son*. A word he hadn't heard in a long time.

"Austin, your daughter seems to me like Mother seemed to you in the Greek play. I'm hoping to see her again. Now, that's an understatement." J. J. laughed at himself.

Austin laughed, too. "Another spoke in the wheel that seems bent on turning. If Georgia has any imperfections, I don't know them. She's true blue. In my experience, you only get that kind of emotion once. Or twice if you're luckier than hell. I was one of those. Now I'm seeing someone pleasant, nice, companionable. Attractive, you know. I think I'll leave it as it is, although she's ready to move in and rearrange the furniture. I'm not sure I want to give up my privacy unless I'm convinced it's for a great piece of happiness."

"I wouldn't consider it, if that's the situation. 'Course I'm the great loner." To his surprise, Austin hugged him.

J. J. had plenty of time to get to his flight. Rush-hour traffic moved along at a clip, without tractors or yokels in pickups to slow the flow. J. J. kept right, not in his usual hurry. He'd seen Georgia on the coastal trail touch the tip of her tongue to a wave-wet shrub, something he and Ginger did. He wondered if Catherine had long ago picked it up from Austin and passed it on to them. He won-

dered if she'd become interested in stones through him and be-
queathed that, too.

What he wanted was to turn back, drive a hundred miles an
hour to that stable where he last saw Georgia sitting on the fence
calling out "Post" to the girls, where sunlight, sifting through the
oaks and kicked-up dust, held the covered ring in sepia light, a light
from the previous century.

July 14

J. J. ARRIVED IN SWAN thirty minutes before they were scheduled to meet the Ireland's hearse at Magnolia Cemetery. Ginger had told Father Tyson that there was to be no ceremony. The less focus, the better. They would witness the burial, stop to see Wills, go to the Sisters for late breakfast, then resume their lives.

With Marco here, she felt more decisive. He had made the long journey to a troubled place for her. Only for her. That he deeply cared, even she could no longer doubt. "This is a great place," he kept saying as she'd driven him around yesterday before dark. "Like a place in a dream. Everything anchored in blue air." She could tell that he liked Lily and Tessie. He'd immediately invited both of them to Italy. She and Marco had stayed up late, talking on the porch. Ginger shivered in the hot night as she told him about the day she came home from school and found her mother. She told him about Wills, his grief, stroke, and unendurable aftermath, and about her survival with J. J. "Later, we'll go out to the cabin. That's where J. J. and I could connect with a source. Here, in the House, we were at home, too, but this is always Big Jim's house. The cabin belonged to *my* family. We kept it as a touchstone. And will."

Motionless in the rocking chair, Marco just listened. Behind her voice, he'd never heard a night so alive. He stared into the dark yard, where for all he knew crocodiles were crawling. Now and then CoCo imitated a hammer knocking off a tailpipe or a drill gun unscrewing lug nuts. Marco had kept his hand over Ginger's on the arm of her chair and she talked and talked.

J. J. CAME UP THE PORCH STEPS with his arms full of gifts. Ginger introduced Marco quickly. "Hey, buddy, I'd have brought you one if I'd known in time that you were here. Welcome to paradise." He clapped Marco on the shoulder and nodded to Ginger, a "not bad" nod she recognized. While they opened his gifts, J. J. regarded Marco. He looks okay, he thought. Solid citizen. Of Italy, of course. Lily and Ginger were shocked at the expensive sweaters. Tessie pressed the soft cotton robe to her face.

"Go change. We'll talk on the way. We can all go in one car." Ginger wanted to get this over with.

"Tessie, are you coming?" Lily asked.

"Nome. I done told Ginger I'm going to get dinner together."

Lily went back for her handbag.

Cass Deal had cleaned the plot, even deadheaded all the spent roses. The coffin already sat next to the hole, now neat and raked smooth. Two hours of scouring had returned Big Jim's grave to pristine white granite. Against the Mason headstone leaned a spray of red roses. Below, someone had left a vase of summer garden flowers. The four of them stood to the side while the men slowly cranked the coffin down into the ground. Could anyone ever believe the pumping red heart just stops; we go in a box and are buried, while those who love us are left to figure out how to endure this brutal subtraction from life? Ginger stooped for a handful of dirt and threw it in, then J. J. did the same.

He brushed off his hand on his trousers and said in a low voice to Ginger, "Are we the only ones to bury our mother twice, both times after fucking disasters?"

"I'd like to say something," Lily said in a quaky voice. She stepped forward, turned around, and looked at them. J. J. saw her swallow twice as she unfolded a piece of paper. Slowly she spoke.

> *Beauty is a thing beyond the grave.*
> *That perfect bright experience*
> *Will never fall to nothing*
> *And time will dim the moon sooner*
> *Than our full consummation here*
> *In this brief life will tarnish or pass away.*

They stood in silence. J. J. clenched his fists hard to keep tears from his eyes. "That's perfect, Lily, thank you."

Ginger put her arm around her, and she and Marco walked her back to the car. Lily started to weep a little. J. J. stood a moment, with his eyes closed and head down, wondering how Lily had happened on a poem by D. H. Lawrence. J. J. suspected there was something more behind it, something she might never tell, or something that would float to the surface in time. Odd, since Ralph had told them that their mother did not kill herself, J. J. had experienced a surge of affection for Lily, as though a stone had been shoved off a spring, allowing water to flow.

While the men shoveled dirt in a mound over the coffin, J. J. read the card on the vase of flowers. *Rest forever in peace, Eleanor Whitefield.* J. J. bent to the red roses and took off the florist's card. *With love from Austin and Georgia.* He thought of Austin flying low, the roses falling on the campus for Catherine. He pocketed the cards. So much to tell Ginger.

GINGER KEPT IT BRIEF in Wills's room. They did not mention Catherine or what had just happened. "Daddy, this is Marco, the man I work with in Italy."

Wills proffered his hand but didn't speak.

"I've heard about you from Ginger, and it is pleasing to me to meet you," Marco said. Lily went down the hall and brought back a Coke for Wills. Marco tried again to get a response. "Ginger tells me you are a doctor. My father is, too. He delivers all the babies in Monte Sant'Egidio."

Wills reached for the Coke, as though he were constantly deprived. Ginger told him about Marco's project, but Wills threw up both hands and said, "Okay, okay."

Abruptly, Ginger said, "We're going now, Daddy. We'll see you tomorrow." Marco extended his hand but Wills ignored him.

J. J. stayed behind. "I'll be right with you." He swung a chair around and straddled it. "Dad, listen. I want to ask you a question. Does the word *Dachau* mean anything to you?"

Wills pulled the straw from his mouth. "Dachau," he repeated. "Terrible, terrible."

"Were you there?"

Wills nodded. "Terrible."

"I heard you were there. You never told us. You were brave."

Wills wiped the sweat from his upper lip on his sleeve. "I was brave," he repeated.

AFTER BREAKFAST AT THE SISTERS, Lily was exhausted. Marco said he, too, wanted to sleep because he was in confused hours. "You can't," Ginger protested. "We're all going to the cabin. And it's called jet lag."

"*Va bene, va bene.* Let me sleep on the way."

"Take me to the House. I want to go visit Eleanor." And after that, Lily thought, I want to stay in bed until dinner.

At the cabin, Marco immediately spotted the arrowhead collection around the fireplace. "Did you find all these? A natural history museum would be proud to have such a display." He admired J. J.'s new fishing spear, then turned to look at the shelves of history and anthropology books.

"We were raised in the boonies, but we did read," Ginger said. She gave Marco a tour of the rest of the cabin, then, after she took him down to the river, she let him sleep in her room. At first she lay down beside him, but she was about to fall off the narrow bed and he fell soundly asleep within seconds. She opened the window, turned the fan on him, and slipped outside, where J. J. sat at his table under the scuppernong vine, looking through a stack of new books.

"I brought you these novels. Good for the long plane trip."

"I can't get over you going shopping. I love the sweater. Sweet J. J." She kissed the top of his head. "Want a dip?"

"Sounds good. Wash away the cares of the world." As they walked down to the dock, Ginger started to sing, as she always had, *Shall we gather at the river, the beautiful, the beautiful rivvvv—eerrr.* She boomed on every stress.

"Was it a week ago that I found Scott sitting here with the news that tilted our little universe? Seems like a year. What do you think Ralph has found out?"

"He was mum. He did say this news might break everything open."

"Christ, good old Sherlock. Go, Ginger." He gave her a push and she jumped in holding her nose.

GINGER, STRETCHED OUT on a decrepit aluminum chaise, spread her hair to dry. J. J. told her about his two days in Palo Alto. "What if Mother had left and taken us to California and we'd been raised there with Austin?" Ginger wondered.

"Then Georgia would not have been born. That would have been a fatal error." J. J. leaned back on his elbows. He told her everything Austin had said about the affair. "We have to ask Lily if you arrived early or late. It could matter, but it looks like you're stuck with Daddyo." He tried to describe Georgia, their glass house with lemon trees, and the big surf spuming from the rocks when he walked the coastal trail with her. He talked about the light at the stable as he drove away. Finally, he told her what Austin said about Wills. "I thought the surprises from Austin, if there were any, would be about Mother. Instead, I walked out staggering over what he said about Dad. This morning when we were at the Columns, I asked him about it. I could tell he remembered something horrific."

"He hardly recalls anything specific. That must have colored every corpuscle in his body." Already she was thinking of ransacking the barn and the stuffed closet in the back room for any record of this, any old Brownie photo or letter. "So he had other sorrows. Unspeakable. I wonder if Lily knows. Probably not. Surely she would have said something, as much as she poor-Wills." She remembered her father sitting alone on the dock at night.

Ginger told J. J. about seeing Mitchell in Athens, then checking with Dr. Schmitt about finishing her degree. "I just may do it! I've gone from thinking I might to thinking how could I not? I remembered so many things about Mitchell when Lily and I were driving home, after barely thinking of him in the past couple of years. Do you know once he brought me an enormous armful of Casablanca lilies? They tinged the whole house with their white perfume. I felt so good to find out he's just fine."

They heard the screen door bang and saw Marco emerge with a large book. He waved and sat down on the porch. "Ginger, Marco seems extra-primo excellent." J. J. turned his thumbs up.

"Maybe our luck has changed. No more turning into pillars of salt. No more seasons in Hades."

"Don't think it. The gods might be huddling right now, preparing the next bolt. They're still standing, those Masons. Hey, I want to go back to California for a while," J. J. said. "I liked it there."

"Georgia on your mind? Is she pretty?"

"Flawless. Something about her."

"Marco, get down here! You've got to swim in the spring," Ginger called. "I think we might drive over to the island tomorrow so I can introduce Marco to Caroline. Want to go? Marco, come *on*. Dinner's at seven and you don't want to miss Tessie's cooking."

J. J. stood up and stretched. "No, I want some time. Take Marco. I'm going up to my room for a while. I need to write down a few notes before they evaporate."

Marco stepped warily down the path, moving through troughs of heat. Ginger had told him about rattlesnakes and water moccasins the size of her thigh. The palmettos, moss-dripping oaks, and the river looked like the Amazon jungle to him. The serene piazza in Monte Sant'Egidio flashed through his mind. He couldn't imagine that he was going to jump into that swirling green water and swim, but he did.

J. J. FILLED HIS PEN with black ink. He found his new notebook in his suitcase and sat down at the window. He reached for a book from his shelves and opened it at random. His finger fell on *here where the moonflowers.* And yes, he'd seen the new curling vine of the moonflowers starting up the porch rail only today. "Marco. Polo. Marco. Polo," he heard Ginger calling. She echoed the hiding game they used to play in the river. But this time she was with a real Marco. He could see them swimming fast toward the bend, where they would get out and climb over the rise to the spring. The late sunlight flashed on their arms arrowing in and out of the water. When J. J. and Ginger were small, they used to seal notes in mayonnaise jars and fling them out as far as they could, hoping the current would sweep them to the ocean. J. J. could still feel the strain in his muscle as he tried to catapult a jar into the current. "Go," Ginger had shouted as the jar flew through the air. They stood on the dock, following each glinting glass until it bobbed under and disappeared. He thought he remembered a voice beside them, Catherine saying *What a good idea.* Someone on a beach in another country would find a jar and twist it open. *We live in Swan, Georgia. If you find this, please write to us. Love, Ginger and J. J. Mason.*

ACKNOWLEDGMENTS

During the writing of this book, I received generous help from Toni Mirosevich, Shotsy Faust, and Josephine Carson. My editor, Charlie Conrad, and the entire staff at Broadway Books are an exemplary publishing team. My luck with being a part of Broadway is due to Peter Ginsberg, my agent and friend. I would like to thank Dr. Robert Mayes Jackson and Dr. Bruce Bonger for their counsel.

I am more than grateful to Edward, my husband, for ten thousand acts of kindness, and to Ashley and Stuart, my daughter and her husband.

My last thanks begin a long way back and go to my family in the South, to my sisters Barbara Mayes Jackson and Nancy Mayes Willcoxon.

ABOUT THE AUTHOR

Author of the international and *New York Times* bestsellers *Under the Tuscan Sun, Bella Tuscany,* and *In Tuscany,* Frances Mayes has also written five books of poetry and a reader's guide, *The Discovery of Poetry.* She edited *Best American Travel Writing,* 2002. A native of Georgia, she now lives in California and Italy with her husband, the poet Edward Mayes.